# BEYOND THE SILK MILLS

# BEYOND THE SILK MILLS

## LESLIE RUPLEY

For permission requests, please address
Dameliam Books
1965 Woodbury Court
Walnut Creek, California 94596

Published 2014 by Dameliam Books
Printed in the United States of America

18 17 16 15 14    1 2 3 4 5

ISBN: 978-0-990426-20-2
Library of Congress Control Number: 2014945710

Publisher's Cataloging-in-Publication Data:

   Rupley, Leslie.
   Beyond the silk mills / Leslie Rupley. -- Walnut Creek, CA : Dameliam Books, © 2014.
   pages ; cm.
   ISBN: 978-0-990426-20-2
   Summary: In 'Beyond the silk mills' Rupley reveals the consequences of immigrant Emma Epstein's desire to provide a better world for her children when it turns to an obsession, to a blind quest for riches, power and social position. The Epstein saga depicts the unique historical era of the early twentieth century and illuminates the roots of modern feminism and today's labor issues.—Publisher.

      1. Women immigrants—United States—History—20th century—Fiction.
      2. Jewish women—United States—History—20th century—Fiction.
      3. United States—Social conditions—20th century—Fiction.
      4. Social mobility—United States—20th century—Fiction.
      5. Social classes—United States—20th century—Fiction.
      6. Social influence—United States—20th century—Fiction.
      7. Wealth—Psychological aspects—20th century—Fiction.
      8. Women—United States—Social conditions—20th century—Fiction.
      9. Feminism—United States—History—20th century—Fiction.
      10. Women employees—United States—Social conditions—20th century—Fiction.
      11. Jewish historical fiction.
      12. Historical fiction. I. Title.

   PS3618.U634 B49 2014          2014945710

   813/.6--dc23          1410

Cover design by Victoria Colotta

In memory of my grandfathers
and all the participants of the
Paterson Silk Strike of 1913

# CONTENTS

# Book Two

# Author's Note

Several characters in this book are based on historical figures. They are composites and do not purport to be true to any individual. When actual historical figures appear as characters, the facts surrounding that person and their quotes are verifiable. Lillian Wald, the founder of the Henry Street Settlement, and Elizabeth Gurley Flynn of the Industrial Workers of the World are principal examples.

If you wish to read references for *Beyond the Silk Mills*, visit my website (http://www.leslierupley.com) or my goodreads page at www.goodreads.com/leslierupley

Leslie Rupley

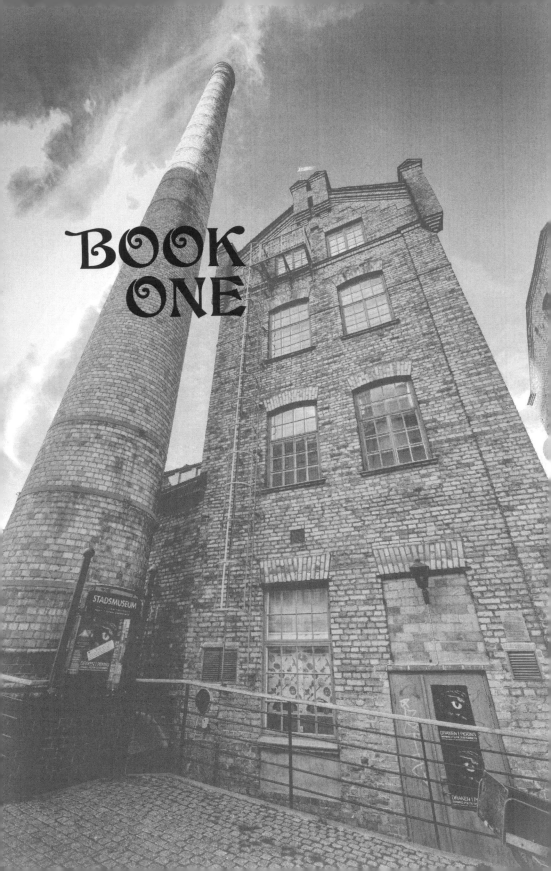

BOOK
ONE

# ONE

## January 1911

**E**mma trudged toward the neglected gray wooden apartment house where the usual five wastrels crowded her Fair Street stoop in Paterson, New Jersey. She wore her still presentable green woolen coat and a flowered kerchief securely tied against the wind. The heavy black leather satchels, one in each hand, slowed her usual quick pace. It had been a long day, and Emma sighed as she kicked a red Gauloises cigarette box out of her way. The street was quiet except for the clip-clop of the ragman's horse on the cobblestones. His wagon was loaded, and he was heading home.

Her sample cases were stuffed with an assortment of Wanamaker rustproof corsets, intended to cram slack-bodied housewives into the shapely cinch-waist form of *Harper's Weekly* models. Emma had shown a dainty DeBevoise figure-forming brassiere and a silk petticoat to her most discriminating customer. "Rosila dear, I brought something especially for you, because with your fine figure you should have such luxury." Rosalie did not buy today, and Emma calculated the lost commission on a five-dollar transaction.

She mulled over her day's sales as she walked. *Mrs. Golden, two dollars. Mrs. Hellman and her daughter, three dollars. Mrs. Beck, two dollars. Not bad.* After paying Bessie her seventy percent for the garments, Emma's commission would be a little over two dollars for the day and about ten for the week. *Soon I'll bring home more than Meyer, God willing.* She frowned while thinking of

5

the money that her husband earned, relatively good pay for a weaver in the silk industry. Even though many garment workers' wives would be happy to have the thirteen dollars each week, Emma had higher aspirations, for the sake of her daughter.

The boys on the stoop squeezed over to make room as they saw her approach the apartment house. She knew they didn't want to catch hell from her wicked tongue today, as they did the last time she scolded them. "It's a real shame you should sit here all day and smoke cigarettes when your parents need some money. You should go to work."

"Hello, Mrs. Epstein." Morris jumped to his feet as she approached. "Can I carry your satchels upstairs?"

"Thank you, Morris," she said, handing them over.

"Hello, Mrs. Epstein," the others muttered as they moved aside to make room for her. "Ass kisser," they whispered to Morris when he edged by them.

The boy led the way into the tiled hallway, black and white tessellation in need of repair. It was bright enough to see, although it was almost time to light the gas wall lamps that illuminated the dark hall and stairwell. Emma looked with disgust at the peeling wallpaper while she followed the boy upstairs. *Stinks from that Sara Bromberg's cabbage every Friday. Anyway, thanks God I get a little respect here.*

She unclenched her cramping fingers, curved and stiff from carrying the sample cases, and scrutinized her long, slender hands with neatly trimmed fingernails. *How long can my hands stay attractive with this life?* Emma had conjured an elegant lifestyle before coming to Paterson from Poland twelve years ago, but *schlepping* corsets door-to-door had not proven to be the path to wealth.

"Thanks to you, Morris. Your mother, God rest her soul, would be proud of your manners. She wanted you should be a *mensch*," Emma said when he deposited her satchels. She smiled, watching Morris nod and race down all three flights of stairs, no doubt to reassert his standing with his buddies.

Emma stood between two pitted wood doors on the third-floor landing. She raised and dropped her shoulders as she turned the knob and walked through the door on the right. Meyer had returned home from the mill and had lit the gas wall lamps in all of the rooms to welcome her home. They shone with a warm yellow glow beneath their frosted glass covers. "Here, Dolly," he said as he met her in their front room. "Let me help you with your coat. I'll put your satchels inside, and you can sit down here on the settee while I get you some tea. Here. Rest."

At that moment, Emma had a fleeting vision of the Meyer she had fallen in love with years ago in her father's home in Lodz. She could see his kindly brown eyes crinkled at the outer edges when he smiled and his black hair brushed back in wavy ridges. His neat, thick black mustache. *He's still taller than me by a few inches.* It was a disconcerting moment, a transposition of time, until the long-ago image lost its hold. In reality he still had his thick curly black hair, kind eyes, and well-trimmed mustache, but at thirty-seven years, more than half of them spent working over a loom, he had lost the vigor of his youth.

As she sat down on the settee with teacup and saucer perched on her lap, she recalled when Meyer had come to her Balut ghetto in Lodz looking for work. Emma's father had hired him to help with the looms because her older brothers Harry and George had gone to America, leaving only the younger twins Dave and Joe to tend them.

Emma was taken by his good looks and his quiet manner, but most of all by his energy, his tension waiting to explode. She flirted; he fell in love. When she was nineteen, Meyer went to America. She was full of hope when he sent for her the next year. She had long dreamed of leaving the crowded alleys of that Jewish ghetto. Now, instead of hope, she had nightmares about returning to Balut, to the draymen's shouting, horses snorting, the never-ending rattle of the weavers' shuttles, the tailors' raspy curses, and the whirring of their treadle machines.

*Ach! Enough.* She put aside her recurring lament that Meyer hadn't chosen to use his vigor and charm to make a worthy life for his family. Instead, he wasted his gifts as a mere weaver, not even a foreman.

She pressed her lips together, relaxed with a sigh, and got up from the settee. With her teacup in hand, she walked through the open double doors into the kitchen. Their four-room apartment was luxurious compared to the one-room wooden shack that had housed nine people back in Lodz, but Emma had expected more than this rundown apartment house in the Paterson immigrant neighborhood.

She noticed that Meyer had added coal, stoked the black cast-iron stove, and set out the large pot of chicken soup she had prepared last evening for tonight's Sabbath dinner. *Thanks God Harry made a gift of this oak icebox to keep the chicken soup from spoiling*, she thought as she opened the back hallway door to retrieve cooked carrots from it. She bit her lower lip hard to avoid yet another comparison of Meyer's disinterest in wealth to her brothers' prosperous business, shaking off her own fleeting remorse for discounting his thoughtfulness.

She peeked into one of the two bedrooms off the kitchen to greet her young daughter. Sophie was seated at her worktable, her head upon her schoolbook, having untied her hair ribbons. Her thick brown curls spilled over the table's surface.

Emma's long curls had been the same when Meyer fell in love with her. Her thick hair was her glory, shiny and flowing, especially in summer when she could wash it more frequently.

"Sophie, wake, my sweet one. Dinner is almost ready."

"Mama, I'm tired."

Emma clicked her tongue and raised her eyebrows. "You wouldn't be tired if you didn't stay awake so late reading your books. Homework is one thing. Cheap novels are another."

"But Mama, these stories are real," she said as her round, deep blue eyes widened. Her dark lashes fluttered with rapid blinks. "They tell how horrible the factories are for the workers. Young girls have to stand all day in bad light and dusty air making shoes or cotton cloth, and even weaving silk right here in Paterson, and Papa says that it is all true. Papa says that something really bad is going to happen…"

"Papa! Papa looks for trouble. Come, eat."

Emma returned to the kitchen to ladle the chicken soup into bowls. Meyer stood over her and picked up the noodles that had slipped from the bowl to have a little appetizer, even before the Sabbath prayers. "Sleeping again," she told her husband as she nodded in the direction of Sophie's room. "Why do you talk about those horrible books with her?"

"Emma, let's not argue about the mills again. Sophie is kindhearted, and she feels for the workers. Let her be."

8

As the family sat down to dinner, the daylight had completely faded and the gaslights flickered on the yellow-papered wall, creating soft shadows. It was a homey kitchen with its Sears and Roebuck oak sideboard and bright cotton rugs on the wooden floor. Emma closed the kitchen curtains to block her view of the peeling paint on the building across the alley. She felt better for having erased the intrusive scene even though she couldn't see it in the darkness.

Meyer exhaled the stress of his day. Every evening he sat back in his kitchen chair to enjoy the warmth of the coal stove and the yellow of the gaslights, the acrid fumes to which the family had become inured. The steam radiator erupted with a clanging noise and then a hiss, as comforting heat from the coal furnace in the cellar made its way up through the pipes and filled the room.

Emma laid her good white linen cloth on the worn oak table and brought out the few pieces of yellowed porcelain plates with delicate pink roses that still called to mind her mother in the old country. These had been her dishes many years ago. There, too, were the knives, forks, and spoons whose silver plating had long ago lost their luster. Her few possessions were merely a shadow of the originals. *And me? Have I lost my luster, too?*

Emma shook off her gloom and called to her daughter. "Sophie, come to the table."

Sophie ambled in and took her seat. The family sat at the kitchen table with eyes closed, welcoming the Sabbath peace. Emma struck a match, covered her eyes with her hands as tradition dictated, and recited the rote blessings as she lit the candles. "*Barukh atah Adonai Eloheinu, melekh ha'olam…*" But even as she praised and thanked God with her mouth, she tainted her prayer with earthly reflections on her meager, worn-out possessions.

She recited the prayer over the bread, broke off a piece of the challah, and passed it to Meyer and Sophie.

"Meyer, my brother Harry told me that again he offered you a better job," she said. "He wants you to watch over the weavers in the mill."

"Emma, bless the wine, and then I want to talk to you about—"

"Why are you so stubborn when we could leave this neighborhood? We might move to a bigger apartment, maybe a little farther uptown…"

"Emma, stop. I don't want to ruin your Sabbath," he said as he poured the wine, held his silver goblet aloft, and blessed the fruit of the vine. As a socialist, he was an unobservant Jew, but he conceded to his wife's upbringing in this way.

"What? What *ruin*?" Emma said as soon as Meyer said, "Amen."

Meyer drew in his breath. He spit out his words with deliberate precision. "I quit my job with Harry this morning. I never want to be a boss."

Emma's face reddened, and she felt a sudden nausea. She put her palms on the table to brace herself, her heart pounding. *This couldn't be.*

"But to quit your job all of a sudden? Where will you go? What is to become of us and our dreams?"

Sophie, spoon in hand, lowered her head over her soup bowl. She squeezed her eyes shut. Splash! Her spoon dropped into the bowl. Then she pushed her chair from the table and fled to her bedroom.

"Look, Emma, what you are doing. How can a child be happy in this angry house? I'll go to her."

"Never mind, Meyer. She can eat later. Tell me how you expect to put bread on the table, never mind pay rent and put clothes on our backs. How can Sophie make her way in the world if she dresses like a poor immigrant? Tell me that."

"Emma, Emma. I'm a good weaver, a good worker, and I'll find work elsewhere. These dreams of riches you speak of—they are your dreams. You have always known that I don't care about money."

"But they are for Sophie now, these dreams," Emma said as she shook her fists.

"Be calm. Sophie is a fine girl. She doesn't need money to make her a better person. You must understand, my love, how wrong it is for me to take your family's money. I have to stand in solidarity with the workers when we rise against the mill owners. What do they give us to show for our labor at the end of the week? Next to nothing."

"Well, that's the truth! Not much to show."

"Emma, I can't stand above my comrades and be a supervisor in your brothers' mill. I will look for work in Doherty's mill on Monday. There I can be a help to my comrades."

"Now I think you are crazy. Why can you never give up on these strikes? What does it get you? We suffer without your pay, and their wives have beautiful new dresses from the seamstress, while I sew my own clothes." *It's the same like in Poland. Always about the workers and strikes.* Emma buried her face in her arms.

"Emma, Emma," he said, patting her shoulders. "You knew when we married who I was. I wish that I could make you happy like we were in Poland and even here in America when Sophie was a baby, but I can't become a capitalist parasite living on the work of others to give you riches."

Emma sat up straight and glowered, her lips curled. "What am I going to tell my brothers? They didn't come to America and slave to build a family business for you to throw their kindness back in their faces."

Meyer didn't respond. Emma stared at her plate as they finished their Sabbath dinner in silence. Then she glanced sideways at Meyer. *He's a stubborn man, this husband of mine.* With her thoughts churning, she struggled to control herself to the end of their meal, and then she left the room without another word.

That night in bed she lay stiff and unyielding next to Meyer, only inches away but elsewhere in her thoughts. She closed her eyes and tried to sleep, but her anger was too close to the surface. *What a fool he is. He'll never change after all these years.*

A sickly bitterness had plagued Emma throughout the weekend, and on Monday morning she lay in bed feigning sleep while her anger continued to roil within. She arose after Meyer left the bed and continued to dwell on her grievances and disappointments as she prepared breakfast. The vision of her brothers in their fine homes on the Eastside plagued her, because she still had to trudge up to an apartment in a filthy downtown tenement. Emma was desperately tired of *schlepping* corsets from house to house. *I need to earn more money. Meyer will never earn enough. But what can I do?*

After a breakfast of tea and a poached egg on dry toast, Emma faced the daily preparation of two oversized satchels that sat on the floor nearby. She slung them onto the kitchen table and pulled out her customer list, trying to ensure that she had the necessary samples in anticipation of the day's sales, but she was distracted by thoughts of the past.

Her cousin Bessie had been a mouse of a girl in Poland, but now she had her own shop. Bessie, with pockmarked skin and a large nose, had cowered in a corner whenever a young man was present. No one thought that she would come to America and marry a rich man. *Humph!*

Emma shook off her distractions and checked that Mrs. Goldman's brassiere was packed. Meyer and Sophie had left the house, and she was ready for the day. She drew on her green coat, tied her kerchief under her chin, and looked around the kitchen. She sighed deeply. The thought of peddling foundations from door to door in the January cold while Bessie sat in her warm store angered Emma.

She snapped her satchels shut, punctuating her aggravation, and slammed the hall door on her way out, tromping down the three flights of stairs, a bulging sample case hanging from each arm.

Sophie had been at the center of her attention during the child's early years, but now that her daughter would soon be thirteen, Emma felt free to focus on her own dreams. As she exited her apartment to face the long, exhausting day ahead, she began to scheme about how to transfer the business to its "rightful" owner, the more capable Emma Epstein who had built up the clientele. *Now I will be the main breadwinner. I will own that store of Bessie's one day, and I'll make of it a stylish shop.*

Meyer, too, had felt the aftereffects of his rancorous argument with Emma. After a weekend in chilly silence, he lay half-awake in bed on Monday morning, thinking about their anger at bedtime and about Sunday's painful distancing of husband and wife, even as his daughter watched the silent duel. He had hoped to make it up with Emma in bed on that Saturday night, longing for a sweet word, a touch, even a smile, but there was no encouragement from her side of the bed. She lay turned away from him— cold as well as silent. He had reached out to touch his wife's shoulder but withdrew his hand before making the gesture, thinking of her icy resentment.

He roused himself from bed and looked at Emma still asleep beside him. Why wasn't she content with this new life? The Lodz ghetto was hardship. Here there was water from a tap, gaslights on the walls, an icebox, a stove, toilets, but what she wanted was a fancy house on the Eastside like her brothers. Once he thought he could make her happy, but he realized she only felt disappointment and bitterness.

*Oy, what am I thinking? Today I find work at a new mill. An important day.*

Meyer shook away his despair, swung his legs over the side of the bed, and reached for his rimless spectacles on the bedside table. He took the woolen trousers from the back of the nearby chair, and still seated on the side of the bed, lifted his nightshirt over his head and pulled on his trousers. He tucked in a clean white shirt with a new stand-up collar, knotted a tie, and pulled his suspenders over his shoulders.

Yet as he drew on his boots and began his morning chores in the kitchen, domestic thoughts continued to intrude on this day that he hoped would be his first in Doherty's mill. He recalled the time in Europe when he first came to work the loom in the Abramowitz cottage and how he had fallen for Emma's alluring ways.

Meyer had never wanted to quit his calling in Poland, nor had he aspired to wealth. He had been an active member of the Jewish Labour Bund, dedicated to a socialist revolution. He was a skilled weaver and a devout socialist. Emma had used her cold silence to bend him to her will. She enticed him with her flirting and then punished him with her remoteness when he refused to consider emigration. Finally, it was the conscription quota and his danger of forced enlistment into the Russian army, a fate heartily feared by vulnerable Jews, that changed his mind.

Turning to the tasks of the day, he went into the kitchen to stoke the coal stove. As he prepared to leave the apartment for Doherty's mill, he called into the bedroom, "Sophie is awake, Emma. She needs your help."

Emma called to her daughter.

"I'm getting ready, Mama, but I need help with my hair, please."

"Yes, my love," she said as she pulled on a dressing gown. "I'll twist your

13

curls, and you can wear a new bow today. *Oy*, you'll be the most beautiful girl in school, my Sophie."

*When she's angry with me she coddles Sophie all the more.* Meyer quietly shut the door to the apartment. Today I'm invisible to her.

When Meyer left his Fair Street apartment that Monday morning, he paused on the front porch, thinking about the Doherty mill, the largest and newest mill in Paterson. He trusted that his friend Manny Shapiro from the old country had put in a word with the foreman. Meyer chose Doherty's mill because of its size and the new improved power looms. If any union organizing were to be done, it would start at Doherty's. He knew that it would be the right place for him to help organize a strike against the four-loom system if it came to that, and this time he would have all the textile trades united into one concerted strike.

He considered the route he would take to Doherty's down on Mill Street, a different direction from the Pope mill, where the Abramowitz brothers had their looms. Observing the breaking dawn from his porch, he predicted he would get to the mill before the light of day.

Meyer looked up and down the street where men and young women, too, trudged off to jobs in the mills, shoulders drawn up against the cold morning air, lunch pails in hand. They would get to the mill after a long, cold walk or a ride on one of the new electric trolleys with those overhead wires, and the bosses would drive up in their shiny new black Packards.

Snow had fallen lightly last evening, but the sidewalks were already covered in dirty footprints. The cobblestone streets were a hazard, slippery and uneven under the new-fallen snow. Meyer shivered as he thought of the gloved drayman delivering blocks of ice for Emma's treasured icebox twice each week. He came like clockwork, summer and winter, up three flights to the back hallway.

Meyer eased his way down the slippery snow-covered front steps and turned to look at the next-door boarding house for single men recently come to America. A sign hung in the window, the same 'To Let' sign that he had seen when he first arrived in Paterson, only fifteen miles as the crow flies from Ellis Island. He had found this house among the advertisements in the *Morning Call* when he came to America before sending for Emma. "BOARDING," the ad read. "A few gentlemen can be accommodated with board in a private family home. Rooms all warm and comfortable."

With a sigh and a wistful smile, Meyer thought of his freedom in those boarding- house days before he sent for Emma. Only go to work, save, and spend leisure time with his *landsmen*, his Lodz friends.

It was a morning for contemplation after the weekend's quarrel. Meyer took in the neighborhood, not without fondness. Dull gray or tan paint buckled and peeled from the wooden framed buildings in this Jewish neighborhood, and the narrow alleys led to small weedy yards crossed by a multitude of clotheslines.

A decaying privy remained in nearly all the yards, even though indoor toilets had been installed. Most buildings had three stories with two or four apartments on each floor. Windows, one atop the other in the same place on every floor, were filmy with dirt. A few had lace curtains like the ones Emma hung.

He buttoned his overcoat and turned west onto Broadway, unlike most who crossed the Erie Railroad tracks, then hurried over to the parallel Van Houten Street, a slightly shorter route to the mill section on the edge of the Passaic River. Meyer preferred the more picturesque walk when he had time.

Most of the important buildings that had been destroyed in the Great Fire of 1902 had been rebuilt, and it was a pleasure for Meyer to study the detailed workmanship of the massive stone façades. Brownstone, granite, and limestone came from local quarries.

He admired the engraving above the doors, the towers, and the columns of carved marble, all decorations of the pretentious French Beaux Arts style. Although a man of simple tastes, he still smiled in appreciation when thinking of the stonemasons' skills or the carpenters' work.

The brownstone Catholic Church, Gothic and imposing, was vastly different from his little *shul* on Godwin Avenue. *Why would God need me to talk to him in such a fancy place?* He inclined his head in deference to two pairs of black-garbed nuns, their arms folded tightly across their midsections. They glided toward him like specters, the white of their wimples illuminating dour faces. It was no wonder that Sophie, terrified, would cross a street to avoid them.

Thus preoccupied, Meyer reached the row of dark redbrick mills with their smoke towers spewing gray clouds into the cold morning air. The stench of the polluted river with its discharge of mill waste and raw sewage had ceased to annoy him, but the acidic fumes had caused the paint to peel from buildings as far as two blocks away.

Ingeniously, pure Passaic River water, ideal for dyeing cotton and silk, was piped from two miles upstream and delivered via raceways to the dye houses that were built over fifty years ago on the banks of the river. The energy generated from the descent of the Great Falls was harnessed from the raceways at each millsite to power the looms.

Meyer pulled up his wool collar and hurried toward his destination. *Us weavers and the dyers and ribbon makers will show those bosses another kind of power once we unite.*

Henry Doherty's mill was the last in line and closest to the falls. Meyer made his way to the office, where he asked about a job as a weaver. Manny had alerted the foreman, who was happy to have another experienced operator, and he set Meyer to work at four unmanned looms across the aisle from his friend.

"I see you have the new looms that stop by themselves if a warp thread breaks," he said to the foreman. "It stops, too, even if a filling thread from the shuttle breaks, no?"

"Yes. We have the newest and the best here at Doherty's," he replied. "Men are damned lucky to work here, I say."

Meyer nodded, and the foreman left him to learn his looms.

There was a break in a neighboring loom soon after Meyer began to tend his own machines. A sudden eerie silence filled the reverberating chamber. The solid brick structure allowed no sound from the outside.

"My God, Manny, it feels like a tomb in here," said Meyer, turning around to see his old friend.

"Do you remember how it took a half day to fix a broken warp thread before these modern looms came?"

"Yah, Manny. Everything is fast nowadays. Some men work four looms now, when it used to be two, and remember, just one loom in the old country. Grinding out the work. Were we better off in Lodz?"

"Here comes the supervisor, that big shot. Turn to your work now, Meyer."

As soon as Meyer refocused on his warp he perceived a purring from the looms. And then the escalation—the drone, next the clatter, and finally the rumbling of the giant machines roaring like an approaching train chugging its way to textile production.

When the lunch whistle blew, some men braved the cold and filed out of the mill with their lunch pails. Others stayed by their looms. Manny guided his friend to a bench under a barren tree where some familiar faces from the Labour Bund in Lodz sat wrapped in their scarves, hats, and heavy woolen coats. Saul took off one glove to grab a thick slab of rye bread from his pail. He reached in for the cheese, drew on his glove, and chewed on his customary meal. As he spoke between bites his breath mingled with the cold air.

"Meyer, welcome to our fine picnic. *Zei Gezunt.* Be well. After all, we are beside the beautiful Passaic River..."

"Where the water rushes in fresh and clean and leaves the mill stinking from its waste and fumes," said Martin.

"You said a mouthful," replied Saul.

"Men, why don't they bolt the looms to the wooden floor? If they would take the trouble, the noise from vibrations wouldn't be as bad," said Meyer.

"We stuff our ears with cotton, but already I lost some hearing," remarked Martin. "The bosses don't care. They say the looms are attached to the over-head timbers, not the floor. That way timbers absorb the vibrations, not the building. What do I know? It's still too noisy."

The whistle blew again before the men could finish their lunch. They packed up their pails, stuffed bread in their mouths, and inhaled their last breaths of freedom as they hurried back to work.

As the afternoon progressed, Meyer rubbed his tired eyes. To block out the noise of the clattering looms, he tried to imagine himself in the quiet of his home and or in the stillness of the early morning air.

He had a moment to survey the long, narrow repository of looms when a broken warp thread stopped the monster machines again. The mechanized silk looms resembled pairs of marchers on a parade ground that Meyer had seen in Europe. Looms lined up two abreast with a menacing assembly of wheels and gears, one on each side of the room's length, meeting at the center of the mill. There was little room to navigate the center aisle between the rotating gears or even along the outer walls.

When the six o'clock whistle blew, Meyer left the mill more dispirited than when he'd arrived. He could see by the other men's gaits that the never-ending vibrations and clanking, as well as the looms' demands, left them drained by day's end.

The Workmen's Circle was Meyer's refuge after a day of work or whenever he had the time to be with his cronies. All the Jewish textile workers belonged to the socialist-leaning brotherhood. They joined together for the welfare of their Jewish brothers as the Italians supported the Sons of Italy. They had their fellowship, they collected for charity, and they put money aside from the dues to help their members in sickness, or during one of the many brief strikes. The Circle connected him to Lodz, his own history, and his *Yiddishkeyt*, that undeniable sense of belonging to the Jewish Nation and to the totality of its experience. When he was there among his friends, he was able to forget Emma's disappointment with him.

It was no wonder that Meyer went to the Workmen's Circle after his first day at Doherty's to unwind with his comrades before going home. Emma would eat with Sophie and save dinner for him.

The meeting room was in the cellar of an industrial building near the mill, a few steps down from the street. Meyer pushed open the heavy wooden door and groaned at the strain in his neck muscles as he bent his head down to avoid the rafter. *Oy, I'm tired.*

He took his old meerschaum pipe from his baggy coat pocket as he navigated the dark stairwell into the packed cellar. Large, black-painted round poker tables with slat-backed rickety chairs claimed every inch of floor space. He found his way through a thick haze of smoky air, pungent with tobacco, and sat down with a group of his friends.

Meyer pulled out his silver tin of "Edgewood Extra High Grade Sliced Tobacco." He crumbled a slice and offered it around in his open palm. As if waiting for this cue, each man pulled out his pipe, nodded thanks to Meyer, and began the ritual of packing tobacco and drawing the flame into the bowl. Meyer smiled as he pocketed the nearly empty tin and briefly envisioned Emma searching for a replacement button in such a container. He liked to think of her caring for him and Sophie by sewing and doing other womanly chores.

With the luxury of the first quiet draws on their pipes, the men closed their eyes momentarily to savor the tobacco flavor. They slumped into relaxation after the day's labor, and the conversation began.

"Meyer, we heard that Manny got you a job over at Doherty's mill."

"*Nu*? Now I am one of a thousand workers in that mill. I work four power looms. It used to be one loom was enough for a man back in the old country where we learned to weave." He sat up straight and raked his fingers through his thick hair.

"Now with the new inventions, we work four looms with little increase in pay, mind you."

"Yah, in the old country, Meyer," remarked Solly. "We worked one loom there, but for eighteen hours a day. At least here it is only ten hours, and half a day on Saturday."

"Solly, why should an owner double his income without giving the worker a fair share? My Sophie knows good English. She read to me a book by this man Edward Bellamy. He died only about twelve years ago. Sophie told me the English words, and I wrote it in Yiddish."

Pulling a rumpled sheet of paper from his coat pocket, Meyer read, "How beautiful life might be if people cooperatively owned and worked and shared the riches of the earth."

"Meyer, Meyer, such a dreamer you are," Solly replied. "Look at what's

19

real. When we don't get all of the crafts together, strikes fail. Look back to '02 when we weavers wouldn't even support the dyers in their strike. The dyers won't help the broadloom weavers or the ribbon weavers. Those fixers and warpers are another story! The throwers aren't worth mentioning."

"But Solly," interrupted Hyman. "Remember 1910 when that Doherty first brought in the four looms. Twice we went out on strike with the AFL."

"Yah, yah, what you say is true, Hyman," said Meyer. "Yet we have to stick together. What about the Italians? What about the other crafts? Everybody strikes or nothing happens."

Solly wasn't convinced. "Sure. We stick together…when the Messiah comes to Paterson!"

But look how far the Ladies' Garment Workers' Union from the shirtwaist factories got last November." Meyer's eyes glowed, and he swiftly combed his fingers through his curly hair as he sat forward in his chair.

"Listen, Hymie, Gompers from the AFL came to New York to get the workers going, and by God, twenty thousand workers, mostly women and girls, went out on strike. They called it the biggest strike in New York's history, 'The Uprising of the Twenty Thousand.' Here we don't need Gompers. We can do it when we all go out on strike together."

"Meyer, it didn't amount…" Hyman started to say.

Meyer kept on. "When little Clara Lemlich called from the podium, 'If not now, when?' they all raised their hands for the old Jewish oath: 'If I turn traitor to the cause I now pledge, may this hand wither from the arm I now raise.' Hyman, we can make the same oath."

Hyman Zitskin sat back in his seat and took a long draw on his briar pipe. The men waited in silence while he paused. They could see the weaver's deeply lined face in the flicker of the oil lamp on the table.

He spoke with deliberation. "Yes, Meyer, they went out on strike in November of last year. Finally, last spring, three hundred owners signed contracts to recognize the union, but ten thousand workers went back to the mills after that long winter to the same conditions they left."

A few grumbles of assent were voiced and then someone said, "How about a little game of pinochle?" Solly dealt the cards.

# Two

## February 1911

**W**ithin the week after Meyer left her brothers' business and began to work at Doherty's mill, Emma was finally certain of what she had always known in her heart. As she walked from the store to her bleak home in the neighborhood of "greenhorns," she rehearsed the declaration she would make to Meyer that evening.

*Meyer, after all these years I believe what you tell me. You will never make money, and I must be the one to earn more than I bring home now. You won't change. You go on strike, and then you lose even the pittance that the boss gives you.*

She stopped and placed her satchels on the sidewalk for a moment to flex her crimped hands. *No more. We will leave this filthy immigrant neighborhood, and I will make sure it happens.*

Angry heat rose beneath her winter coat and she could hear her heart thumping in her ears as she tramped homeward. *A miserable life, damp halls, roaches. I'm too long in that horrible apartment building.* Lost in thought, she slipped on a hidden patch of ice and sprawled to the ground. Emma sat for a moment to assess her condition, and when she decided that no harm had come to her body, she turned onto her hands and knees and pushed herself to her feet. She untangled her ankle-length dark woolen skirt and smoothed her coat over it.

Emma picked up her satchels, threw her shoulders back, and looked around to make sure no one had seen her, but there was a bearded Hasid in his long black coat and fur hat looking at her with concern.

"You never see a woman fall? You couldn't help me to my feet?" The man turned away with a jerk of the head, and she recalled that such a religious man is not permitted to touch a woman other than his wife. She scowled and resumed her angry reflections.

To soothe her anxiety, Emma called to mind the image of her brother Harry's two-story house on Wall Avenue, because she was certain that someday she too would live in splendor above the downtown rabble. This mental picture was forever a symbol before her eyes.

Wall Avenue in Paterson, New Jersey, invoked the wealth of its Manhattan namesake. Harry's palatial limestone house had a columned front entrance, large windows topped with arches, and a magnificent terraced lawn. She thought of the lawn and garden as "the grounds" for Harry's family to enjoy like a private park.

Emma visualized her own future manor house while she walked. Harry had many rooms upstairs and down, too many to use. She wouldn't make her house the same as Harry's with columns in front. No, hers would be different. Brick maybe, not limestone, and she'd have flower gardens instead of lawn. Sophie would have a big room with a fireplace. And Meyer…As Meyer entered her thoughts she lost the train of reverie and refocused on her journey home.

The weight of her bags felt more burdensome the closer she got to home, and to distract herself she thought about a possible first step in her campaign to acquire cousin Bessie's store for herself. *If I am not for myself, who will be for me? That is what Meyer says about the workers.* As she thought about it now, her cold and discomfort vanished, and she continued on with renewed vigor.

The following week, Emma went to the shop to settle her accounts, but she had a great deal more in mind. Unseen, she peeked through the window to observe her cousin. She straightened her shoulders and adjusted her smile before entering the store.

Bessie was sitting in a chair behind the almost empty display case. Her graying hair was pulled back into a bun, and a simple tortoiseshell comb on either side held wispy hairs in place. She wore a serviceable woolen dress with the waistline under her bosom, pushed upward by her stout middle.

Emma looked around the tired shop, trying to hide her disdain. Bessie glanced up and smiled. "*Nu*, Emma. Did you have a good day?"

"Ordinary, Bessie, but I have an idea how we can make more money."

"Emma, you make good sales as it is. What do you mean, 'more money'?"

"We don't draw in enough wealthy clientele. I can't walk with my garments all the way up to the east side of town. They have to drive their cars down here."

"Yah, Emma. From your mouth to God's ears!"

"We can't wait for God to work. We have to do some things on our own. We have to make from this shop a beautiful attraction."

"Emma, who is this 'we'?"

"Naturally, Bessie, you and me. I have some good ideas about this."

"*Nu*? What are your good ideas?"

"Oy, it's getting dark. I'm sorry, Bessie dear, Meyer and Sophie are waiting for dinner. I'll see you tomorrow."

The trap was set. *Let Bessie stew for a day or two, silly woman…a miracle she can even pay the rent. What does she know about business?*

Emma recollected the timeworn shop on her way home. A battered sign above the door read "Foundations."

There were large display windows on either side of the old wooden door, but they were cloudy, and not a slip or a corset was displayed on the window-level shelf. Inside the dingy shop, the walls were still painted in the dull gray of the prior owners. There were glass cases on which random articles of underthings lay, but the bulk of the stock was folded in piles or stored in the cases.

She imagined an elegant remake of the dreary store. She would wash the front windows, lay out the merchandise, and put up a shiny new sign saying "Emma's Fine Foundations." She thought of buying the new type of wax mannequins to show off the camisoles and having tables to display the brassieres and pantaloons. *When that store is mine, all the uptown women will flock to me. Bessie will be shocked at the money I make.*

Sophie sat sideways across the ledge, leaning on the side jamb of her open third-floor bedroom window. She looked out to the empty clothesline stretched taut on a pulley between the window and the telephone pole at the rear of the yard. Clean trousers and shirts flapped below on her neighbor Dottie's line.

She knew that it was almost lunchtime, but still Sophie stared at a wet load of wash, knowing that her mother would be angry at the delay. *I can hear her now. "Nu?" she'll say. "You want to wait maybe till the sun goes in, so tonight you can take in the clothes stiff like ice?"*

She breathed in a deep sigh and got up from the window ledge to hang the wet clothes. First, Sophie picked up one of Papa's shirts from the basket and shook it out to free the wrinkles. *I wish Mama would be more kind to him.* She turned the shirt upside down and fastened each side to the line with wooden pins. There were always arguments. Last night Emma had thumped Meyer's bowl on the table hard enough to make the soup splash. He hadn't said a word, but Sophie saw his sad, resolute smile.

The sound of a rap on her door startled her. "Sophie, *Sheinela*, are you in there?  I'm home from work already. It's half-day Saturday."

Sophie dropped the laundry and ran to welcome her papa home. She pushed her nose into the rough nap of his gray wool coat to inhale the sweet tobacco scent and then bent down to remove his shoes after he lowered himself onto a kitchen chair. Sophie sat next to him. "Papa, tell me a story about your day."

"Yesterday a fat crow sat on the mill gate before I go in to work. Come lunchtime I take my pail outside and there was that black crow again. I'm calling him Blackie." Papa laughed out loud.

Sophie giggled. "Did you tip your hat and say, "*'Scholem-aleichem,* Blackie!'?"

"Yah, that's a good one. On Monday I'll bring him a little piece of bread and get Blackie to come down to me from the gate. Now you go finish with the clothes and help Mama in the kitchen."

Later that day Sophie was trying to read some of the *Paterson Evening News* to Papa in the parlor while Emma began to prepare dinner with a banging and clanging of pots. "United States Army Drops…"

"Sophie, I can't hear you," said Meyer, pointing to the kitchen with his chin. Sophie looked heavenward, motioned Papa with a roll of her eyes, and the two tiptoed through the kitchen behind Emma's turned back to Sophie's room off the other side of the kitchen.

Now, sitting on the edge of her bed with her door closed against the kitchen noise, she read, "***United States Army Drops the First Live Bomb From an Aeroplane***." It was a test conducted by Lieutenant Myron Sydney Crissy in San Francisco. The girl stopped reading for a moment and sat lost in thought. She shook her head and pulled the large cream-colored silk ribbon from her hair, laying it beside her on the bed.

"Papa," she asked. "What 's a bomb?"

"*Sheinela*, my little beauty, you should not know from such things. A bomb is a new way to kill people. They don't kill enough yet with swords and guns. Now they drop a big ball from an aeroplane. When it falls to the ground, it explodes, and people die. It's not enough people die from accidents and sickness. Sophie, Sophie, the world will be a better place when socialism comes. Everyone will be equal with no bosses and workers, and then we won't need bombs."

Sophie was quiet for a moment, her thoughts turned inward, but then she began her anxious rapid eye-blinking and said, "Papa, I wish people didn't fight at all…even in our house."

"I know, *Liebe*. I know." Meyer looked at his adolescent daughter sitting next to him with her arms outstretched, palms facing upward in question. A frown masked the beauty of her wide-set, deep blue eyes and long dark lashes.

Sophie turned toward the kitchen and said, "Papa. I don't understand why *she* hates the workers so—"

"Sophie, respect your mama, and don't call her *she*. Remember she is your mother."

"Yes, Papa." *But it's true. You know Mama really hates the workers.* Sophie wrapped her arms around Meyer's neck, kissed him on his bristly cheek, and then lay back on the bed, her pleated sailor-style dress rumpled about her.

Meyer's expression softened with the kiss, and Sophie gazed at him. "Papa, I love you more than anything. I can't understand why you don't answer back when Mama gets angry."

The pair sat in silence for a few moments and then Meyer said, "Sophie, I used to talk to your mother about our labor struggles in Poland. She doesn't want to hear anymore. She wants a new and better life."

"You can tell me about them, Papa," she said as she sat up straight.

Meyer didn't need a second invitation. "The Industrial Workers of the World or the IWW...they call them the Wobblies...have a constitution. Wait, I'll get it for you." Meyer retrieved the pamphlet and returned to sit beside Sophie. He read in Yiddish to his daughter.

"The working class and the employing class have nothing in common. There can be no peace as long as hunger and want are found among millions of working people and the few, who make up the employing class, have all the good things of life."

He swallowed and Sophie saw his eyes grow cloudy. He blinked and continued. "Between these two classes a struggle must go on until the workers of the world organize as a class, take possession of the earth and the machinery of production, and abolish the wage system."

"I guess you won't bring any money home when they abolish the wages. Mama won't be happy."

"No, my child. You don't understand. Everyone will have what we need. Big bosses won't have riches while the rest of us starve."

"I don't think that will happen soon."

Meyer got up and went to the chair beside Sophie's worktable. He sat down and studied the lettering on her schoolbook, the one on top of the neat pile, as if it might hold an explanation for Sophie. He frowned, picked up the book, and felt its heft before replacing it. He looked around at the pink-and-gray-flowered wallpaper while Sophie studied him, impatient for a response.

Meyer took a breath, reached for his pipe in his breast pocket, and held it. He took it out by the bowl and began to speak. "Sophie, the IWW helped the Brooklyn shoe workers to strike last week. You remember the Ladies' Garment Workers' strike in New York City last year, yah?"

"I remember that one, Papa. They're the Wobblies. Right? All the ladies and girls walked out to make the bosses give them better lighting to see their sewing machines. They wanted the bosses to unlock the doors, so they could go to the toilet when they had to."

"Yah, in New York."

"Papa, you said those factory girls are even younger than I am."

"Yah, some are only twelve years…right here in Paterson, too."

"I want to strike with you Papa, to help those girls. I don't understand why Mama thinks that strikes are bad."

Sophie rose from her bed and sat on a footstool near her father. "She says that the mill owners take all the risk. That's why they should take the rewards. You say the workers make all the money for the owners, and they should share the profits with the owners. It's confusing—"

Emma's call from the kitchen interrupted their talk. "Sophie, come to dinner and tell your papa to come, too."

*Mama, you tell him.* She motioned for her Papa to come to the table.

Sophie customarily read some of the *The New York Times* to Meyer on Sunday mornings and then spent time with her mother cleaning house and doing handwork while Meyer read the Yiddish papers.

On this snowy Sunday morning, Emma and Sophie prepared to sit down in the parlor to knit when Emma asked, "Sophie, did you polish the wood on my settee with linseed oil this morning?"

"Yes, Mama. I know how you like to take care of your good mahogany settee."

Sophie sat down beside Emma on the red velvet cushion and put her knitting basket on the floor nearby. The ornate piece of furniture sat beneath the two lace-curtained windows that faced the street. Sophie knew that Emma was equally proud of the new gray-green wallpaper with gold leaves and tiny red flowers for which she had scrimped, and over which she had supervised Meyer's hanging of the precious rolls.

"Ah, Sophie, someday we'll have more furniture like this settee instead of cheap oak furniture from the Montgomery Ward catalog."

"I like your embroidery on the seat cushions better than this velvet, Mama."

"What do you know about quality? Embroidery costs me nothing. But the settee…"

"Yes, Mama, I know how much you paid for it."

The two picked up their knitting, each with her own thoughts, until Sophie spoke.

"I had a dream last night, Mama. I was looking up at a giant wood door. Mama, it was as tall as a whole house, and the handle was so high! It was a fancy door with carving, maybe one of those horses with a horn on its forehead. I don't know what was on the other side, but I knew I had to get in there."

"*Nu?* What did you do?"

"I knocked, but my sound was so tiny. I found a big rock and threw it against the door to make someone hear, but it landed with a plop on the step. I started to cry and I kicked at the door. Then something strange happened."

"Yah?"

"I stood on tiptoe and stretched so high, higher than I thought I could reach. I almost touched the handle. I was almost there, Mama, but I woke up. What did it mean, Mama? What was behind the door?"

"Maybe you're not ready to see what is behind the door, Sophie."

"But what was behind the door?"

"Maybe your future. Maybe you'll see behind the door when you're ready."

"But Mama, I'm ready now."

Sophie thought about this idea of her future, which led her to ponder the difference in outlook between her parents. Mama doesn't really see who I am, she thought. Sophie perceived her mother's dream for the future as having more and better possessions. There would be no change, only more of the present. She compared it to her papa's glorious vision of a new and very different future.

As she reflected on this schism between her parents, her stomach tightened and her features stiffened. She clutched her knitting needles tightly, unable to allow the smooth flow of stitches from one needle to the other. She put her work in her lap and looked down at it.

"*Nu*, Sophie? You have nothing more to say?"

"No, Mama, I was still thinking about my dream."

Emma felt the tension and searched for a way to engage her daughter. "Do you still do the finger exercises that I taught you, Sophie? I do them every day to keep my fingers strong and nimble. Hold up your hands and show me how you do it."

"Oh, Mama, not now…Oh, all right." She began the drill despite her reticence. She held her hands palms facing inward and fingers together. She separated one finger at a time and brought it back to meet the others. Then she did the same thing by twos.

"*Gut.* You can make each finger work for you, and that's what makes you handy—just like me."

"Yah. Just like you." Sophie tried to smile, but the corners of her mouth wouldn't move that way.

"Someday, Sophie, we will be rich. I have a plan to own a fancy store downtown, so I can make a lot of money from those rich Eastside ladies. I'll buy you plenty of pretty things."

"Yah, Mama. Is that what's behind the big door in my dream?"

# THREE

## February 1911

**E**mma calculated that she had given Bessie sufficient time to mull over her tantalizing idea of earning more money. She arrived at Bessie's store on a Monday to execute the next step of her plan to acquire her cousin's store for herself. As soon as she set foot in the shop Bessie asked, "What are your ideas, Emma, to make more money?"

*Sarah Bernhardt I'm not, but I got my audience.* "Well, to tell you the truth, Bessie, it will take money to make money. We have to clean up the windows and buy some displays. No one wants to come into a shabby store."

"But, wait, Emma. What do you mean 'shabby'? I clean, and I wash the counter."

"Yah, that's true."

Emma sniffed the air. *Smells like a musty closet in here.* She walked through the storefront to the cluttered stockroom in the rear of the store where boxes of garments were strewn about the floor. Emma pushed them aside with her foot. She had often considered organizing the merchandise, but she had put the thought aside and instead added it to her mental list of criticisms.

"Bessie, you don't mind I open the door? Only a little."

"It's too cold, Emma."

*It's too cold? It stinks in here!* "I know you wash the counter, but it's more than cleaning, Bessie. We have to make it look elegant to attract rich ladies," she continued. "We must advertise, have a 'try-on' room, and make from this shop a gorgeous showroom that will bring in the elite of the Paterson ladies. That's to start."

"Emma, a 'try-on' room? The ladies will put the brassieres on here, in the store?"

"Well, sure, Bessie. Maybe they pick the wrong size, and they need to try another one. That way I wouldn't have to go back to their house to bring a different size."

"I see, Emma, but you said, 'shabby.'"

"Bessie, not to insult you, but the colors in here are faded and dull, and there is no way to show off the merchandise."

Emma walked around the perimeter of the store, noting the stained and peeling paint. "For instance, Bessie. Look at these gray walls. With a little money we can paint them a bright yellow."

Bessie nodded, but her usual smile faded, causing her pockmarked jowls to sag. For a moment Emma felt empathy for her aging cousin, but she pressed on with her litany. "There is only one chair in the store for customers, and the stuffing is coming out of the seat. When the ladies bring their friends, where will they sit?

"And do you think we can serve a little tea? You have no mannequins. You know, Bessie, mannequins are the newest way to show off the merchandise..."

"Emma, stop already. If I have to buy display tables and chairs and pay to advertise, I will need money, like you said. I can't ask Mordechai for money. Already he thinks I don't make enough from his investment."

"Bessie, we can talk about this later." *Keep her in suspense.* "Here are the sales I made today. I sold eight dollars, less my thirty percent. I owe you five dollars and sixty cents. I'll need another brassiere, another corset, and one pantaloon. I'll go in the back and find what I need, and then I have to go."

Emma rushed from the store before Bessie could say another word. With her two dollars and forty cents, she went to Washington Street where all of the kosher shops and stalls lined the streets. She haggled over the price of a freshly butchered chicken, remembering how in Lodz her family of seven considered one *Shabbos* chicken a treat for the whole family. Shaking her thoughts from the past, she hurried home with her mind once again free to think about her plans for Bessie's store.

Emma assumed that Harry would lend her the money to buy into the store, but she wouldn't let on to Bessie until she had done her research. She sent for the *John Wanamaker*, the *Lovelee*, and *The Bedell Company* catalogs from New York, all well-known manufacturers of ladies undergarments. Each evening after dinner she piled her kitchen table in the Fair Street apartment with the catalogs and copies of the "big six" women's magazines—*Ladies' Home Journal*, *McCall's*, *Delineator*, *Woman's Home Companion*, *Pictorial Review*, and *Good Housekeeping*.

"Listen, Meyer," she said as she pored over the publications. "I'm going to buy a share of Bessie's store."

"From where did you get such an idea?"

"For a long time I am thinking that Bessie is no saleswoman. I told you how shabby that store is. Now I'm going to make of it a fancy shop."

"I shouldn't ask, but how do you think to do this?"

"Already I am thinking to get the money…"

"I know. From Harry or George."

"Why not? Harry is happy to help. I'll have four hundred dollars to buy a half share from Bessie. She doesn't know everything yet."

"Poor Bessie. She doesn't know from an Emma who has made up her mind."

"Why 'poor Bessie'? She'll make more money with me than she could before."

"Emma, Emma. Go ahead. Make money." Meyer sighed, looked heavenward, and resumed his reading of *The Jewish Daily Forward*.

On Sunday, Emma went with Sophie in tow to visit her brother Harry, who had sent his chauffeur for them. She never failed to feel like a woman of means when she sat erect on the cushy, black leather rear seat of Harry's Model T with Sophie at her side, dressed in her prettiest lace dress, a huge silk ribbon in her hair.

Today she would ask Harry for a loan of four hundred dollars to buy in as a partner in Bessie's store. Harry would be sympathetic since Meyer quit his mill without a thought for how to support his family. He had looked after Emma ever since she was a little girl in their one-room ghetto home.

The Abramowitz's aproned servant opened the door, and the sweet aroma of Sophie's favorite pot roast, tsimmes with prunes, wafted outward. Sophie whispered in Emma's ear, "I hope they serve apple strudel, Mama."

"Yah, Sophie," she answered as the two walked into the house. "Say hello to your aunts, and then you can go with your cousin for a while."

Sophie said her hellos and then went in search of Charlotte, her cousin and closest friend. Emma looked into the salon that opened to the right of the entryway where her eldest brothers, Harry and George, sat with their wives, Selma and Rose, on lush, green velvet settees. The men rose to greet their sister and then left the room to smoke in the library across the hall.

"Sophie looks lovely with her thick curls, bless her," Rose offered.

"She should only grow healthy," said Emma.

"*Nu*, Emma. Why not?"

The sisters-in-law returned to their discussion of fashion, and of all things, thought Emma, the right of women to vote.

"They have always been ahead of us in the western territories." Rose picked up the thread of their previous discussion. "Women in Wyoming and Colorado all vote. Pioneers, I think. Yah? The state of Washington granted suffrage just last year."

"In 1776 when the New Jersey constitution was written, the drafters had the good sense to allow the vote to everyone, including women. The catch was that the person had to be worth fifty pounds," said Selma.

"I'm worth more than that! I didn't know we could vote, Selma!" said Rose.

"Rose, those New Jersey politicians took the vote away in 1807. They got nervous about all the women with power."

Selma turned to Emma. "I've been helping to organize the WPU's New York march for suffrage next week, Emma. It's the first of its kind in this country, and we expect at least three thousand women with street speakers and pickets. Would you like to join us on Wednesday?"

"What WPU?" asked Emma.

"You know, Harriot Stanton Blatch's work. It's the Women's Political Union."

"Oh, that WPU," said Emma, trying to conceal her ignorance.

Selma saw Emma's confusion and quickly changed the topic. "Emma, have you finished that lovely afghan you were working on?" she said.

"Not yet. It's a complicated pattern." Emma answered tersely as she suppressed disdain for the suffrage work of her sisters-in-law. *What good would the right to vote do me? I already have the right to earn money, and I can make myself a Somebody without a vote.*

When Anna the housekeeper came in to announce dinner, Emma got up quickly to seat herself next to Harry.

Once the meal was served and conversation begun, Emma asked her brother for a private moment after dinner. Harry nodded and said that he would talk to her in his office later.

Following the main meal, Emma made short work of her strudel and poked Harry meaningfully with her elbow.

"Okay, Emma. We get up now."

As they walked toward the other room, Emma put her arm through his and drew him near. "Harry, you know Cousin Bessie. She is making nothing from that shop of hers. I make money from selling her goods, but I could make much more from running that shop..."

"Wait, Emma. Let's sit down first, and I'll pour us some brandy. Relax a little." He moved toward the table where he had a decanter and glasses.

"I don't need brandy. I want to ask you something," she said as she sat down on the settee.

"All right. No brandy." Harry was used to Emma's ways, so sat in a nearby chair and got to the point. "What do you want from me, Emma?"

"Harry, I need four hundred dollars to buy a half share in Bessie's shop. Enough dragging those satchels through the streets. I'll make a first-class business from her store, and when she retires, I'll buy her out. We both know Meyer will never amount to anything. I need to make the living."

"Emma, you have a plan?"

"Yah. I know what I have to do."

He repositioned himself in his leather chair and looked directly at Emma. "I can see your jaw set in place. There is no getting in your way when you look like that. As a young girl in Poland you got that look on your face, and you always got your way. Remember before the twins were born when George and I slept on our mats near the wall oven?"

"Yah, Harry. I remember, but..."

"Mama didn't want you to sleep on the dirt floor, because you were too young," he said. "She made you sleep at the foot of our parents' bed. You set your jaw and said, 'I want to sleep near my brothers.' You got your way. Stubborn is what you are."

"*Nu?* I don't like every time to run to you for money, but what can I do? You and George are the only ones I can go to." *But someday…someday I won't have to go to anyone for money. I'll make it for myself.*

"All right, Emma. I'll loan you the money, and you start to pay me back when you can."

"Harry, you won't feel sorry about this. I take your money with thanks, and from it I'll make a good business."

"Yah, Emma. I think you will."

With a four-hundred-dollar check written to Emma Epstein from National City Bank, all that was left to do was to convince the naïve Bessie that she needed a partner.

Several weeks later, Emma and Bessie's partnership was an accomplished fact. Bessie's husband, who anticipated better profits as a result of Emma's skill and determination, saw to that.

The two women sat in the newly painted shop on Broadway after closing time. The stockroom had been remodeled to include a fitting room, and the wax mannequins that Emma ordered were brazenly nude, awaiting their new silk shirts. Emma compromised with Bessie on the parlor suite that had been purchased from the Montgomery Ward catalog, spending much less than she had hoped. They bought an ornate carved settee and two armchairs made of imitation mahogany with red and gold damask-upholstered seats for $17.85. The legs were gracefully curved and the seats and backs were tufted and buttoned. No one had to know they were catalog pieces.

Emma had done some comparison shopping. "Quackenbush's department store always runs full-page ads in the *Paterson Evening News*. Their cambric is schlock. It won't keep its shiny stiffness, and the seams aren't reinforced. Even with their sale on drawers for twenty-two cents, we'll have no trouble selling good quality cambric drawers for forty-nine cents."

"But Emma, so much money?" asked Bessie.

"Our customers will pay for the quality and the fuss we make over them."

"How much fuss can we make over a cotton brassiere?"

"We don't have to sell only brassieres and corsets when we can buy these beautiful silk shirts to wear under the new style of long jackets and gored skirts. Look at this picture, Bessie. It says, 'Silk waist, buttons in back. Made of silk taffeta. Circular lace, yoke front and back, elaborately trimmed with Venice silk braid, silk lace and silk piping. Choice of black or white, and choice of long or three-quarter-length sleeves.'"

"I can read English, Emma."

Ignoring Bessie's annoyance, Emma proceeded with her plans. "Now Bessie, the new wax mannequins can't stay too long in the window. You know they'll start to melt in the hot sun, so we'll move them back into the store. What can we put in the window to attract our clients in the hot months?"

Bessie's eyes darted around the shop looking for an answer to Emma's question, but before she could open her mouth, Emma continued.

"Hats! We'll buy a supply of those wide-brimmed hats with colorful flowers— and ones with feathers, too. They will bring in the ladies. *Nu?* Bessie, why don't you say something?"

# FOUR

## March 1911

**There** was a crowd in Max's candy store this Sunday morning when Sophie went to buy *The New York Times*. She wondered what happened to bring in this abnormal glut of customers. As the crowd pushed her thin frame forward, she heard their murmurs.

"A *shandeh*! A real shame such a thing could happen," said an elderly neighbor from her building.

"They all died? How many?" asked another.

"Let me through," cried another neighbor. "My cousin works in that factory."

When Sophie finally reached the newsstand, she grabbed for the last of two newspapers on the rack and paid her five cents. She shouldered her way out and walked onto the street where she might be able to read the front page. There was a picture of a flaming factory building, focused on a ladder that was too short to reach the top floor where frantic workers were trapped by flames. She sat down on the curb to read the description of the shirtwaist factory fire, and when she could no longer contain her tears, she ran home with the paper, threw it on her bedroom floor, and flung herself onto her bed, sobbing into her pillow.

Meyer was out when she arrived home with the paper, but Emma came running when she heard Sophie crying, and she stepped unaware over the ghastly headlines on the floor.

### 141 Men And Girls Die In Shirtwaist Factory Fire
### Trapped High Up In Washington Place Building
### Street Strewn With Bodies; Piles Of Dead Inside

She sat mute on the bed beside her daughter and reached out, placing her hand on Sophie's back. "Don't cry, Sophie. Why do you cry, darling?"

Sophie continued with unabated tears. Emma remained on the bedside, a tentative hand on Sophie's back, lips pursed, and squinting back tears of frustration from her own eyes. She inhaled deeply and released a sibilant flow of air, raised and dropped her shoulders in resignation, and stepped once more over the newspaper without noticing the headlines as she left the room.

Minutes later, Meyer returned from his walk and went to Sophie when he heard her sobs. He glanced at the papers and couldn't make out the English, but there was no mistaking the striking photo of fire at the upper levels of a ten-story factory with the firemen's aerial ladders only reaching between the sixth and seventh floors.

"Sophie, *Meine Liebe*, is it this picture that makes you cry?" he asked as he turned her shoulder to face him and reached for her with his arms.

He held and comforted her for several minutes before she was calm enough to read some of the article to him. Emma stood at the doorway while her daughter read the news.

"One hundred twenty-five of the six hundred sweatshop victims were girls between sixteen and twenty-five years, many, heads of immigrant families…The pieceworkers died trying to exit a door that had been locked from the outside to prevent them from leaving the work floor during their work hours…One of the two elevators was not working, and the single fire escape had collapsed, so they jumped from the tenth floor or else they died in the fire."

"Papa, what can we do to help these poor families? The paper says that some of them have no one to support them anymore."

"Tomorrow I ask at the Workmen's Circle. Maybe there is something we can do."

"Papa, please can we go to see the Triangle Shirtwaist Factory? I want to see for myself. I can bring my savings from the doilies that I sold in Mama's shop."

"This is a terrible tragedy," exclaimed Emma when she heard this request. "But to go all the way to New York? Miss school? Miss work? Can you change what has been done?"

"You know your mama," Meyer whispered in Sophie's ear. "We won't have any peace if you stay out of school. We can help maybe another way."

On Tuesday Meyer learned that the International Ladies' Garment Workers' Union had organized its own relief committee in concert with the Workmen's Circle. Sophie gave Meyer her savings of three dollars for the relief fund.

That Tuesday evening, the thirteen-year-old girl and her father sat arm in arm on the backyard stoop with well-worn chair pads for comfort. The air still held the memory of winter on that late March evening. Icicles dripped from the eaves above them with a steady splat onto the pavement. Snow had receded from the withered lawn except for a small gray patch in a shady corner, and a lone lilac tree held its hopeful limbs erect while building strength to sprout its fragrant buds.

"Before you know it, the time will come to plant our tomato seeds. I saw in the store a packet," commented Meyer.

"Last year we had good luck. I love the smell of the leaves on my hands when we trim our plants," said Sophie.

"Yah. Spring is coming soon. New hope for every living thing."

"Papa, remember you told me about the strikes of the shirtwaist factory girls so long ago? You called it 'The Uprising of the Twenty Thousand.' Why didn't they listen to those girls then, Papa? Why didn't they unlock the doors so the girls could get out? They wouldn't have stole, like the bosses said. They wouldn't be dead now, Papa."

"It's not easy to make those bosses give more money. Now, I think after this big fire, change will come. We'll read *The Forward* and the other papers, and we'll see what happens. Maybe these deaths will shame the owners to make the factory safe."

"Will the workers ever get an eight-hour day, Papa? Will they give it now, Papa?"

Meyer took his daughter's hand in his, and with a sad smile he squeezed it and shook his head up and down, but his eyes did not smile.

# January 1912

**E**mma yearned for a quiet evening at home, alone with her teacup and her thoughts, her catalogs, her dreams. She had struggled with Bessie throughout the fall about adding new styles and keeping inventory organized and accessible. Now, in the middle of winter, they fought over the heating bill, Bessie in her tatty woolen sweater turning the heat down each time Emma turned her back.

"Bessie, we must keep the shop warm and comfortable for our customers to try on garments," she had repeated to no avail.

This evening as Emma prepared to relax at home, she thought about Bessie's eventual retirement, and a smile replaced her scowl. The kitchen was quiet and clean after dinner. Sophie was doing homework, and Meyer, blessedly, was at the Workmen's Circle. Emma had changed into her satin padded housecoat, the violet one with the lovely quilted design on the collar and cuffs, the one that made her feel like a lady. She took out one of her mother's china cups and brewed herself a cup of Lipton tea, the Quality No.1 from a bright yellow packet.

She laid out the latest *Wanamaker's* catalog, sat down, and began to leaf through the current styles, stopping at a page with a modern French corset of ivory silk and bone with garters attached. "That quality would suit my wealthiest customers," she thought, but the image vanished like a bolt of lightning when the kitchen door flew open and Meyer appeared, much earlier than usual. He pulled off his overcoat, hung it over a kitchen chair, and sat down across from Emma.

"They finally lowered the workweek in the Lawrence woolen mills from fifty-six to fifty-four hours, and those shysters had to take the difference out of the workers' pay. That's thirty-two cents a week from their nine dollars—a few loaves of bread it could buy. Yesterday some women left that mill, shouting, 'Short pay, short pay!'"

Emma looked up from her catalog, frowned, and clicked her tongue.

"They went on strike! Do you hear me, Emma? More will join them. I tell you a real strike will come to our mills here. Our time will come. Remember in Poland—"

"Don't tell me about Poland, Meyer," she said as she turned a page. "I am tired of hearing about 'the workers.'"

"Emma, this is news. We were talking about it at the Workmen's Circle. The IWW has been organizing for years to make this happen in Massachusetts, but we don't need the IWW to organize here. We'll be ready when the time comes."

"Meyer, I'm working to make a new life. Here," she said, pointing to her catalog, "this is where I make the money. When we left the old country we had a dream to come to America for a new life." Emma slammed her catalog shut.

"Emma, please let me—"

"Can't you let me live in peace without your talk of strikes?" she yelled as she stood and gathered her robe around her.

Before leaving the room, she threw out her last barb. "God in Heaven! What did you do? You and your friends brought Lodz to Paterson. Why couldn't you leave the workers' movement back in Poland?"

"Will you never understand?" Meyer cried as he pushed away from the table, nearly knocking over a chair on his way to the front room. He sat back into a Morris chair, pulled out his pipe, and opened *The Daily Forward.* After a moment he snapped the newspaper shut and returned to follow Emma into the bedroom.

"Why should the weavers run four looms without getting more pay? Tell me that, Emma."

"Your trouble is you can't see what the owner needs to make a success. They have to pay for the raw silk, the brokers, the rent, the upkeep, the workers' pay, the modernizing…"

"Emma, it's not right. We work too hard for too little."

"You are right about that, but the workers won't win in Paterson. The bosses will win. This great 'Silk City' will die before the owners let the workers run their mills. Mark my words, Meyer. Mark my words."

The day after Meyer told Emma about the woolen mill strike in Lawrence, Massachusetts, he was in need of camaraderie. When his day at Doherty's ended, he hastened to the Workmen's Circle to see what news had transpired that day. He descended the narrow steps to the cement-floored cellar room, excusing himself and squeezing between the closely packed tables to join an active conversation with his friends. Seven men sat around the heavy black wooden table, its outer channel filled with poker chips. Solly Bergman, Hymie Minsk, Isaac Shmuel, and Manny Shapiro, Meyer's closest friend, were among the group.

A smoky haze hung in the air from men who puffed on their pipes or cigars in a room of twenty poker tables, where ten would have been comfortable. Their damp, wool winter coats absorbed the tobacco aroma that each man carried home at night.

When Meyer sat down in the last available chair, his group was straining to hear Manny talk above the other card players' calls and the clacking poker chips. He was holding a copy of *Solidarity*, the Industrial Workers of the World publication.

"The Wobblies helped the woolen mill workers in Lawrence, Massachusetts, organize for a strike. It started with ten thousand workers, and soon they had twenty thousand," said Manny.

"I hear it's worse up there than even we have it. They have *kinderlekh*, little children, working like grown women in that American Woolen Company," said Hyman.

"Yah, Hymie. Half those workers are girls not yet eighteen, and some are even less than fourteen. Meyer, your little Sophie could be working there."

"My Sophie? God forbid!"

"It's the work speedup that's the problem," interrupted a new voice at the table. Isaac Shmuel spoke up. "With two new looms, those mill owners produced more goods and laid off the rest of the workers. We see it right here in Paterson, and it could get worse if all the mill bosses make us work four looms. We could lose our jobs here, I tell you."

"Look who's talking! You finally open your mouth, Isaac, and out come pearls," said Hyman. "He's talking the truth. My wife's cousin was working up there until we brought her family to Paterson. The apartment was a *shandeh*! Twelve people in three tiny rooms. Bread, molasses, and beans to eat. No meat. No chicken, even on *Shabbos*.

"My Malke found them a place to live on Governor Street. Manny got her husband a job at Doherty's like he put in for you, Meyer. Do you know him, Velvil Hamish? His wife is Malke's cousin."

"I didn't meet him yet," said Meyer. "I heard that young *shikseh* Flynn is up there now. Such a mouth she has! She reminds me like that little Clara Lemlich in the Triangle Shirtwaist Factory. What is her name, Hymie? You remember."

"Yah. Elizabeth Gurley Flynn from the IWW."

"That's the one. She's a child herself. And it's a good thing, too, she should be there," said Meyer. "*The Forward* said that thirty-six out of every hundred workers in that mill die before age twenty-five. Oy! Half the children die from hunger and sickness before six years. Mind you, the lint from the wool is bad for the lungs. Thanks God the silk don't shed lint like wool."

"Wait a minute, Meyer. Are you saying we have it good here?" Solly asked.

"Solly, you know me better. I think maybe we need the Wobblies to help here in Paterson."

Manny chimed in. "Yah. We join all our trades together for a mass strike. Then we call in the Wobblies. If they get better hours and fair pay in Lawrence, we should do the same."

Meyer had privately decided that the IWW Local 152 could help to unite the dyers, the broad silk workers, and the ribbon workers in Paterson. He knew that the decision might not be popular with some of his *landsmen* who were staunch supporters of the AFL. They thought the IWW was too radical, but he made up his mind to speak.

"My friends, already I joined the IWW Local 152," said Meyer. "I think maybe they can help us better than the AFL that keeps our trades apart."

Silence. Manny smiled at his close friend, but Solly's mouth dropped open. He would be the tough one to win over. The men sat forward as Meyer drew on his pipe and exhaled with a great expulsion of smoke.

"Listen. Joseph Ettor from the IWW was organizing up there in the woolen mills for months before the strike. Then he and that Italian, Giovannitti, made up a committee with two people from each group—you know, two Poles, two Italians, two Irish, two Jews…"

"Yah, yah, go on."

"There were twenty-five languages spoken at that first meeting, and they had—what you call it?—an interpreter for each language so everybody was equal. They figured out their demands."

"Yah," called out Manny. "I heard they are asking for a fifty-four-hour workweek and a fifteen percent raise! They want double-time pay for overtime, and they want a promise of no revenge against the strikers."

"It's a dangerous thing they're doing," Isaac ventured. "The Lawrence mayor called out the local cops, and the strikers called out thousands of picketers. Then the owners turned fire hoses on the picketers."

"It could get very dirty," cautioned Meyer. "People lose their tempers. They break windows, they throw things, and then they go to jail. It's a war up there, and the judge wants to teach them a lesson. The governor even sent out the state police. I think we should wait to see how it goes. If the Wobblies help them to win, then we get our own workers together."

"We can make a strong strike committee if we pull enough of our own Lodz brothers together," Manny was quick to add.

On Sunday, Emma and Sophie went to visit the Abramowitz family at Uncle George's house, giving Sophie a chance to talk in private with her cousin Charlotte. The girls adored each other, even though Emma's constant comparing of the two annoyed Sophie.

"Your cousin Charlotte knows what is good for a young girl. She plans to go to college and marry a man of position. What? You're not as smart as she?" Emma would say. "You could do the same."

The friends lay across Charlotte's large brass bed with the lacy white canopy, Charlotte on her back and Sophie on her side facing her cousin, head propped on her palm. She was quiet today, after hearing her parents argue about the Lawrence strike.

"Oh, Charlotte, I wish I could be like you. Mama would be so happy if I could go to college with you and then get married right away…"

Charlotte sat up and said, "Don't talk like that, Coz. You're much smarter than I am. You can do great things in your life besides getting married and raising children."

"But, Char, you really want a husband and a home. You'll be a wonderful mother, and I'll be the auntie."

"Oh, stop. You'll have children too, Sophie. Anyway, we're only in high school. You won't even be fourteen till next month. We have lots of time to think about it, even though some girls have boyfriends already."

"Yes, but not the Jewish girls, or even the Italians. Our parents are so strict."

Charlotte lay on her back again, stretched her leg upward, and pointed her toe, revealing a muscled calf. She jumped up and grasped the barre that her mother had installed for her on a mirrored wall, extended her leg high above her head, lowered it to the ballet fourth position, made a plié, and turned a sharp pirouette. Her loose skirt wrapped itself around her legs as she spun.

"Come on, Sophie, you try."

"Not me, Char. Especially after you told me about your ballet mistress who bangs on the floor with that big stick to keep time. I have enough strictness at home. I was thinking about something else. Did you read the newspapers about the strike in Lawrence, Massachusetts?"

"No. I didn't read it. My papa takes the newspapers to his office and I never see anything," she said, lifting her leg onto the barre and stretching forward.

"Papa and Mama were fighting about it the other day when I was in my room doing homework. They don't seem to care if I listen. They almost scream."

Charlotte left the barre to sit on the bed next to Sophie. She leaned close to her cousin and waited for the news that had caused another fight in the Epstein household.

"Papa was talking about the strike in a woolen mill, and he was saying that a strike would come to Paterson, too. He got very excited and talked louder and louder. Sometimes I put a pillow over my head, but this time I had too much homework to do. He was saying that the weavers need more money, and they work too many hours."

"You wouldn't hear that kind of talk in this house. What did your mama say?"

"She yelled back that he doesn't make enough money. She said that the bosses won't give in to strikers."

Charlotte put her arm around Sophie's shoulder and squeezed. "I'm sorry that you have to listen to all of that."

Both girls sat with hanging heads, silent. Charlotte breathed deeply. "Maybe you should come and live with us, Sophie."

"It's not that bad. I couldn't imagine being away from Papa."

When they went downstairs for dinner, Sophie tried to smile, but she couldn't get the sound of her mother's voice out of her head. "Those bosses will never give in to strikers. Mark my words," she had said. "They won't give away control of their mills."

# FIVE

## February 1913

**S**ophie smiled and nodded her understanding to Mr. Stechman as he droned on about the Civil War, but her mind was elsewhere. This sophomore history class had once been her favorite, but school had lost its interest for her since the night her father came home after leading his comrades out of Doherty's mill. Mr. Doherty had once more tried to impose the four-loom system on the workers.

Meyer had seemed unable to stop talking. Sophie cracked the doorway of her bedroom and watched him talk to her mother in the kitchen. Her eyes widened as she gazed in disbelief at Meyer outtalking Mama. Even in her parents' worst arguments, she had never seen her father in such a state of agitation. The usually quiet man seemed more animated, speaking in a frenzied monologue about the future of the strike and about how the other crafts would join the broadloom weavers.

He was beginning to perspire and removed his shirt collar while continuing his excited display.

*I never saw him so forward with Mama.* She watched her mother seated on a kitchen chair while her papa paced back and forth, energized beyond recognition. *Mama, where is your tongue?* Emma sat back in her chair, her jaw tight, unable to insert a word.

Meyer's voice escalated, and he pounded on the kitchen table with his fist. "The Central Committee and the Executive Committee called the strike today and five thousand weavers walked out! Five thousand weavers, do you hear? For a long time we planned it, and it worked. And, Emma, the dyers' helpers will walk off tomorrow. Finally! Finally! The different crafts will stick together this time."

Sophie stood transfixed. She blushed with excitement. *This is my quiet papa? He's telling her!* Meyer paced back and forth between the kitchen and the adjoining front room with deliberate speed, each placement of his booted foot landing firmly on the hardwood floor.

Finally, when it appeared that he had exhausted his energy, he stood erect before his seated wife. Sophie opened the crack to get a better look at her papa. She saw his shoulders sag, his beseeching eyes, and her mother's relenting smile as he took her arm and led her into their bedroom.

Sophie closed her door and listened to the poignant stillness in the apartment. After preparing for bed, she put her ear to her parents' common wall, not without guilt. The only thing she heard was the creaking springs of their bed.

# March 1913

The days of the strike wore on, and the number of strikers swelled to 24,000 men and women. The IWW leaders had arrived in Paterson in mid-February. They helped set up the Central Strike Committee to unite the various crafts and ethnic groups. The committee's job was to handle communications, organize mass meetings, manage a strike relief fund, and provide legal help for arrested strikers.

Sophie thrilled to Meyer's evening reports about the movement. "Please, Papa, can I come to a meeting for the strikers? I only want to see the leaders at a rally. I'll finish all of my schoolwork. I promise, Papa."

"You know how your mama feels about your education. I will tell you everything, so you know about the strike."

"I know how the IWW leaders came to help. And you're on the Executive Committee, right Papa?"

"Yah, and the Central Strike Committee."

"What are Big Bill and the others like?"

"Big Bill Haywood was in on the Lawrence mill strike, and he came here last week. He's a big Texas man with one of those Stetson hats.

"I saw a new book called *Riders of the Purple Sage* with pictures of cowboys. Was it like that, Papa?"

"I don't know, Sophie, but Bill Haywood knows how to run a strike, and with him came Carlo Tresca. He speaks Italian. Best is that little Elizabeth Gurley Flynn, only twenty-two years old and already experienced with strikes since when she was sixteen. She looks like you might knock her over, so tiny a girl. They sometimes call her 'Gurley.' Next to Big Bill, she's maybe like a big doll. But she makes all the strikers pay attention and sing out and cheer. No matter what language they speak. No matter their job. We all sing together."

Within a week of the February twenty-fifth walkout, Meyer's dream to unite workers of all nationalities and textile crafts was realized. The broadloom weavers, the ribbon weavers, the dyers, the dyers' helpers, the throwers, the twisters, the pickers—all joined forces for the first time. They picketed the mills every day, soon affecting 75,000 of Paterson's 124,000 people, including the almost 24,000 strikers and their families, as well as small-business owners and other creditors.

The remaining 50,000 people of Paterson who were not directly involved were forced to take sides in the strike. Some were connected to the mill owners or the city government or the police, while others were tradesmen, sympathetic to the working folks. No one was free from the conflict between the workers and the silk manufacturers, least of all the Epstein family.

Sophie could tell that Emma was caught between the Abramowitz business interests and her husband's cause. "Sophie, we won't go this week to Harry's house," she announced.

"But I was looking forward to seeing Charlotte."

"Sophie, it is not a good time," was all she had said. Charlotte had let her cousin know that the brothers were afraid to talk freely in front of Emma, because she might let something slip to Meyer. They were wary of any contact with the strikers.

Sophie recalled squeezing her eyelids to prevent tears from escaping. It seemed that her tears were often at the ready, her stomach was achy-tight, and she felt the frustration of energy with no outlet for action. Her thoughts were with the mill workers, but she was unable to formulate a plan to help.

Each night she asked her father, "Are we going to have time for the newspapers after dinner?"

"Yah, sure," he would say, and he read aloud in Yiddish from *The Worker* and she in English from the IWW's *Solidarity* newsletter. She assimilated socialist doctrines that attacked the bosses who reputedly cared for nothing but enriching their bank accounts at the laborers' expense. Meyer's daughter was as ready for this strike as any oppressed worker.

Sophie lay awake most nights, thinking of the families who suffered from loss of income. More vulnerable than usual from lack of sleep, she traipsed to school each morning with an anxious knot in the depth of her stomach. The unembellished façade of Eastside High School, a mammoth three-story red-brick building erected upon the ruins of an Indian burial ground, did nothing to assuage her unease. The vast paved yards that surrounded the building couldn't erase the fact that she was trespassing upon the ancient graves of the Lenni-Lenape Indians. Eastside's unruly football players, The Ghosts, presented another affront to those long-buried natives beneath their field.

Until now it wasn't entirely from this travesty, and surely not from aversion to her studies that made school difficult, but more recently she disliked the tumult of the passing time between classes. Cold stone floors and walls provided no cushion for the clamor and pushing, shouting and teasing that rattled her sensibilities and assaulted her overtired senses.

Boys of every nationality called to each other in their native tongue—Italian, Irish, Polish, Yiddish.

"Noon at Ben's candy store!"

"Tonight at the 'Y.'"

"Out of my way! Move over. Where ya goin', to a funeral?"

They crowded and elbowed anyone in their path. Some of the girls were as boisterous, but not Sophie, who, books held close to her chest, made efficient progress along the sidelines.

Now with the strike on her mind, she had no patience for her teachers or for enduring the anxiety of mingling with hordes of rowdy boys between classes. She had always loved the study of Latin, history, and English. She read late into the night. But now those pleasures were insignificant compared to the allure of the strikers' songs and slogans that Meyer brought with him in the evening. To Emma's horror, she sang along with him to "The Commonwealth of Toil."

In the gloom of mighty cities
Mid the roar of whirling wheels,
We are toiling on like chattel slaves of old,
And our masters hope to keep us
Ever thus beneath their heels,
And to coin our very lifeblood into gold.

But we have a glowing dream
Of how fair the world will seem
When each man can live his life secure and free.
When the earth is owned by Labor
And there's joy and peace for all
In the commonwealth of Toil that is to be.

As she listened to her father recount the day's activities, Sophie hungered to be in the picket lines, chanting those words. Each morning he went to Turn Hall at the corner of Cross and Ellison Streets, where the mass meetings were held. Then he went to the shop meetings to help develop daily tactics and instructions for the noontime pickets. He encouraged the men and women on the line and came home late, full of stories—who was dragged to prison, who showed bravery, who yelled the slogan the loudest, who said something clever, and most interesting of all, what Elizabeth Gurley Flynn did and said.

Sophie repeatedly begged her papa to allow her to attend a day of the strike, but he said, "Too dangerous for a little girl like you. A young girl must be in school."

"Papa, I'm not a little girl. I'm fourteen years old. I'm almost as old as some of the girls on strike."

Meyer finally agreed, and by some miracle, he convinced Emma to allow him to take Sophie to a Sunday gathering in Haledon where the socialist mayor William Brueckmann was sympathetic to the IWW's ideals. Pietro Botto, an Italian immigrant weaver, had a new house built for his family in Haledon, and he made his balcony available for Sunday meetings, which had been banned by the City of Paterson's blue laws. Workers gathered on the undeveloped tract of land near the Botto home, dubbing it "The Green."

Meyer held Sophie close to him on the crowded Haledon trolley. She reached up to whisper in his ear, "Papa, will Elizabeth Gurley Flynn speak today?"

Then she looked up at him with her deep blue eyes and long thick lashes that nearly touched her full eyebrows. Her adoring father studied her intense face as she asked about her idol. *When did she grow to be beautiful like a woman?*

She noticed his gaze and asked, "What is it, Papa?"

"Nothing, my daughter. Only you have grown so beautiful. You must take care of yourself."

"Thank you, Papa. I always take care. Will she speak today?"

"Yah, Sophie. Elizabeth speaks on Sundays. You never saw her before, that young girl with so much power in her voice."

"No, Papa. That's why I wanted to come with you."

The trolleys disgorged thousands of workers and their families from crowded Paterson neighborhoods into this new suburb. There were speeches, singing, chanting, dancing, and music, all planned by the Central Strike Committee to maintain the workers' high spirits through the trying times of the strike.

The radiant sun had chased March clouds. The air was crisp and clean with the promise of spring. A crowd of about five thousand strikers and their families trod the last patches of dirty brown snow into the damp grass, and icicles that still hung from the eaves dripped rhythmically to the ground.

The land in front of the Botto house was packed with bodies jammed one against another. Children wiggled in their parents' arms. A low hum emanated from the crowd, peaceful, but anticipatory.

Meyer pulled himself to his full five-foot eight-inch height and raised his chin to survey his fellow strikers, each one a comrade. He smiled, more content than he had been in months as he held Sophie's hand. Aware of a stirring in the crowd, he nudged her and pointed to Botto's daughter Eva, who was guiding Elizabeth Gurley Flynn through a crushing mass of bodies into the house and up to a second-story balcony, where she would deliver her address.

"Sophie, some weeks there are twice this number of people."

The crowd began to chant, "Gurley, Gurley, Gurley!" and then a hush swept through the mass, when one by one they recognized the young woman leaning over the balcony in her long black skirt, white shirtwaist, and black string tie. Her hair was parted in the center and pulled back from her face, a traditional demeanor belying her politics. She raised her fist high in the air, and a roar of cheers filled the Green. She shouted, "Eight-hour day!" and the crowd echoed the chant until she held up her hand for them to stop.

Her tiny body projected a voice as fierce as a man twice her size. She had learned from her IWW training how to modulate her voice so that a multitude of even ten thousand could hear it. She mesmerized the crowd. When she smiled, the people smiled; when she frowned, the people frowned.

Sophie stood transfixed as she listened to the passionate young woman.

"Papa, I want to be a part of this strike, not only on Sunday."

"Now, Sophie…"

"No, Papa. I want a *Little Red Songbook*, and I want to sing out with the strikers in this battle for workers' freedom. I want to hear the songs in all different languages from all of the immigrants. I want to hold a picket and demand an eight-hour day. I want to help the younger workers especially to get fair pay for their work. I…"

Meyer wondered if he had made a mistake by bringing his ardent daughter to the picnic. "Enough. You come on Sundays. That is all."

After another week of school, Sophie couldn't bring herself to pass through Eastside's halls or sit in another class. As soon as the bell rang for lunch, she made for the rows of tall steel basement lockers, arriving there before most of the lunch crowd. She turned her combination lock automatically, although she often worried that she would forget the right numbers and turns. Sophie reached to the upper shelf for her scarf, wrapped it around her neck, put on her coat, and slipped from the building, feeling some regret that the class she would miss was Mr. Stechman's.

She hastened down Park Avenue, one of the loveliest residential streets she knew, but didn't spend her usual amount of time admiring the mansions. The day was cold but clear. Mild winds dispersed the fumes of an occasional Model T. A rare patch of dirty brown snow still littered the nascent lawns, but a few determined spring robins pecked for worms. Winter gloom was on the wane. If Sophie had looked closely, she might have seen the newly formed buds on the windblown maples and oaks.

Within a short time, she arrived at city hall, that great building on Market Street whose niches, within the upper façade of the ornate clock tower, were home to flocks of noisy pigeons. The birds bobbed and pecked at the naked ground. No one was feeding them today. The few people who passed city hall had their coats buttoned, shoulders hunched against the chill, and hands pushed deep into their pockets.

Sophie heard shouts from the crowds after she walked a few more blocks down Market Street. Looking overhead where American flags hung from the buildings, she saw an immense banner stretched across the street which read, "We live under this flag. We work under this flag. We will defend this flag."

*What does that sign mean? Defend the flag?* She didn't think it rang true to the strikers' tone, so she looked forward to questioning her papa without letting on that she saw the sign. Sophie made a deep sigh and continued her walk downtown, sorry to deceive her father.

Immense redbrick mills towered ahead as she approached the mill area. *They look like prisons, not workplaces.* She looked upward, scanning the clouded windows of the multistoried monuments to industry, and she shivered. She wiped the tears away from her eyes with the back of her hand. *It's so cold.* Sorrow overwhelmed her as she imagined her papa and thousands of others locked inside those dreary walls for ten hours a day. She sniffed and wiped her eyes again.

Now as she looked across the way, Sophie saw a throng of clamoring workers elbowing their way out of Turn Hall. Most men wore a long woolen coat, buttoned high at the neck with either a bowler or a woolen peaked cap. The Central Committee held daily mass meetings here to galvanize the strikers and to keep them energized for the fight. Groups of workers received their instructions for the day and were now organizing for the noontime picket lines.

She stood on the opposite side of the cobblestoned street among a group of onlookers who were watching the dispersing strikers. Vigilant foot policemen and haughty ones on horseback mingled among the strikers.

The crowd would soon be close enough to envelop her.

*Should I join in? Someone might see me and tell Papa.* She held back, an observer, wondering how she had had the nerve to leave school.

"Thank God I didn't cross the street," she muttered audibly when she saw several policemen on foot wield their nightsticks among the forming picket line. Others sat erect on horseback, wearing long double-breasted coats with two rows of brass buttons and a shiny badge. In contrast to the strikers' bowlers or woolen caps, they wore shiny stovepipe hats that added to their fearsome height above the striking laborers.

Every manner of person, men and women from among a dozen nationalities, assembled and held a picket sign despite the threat of nightsticks. "Eighthour day," they cried.

Rather than endure estrangement from the action, she left the hubbub and scurried down to the Passaic River where the Great Falls rushed into the raceways, within which a century-old system of waterwheels created power for the looms, the locomotive factories, and even for Colt's revolver factory. Wind carried a spray of water from the Passaic falls, which appeared artfully framed beneath one of the nine arched iron bridges that spanned the river. A rainbow, eerily visible every day, glimmered above it. Sophie stood captivated at the miraculous scene until she was forced to squeeze her eyes against the freezing droplets and wipe her face dry with her scarf.

She paced back and forth on the walkway above the river and then stopped to look across at the Great Falls hydroelectric power plant, the new brick building below the falls that was recently installed by Thomas Edison's electric company.

A plaque marked the place where in 1792 Alexander Hamilton had decided that Paterson's Great Falls would be the center of a new industrial city. Sophie wondered what he would he think of the servitude created by progress.

She sat down on a bench and drifted into reverie. The view reminded her of an automobile tour last summer when her Uncle George took her and Cousin Charlotte into the northern countryside. She recalled that the tributary rivers flowed from the mountains into the Passaic and she tried to name them all. The Whippany, the Rockaway, the Pequannock, Wanaque, Ramapo, and after a moment of hesitation, the Pompton. Indian names.

Thinking of the Indians who predated the harnessing of the Passaic, she imagined how they might have paddled canoes like the rented ones she had seen on Sunday afternoons in the park above the falls.

A sudden explosion of chanting from picketers who had marched to the river interrupted her daydream. "We wove the flag. We dyed the flag. We live under the flag. We won't scab under the flag."

Sophie now understood the meaning of the banner she had seen hanging across Market Street. The chanting was the strikers' retort to the bosses' attempt to lure the workers back to the mills by calling on their patriotism. *What will Papa have to say about that tonight?*

Emma overheard her husband and daughter discussing details of the IWW strategy as she sat with her needlework in the parlor. They were at the kitchen table with a kerosene lamp to light their copy of *Solidarity.*

She put down her knitting for a moment to listen more carefully. "Those foolish bosses gave away frankfurters at the Weidmann dye plant. *Nu?* The strikers went in and ate the food. Then they turned around and went back to the picket line, just like that! I think they were polite yet," he laughed.

"Bosses thought they would stay and work?" asked Sophie.

"Yah!" he said, and laughed some more.

Emma even laughed at that one before she picked up her knitting, but her amusement soon turned to anger as she listened to their complicity.

"People don't have money for undergarments from my store," she called to them in the kitchen. "Even the wealthy ones don't have extra to spend with the mills shut down. You call the bosses foolish, but we have no money coming into the house. Who is the foolish one?"

No answer came from the kitchen.

"Almost half the city is on strike. No one has money to buy. Did you hear me?" Emma called.

"Yah, Emma," answered Meyer.

"From where do you think the landlords will get the rent? From a stone, maybe? What about the grocer? This strike is killing business."

"I know, Emma. We talk later," called Meyer.

Emma snorted and continued to seethe about the lack of money. *What does he care about Sophie and me? The strike, the workers. That's all he thinks of.* She lamented Sophie's fate if she were to follow Meyer's passion. She would lose her daughter to the cause, and the dreams that she had for her—a good marriage, a beautiful home, a life of privilege—would vanish. The agonizing ache of this loss triggered her hands to stiffen on the knitting needles, and the smooth flow of stitches from needle to needle turned tight and resistant. Emma stuck the offending needles into the ball of yarn and shoved them into her wood-framed brocade knitting bag.

Emma exploded as she and Meyer prepared for bed that night.

"Well, Meyer. Our savings are almost gone, and there is no end in sight for the strike. I have no salary from the store. There is only enough income to pay the rent and overhead, and I can't ask my brothers for money when you are the reason for this strike."

"Wait a minute, Emma." Meyer's voice rose in anger. "The reason for this strike is low pay and too many hours, not me or the workers."

"*Shah,* Meyer. You'll wake Sophie."

"She knows already that we argue. Do you think she is deaf and blind?"

"Listen, it would kill me to go for charity, to stand on a breadline. You will have to care for your family, Meyer, and go to the General Relief Committee. Talk to the landlord about the rent. Plenty people don't pay rent already. Do you think he will throw us out? Who could afford to take our place?"

"Emma, I…"

"Time to stop dreaming now and feed your family. You have to go and stand on the food lines for groceries. You paid your five dollars to buy into the Purity Bakery Cooperative when Jews opened the business. Now you can get bread from them."

"Emma, you are right. It's time, now that our savings are gone."

"You can't depend on me while this strike is crippling my business, Meyer."

"Yah, I go tomorrow."

Bread for the table and Sophie's defection were only a part of the agony that Emma felt. Her brothers and even their wives shunned her because of Meyer's devotion to the strike, and the Abramowitz family had no doubt been relieved that Emma had begged off from Sunday dinners.

Equally bad, her neighbors recognized that despite Meyer's prominence in the strike, she wouldn't help the strikers. Most everyone in her building and in the whole Jewish neighborhood had chosen the workers' side, and they knew that Emma, a businesswoman, was a loyal member of the Abramowitz family of mill owners. She could feel their derision as she passed them in the hallway and on the street with their faces averted. There were no more greetings or neighborly chats. Worse yet, the names of everyone who had contributed to the strike fund were published in the as yet neutral *Paterson Evening News*. She was branded by her omission.

Emma wondered if she should make a small contribution to the strike fund through her business. *No, impossible.* She knew Harry would be furious to see her name on the list of strike contributors while she still owed him four hundred dollars.

The predicament plagued her. Her loyalty was to the silk manufacturers, but now she would be forced to take credit from her landlord and the grocer who supported the workers. There was no peace to be made with either side. Should she make a show of supporting her husband, or remain clearly on the side of her brothers and the other entrepreneurs?

With no way to resolve her discomfort, Emma approached Meyer with her dilemma.

"Meyer, sit a minute more. I need to talk to you," she said one evening while drinking tea after dinner.

"Don't worry, I'm not angry with you," she was quick to say when she saw the look of reluctance on his face.

"What is it Emma. Is there trouble?"

"Meyer. I have a problem."

"What, Dolly?"

"Meyer, I am a person no one will talk to. The people in our building look the other way when they see me. My family doesn't invite me to the house now, and I am alone with my conscience. I can't support the strike because of my brothers and the money that I still owe Harry. But I suffer living here and being the only one on the outside."

"Emma, do you think you would give support to the strike if you didn't have your rich brothers?"

"Such a question, Meyer. I see the business side, and yah, I see how hard you work for so little."

The two sat in rare companionable silence, finishing their tea and pondering a solution. As darkness enveloped the kitchen and Meyer lit the lamps, the coal stove emanated a warmth that contributed to a comfortable, protective feeling.

*It's good to sit a minute with my husband.*

The hiatus seemed to invigorate their intimacy. "Emma, we don't have extra money to give, but you might come to the benefit dance next Saturday night and help to serve the food or take hats at the door. Workers would see you there and maybe feel a little better toward you."

Emma was at first repulsed by the thought of serving, but thought better of speaking too soon. *This is not for me.* Then she thought about the wealthy ladies who sometimes help to cook and serve at their own charity benefits.

"Meyer, I have to say you have a good idea this time. I'll come to work in the kitchen where my clientele won't see me, but our neighbors will. Maybe they'll think better of me. Maybe I'll get a smile once in a while."

# Six

## April 1913

A stealthy routine became easier for Sophie after her initial truancy. She attended her first two classes and left in time for the ten AM meetings at Turn Hall. First she ventured to the basement where her tall metal locker was indistinguishable from the hundreds of others with their combination locks. Only its position in the row, the number on a tiny tag at the top, and an angry dent in the end locker made her own easy to find.

I'm glad to be getting taller, she thought as she reached to the top shelf where she stowed her books to retrieve them later in the day.

Sophie was burdened by fear of her mother's discovery and guilt over the angst it would cause her papa. She hated to disappoint Mr. Stechman, her favorite teacher, but she had no alternative. *I have to do this. I have to be at the pickets.*

She put on her coat and hurried out of the building on the Park Avenue side, heading downtown to Ellison Street where Turn Hall had been the favored meeting place of the dyers and broadloom weavers even before the strike. Its barroom proprietors offered a space large enough to accommodate the mass of strikers. The imposing stone building featured a two-story arch under which a massive wooden door opened onto the street. It stood next to a smaller wood-shingled shop with a tattered awning.

Sophie attended the meetings inside Turn Hall where the IWW now rented space for their Executive Committee and general meetings, but she avoided the picket lines for fear of being arrested. The thrill of being a part of thousands chanting with one united voice energized her. She was lifted almost to a state of ecstasy.

This day she stood on the main floor in Turn Hall, crushed shoulder to shoulder among the crowd. She looked up at the shouting throng of onlookers in the gallery above, smiled, and joined the chorus of "Eight-hour day!"

She felt a tap on her shoulder and turned to see a tall young man with an olive complexion and black curly hair looking down at her. Glancing up, she was astonished at the intensity of his almond-shaped green eyes.

"Who is that talking on the platform?" he asked.

"That's Hannah Silverman," she responded. "She's only seventeen, so brave and dedicated."

"Yah. Did you hear Gurley yesterday?"

"No, but I heard her in Haledon one Sunday."

At that moment Hannah stopped speaking and led the group in "The Commonwealth of Toil" to the tune of "Darling Nelly Gray." The young man held his copy of *The Little Red Songbook* open and stretched over to share the words with Sophie, who knew the chorus from evenings with her father. She reddened as she glanced sideways at him, but joined in the song with full voice.

Big Bill Haywood strode onto the stage. He held up his hand, and with five fingers stretched far apart said, "This is how we are when the AFL keeps us in separate trade unions, one for the dyers, one for the weavers. And this is how we are when we join the IWW!" He held his mighty fist high in the air and shook it at the invisible bosses. "We must stick together to be strong!"

Sophie joined the chorus of "IWW! Solidarity Forever!"

Perspiring in her heavy winter coat and hoarse from a morning of chanting and singing, she started to leave the hall when the meeting ended, but the young man reached for her arm. "Are you going to the picket lines?"

"I can't go to the picketing." She blushed and looked down at her toes.

"But they give us lunch first, and we stand together. I'll show you."

"I'd like to, but I can't."

"I don't understand," the young man said. "You seem like one of us."

"Yes," she replied, growing redder and more embarrassed. "You see, I sneaked out of school to come here. My father is on strike, but he wants me to finish school."

"What's your name?"

"Sophie Epstein."

He paused and wrinkled his brow. "Ah. Your father is Meyer? They are friends, my father and yours! We are *landsmen*! I'm Isador Shapiro. Our fathers knew each other in Lodz."

"That's Manny? They have looms next to each other at Doherty's."

"I didn't know Meyer had a daughter. He doesn't know you are here?"

"No. I think it would hurt him that I'm not in school."

"I quit school to join the strike. I promised my father that I would go and finish after the strike. I only have one year after this."

"I'm a sophomore. I go to school enough to take the exams. I still study at night and no one knows that I don't go to school."

"Except your teachers. Your parents will find out, Sophie."

"I hope not, but I am always looking around for my father, so he won't see me at the meetings. If I picket, he'll be sure to know."

"Well, come with me to get some food, and then you can go. Maybe I could meet you at Ben's candy store tomorrow and walk with you to Turn Hall. Would you meet me?"

"I'll be there a few minutes after ten tomorrow morning, Isador."

Isador's warning was prophetic. That day, an official letter had arrived for Mr. and Mrs. M. Epstein. Mr. Stechman had pointed out to Principal Goldman that he hadn't seen Sophie in class for some time. She hadn't dropped out of school officially, but at fifteen she was at the legal age to do so. Emma was holding the open letter in her hand when Sophie came home.

*Dear Mr. and Mrs. Epstein,*

*It has come to my attention that Sophie has not been in regular attendance at school. Since March 8, 1913, she has been absent from her afternoon classes for all but three days, those on which examinations were given. Please visit my office to discuss her absences.*

*Yours truly,*
*Hyman H. Goldman*
*Principal, Eastside High School*

Emma's face was white, her eyes were wild, and the opened letter was shaking in her outstretched hand. "This is what I work for? This is how you thank your mother and father for their hard work? Every morning you leave this house with your schoolbooks, and where is it you go? Tell me, Sophie. Where do you go?"

"Mama, I go to the picket lines to support the workers."

"Oh, my God! You go to the picket lines. And you don't know that dozens of picketers are taken to jail every day? You don't know that a policeman's club could easy come down on your head as on another person? You are my sweet daughter. What is to become of you? You are my hope."

"What hope, Mama? What am I your hope for? To be a rich lady? To drive in a Ford car? To live on Wall Avenue? Look at me, Mama. I am not your hope for those things. My only hope is to do some good in this sad world. Elizabeth Flynn said…"

"Do you think I care about what that *shikseh*, that little gentile girl, has to say? I have enough trouble already from this strike, and now you, too."

"Mama, you know I love you. I don't want to bring more trouble to you, but I can't be in school now, Mama. I can't think when I am in class. I only want to be with the workers."

"Sophie, you will come with me tomorrow to see Mr. Goldman. We will see what he has to say."

Sophie passed a questioning look at her silent father, who with compassionate eyes and a very slight smile, said not a word.

The following morning at seven o'clock, two figures could be seen picking their way between puddles on Straight Street, one fairly pulling the other along, Emma in her green coat and babushka, and Sophie in her navy blue winter coat. The force of the wind and rain turned their umbrellas inside out, impeding progress as they stopped to right them. Not a word was exchanged between the two. There was only the sound of the wind and the pelting rain. Emma's jaw was set tight. Sophie's tears were indistinguishable from the rain. The two had never experienced as serious a confrontation.

As they approached Eastside's office door, Sophie straightened her posture, wiped her eyes, and lifted her chin, determined in her plan to drop from school. She knew from Emma's tight jaw and her erect posture that her mother was equally determined to collaborate with Mr. Goldman about forcing her to remain in school. They stood under the eave, shook out their umbrellas, and wrapped them shut. Emma opened the double door and marched into the office with Sophie in tow.

"Good morning. How may I help you?" inquired a bird-like woman behind the visitor's partition. She was clutching her black knitted shawl tightly around her thin body and appeared worn out, even before the start of the day. The minute hand on the round, black-rimmed school clock above her desk jerked a notch.

"How could such a scarecrow run an efficient office?" whispered Emma as she said aloud, "We are here to see Mr. Goldman."

"May I ask if he is expecting you?"

"I am Emma Abramowitz Epstein."

"Mama, must you always say 'Abramowitz'?" Sophie whispered.

"That is who I am, Sophie. Your uncles are very well known in Paterson, and their name is worth something."

"Please go in, Mrs. Epstein, and Sophie."

Emma announced herself again. "I am Emma Abramowitz Epstein."

Mr. Goldman was a German Jew whose family had preceded the latest wave of Eastern European Jewish immigrants. Emma couldn't know that to him, her maiden name evoked the often-unwelcome tide of the more recent and embarrassing greenhorns.

"Sophie, sit here across from me," he said, and pointed to a corner chair for

Mrs. Epstein. Mr. Goldman addressed Sophie directly. "Sophie, Mr. Stechman said that you have been missing his class for several weeks. I asked your other teachers, and it seems that you have a pattern of leaving after second period."

Sophie stared down at her clasped hands and responded with a nod.

"Yet your grades are all excellent. You never miss an examination, and you always score above ninety percent. How do you manage that, may I ask?"

Sophie looked up. "I read the textbooks and study at night, Mr. Goldman."

"So you are telling me that you learn the material without going to class?"

"Yes."

"I see. And now will you tell me the reason for missing your classes?"

"I go to the meetings at Turn Hall to support the strikers."

"And?"

"What do you mean, Mr. Goldman?"

"Would you like to tell me why this is more important than your classes?" He leaned toward her.

"Yes," Sophie asserted as she sat up. She startled herself, but went on with the words and images that flooded her mind. She repeated the ideas that she heard at the IWW meetings. "This is the first time that all of the trades in the textile industry are united under one union. The IWW helped the workers in Lawrence to settle, and they can help us to win better conditions for our workers here in Paterson."

Sensing that her principal was not unsympathetic, she paused for a moment and waited for his nod to continue.

"It's solidarity that makes a difference—like all the teachers in every department here at Eastside working together, Mr. Goldman. The entire economy of the city would benefit if the textile workers made more money and worked fewer hours. There would be less unemployment, and my father would only have to work for eight hours instead of ten every day."

"Go on," said Mr. Goldman as he adjusted himself in his chair.

Sophie had forgotten herself as she warmed to her topic. "The mill workers could spend time with their families in the evening if they only had to work eight hours a day. Owners can't continue to exploit the men, women, and young people who toil for them. The time has come for change, and I want to help, to be a part of it."

The principal interrupted Sophie as Emma struggled to recover herself.

She had been sitting with her mouth agape, seemingly unable to integrate the image of this new young woman with the Sophie she had raised.

"Sophie, you are working for a good cause, but you are only a sophomore. You must be aware that you are one of the brightest students in your class, and that you have the ability to go to college. Mr. Stechman and I have talked about you, and we have hopes for your future."

Still, Emma sat wide-eyed, but finally managed to add, "*Nu*, Sophie. I told you." She closed her mouth again when she received a sharp admonitory glance from Mr. Goldman.

The principal continued. "Sophie, what kind of a future do you see for yourself with this labor organizing? Do you want to throw away the chance to go to college?"

Silence prevailed for a few moments as Sophie became aware of pulsing in her temples. She tried to control the energy that she had unleashed, took a few deep breaths, and unclenched her fists. After a while she began the speech that she had rehearsed in her mind the night before.

"I am fifteen and old enough to quit school. I don't want to quit. I only want to stop going to school until the strike is settled."

The principal hung on her word "until."

"Sophie, you would come back and finish school after the strike is over?"

"Oh yes, Mr. Goldman."

"You are asking for a leave of absence from school." He rephrased her intention as he looked directly at Emma and inclined his head slightly to indicate consent.

"Do I have your word that you will return after the strike?"

"Yes."

"But that is not all. I am going to ask you to do something that hasn't been done before. Personally, I will be taking a big chance on you, because I don't want you to be among the dropouts."

"But, Mr. Goldman—"

"Don't interrupt. There are about eight weeks left of this semester. I want you to speak with each teacher and work out what you will have to do on your own to complete your courses if the strike continues. Obviously you can do that. I'll talk to your teachers; otherwise, they would refuse."

Sophie looked over her shoulder at her mother who had been noticeably outmaneuvered. "Mama?"

Emma pursed her lips, nodded her assent, and rose to go. "Thanks to you, Mr. Goldman. Come, Sophie."

The way home was as silent as the walk to school with both mother and daughter absorbed in thought. Turbulent rain and wind accompanied them home.

Sophie glanced sideways at her mother, trying to gauge her anger. At that moment it appeared to Sophie from her mother's posture that she was far older than her thirty-five years. Seldom had the girl seen her mama in quiet defeat. For a brief moment before mulling over her own circumstances, Sophie was shocked to see Emma depleted. The confident energy that had been an integral part of her being was for the moment lost.

Meyer was not at home when the two arrived, so each went her separate way. Sophie recalled her commitment to Isador, and she questioned how she could have put him out of her mind. There was still time to meet him, and she prepared to leave the house again, shaking out her damp hair and replacing the pins that held it in a neat bun. She looked in the mirror, evaluating herself in an unfamiliar way. *Will he like the way I look?*

Sophie's coat was still damp, and her umbrella dripped from the morning's storm when she left the apartment, having called good-bye to her unresponsive mother. When she reached the outside landing, she glanced up and down Fair Street, noticing the shabbiness of the wooden apartment buildings and rooming houses. The unpaved strips between the sidewalk and the curb were weedy, with no grass or flowers, no sign of tended gardens like in the wealthier neighborhoods. One or two private homes on her street had small gardens, but otherwise the neighborhood was visually impoverished. She put her thoughts of poverty aside when she realized that the wind had died down, and the storm seemed to have passed for the time. She folded her umbrella.

The street was quiet, everyone either at work or at school. Storm-blown twigs and branches from ancient oak trees littered the road. Sophie inhaled the air, cleaned by the rain and fragrant from the scents of spring. She jogged down the steps and headed for Ben's candy store, her mood suddenly altered for the better.

Isador was waiting in front of Ben's store when Sophie arrived, and they fell into place beside each other, oddly comfortable. As they walked down Park Avenue, Sophie related the events of last evening and this morning.

"Isador, she was so angry. Sometimes my mother gets mad at Papa, but never at me. I was frightened, and I turned to Papa for support, but he didn't say a word. I think he was smiling at me, but I couldn't be sure."

"Did he say anything?"

"No. He let my mama fume about the strike, and how I would be hurt in the picket line, and what had I done to her hopes for me. It has always been her hopes for me. She never asks what hopes I have for myself."

"What are your hopes, Sophie?"

"I don't know for sure. I only know that I don't want to be a rich and useless lady. I want to do something important with my life, help to make the world better, like my aunt Selma who works for the suffragists. She's the only woman I know who follows her beliefs except Hannah Silverman, Gurley, and those women on strike. My aunt Rose goes with her to the meetings, but I don't think she really cares about the vote for women. I think she has nothing better to do."

"And you, Isador? What are your hopes?"

"You can call me Izzy. I want to go to law school. I think about how the labor unions need legal help."

"Mmm. That would be wonderful. We're almost near the picket lines," Sophie said as her eyes darted around. "I hope we don't run into my father. I'm not ready. I need to talk to him alone before he sees me here."

"You haven't run into him at Turn Hall yet?" Isador queried after a period of silence.

"I guess if I go to the lunch line or the picket line I might see him."

"Well, I'll get you some lunch and you can figure out what to do next."

"I want to talk to Hannah Silverman and ask her how I can help. There must be plenty for me to do. I was thinking about the Purity Bakery. They give flour to the Relief Committee, and volunteers make bread for the workers and their families. I might work at the Relief Committee's store where they give the bread away."

"Maybe we should look for Hannah after the meeting this morning. Then I'll go to the picket line."

"Thank you, Isador," she said, wondering what the young man wanted with her.

As the newfound friends approached Turn Hall, vigorous jostling brought Sophie to the present. Ellison Street was mobbed with workers. The men still wore their waistcoats with trousers held up by suspenders, even though the collars and cuffs were long past fresh. Many wore cloth caps, and others their bowlers. The strikers kept their appearance as neat as they were able, and unlike stories that were told in homes of the wealthy, they didn't carry guns or weapons. The IWW made special effort to ensure that if there were to be violence, it would not be started by their members.

Isador took Sophie's arm and led her to the front of the hall where she might have a better view of the speakers and be closer to Hannah if she spoke today. She looked up at this tall, lean young man, feeling his warmth and aware that she was blushing.

Carlo Tresca came to the podium to talk to the Italian workers in their language. Sophie, her romantic feelings newly stimulated, had learned a bit of intrigue through Charlotte, who heard from her own mother, that the handsome Italian and Gurley were lovers.

There was a lot of chanting, some in Italian, until Gurley stepped onto the podium. In her long black skirt and familiar white shirtwaist, a little black tie at the neck, she looked like any one of the other young women. Her presence during the strike had been constant, and unlike Big Bill Haywood who drifted in and out of Paterson, Elizabeth Gurley Flynn had become the spirit of the strike. The women and children adored her, and the men respected her.

She leaned way over the edge of the stage and pointed her finger toward the crowd. She gesticulated. She paced. She cried, "I'm not the leader of this strike! Who is the leader of the strike?"

"We are the leaders of the strike!" the crowd shouted. A brass band began to play, and the crowd sang the French song made famous by Joe Hill, the "Internationale," from *The Little Red Songbook*. Those who didn't know the words or didn't have a copy of the songbook hummed the tune.

Arise, you prisoners of starvation!
Arise, you wretched of the earth!
For justice thunders condemnation.
A better world's in birth.
No more tradition's chains shall bind us.
Arise, you slaves, no more in thrall!
The earth shall rise on new foundations.
We have been naught, we shall be all.
Tis the final conflict;
Let each stand in his place.
The international working class
Shall be the human race.

Gurley had spoken at seventeen meetings the last week alone, and these meetings kept the strike alive. There were speakers during the day and again at night.

Sophie noticed Hannah Silverman standing at the side of the platform. She kept her eye on Hannah so that she could follow her after the meeting, and when the hall began to empty, Sophie and Isador approached the girl.

"Miss Silverman," Sophie ventured.

"Hannah, please. We haven't met."

"Yes, uh…Hannah. I would like to help the strike. I left school to help."

Hannah inquired about Sophie and her background. "Meyer Epstein is your father?" she asked in awe.

Again Sophie was surprised to hear that someone else knew and respected her father. Meyer's passion about socialism and the treatment of laborers characterized him, and she knew that he was involved in the committees, but had not known how deeply he was engaged in a life beyond her family. She had thought that her papa was too loving and gentle to oppose her mother, and had pitied him. Now she saw there was no need for that.

Sophie was glad to hear that there was much for her to do. There were women's meetings every Tuesday night, and meetings for the children as well. Along with shepherding the little ones from school to their groups, there were younger ones who needed tending while their mothers were on the picket line.

She also learned that it took three thousand dollars a week for the Relief Committee to feed and meet the needs of the strikers. One thousand dollars a week was pledged by The Sons of Italy, but the remainder had to be raised through contributions from IWW members in other cities and from other sources. Sophie could help to raise money, and she could also work in the Relief Committee's ad hoc store to distribute food to needy families.

For a moment she recalled her mother's attempt to help the cause by working at a dance to raise money, but it hadn't changed anything. Emma was still against the strike and as much an outcast in her neighborhood as before.

Isador watched Sophie who seemed lost in thought, and he took her hand to lead her outside, but dropped it quickly when he realized what he had done. "I'm sorry to be so forward, Sophie."

She placed her delicate fingers within his hand again and smiled as she looked up at him. Swiftly she looked down, her thick black lashes covering the deep blue vivacity of her eyes. She felt the tiniest pressure of his elegant hand enclosing hers.

After Isador affirmed their date to meet in the morning, he went to the picket lines. Sophie stood still for a moment. Her face was flushed, and she could feel her temples throbbing. A buzzing sound threatened to overtake her consciousness. Her sight began to blur, and she picked her way back into the hall to sit on a bench. With deep breathing, Sophie was able to prevent a faint. She knew that the excitement of the entire day, of the meeting with Mr. Goldman, of seeing Isador again, and of meeting Hannah was catching up with her. She still had her father to face at home.

Hunger pains reminded her of the missed opportunity to eat lunch with Isador. "Well, too bad," she thought. "Others go hungry every day."

Sophie rose slowly to test her strength, and when she felt comfortable, she made her way to the relief store where she knew she might get some bread before going home. *Big day. I can help the strike, and Isador held my hand. Isador. Izzy. Tomorrow.*

Sophie was energized and beamed with pride about her papa's part in the strike as she headed for home to talk to him about it. She wouldn't have walked with the same determination had she recalled the defeat her mother experienced that morning in Mr. Goldman's office. Emma was banging pots and pans in the kitchen when Sophie opened the door.

"Hello, Mama."

Silence.

"Hello, Mama, I said."

Silence.

"You are not talking to me, Mama? I promised to go back to school when the strike is settled. You heard me, Mama. Mr. Goldman agreed. Mama!"

Sophie wiped a tear from her eye before it dropped onto her cheek. She went into her room and lay on the bed. She knew that this was her mother's tactic to get her way. She had seen it used often enough with her father, but she couldn't go back to school now. Her path was set, and there was no way to avoid the pain with Emma.

When Meyer came home, the real battle began. "I know you are at the bottom of this, Meyer. You put ideas into her head about working for the strike. Now look what has come of it! She quit school, and then what is to become of her?"

Meyer had learned to minimize Emma's drama. He asked, "Emma dear, what happened this morning?"

"She quit school. That's what happened! Now she can run in the streets, and God knows what will happen. Oy, my heart!" Emma cried as she clutched her bosom and made for a chair.

"Dolly, what is it? You are in pain?"

"No, Meyer. *Loz mir aleyn*. Leave me to think."

Meyer went to talk with Sophie, and the two went into the back hallway and downstairs to sit on the stoop in the yard.

"*Nu*, Sophie? What is this news?"

"Papa, it's not so bad as Mama says. Mr. Goldman gave me a leave from school. I have to do the schoolwork on my own, and then I can go back when we win the strike."

Meyer's eyes twinkled, his barrel chest puffed up, and he encircled Sophie's shoulders with his stocky arm. She glanced sideways and saw his mustache twitch as it did when he smiled. "Sophie, my love, there is plenty for you to do. Only stay away from the pickets."

"I know, Papa. I talked to Hannah Silverman today, and she knows you, Papa. I met Isador Shapiro, too. His papa told him what you are doing in the strike. I think a lot of people know who you are."

"So, you met Isador? Manny has *nakhes*, much pleasure from that boy. He is a fine student, and he also left school to work for the strike."

"He's very kind, Papa."

"Yah, yah, my little girl."

# Seven

## May 1913

**E**mma's younger brother, Joe, was one of the few contented Patersonians. As a single young man he had a comfortable attic room with his older brother George's family. The Abramowitz parents in Poland were happy to know that the family took care of their youngest children, the twins Joe and Dave. Dave, the aberrant Abramowitz, lived with Harry's family, but he shied away from family gatherings, keeping to himself. He was always dealing at the edges of propriety, always looking for a slick way to make a buck.

Today Joe sat on the edge of his bed and reflected on his work and his future before getting up to face another idle day. Without a family to support, he had amassed a good amount of savings and had been living on them like the few others who were as fortunate.

Joe had a good reason for his newfound happiness. He had met Flora, his true love, after more than a decade of loneliness in Paterson. Emma had Meyer, and the others had wives, but thirty-year-old Joe had been alone until now. *I found joy again with my Flora for the first time since I left Lodz so many years ago*, he thought as he reached for his trousers, the larger ones he bought to fit his growing middle.

He recalled his long-ago envy of Meyer because of his expertise and love of weaving. *Meyer was a better weaver than me.* Joe didn't care for the work, but he watched Meyer and saw something happen to him when he was at the loom. He bent over it and listened to the vibration of the warp as he threw the shuttle. He even knew when a thread was getting ready to break. Then this fine weaver took Emma's attention away from him.

He thought about his job as he bent to put on a sock, taking pride in running his brothers' mill with fairness to all of the weavers. He never gave the better silk to favorites, because when a worker is paid by the yardage, good silk could mean more money in the pocket. He made up the work shifts and checked the goods on the warp. Joe knew that his brothers were fortunate in his careful stewardship.

He got up to put on his trousers, letting his suspenders hang under each arm until he put on his shirt and tucked it in. *I do all this work, but even with the money in my pockets, I feel nothing for it.* Unlike Meyer who loved the weaving, and his brothers who relished the business, he alone was without a visceral connection to the work.

*What do I like?* He smiled as he adjusted his collar. *A walk along the river, a park bench, a Cuban cigar, a good meal, a bisl schnapps…but I always longed for a good woman.*

"I was a lonely man, but no more. I found my Flora, my love," he spoke to his image in the mirror as he parted his wavy brown hair in the center. "My brothers be damned. They call her '*shikseh*' and tell me not to marry out of our religion, but they can't change what has happened between Flora and me. Thank God for Emma. She's the only one who is happy for me."

Joe and Emma were alone at the Epstein kitchen table one evening after dinner. She asked him, "How did you meet a gentile girl with all the Yiddish *meidleh* in Paterson? You know the brothers don't approve."

Joe leaned back in his chair and smiled despite his disappointment with the others' withheld consent. He loved to tell a good story, and in preparation he poured himself a full jigger of schnapps, took a drink, and savored the alcohol as its essence burst in his mouth. He swished it around, swallowed, and began.

"I tell you, Emma. It's simple. One lunch hour last month I go to feed the pigeons in the city hall plaza. Harry's maid, she gives me some stale bread for the birds when I leave the house. So like regular, the plaza was filled with people, idle people who are out of work, not the strikers. I'm sitting on a bench with my coat open, enjoying the sunshine. I push my derby back on my head and lean back."

"Yah, and you heard the bells in the city hall tower strike twelve times. I know you like those bells," Emma interrupted.

"Yah, Emma. You know me. Now I tell you the important part. I bend over to toss some crumbs for the birds. I sit up, and all of a sudden a woman is sitting next to me on the bench. She opens her pocketbook and takes out from a handkerchief a piece of bread."

"That was Flora?"

"Yah, Flora. I look at her, and she looks at me, and we laugh. Such a big happy face! Such a big laugh! Not a little one hidden in the handkerchief. Then she stops laughing, and her smile covers her whole face. I smile, too, like a big *schlemiel*.

I see her blonde hair without curls like yours, Emma, her blue eyes, and her wide face. 'A Pole,' I think to myself, 'not a Jew.' What does it matter? She's a big woman, no Emma? Big bosom and strong hands. *Zaftig* and healthy."

"Joe, such a big woman should come to the store to get a good fit. I'll fix her with good foundations."

Joe whisked up and ate the last crumbs of the cinnamon and raisin babka he had brought to the family. He licked his pudgy fingers, smiled, and took another swig of schnapps.

"So I tell you more of the story. We smile some more, and after I turn my pocket inside out to empty the last crumb, I stand up tall and suck in the fat belly that I get here in America. I ask her, '"Can I walk with you somewhere?"'

Emma began to clear the table while Joe narrated. She put the schnapps away and moved to the sink. Joe took that as a sign of Emma's impatience and he closed his eyes for a moment to reflect on that day.

Joe thought about their walk down Main Street, their strides matching perfectly—a portly man and a healthy woman of equal height. When they reached her workplace, Joe bowed deeply from the waist and removed the ever-present white carnation from his lapel, offering it with a flourish. Flora grew wide-eyed. It was strange to see such a sturdy woman blush, he remembered. Then he asked to call on her at home.

"Emma," he said to her back as she washed the dishes, "you know Flora, she lives with her parents and two younger sisters. The father worked for a carpenter, but the man has no business for Mr. Walinski. When I go to her house for dinner, I bring some chicken or some meat, and it makes me happy they accept it. When I'm with them, I feel like I belong, more than I do with my brothers. Flora is the right one for me, Gentile or no."

Emma turned around and smiled at her favorite brother. "That's good, Joe. Everyone should have somebody, and you're not getting younger. You'll bring her here for a meal on Friday? We don't have much food like we did before the strike, but plenty to share."

"Thanks, Emma. I don't think the others will be inviting me anymore when they hear about Flora and me. You know. About getting the downstairs apartment together when the Lerners leave this building. She can still give her salary to the family until the strike is over. I have money yet. But Emma, before I go, I think maybe you don't look right. You worry about something?"

"Well you know, Joe. The strike... "

"No, Emma. It's something more. I know you too good."

"Well, Joe. I'm not sure yet, but maybe...*oy*. I think I'm in the family way."

"Emma! Joe pushed himself up from the table and took his sister's hand. Does Meyer know? He wants another child?"

"No. No one would want a child in this time. We hardly have enough for the three of us, but he was so amorous when the strike started...like he was in Lodz."

"I remember how you two cooed at each other in Lodz, and I saw you sneak off together."

She shook her head from side to side. "Joe, I'm thirty-five. Too old, but already I missed three months."

Charlotte came to the dining room for breakfast, which was always served as formally as dinner in George Abramowitz's Wall Avenue home. She had planned to meet her cousin Sophie at a park near school after her last class and after Sophie's strike activities. Now she needed to arrange it with their driver Leon to pick her up from school later than usual, under the pretense of attending a school function.

Anna Severini carried a tray of scrambled eggs and rye toast into the dining room where George, his wife Rose, and Charlotte were already drinking juice. She left and returned with a teapot for Charlotte and cups of instant coffee for the adults. Anna, the wife of Rocco Severini, a striking ribbon worker, finished serving and left the room, but she hesitated outside the door.

"Rose, I think we need to let Anna go," whispered George. "I can't talk freely in my own house knowing that she will bring everything home to her husband. Sure, we don't talk business here, but what is to stop her from gossiping to the strikers about how we live? And come to think of it, where is Joe?"

"Uncle leaves early, Papa. You know he's hardly ever here," said Charlotte.

"Yah, I know, but what about Anna?"

"George, they have so little, and Anna has children. What will they do if she doesn't bring in money?" said Rose.

"She can go to the Sons of Italy, like the rest of those anarchists!"

"Papa, they're not anarchists, they're socialists," interrupted Charlotte.

"Socialists, schmocialists, what's the difference? All they want is ownership of what took me years of sweat to build. I came here with nothing and…what do you know from socialists? Is it that cousin of yours, Sophie?"

"I love my cousin. I know you love her too, Papa. Why do you talk that way now?"

"Charlotte, listen to Papa," Rose said.

George continued. "You don't know that she dropped out of school? She has been going to their meetings all along—those workers at Turn Hall. She's not in class with you, is she?"

"No, Papa." Charlotte thought about how difficult it was getting to meet Sophie, but she knew that her cousin had no other confidant to share the details of her growing relationship with Izzy. On the other hand, she felt traitorous to her father telling Sophie about the tidbits she overheard at home, and she suffered with the complexity of what was once a quiet and predictable life.

Her father interrupted her brooding. "You won't see her anymore. She dropped out of school to join her father. I want you to stay away from Sophie while this strike lasts. She'll bring you no good. Meyer has her tight in his grip. Stay away, I tell you."

"Papa, how can you be so hard?"

"Hard? You call me hard? In April a man was killed because of those strikers. Some *dago* was sitting on his porch down there, and he was shot dead. I only worry about you."

"You don't know the story, Papa. I heard in school that the O'Brien detectives shot him by mistake when they pointed their guns at the picketers. He was shot in the back and he wasn't even on strike. He was only sitting on his front stoop."

"Go to school, Charlotte, and stay away from Sophie. Leon, where the hell are you? Where's that driver now? Leon, Leon, take Charlotte to school," said George.

"I'll find him, Papa," she said as she ran to gather her schoolbooks.

"Calm yourself, George. Maybe you are right about Anna. The whole thing is getting dangerous. So far Charlotte is fine, knock on wood. As much as I love Sophie, maybe she has gone too far."

"I'll talk to Anna, and I'll give her an extra week's pay. Thank God we have the mills in Carbondale. We would be in bigger trouble without the income from the Pennsylvania mills. It was a smart thing that Harry and I did a few years ago. We can't run a business with all this striking in Paterson. God help my brothers Dave and Joe, two lovable *schmuks*. Joe wanders the streets with nothing to do while the mill is closed. Dave is off doing God knows what."

"Joe is going to marry that *shikseh*, Flora. We'll have to make a party for them."

"It's a bad time for a party, Rose. Joe should wait. Maybe I'll send him to Carbondale to help run the mill there. He can keep the looms running."

"I went to the shop yesterday to buy something from Emma, and she told me that Joe and Flora plan to take rooms in her building on Fair Street. It's a *shandeh*, not even married. I don't think he'll go to Pennsylvania now," said Rose.

"That's not my worry. Rose, how did it come to this? Lodz right here in

Paterson, only this time we take money to the bank, and the other *dummkopfs* like Meyer with their Lodz talk of a workers' revolution, still knock their heads against the wall."

Charlotte managed to meet Sophie after school at a nearby park. Her cousin was slouched on a bench, eyes downcast as Charlotte approached. *I hope nothing is wrong with Izzy.*

She hastened her step and reached out to hug Sophie. "What is wrong? Did you and Izzy have a spat?"

"No, Char. Everything is dreamy with Isador. It's the strike I'm worried about. It's been so long, longer than they thought, and people are suffering. Not just the strikers, Char, everyone, especially the children."

"I know. Papa fired Anna after all these years, because he's worried about what she might tell her husband about our family. Now her family has no income. It's not fair, Sophie. Not fair for anyone, I guess."

Charlotte knew that her father didn't believe he had a choice in firing Anna. She, too, had begun to feel that Anna was listening to every word, yet she anguished over the Severinis' poverty.

"Mmm," said Sophie with a solemn nod. "You see why the workers are losing heart. You remember in the beginning how I told you about Police Chief Bimson?"

"My father thinks he's helping to end the strike."

"He's helping, all right, by sending his police to harass the strikers. He's working for the big bosses. So is the mayor," Sophie said, a little too harshly for Charlotte, who took it in with an effort not to judge her cousin.

"In the beginning he would send the paddy wagon to the picket line every day," continued Sophie. "The strikers would jump on. Back then, going to prison was a mark of honor. Workers sang songs and chanted all night in jail to the annoyance of the police."

Charlotte noted a palpable change in her cousin's exhilaration since February when the weavers pulled off a united front. Sophie was hunched over, her elbows on her thighs and her head in her hands. She wasn't smiling at the sight of golden forsythia, or inhaling the sweet scent of lilac that normally lifted her mood. She seemed distant.

"No more singing, Sophie?"

"No more, Char. Now they go to jail for a free meal, but their jail keep is becoming too expensive for the city. I saw policemen throwing picketers off the paddy wagon. They pushed and yelled, 'You get off. You were here yesterday.'"

"Everyone is grumbling, not only the strikers, Sophie. The small-business owners and the shopkeepers don't get much trade. You know that your mama's business is off. People can't even afford to go to the dentist or the doctor."

Charlotte began to worry whether the Epsteins even had enough food, but she was unwilling to ask. She thought to question her Uncle Joe who visited them often. He would know how to help if necessary.

Sophie was silent for a few moments, apparently lost in thought. Then she said, "It doesn't seem to me that the mill owners really want to end the strike. They reject everything the strikers ask for in negotiations."

"But Sophie…"

"People are hungry, Char. The silence of the mill whistles and the absence of the black soot from the smokestacks used to make strikers feel powerful. Now I think they almost wish to see that soot spewing out again."

"My papa says that he and the other mill owners can hold out all summer long, even if they lose their fall line of dress fabric for the coming season. They have money coming in from their mills in Pennsylvania, and they can sell off their surplus silk."

"Is it true that they threaten the small mill owners not to settle on their own?"

"Yes, Sophie. I heard Papa and Uncle Harry talking about it. The big owners don't want to break ranks, and they threaten the little owners. They have power with the New York buyers and they can put the small guys out of business. The mistake they made in the past was to settle with the separate unions. Now they won't do that."

"But the small owners who have only a few looms can barely make a go of it working their whole families, their children and their wives, to try to keep afloat," said Sophie. "They're going broke and closing down. And Charlotte, did you know that they call the small family businesses 'cockroach shops'?"

"That's disgusting, but I've heard it. I hate our families being on oppo-site sides," said Charlotte, turning red. She rubbed a tear from her eye and reached out to hug Sophie.

"I miss getting together on Sundays. Please, Char, don't let us grow apart."

"Today I thought maybe you were angry at me."

"Angry at the world. Angry at injustice, but never at you."

"Well then, Sophie, tell me about Izzy."

"Char, I love his eyes, and that adorable little space under his bottom lip."

"Did he meet Aunt Emma yesterday?"

"Not yesterday. He came to pick me up at home this morning for the first time. She saw him. She didn't say anything."

"I hope she doesn't make a fuss, Sophie."

"Papa loves him, Manny's son."

"That's what I mean. If your father loves him…"

"I know. I don't care about what she thinks."

The effort to raise money to help the strikers was losing momentum, and the IWW was desperate. Sophie was alert to the hunger, and she worried that it would kill the strike. Bodies were lean, and clothes were threadbare. She saw hunger in the gaunt faces of the older children who sometimes came to the get bread from the Relief Committee where she worked.

Her father had told her of Big Bill Haywood's startling proposition to ameliorate the desperate food shortage. One hundred New York families had offered to care for children of the strikers for the duration. Mostly they were wealthy families who offered to clothe and feed the youngsters of parents who might be willing to send their children away. The resulting publicity from this tactic had been a decisive factor in the quick settlement of the Lawrence, Massachusetts, strike. Many of the same New York families who had housed children from Massachusetts volunteered again.

Sophie attended a mass meeting where Elizabeth Flynn campaigned for the proposal. She explained how it had worked in Lawrence, but while she was talking, Sophie overheard some of the people in the crowd.

"Yeah, we send our children and what will the bosses do to us? They won't forget," yelled one man. Many more echoed his response.

Another woman whispered to her friend, "I'm not so poor that I can't take care of my own."

Her friend added, "How do we know if they'll treat my boy good? No one can care for my Sergio like his mama."

After all of the talk and parental resistance, six hundred children were sent to live with foster parents outside of Paterson, but the impact was not as great as it had been in the Lawrence strike where the police had tried to prevent mothers from putting their children on the train. Here in Paterson, the police were wise to the publicity that the intervention had created, and they didn't allow the exodus of children to become a symbol for the strikers.

The Executive Committee scrambled to find sources of support for the strikers who were now in their third month of financial hardship. The plight of labor in Paterson would become more desperate without positive publicity to generate donations from the broader pro-labor community.

Haywood, Tresca, and Flynn had tried to get New York newspapers to launch an affirmative appeal to New Yorkers for Paterson strike relief, but the papers' hostility to the IWW prevented them from providing information to the public about the strong role the silk workers had in initiating and running the strike.

As the plight of the silk workers continued to deteriorate, Bill Haywood and other IWW members shared their anxiety with the Greenwich Village socialists, artists, and poets who had been supportive of the Lawrence strike. While Haywood was at a small gathering one evening in the Village, these members of the intelligentsia conceived of a pageant in which the Paterson strikers could enact their tribulations through a series of vignettes presented in Madison Square Garden to an audience of fifteen or sixteen thousand. This, they thought, would surely engender sympathy for the strikers.

Izzy and Sophie were present when Bill Haywood introduced John "Jack" Reed, a New York newspaper correspondent and former Harvard cheering squad member. He would orchestrate the pageant and help to raise money for the rental of Madison Square Garden and the building of the stage and sets. Sophie was convinced that the speech he gave to solicit support for the pageant would generate favorable publicity and subsequent donations, but like others in the crowd, she also hoped that admission receipts and program sales from fifteen thousand audience members would give the strike a needed boost.

Sophie's exuberance built as she listened to the scheme. When John Reed finished his description, she turned to Izzy, her eyes blinking rapidly and her hands outstretched. "Isn't that wonderful, Izzy? We can all participate in a pageant to show the world how the workers are suffering."

Izzy didn't answer at first, but when they left the crowded meeting and walked into the May sunshine, he frowned and rubbed the back of his neck. "Sophie, I'm not sure that it's a good idea to divert energy from the picket line to rehearse for a pageant. It doesn't make sense to take more than a thousand pickets from the lines for three weeks to act in a play."

"But Izzy, imagine all the publicity the strike will get in New York. We could get more donors, and we're sure to have more relief funds."

Izzy shoved his hands into his pockets as they walked home from the meeting. He pressed his lips together, then wet them with his tongue before speaking. "We both have work to do here in Paterson for the next three weeks while the rehearsals are going on. Do you really want to stop working at the relief center to act in a play? You have all of your homework to keep up with, too."

Sophie put her arm through Izzy's and stepped closer to him. She was quiet for a few minutes, and then she stopped and turned to face him. "I guess there are plenty of other people who might want to act in a play. When I think about it carefully, I suppose I'd rather not be in the pageant, but I would like to see it."

"Well that settles it for me," said Izzy. "We'll attend the pageant to support our comrades and keep out of it until then."

# EIGHT

## June 1913

As Izzy had predicted, work on the pageant superseded everything for the three weeks until its performance on June seventh. During that time more than eighty volunteers from Greenwich Village worked on the stage and sets. In the end, twelve hundred people participated. They amassed in the morning, took a train to New York, and marched up Fifth Avenue to Madison Square Garden, cheered on by the spectators. The final rehearsal was at two o'clock.

On that evening, Sophie and Izzy waited in line for an hour to get into the Garden. When they reached the entrance, they had only to show their "little red card" to gain admission. They noted that others paid as little as twenty-five cents. Sophie wondered how the pageant could make a profit on admissions if most people got in free or for less than a dollar.

Once inside, she marveled at the massive stage with a two-hundred-foot drop depicting the front of a Paterson silk mill, as dismal in re-creation as it was in reality. "Look," she said as she poked Izzy. "See the lights through the mill window on the stage?"

"Impressive," said Izzy, but he was scrutinizing the décor. Red was the color of choice. Little children wore red. IWW banners featured red. Program sellers wore red bows in their hair. He turned to the top gallery on one side of the auditorium and saw a banner reading "No God, No Master" before the

IWW leadership wisely climbed up and tore it down. They didn't want it to engender the antagonism it had in Lawrence.

Eyes turned to the performers who marched from the building entrance to the stage, passing through the audience via a specially built walkway. The workers on stage reenacted scenes from the strike, and while they couldn't dramatize the actual "murder," pallbearers carried a coffin for the funeral of the slain Italian Modestino, the bystander who had been shot by a stray bullet during a scuffle between the O'Brien detective agency and the strikers. The agency had been hired to guard the property of the Weidmann Silk Dyeing Company, and though the strikers never carried weapons, the mayor had issued permits for the detectives to carry guns.

There were six scenes in all, with much singing of IWW songs, pickets, scuffles, speeches by strike leaders, and a scene showing Elizabeth Gurley Flynn escorting the red-clad children of Paterson to their foster homes in New York.

After the very long performance, the crowds emerged into the evening air and dispersed to find their way home. Sophie and Izzy walked back down Fifth Avenue the way they had come and took the Erie train back to Paterson.

Sophie slept, her head on Izzy's shoulder during the train ride, but Izzy, who had promised the Epsteins that he would take responsibility for Sophie's safe arrival home, struggled to stay awake. When the train arrived at the River Street Station, he woke her with a gentle caress and escorted her home to Fair Street.

Both were tired and emotionally drained, unprepared for what awaited them. Emma was at the door before Sophie could reach for her key.

"Mama, what are you doing awake at this hour?"

"*Nu?* I could sleep when my daughter is out all night? Your papa sleeps. I drank tea and watched the clock. It was a success, the pageant?" she asked while pulling Sophie inside and leaving Izzy in the doorway.

"Mrs. Epstein, it's hard to tell…"

"Mama, the show was magnificent. I was so proud of our workers."

"I'm not sure what good it accomplished," said Izzy. "Maybe we'll get the publicity we want, but I don't know about the cash we need to keep the strike going."

"Maybe it's time to end this strike, Isador," Emma said. She began to close the door against him, but Sophie bypassed her mother, ran outside, and whispered into Izzy's ear, "Thank you for the evening."

Izzy smiled, and turned to leave as Emma reached to pull her daughter back inside.

Mayor McBride, the police, their detectives, and the manufacturers effectively cut the strikers off from communication within their ranks. By late May, the *Paterson Evening News* had turned against the strikers, Turn and Helvetica Halls were closed to them, and rumors spread that some strikers were defecting and returning to work.

Meyer, as a member of the Executive Committee, knew that the rumors were untrue, but without a central meeting place to get the word out, a few of the strikers acted on misinformation by returning to work.

They were attacked on all fronts. Hospitals discharged patients who couldn't pay, especially those whose visitors wore an IWW button. More than six hundred strikers had been arrested in May. The detective who shot and killed Modestino went unpunished, and the IWW leader Quinlan was convicted of inciting a riot, even though a preponderance of witnesses testified to his innocence.

On this day in late June, Meyer and Manny headed toward the Workmen's Circle to let off steam with the *landsmen*. The usual cronies and Saul and Martin from Doherty's were seated at the table. Manny and Meyer came in together and joined them. The men were not so free with their tobacco as had been their custom. A few had stopped smoking, and the rest sat with half-filled, unlit pipes.

"*Nu*," said Manny as he sat down. "This is how you look, Hyman? First time I see you without so much smoke in your face!" The men chuckled, trying to insert a little humor into their desperate circumstances.

The men sat in silence after the chuckles subsided, reverting to their visages of grave concern. Hyman's lined face had become gaunt. Manny's forehead appeared more etched. Meyer continually drew his hands through his graying hair, and the tail of Solly's belt had grown several notches longer.

"It's one thing and then another piled on," said Solly.

"My wife is nagging me already to go back to work," said Martin.

"Meyer, you're on the Executive Committee. What do you think of the IWW now?" asked Hyman.

After a pause Meyer said, "Flynn, she don't give an inch yet. 'All or nothing' is what she wants. All the trades stay on strike and no bargaining one by one."

It was true that Flynn in particular had stepped up her verbal agitations against the employers, making the Executive Committee uneasy, but even as the strikers were starving and the relief committee was trying to support thousands, the silk workers remained for the most part remarkably resilient and dedicated.

"Yah," said Manny. "We voted again to stick together."

Solly wasn't sure this was a good idea. "Some bosses like Aronsohn will bargain. Maybe we…"

"You go back to work, Solly?" asked Manny.

He looked around at his stern-faced *landsmen*. "Maybe I stay out a while yet, but that pageant didn't help. From where can we get relief?"

Solly knew that the pageant had been a huge artistic and publicity success, but the meager profits went toward the high cost of production and hadn't provided relief to the workers who relied on the expected income for food. The Executive Committee saw more donations from outside Paterson in June, but not enough to rejuvenate the Relief Committee's funds.

By mid-June, the Central Strike Committee was actively seeking ways to cut relief costs. They decided to offer bus fare to single men who would go to another city for work and then return after the strike. Almost five thousand men left Paterson to find work in surrounding cities so that families with children would have more food.

Meyer lapsed into silence as he recalled his last confrontation with Emma. She had joined with the other small-business owners to put their weight behind the big bosses. Her last words to Meyer as he left the house were, "Where will we be when you, the big *makher*, the big shot of the Executive Committee, have your name on the blacklist?"

# July 1913

**J**uly was a dispiriting month for the silk workers. The larger manufacturers could hold out longer. They shipped silk to their mills in Pennsylvania, and they took in money from their commission agents or middlemen who had been holding broad goods from the prior year. In a market desperate for a fall line, the agents sold high, cleaning out stock and paying the manufacturers the remainder of their sales price less their original draw.

Sophie opened the Relief Committee store every day, even though the other girls had stopped coming. There wasn't enough to do given the shortage of food. She sat down on the rickety chair and surveyed the shop one morning in mid-July. A few sacks of flour. A few cans of beans. *How can I divide this among the needy? What am I going to say?*

The door opened behind her, and she shuddered, thinking it might be the first family of the day coming for food. She stood and turned to the door, her arms hanging and shoulders sloping, so unlike the vivacious girl she had been.

"Izzy! Why did you come to the store today? Aren't you picketing?" she asked as she quickly wiped her eyes.

"I came to see you. The ribbon workers compromised. They voted to take a nine- hour day. It looks like they will go back to work soon," he said in a flat tone. He dropped into the vacant chair, nearly breaking the unhinged legs. Sophie sat down on a sack of flour. She looked down at the idle hands in her lap, too dispirited even to cry.

"What does your papa say, Sophie?"

"He thinks we'll have to close the relief store soon. All the appeals to New York for donations didn't give us much. We had to share with the strikers in New York. Our dresses hide thin bodies. You men show all your bones. Look at you, Izzy. You've tightened your belt again. I can't bear to see you so thin."

He got up and sat next to Sophie on the sack and put his arm around her. She leaned toward him, felt his bony shoulder against her cheek, and suppressed an agonized sob.

"Oh, we'll fatten up when this is over, Sophie. You'll see."

"Maybe Mama's shop will begin to make money again, but what about the strikers on the losing end? What about the ones like Hannah Silverman who has been threatened with being blacklisted and even being sent to the State Home for Girls?"

"My papa is buying looms to have a family shop. He'll rent some space in a mill. Maybe others will do that."

"Yah, maybe," said Sophie, who suffered for the men and women who might be blacklisted and looking for work. "Life here in Paterson will never be the same, Izzy."

On July twenty-third, the Relief Committee closed its doors, and two days later the ribbon workers voted to go back to work. The strike drifted to an undignified end and was called to a halt on August second. While some ribbon workers got a nine-hour day concession, the majority of workers didn't achieve their eight-hour objective. Some employers offered pay raises in July, raises that the workers would continue to strike to uphold. The IWW, however, achieved a lasting victory. They defeated the "stretch-out" to the four-loom system, and two looms per worker remained the standard in Paterson for years to come.

# August 1913

The sun had long since set, but the heat of the day would not relinquish its hold. It had been a hellish, humid day, temperatures soaring above 100 degrees. The Epstein apartment was still unbearably hot, surely too hot to sleep, especially for Emma who was with child. Heat drove the family to the back stoop to cool off. Meyer had removed his shirt, something he rarely did in front of Sophie. Regardless, he was wet with perspiration. Sophie's damp hair was tied above her neck with a ribbon. Emma was cooling herself with her favorite painted fan, despairing of her child who would be born into this steamy immigrant neighborhood.

No clouds blotted the gleaming stars, whose twinkling served as a reminder that no rain was forthcoming. Fireflies blinked intermittently throughout the yard. "Remember how we caught those lightning bugs in jars, Sophie?" asked Meyer.

"Yah, Papa. You helped me put them into a jar for my bedside. I always put grass in the bottom to make them feel at home, and they twinkled until I fell asleep. They were gone in the morning, and I never questioned that, but I had suspicions."

"Yes. I let them go as soon as you fell asleep," Meyer said.

"Oh, Papa. I'm glad. I never thought about their dying when I was little."

The three were silent again, listening to the crickets and an occasional barking dog. It was even too hot to talk. Meyer reached over and patted Emma's growing middle. Her baby had quickened for the first time a few weeks ago.

"What will we name our baby?" Sophie asked.

"We'll call him Aaron, after my grandfather." Emma was confident that she would have a son, and she wouldn't consider a girl's name.

"But if it is a girl, can we call her Elizabeth?" asked Sophie.

"*Nu*? You can't forget that troublemaker? The strike is over, and thanks to God, she is gone."

Meyer poked his daughter, a signal to retreat from the conversation, but the damage had already been done. Emma's reawakened fury pierced the peaceful stillness of the night.

"Now maybe my customers will come again. We need that money to pay our debts. Five months of striking and for what? *Gornischt!* The bosses always win, I tell you. All that debt, all the suffering, and for nothing. *Gornischt!* And what will come of you, Meyer, now that you are on the blacklist? There will be no work for Meyer Epstein in any silk mill."

"I'm not sure yet, Emma. Manny is buying looms to take in silk on commission. They plan to weave broad goods on a contract, and they asked me to join them."

"Where will you get the money?"

"I don't need the money. Don't you know yet that I will never be a boss? I cannot do it. Maybe I'll work for them."

"Meyer, if they hire you from the blacklist, will they get any silk on commission?"

"I think maybe they are too small to worry the big owners."

"But Papa, you don't have to work in the mills anymore. It's a good thing." Sophie looked at her father, her hands wide apart and palms upward, the gesture that could express a myriad of emotions, but at this moment, joy.

"Sophie, Sophie, how do you think your father will earn a living?"

"I don't know. Some other way. It's too hot to think," answered Sophie, dropping her arms to her side.

"Yah, it's too hot, Meyer," said Emma.

A crashing sound in the alleyway startled them. Someone had come in and upset the ash cans in the dark. Isador called out, and came into the yard. "I tried your doorbell."

"Here we are, Isador. Sit," said Meyer as he patted the step next to him.

Isador looked awkwardly at Sophie who was sequestered between her parents. She rose and sat on the step below them, and he sat beside her. "I thought it would rain," he said.

"Yah," said Meyer.

"Maybe tomorrow," he ventured.

"Yah. Maybe tomorrow."

"We need the rain." Isador attempted to start a conversation, but he soon realized that the night air was filled with tension.

Sophie inhaled and released audible breath. "Maybe we could walk. Yes, Mama?"

"Yes. You and Isador walk."

The two young people were often together, and Emma and Meyer didn't object to Manny's son as a friend for their daughter. He was a smart boy, soon to be a college student. Perhaps all wasn't lost with Sophie. The strike was over, she would be going back to school in September, and she had found a suitable young man.

Meyer reached for Emma's arms to help her stand, and he led the way up the back stairs to their apartment, signaling a temporary truce.

Harry and George relaxed in the former's office this Friday afternoon. Selma was helping their maid to prepare for *Shabbos*, and the nurturing aroma of chicken soup suffused the air. Harry fingered the brass studs along the outside arm of his maroon leather chair. He reached down the arm, and then up again, circling each small nub in its turn.

"How about a *bisl* schnapps?" he offered as he went to the sideboard.

George took the proffered shot glass. "The city is starting to come back from the strike, no?"

"Yah. Yesterday I saw the dentist. He's happy. People can afford to pay him now."

"Black soot from the smokestacks again. Nothing better than the shaking of the looms," said George. "Rose says the grocers are finally getting what's owed to them."

"It's only those damned blacklisted strikers, a thousand of them yet, who are a problem," said Harry. "Our manufacturers' association learned their lesson this time. Those strikers showed us what solidarity is, by God! We can stick together, too, and not hire from that blacklist."

"Yah, it's good we all agreed, the dye houses and the broadloom manufacturers too. Even the ribbon companies. No one will hire those Wobblies," said George.

"The only thorn in our side is Meyer. Brother, what can we do about Meyer? Emma is about to give birth and he has no work," Harry said. *If only she hadn't married that schmuk.*

"There is nothing to be done. Even if he wanted to come to work for us again, we would be finished with the other owners. No dye house would take our goods if we hire him," George complained. "Yet Emma is begging for her husband, the *schmuk*."

Harry got up and paced the room. "*Schmuk* or no, he is family," he countered, feeling not at all as charitable as he appeared. "I'll tell you what we do. We tell him to change his name and find work in Pennsylvania. We won't interfere. We don't know nothing about this person if the other owners ask."

"What, send him away?" asked George.

"What else can we do? We can't do anything for him in Paterson. Plenty men are leaving from this blacklisting, George. I'll tell Emma."

Harry had resigned himself.

# NINE

## December 1915

**Izzy** was home from college for the winter holiday and spent every possible moment with Sophie. The two walked hand in hand up Broadway toward the fashionable east side of town, unaware of their surroundings. Izzy wore the now familiar and endearing brown derby that he bought when he started Columbia University in Manhattan. With his hat pushed back, a fringe of curly black hair around his ears and a widow's peak on his forehead gave him an impish look. Sophie enjoyed his new quirky mannerisms, and she also liked the brown wool-tweed vest that he habitually wore.

A Model T roadster passed them and signaled its "aroogah" brass horn. Isador laughed and squeezed Sophie's hand. "We'll have an automobile one day," he whispered into her ear.

"I miss you when you are away at school," she responded.

"That's why you should study at Barnard College, Sophie. So we can be near each other in New York. I know that your uncle wants you to go to Bryn Mawr with Charlotte, but try to stand up to him. We could be so close to each other with me at Columbia just across the Boulevard."

"It's my mother, Izzy. If I go to Barnard, she will want me to live at home and take the train to school. She'll want me to keep working in the store on Saturdays. It would be easier to leave home if I went to Bryn Mawr. Uncle

George would convince her to let me go, so that Charlotte could have a companion. After all, he and Uncle Harry are paying."

Silence. The two walked on. Isador pulled Sophie close to him when a cold gust of wind threatened her warmth. "You only have two more weeks at home," she said.

"Yah."

"I could persuade Mama to let me visit you on a Sunday if I took Charlotte with me."

"Yah."

"Is that all you can say? Yah?"

"What can I say, Sophie? I'm gloomy when I'm away from you. It's not easy to keep my mind on my studies."

"Yah," she said. And they laughed.

"I'll try, Izzy. If only Papa could make the decision himself, it would be better. Mama wants Charlotte's life for me. I'm not Charlotte, though her life would be easier. She'll be so content at home with children."

A sudden note of anxiety crept into Isador's words. "Won't you be happy with our children?"

"Of course I will. You know that. It's…well, it's what we have always talked about. You know how important workers' rights are to me. And now, with the suffragists…"

"I get frightened sometimes, Sophie. I get frightened that I won't be enough for you, that you'll want to go off like Gurley and travel around the country to support strikes."

"I can't be away from you, Izzy. I love you. There's plenty to do right here."

He squeezed her close, kissed her frosty cheek, and turned around in the direction of their homes. Sophie knew that Isador had loved her since they'd met during the big strike, but that he sometimes felt neglected when the suffragettes took her time. She also sensed his unspoken hope that she would be at home with their children, and she suspected that what he said next was only to be valiant. "You march on the picket lines, and me, the union lawyer, I'll bail you out of jail."

Sophie lay awake in bed that night pondering her options. She prayed to be with Izzy in New York, but ruminated about each family member pulling her in a different direction. Her papa would care only about her happiness, and Emma would be fine with Barnard provided Sophie slept at home every night and worked in the shop on Saturdays. Uncle George, on the other hand, hoped that Sophie would accompany Charlotte to Bryn Mawr.

Mama might reluctantly concede to Uncle George. *But Bryn Mawr! That's farther away from Izzy than Paterson, New Jersey.* The longer she deliberated, the more certain she grew about living in Manhattan to go to Barnard College. *How could that work out?* Sleep overtook her, but no solution was at hand.

When she awoke the next morning, Sophie went into the kitchen for breakfast. Her father had not yet gone to work, but Emma was downstairs giving Aunt Flora instructions for the day about her little brother Aaron. She kissed her papa, and sat down at the table.

Companionable moments like this were rare. Meyer had prepared tea, and Sophie padded around the kitchen making their oatmeal and setting the table. Once they were seated, Sophie unburdened herself to Meyer.

"What can I do, Papa? How can I convince Mama to give me her blessing to go to Barnard College and live at their new residence hall? Besides being close to Izzy, I think I will need to study there at night. She'll never say yes. All she wants is for me to work at the store."

"*Liebe*, don't be hard on your mother. I think maybe she is afraid for you. You and Izzy are the first of our *landsmen* to go to college. Such a thing—a girl in college. You are young, but we saw troubles. Jews couldn't go to college in the old country, never mind a girl. Mama wants only what is best for you. She thinks maybe you stay safe when you work in the store."

This shed a new light on Emma. Conceivably her mother was feeling protective, but how could she convince her that Barnard College was a safe place to be, if that were the issue? "Papa, who will stand up for me? I know that you will help, but, well, you know how she is."

"She's the one with opinions, yah?"

"Oh, Papa," Sophie cried as she leaned over to hug him. "I love you."

"I wipe those tears," he said as he gently kissed each of her eyes. "Here, *Meine Liebe*, enough tears. We think. Who could help us?"

"Maybe my principal could talk to her. She likes him, because I went back to school after the strike."

Meyer paused, smiled, and then said, "Your Aunt Selma, she loves you, no? I think maybe she understands better what is best for you. Talk to her, *Liebe*. Now I hear your mama on the stairs."

"Thank you, Papa," said Sophie as she rose to kiss his cheek. "You have to go to the bakery now. I'm glad you are with Purity Cooperative and not the mills, but I know that it still makes you sad not to be among the weavers. I'll think about Aunt Selma some more."

# January 1916

Selma Abramowitz, born in America, was an elegant woman. She was a real beauty, tall and thin in her stylish suits. She was the first woman Sophie had seen in a dress as high as mid-calf. It was still a bit of a scandal, but Selma, undaunted, was always on the forefront of style. She wore her hair cut short and used henna to color it. Rose grumbled her disapproval to George, but if truth were told, her husband knew she didn't have the poise to match Selma's panache.

Emma, who had now become full owner of the store after Bessie's retirement, delighted in Selma's visits to her shop, Emma's Fine Foundations, because it always gave her an opportunity to fit Selma with the latest undergarments. She had hinted that the newly patented "bra" would surely catch on if Selma shared this fashion find with her wealthy friends.

Aunt Selma had integrity, and Sophie admired her because of it. She was strong enough to overcome Harry's objections to her suffragist activities, and she had marched in parades in New York for three years now. Since the time Sophie had participated in the silk workers' strike, she found that she could confide in her aunt Selma. Now she had good reason to seek her out.

The two were enjoying the fireplace warmth in the smaller of the home's two sitting rooms, the one that was exclusively Selma's. Teacups warmed their hands, and they extended their stocking feet close to the fire. Sophie looked around the delicate floral-papered room and rearranged a plump, green pillow behind her.

She tried to explain her plight. "Aunt Selma, Charlotte is my closest and dearest friend, and I'm happy that she is going to Bryn Mawr, but I can't go with her. It's not the right place for me," Sophie blurted.

"I know, dear."

"What do you know?"

"I have three wonderful sons, and when they grow up they will most likely go into the family business. That's how they are. But if I had a daughter, I think she would be like you. We aren't related by blood, but we have some things in common. I know you're fervent about women's rights and labor issues. During the time you were marching with the strikers, I could feel your energy. It's like that for me when I am with the suffragists. When I stand with those women, I am proud that we are working together for the equality that every person deserves by right of birth."

"Oh, Aunt Selma, I wish I were your daughter!" cried Sophie as she leaned over to embrace her aunt. "Papa understands, but how can I make Mama see how I feel?"

"Sophie, your mother loves you fiercely. She is a strong-willed person, as you are. She only wants your happiness, and she believes that her vision is right for you, too."

Sophie sighed and leaned back against her cushion.

"Emma must know that you need her acceptance and understanding."

"Yes. That's why she's holding out for her way. I know she loves me, but it doesn't help. At Barnard I could study and still be able to help the suffragists. I can't live as far away from the city as Bryn Mawr." Sophie put down her teacup, blew into her handkerchief, and put it in her pocket.

"You can't live as far from Isador either, I imagine."

"I miss him," she said as she lifted her teacup.

In the silence that followed, Sophie sipped her tea and allowed her tension to subside with each audible breath. She leaned back on the cushy settee and reached her toes closer to the fire as Selma, too, relaxed. Strangely, Sophie enjoyed being in Uncle Harry's house today, as she hadn't all the years of growing up and sharing Sunday dinners with the family. The big house was quiet. Her cousins had been chauffeured to their sporting events, and Uncle Harry was still at his office. The house had a different feeling when Emma wasn't hovering.

"Have you talked to Charlotte about this?" Selma ventured.

"I don't want to hurt her feelings," Sophie answered. Even as she voiced this, she knew that Charlotte would have to be on her side, and she began to rehearse the words to her cousin. Charlotte would understand about Isador, and there was no need to bring up anything about her desire to be in New York, where support for her socialist vision and the suffrage movement was strong.

"Charlotte will support me, but Mama sees no need for me to be away from home at night, even if I go to Barnard," she continued. "I don't know what kind of campaign would change her mind. It would take an army to work out a battle plan!"

"Maybe we can work out our own campaign," said Selma. "I don't like being in the middle, Sophie, but I can see you truly need some help. I'll convince Harry to talk to George. He'll understand that your companionship at Bryn Mawr would make Charlotte too dependent on you. She is already shy of being on her own in new situations without you at her side. A little more self-reliance would be a good thing."

"Barnard is less expensive than Bryn Mawr, Aunt Selma," added Sophie.

"True. The first step is to see if your uncles will pay for Barnard instead of Bryn Mawr. Then we'll tackle the residence question."

"I'll speak to Charlotte," said Sophie. "When she sees what it means to me, she'll be fine."

Sophie kissed Aunt Selma good-bye and left the house with a lighter step than when she had arrived. She buttoned her coat, wrapped her scarf around her neck, and walked briskly down Broadway to her home. For the first time since Isador had left for Columbia, she felt a sense of hope. If George and Harry would pay for Barnard as they offered to pay for Bryn Mawr, she would only have her mother to convince.

Sophie was working in Emma's shop on the Saturday after her visit to Selma. When Emma stepped out to do an errand, Sophie used the opportunity to call her aunt Selma on the store's recently installed candlestick telephone.

Selma had good news. The uncles had succumbed to her persuasion, and both Harry and George were willing to support Sophie at school in New York. Charlotte had already agreed that her cousin should go to Barnard. All that remained was Emma.

Isador was still ignorant of all the behind-the-scenes dealing. He would be leaving for school in another week, and Sophie didn't want to send him back to New York without some positive news.

Sophie began to tremble with excitement over the possibility of moving to New York. On the other hand, she felt a dreadful anxiety about confronting her mother, compounded by guilt over her secret plotting.

With conflicting thoughts, she couldn't decide how to approach her plan. *Should I talk to Mama in private or include Papa?* Then she thought it might be better to ask Aunt Selma to do the talking. *No, that's not right. How can I make Mama understand?*

Sophie craved her mother's support and acceptance of a way of life different from Emma's vision of a well-to-do homemaker. I suppose, she thought, that I should approach one thing at a time. If I could get her to agree to my living at Barnard now, I would be happy. Who can tell what the future will bring?

Emma reappeared in the shop, and a new customer came in, putting an end to Sophie's contemplation. She spent the remainder of the day waiting on ladies as they decided which undergarments to purchase. Many women came into the shop to see and perhaps have the courage to try on the new "bra" design that was the talk of the undergarment industry.

When the store closed, Sophie said, "Many women came in today simply to try on, but I couldn't keep track of them all."

"You should learn from your mother," Emma said. "I write the names in my notebook so that I remember to send every shopper a little thank-you card for visiting the store. That's how you make a business, Sophie."

Sophie's mind was elsewhere. During the walk home that evening she rehearsed her scenarios. What would she risk by insisting on Barnard? It had become so entangled with covert negotiating that she could unwittingly betray Aunt Selma. Papa is bound to be in the middle between Mama and me. As she deliberated, she clarified her intentions. She would go to Barnard, and she would stay in Manhattan at the residence hall, but at what price?

After Sunday breakfast, Sophie helped her mother clean the kitchen. At her private request to Papa, he had taken little Aaron for a walk.

Sophie ventured, "Mama, I have been thinking more about going to Barnard and not Bryn Mawr next fall."

"*Nu*? You know that is not possible."

"Why do you say that, Mama? Barnard is a good school, and it is closer to home."

"If you want to go to college, your uncle George would be happy for Charlotte to have a companion. It is settled."

"Mama, I'm not a paid chaperone for Charlotte. Uncle George wants what is best for me, too. Barnard has a social science department. I can study social work there, but not at Bryn Mawr. They don't study government or economics or social science at Bryn Mawr. They study only the classics."

"Consider your place, Sophie. You will do as your uncles wish."

Sophie held her tongue. She didn't want to fight with her mother. She was quiet for a moment, but her eagerness boiled over, and what came out next was not in her plan.

"Charlotte thinks I should go to Barnard. She knows that I could learn more about social work there. Her papa would agree to pay for Barnard."

"I have heard nothing of this. Bryn Mawr is a safer school for a young lady. If you are so sure you want to leave your family behind, then you will go to a school for young ladies, not to turmoil in a big city with God knows what going on! Who has heard of this social science? Do you want to confuse your mind, or become an educated, eligible woman?"

"Mama, that is unfair. You know I want to be a social worker. Izzy understands."

"So that's it? Izzy understands? And not your own mama? Izzy knows what's best for my daughter?"

"Please, Mama, try to see things my way. I want to go to school where I will learn about the world today, not only the world of the past. I want to study with other women who are like me, and I want to stay in the residence hall where I can study at night…"

"You want. You want. What a young girl wants is not always the best for her. You will not go to Barnard. If you go to college, you will go to Bryn Mawr with Charlotte or not at all. You can work in the store and learn about today's world right here."

Sophie squeezed her eyes shut and lips tight for a moment. "Mama, I will go to Barnard, and I will live there, too—with or without your blessing!"

Emma stepped back and held her hand to her mouth, eyebrows lifted. Her eyes were cold, and her anger erupted. "Is that how you talk to a mother? After all these years? I have always done what is best for you, and now you dare to talk to me that way? Shame! That's what it is. A *shandeh*!" With that she grabbed the dishtowel from Sophie and began fiercely wiping the dish. It slipped from her hand and crashed to the floor.

# May 1916

**S**ophie raced up the three flights of steps with her skirt entangled, and arrived in the kitchen out of breath and trembling. Her left arm encircled a pile of schoolbooks held close to her chest, and her chin anchored a torn envelop on top. In her free hand she clasped the opened letter, intending to lie on her bed and reread it. As it was late afternoon, she expected her parents to be at work and little Aaron to be downstairs with Flora, but when she opened the door she was surprised to see Emma at the table.

"Mama, you're home."

"Yah. I left early to do the bookkeeping at home."

"Oh." Sophie hesitated and remained near the door but looked toward her bedroom.

"You're not happy to see your mother?"

"Of course I am, Mama. Only I didn't expect to see you." She gave Emma a perfunctory kiss on the cheek and sat down beside her at the table. Sophie squirmed in her chair and turned again to look toward her bedroom.

*I have to tell her now.*

"I got my letter, Mama."

"Your letter? What letter do you have?" said Emma as she looked up from her ledgers.

"I told you long ago that I applied to Barnard. This is my acceptance."

"Yah, sure. You applied, but you can't..."

"Mama, I told you that I am going to school there."

Emma got up from the table, standing imperious and angry. She looked down at her seated daughter. Her eyes squinted, her teeth clenched, and the tension radiated from her protruding lower jaw. Sophie glared back at her mother.

"You told me? And I tell you that you are not going to live in New York."

"Mama, Uncle George has agreed to pay. You know that," said Sophie as she rose to meet Emma face-to-face.

Emma slammed her fist on the table. "George did that without me. If he asked me I would have told him you cannot go to New York."

"Mama, I am eighteen years old. You can't treat me like a child. Barnard is the best school for me. It has the programs I want to study, and I plan to go there in September. I don't want to go against you, but you can't hold me back. Papa knows it's the right thing for me."

"Papa would give in to you every time, but I won't have it."

"Well, I'm going," she said as she ran out of the kitchen and slammed the door behind her.

In tears Sophie went down to the next floor to seek solace from her aunt Flora. She opened the door and called, "*Tante* Flora."

When Aaron saw Sophie, he jumped into her arms before she could wipe her eyes.

"Sophie, are you crying?" he asked.

"Just a little bit," she said as she brushed away her tears and knelt down to embrace her brother. "Sometimes people cry because they are excited."

Flora bustled into the kitchen from the front room and put her dustrag aside. "Oh, Sophie. It's good to see you. Come, sit down with us."

"*Tante* Flora, Sophie is crying. She's 'cited,'" said Aaron, climbing onto his sister's lap.

"I can see that," said Flora, who eyed the letter.

Sophie turned it over to Flora who read it and looked up at her niece with a sad smile.

"You showed it to your mama?"

Sophie nodded. "I guess I'll go to see Charlotte until Papa comes home," she said as she lifted Aaron off her lap and kissed him on both cheeks.

"I'll see you at dinnertime, Aaron. Now I have to go out, and you must let go of my legs."

Flora came to wrest the little boy from his sister. "Now, now, little man, I think we have some cleaning up to do. Let's put your toys away before you go home."

Sophie whispered into Flora's ear, "Can we talk tonight?"

With a nod from her aunt, Sophie kissed the boy on the forehead and squeezed out of the back door before he could stop her. She trod down the remaining stairs and sat on the back stoop with her head in her hands. She reread the acceptance letter.

It was getting too late for a long walk or bus ride to Charlotte's house, so she remained inert, staring at the open letter in her lap. She startled, imagining a presence behind her, and then smiled as she envisioned Izzy looking over her shoulder at the letter. He had fretted for the entire school year, missing her and waiting for her to finalize her enrollment at Barnard. "Yes?" she would hear him ask. "Yes," she would answer.

Izzy was planning to come home for a visit on the weekend. Three days away. He would come to her apartment on Friday night as he had always done, greet her family, and then the two would walk to his home for Sabbath dinner with the Shapiros.

A vision of her mother's fury gripped her. Sophie's stomach tightened; she twisted her fingers, and her lower lip trembled. No, she wouldn't cry again. *It's my life. I won't back down.* She bit her lip and sat straight up, her fists clenched.

Sophie tried to calm herself and predict a scenario for Izzy's visit on Friday night. She would go to him at the door and take his arm, but he would see Emma's anger.

Mama might accuse him. "You are the cause of my daughter's disobedience. You are the reason that she wants to leave home," she would say.

*No. It can't happen that way.* Sophie tried to think of how to avoid the scene and decided at last to meet Izzy at the door and leave with him before he could come inside.

She remained on the stoop picturing her impending nearness to Izzy in New York. She had visited him on two occasions accompanied by her cousin Charlotte, Emma's annoyance notwithstanding. Yet knowledge of campus or academic life at Barnard was still vague. She turned to the familiar reverie of her time with Izzy on the Columbia campus.

Nothing distracted her until she heard the church bells chime five times. *Papa will be home soon.*

Tonight would be another of those scenes with Emma raging and Meyer consoling, diffusing the tension. The arguing had become too familiar, and Sophie wished for Aaron's sake that she could avoid another confrontation on Friday night.

Precisely as Sophie had foreseen, Emma greeted her with stern silence when she came back into the house. This will be a very long summer, thought Sophie.

# TEN

## September 1916

"**What** are you doing here at Auntie's house now, my darling? Does your mama know where you are? Did Mama tell you to come here, Aaron?"

"No, *Tante* Flora. I came by myself."

"Your mama won't like that. It's dinnertime. Come, I'll take you upstairs. Up you go," said Flora as she hoisted the toddler onto her ample hip. "Joe, I'm going upstairs for a minute. Aaron came down by himself again."

Emma was stirring noodles on the stove when she called out to her son. "Aaron, where did you go? Are you in your room?"

"Meyer," she called into the parlor. "Is Aaron with you?"

"No, he isn't in the bedroom?" Meyer came into the kitchen and then looked in both bedrooms and the bathroom. Maybe he went downstairs, he thought as he opened the back door.

Flora stood at the door, Aaron on her hip, her fist poised to knock.

"I was coming for him, Flora dear. It's not good he goes…," said Meyer as he reached out to hold his son.

"There you are! Enough already!" Emma interrupted. "I told you not to go downstairs by yourself. I'm sorry, Flora. You shouldn't be bothered now after watching him all day," Emma said when she saw her sister-in-law.

"Emma, you know how much Joe and I love Aaron."

"Yah, Flora. Say good-bye to Auntie, Aaron," said Emma.

"Bye, bye, Auntie," whispered Aaron as he snuggled into his father's shoulder and peeked out at her from under his thick lashes.

"Son, *Tante* Flora eats her dinner with *Feter* Joe. You eat your dinner here. Thank you, Flora. *Gut nacht*," said Meyer.

"*Nu*, Meyer, everything is *Tante* Flora. He sneaks down there like we don't have toys enough for him here."

"The boy is with her all day. If you would stay home from the store sometimes, he would like that."

"And then who would put food on the table?"

"Emma, you don't like it when I talk to you about the store, but when Aaron goes to bed, we will talk." Meyer settled Aaron onto a chair piled with books, tied a bib around his son's neck, and sat down.

"Where is Sophie, Mama?" Aaron asked when Emma placed the lamb chops on the table.

"You know Sophie went away to school. Sophie is at school."

"But school is over. Sophie has to eat dinner. Does Sophie like lamb?"

"Aaron, Sophie went far away, and she sleeps at the Barnard school," said Emma.

"I miss Sophie, too, little one," consoled Meyer. "Our girl has grown up."

Meyer lifted Aaron from the table after dinner and carried him into the bedroom where his crib remained at the foot of Emma and Meyer's bed. "Mama dresses you like a little prince, boy. Let's take off these knickers and get ready for bed. Maybe when you grow a little bigger, you can sleep in Sophie's bed."

"Where will Sophie sleep, Papa?"

"Sophie is away, Aaron. You can sleep in her bed."

"Papa, tell me a story."

Meyer began, "Once there was a mean mill owner. The workers were tired at the end of the day, but sometimes he made them work longer with no supper. The mama didn't have money enough to buy good food…"

"Meyer, stop with that nonsense," Emma called from the kitchen.

"Time to sleep, son," said Meyer, tucking the little boy into the crib. He sat beside the crib as Aaron's eyes became heavy, and then he reached in between the slats to pat the curly black hair so much like his own. He put his finger on the cleft of the child's chin, again like his own. "May God bless you and keep you," he whispered. "May his face shine upon you." He sat a while longer admiring the sleeping child and praying. *Dear God in heaven, give him health. Give my son strength, so he should think and act on his own.*

After a few moments Meyer returned to the kitchen. He motioned Emma to a chair and sat down beside her. Emma waited for a moment, watching her husband run his hands through his hair. He pulled out his pipe, but didn't reach for a match. "Dolly, ever since Bessie retired you work too hard. Why don't you take a day from the shop to be with your little one? He needs his mama."

"Meyer, you know how I have to work to make my shop the best in Paterson. It takes time."

"It's not the money, is it Emma?"

"Yah, it's the money. I need the money to be a Somebody! I want to be a Somebody," Emma exploded.

"Aaron and I, we think you are a Somebody." He was careful not to mention Sophie, who was by now a dark shadow in Emma's thoughts.

"Meyer, you work, and yah, that is fine. Thank God the bakery workers don't strike. Still we cannot afford to move to the Eastside. Enough of Fair Street and these greenhorns. Enough with their Polish and their Italian, yelling and fighting. It's time for Jews to leave this ghetto."

Meyer put down his unlit pipe and stared at his wife, gripping his hands in his lap. She had grown red in the face and jumped from the table, holding her elbows at her side to control her shaking fists.

"What are you looking at? You can't say something?" she continued.

Meyer shivered with the realization of his wife's ambition. *Now she wants more than the money. She wants to be a big shot, so everyone can see.* He saw that she was overwrought, and with measured deliberation, he rose and left the room.

*Barnard College*

*September 12, 1916*

*Dear Mama and Papa,*

*I am in my beautiful room in Brooks Hall sitting in a cozy corner near the bay window that opens to the Hudson River. The window has a seat built into it with yellow chintz cushions. The furniture is plain and useful, like the kind we buy from the catalogs in Grand Rapids, but everything fits so nicely. My roommate Eleanor and I each have a bed, a desk, and a dresser with a mirror. The wallpaper has stripes with yellow flowers on it.*

*Who could have imagined that such a Hudson River view would be mine to enjoy—sailboats, tugs, ferries, and cargo boats glide along the river. In the evening fiery red sunsets fade into soft pastels as they light the western sky beyond the river, and beyond the Hudson, not so very far away, is Paterson. I hold you in my heart, even though I cannot see you.*

*Tell Aaron that Barnard Hall has a gymnasium with a swimming pool! (I'm afraid to swim, but I must try.) The doctor's office is there. So are undergraduate study rooms and offices for student organizations.*

*Eleanor Reichman, my roommate, is so beautiful, Mama. Her hair is wavy like mine and as black as the crow that Papa used to talk to at the mill. She has huge, brown sparkling eyes, and she's a little taller than I am.*

*When she started to unpack her trunk, I was amazed to see so many clothes. I never knew one girl to have so many dresses. My suitcase was unpacked and put away in no time, but she spent the whole afternoon arranging her skirts, suits, dresses, undergarments, and shoes. Even though she is taller, we wear the same size, and she said I could wear some of her shirtwaists!*

*Best of all, she is friendly. We go downstairs to the dining hall together, and we see our other friends there.*

*Eleanor's great uncle, Jacob Schiff, donated money to build the new Students' Hall, and there's a plaque inside the front entrance with his name. Everyone meets between the pillars where the plaque is hung, and they call it "Jake." They say, "Meet me at Jake."*

*I wondered why such a wealthy girl has to share a room in Brooks Hall, until Eleanor told me that her father doesn't want her to be different from the others because he is wealthy. "Remember," he told her, "you have an obligation to use your wealth for good, not to put yourself above others."*

*Another new friend, Rose Braverman, has a room that looks out to the east at Columbia College with its lawns along the Boulevard. I'll tell you more about Rose another time. We are ninety-seven women living in this new building. We have a dining room on the first floor and an infirmary, Mama, you'll be glad to hear, on the top floor. Miss Weeks is in charge here, and she has an open-house tea every Thursday for friends and other students.*

*I didn't tell you about all my classes. I have a class called The History of Western Civilization, and also a biology class. I will continue with my Latin studies, as I had a good start at Eastside High School. I have to study mathematics, and also I need to learn French or German, so I'll try German, because I know so much from Yiddish.*

*Most girls are not so lucky to stay here, because they live nearby and can take the subway to school. I couldn't have done it, Mama. It would have taken hours each way to take the train and a subway to school if I had stayed at home. Now I can study in the library in the evening and between my classes. I hope you forgive me for leaving. I love you both.*

*Please kiss little Aaron, Aunt Flora, and Uncle Joe for me, and tell them that I love them.*

*Your faithful daughter,*
*Sophie*

# October 1916

*Barnard College*
*October 10, 1916*

*Dear Papa,*

*I dislike writing to you in care of Izzy's papa because Mama would not approve of my interests, but I need so much to share my work with you. Tell me about the strike in the Passaic silk mills. I get my news from Izzy through his father. I heard that when you drive the bread delivery wagon, you stop at the silk mill to encourage the workers. It's a good thing that you work for the cooperative, so that you still keep your hand in the union affairs.*

*Izzy and I study together at the library, and he always walks me back to Brooks Hall. You can be sure that he keeps me safe. Papa, I love him. He isn't happy that I belong to the Barnard Suffrage Club. It's not that he objects to women having equal rights to vote. He doesn't want me to march in any parades. He thinks that I might get arrested or trampled to death! So silly of him, but for now I only work in the suffrage office to make him happy. I see Aunt Selma there.*

*Please write to me about the mills and what you are doing.*

*With love from your devoted daughter,*
*Sophie*

*Purity Bakery*
*October 30, 1916*

*Meine Liebe,*

*You know that to write is not easy for me, but I try. Hamsel is at last to be retired. Our old bakery horse pulled the delivery wagon for me since I started to work for the bakery after the strike. Now he cannot pull so hard. One day, I got out from my seat and pulled my old friend by the reins. I walked next to him all day, and now your papa and Hamsel are tired. Morty and Sam talked about it a long time. They made a new answer for the bakery. Hamsel will move to the Vanderdam farm in Haledon where he can rest. We are to buy a truck!*

*Today I got up early and harnessed our Hamsel for the last time. We delivered Purity bread to all the stores. Still I had to walk along next to Hamsel. I tell him, "Hamsel, this is your last day of work, so pull hard. Make me proud." We stopped at every store so people could come outside to say good-bye to him. They pat him. They say good-bye, and some people cried. Mostly the old folks cried. Young people want progress. Soon there will be no more horses in Paterson to clip-clop on the cobblestones. That sound will be no more. Even the bell on the wagons will be gone, and we'll have a loud horn instead. One day only machines will be on the streets. Times change, Meine Liebe, and now I will learn how to drive our truck.*

*I stopped at Max's candy store, and he sends kind regards to you. The landsmen at the Workmen's Circle ask about you and Izzy, too. Manny and me, we get such nakhes from you and Izzy. Think, to have our children in college!*

*Aaron is growing fast. He talks such good English now that he forgets his Yiddish. Flora speaks only English to him, but we still talk Yiddish at home. Your mama dresses him like a little mensch. Always she sends him to Flora with clean shirt and knickers. She thinks maybe we should move where he could go to school uptown. Such a worry! She can't get from her mind the rich life. Nu? Maybe we will move. You know when she gets an idea no one can stop her. Liebe, you are not so different.*

*I stop at the mill in Passaic on my route and meet with the union people. The eight-hour day will be coming soon, I know. I am sad when I see such hard labor, and for what? To take home so little pay for so long work? But to tell the truth, Dolly, I miss the silk mills. Now I earn more money, and my back does not hurt so much from stooping over the loom, but my fingers itch to run over the textiles again.*

*Take care about the suffrage work. Aunt Selma is in very deep to her neck. You must study and not think too hard about this now.*

*I send you my love,*
*Papa*

# November 1916

*Barnard College*
*November 10, 1916*

*Dear Uncle George and Uncle Harry,*

*I am sending this letter to Uncle George, but it is really for both of you. I am so happy here at Barnard, and I thank you both many times over for sending me here. I know that Charlotte is cheerful at Bryn Mawr, and so it is all right for me to be away from her. I will study hard and make you both proud that you sent me. Maybe next year I can work to pay for some of the cost.*

*People are talking about the war in Europe ever since the Germans sunk the Lusitania last May. It makes me afraid. Do you think that we will enter the war? There is a club here at Barnard of women who are against the war, and I think I should join. Is it really our business to fight so far away from home? Please tell me what you think.*

*With love,*
*Sophie*

*November 20, 1916*

*Dearest Sophie,*

*Your Uncle Harry and I, we read your letter, and we are glad that you study hard. Your mama and papa are proud of you. They tell us about your classes. Do not worry about the money. While we have, we give gladly. The war demand for silk is making us a lot of money.*

*You worry about the war. You want peace. Everyone wants peace, but there are many reasons why we must help the English and the French.*

*When I talk to the bankers and the ones with money, they say that those countries owe us money, more than you could count. If they lose the war, they won't pay us back, but war or no, we make money from our broad goods.*

*Love from your Uncle George*

# ELEVEN

## February 1917

**S**ophie moaned and wriggled closer to Izzy, warming to the intimacy of his tongue as it caressed the inside of her lips. A dizzy feeling came over her, and she felt that she could melt into his body. They stood this way, kissing, swaying, moaning, linked together yet standing fully clothed in Izzy's rooming house for a very long time until Izzy guided her toward his narrow bed.

"No, Izzy, we can't."

"It's fine, Sophie. I promise. We'll wait, but we can lie here next to each other."

They lay entwined on Izzy's cot, momentarily hesitant because of the risk of their nearness. Sophie rested her head on Izzy's chest while he stroked her hair. The green wool of her shirtwaist skirt was tangled in their jumble of legs. Struggling with their impulses, they listened to the familiar sounds of the city below—horses, automobile horns, and clanging electric streetcars—all the more audible above their silence.

Izzy sought Sophie's lips, and they kissed more fervently than before. Izzy rolled on top of Sophie and pressed his hips toward hers. She felt his fullness bearing upon her pubic bone through her petticoat and full skirt. The sound of their breathing replaced the din of the city, and she sensed an aching down there, a tingling, and a wetness in her own drawers that no longer surprised her. As their passion grew, Izzy pressed harder upon her, and then stillness.

121

He sighed and rolled to his back, the front of his gray wool trousers wet with his spent love.

Sophie rolled to her side and reached over to trace the outline of his lips. She adored the way his full lower lip rolled downward to create a tiny crevice underneath it, a tiny little space where she could put her finger. She looked at his peacefully closed eyelids and thought about how his green eyes sparkled when he laughed. *They look like glowing emeralds in their almond-shaped sockets.*

Suddenly she sat erect and listened for a sound. "*Shah.* Izzy, I hear someone. Footsteps coming this way."

"No one but my friend Allen comes this way to go to his room. Don't worry."

She smiled and lay down again, comforted.

Izzy had a furnished room on the second story of Mrs. McLean's converted home. Once when her husband had a fine job, they bought this large house on West 121st Street near Amsterdam Avenue for their family of ten.

The house was convenient to Kent Hall, Columbia's law school, five blocks south on West 116th Street at Amsterdam, so when Mr. McLean died and the children grew, the widow began to rent the upstairs bedrooms to students and to serve meals as an option. There was a butler's stairway in the back of the house near the kitchen, as well as the front door access to the home.

Female guests were forbidden in the men's rooms, and it was this back staircase that Sophie and Izzy climbed when they were certain that no one was in the kitchen. They mounted twelve carpeted steps to a landing, then five more creaky wooden steps to the long hallway with three bedrooms on each side and a bathroom at the end. It was those last five steps that were nerve-racking until they reached the carpeted hall. Then they quickly tiptoed to the last door on the right, the end room near the bathroom. The neighboring room belonged to Allen Levy, Izzy's closest friend at Columbia.

From her prone position, Sophie looked around the sparsely furnished room with some built-in shelves above the bed, an oak armoire on the opposite wall, and a rickety red painted desk near the window that had belonged to one of the McLean boys. Izzy's schoolbooks, some work by Upton Sinclair, and socialist magazines were lined neatly on the shelves, along with a formal family portrait that was his parents' parting gift.

The original tan, grass wallpaper was beginning to peel at the seams, and an irregular water stain above the front-facing window was a sign of the leaky roof. Bedraggled lace curtains hung unevenly on either side of the window. Izzy's mother had sent his goose-down featherbed with him, the only bit of luxury that he possessed. Naturally, his signature tweed vest and derby hat were hung on a wall hook.

Izzy got up, reddened as he looked down at his trousers, and fumbled in his armoire for a change of clothes. "We'll have a nice home someday, not a student's hovel," he said as he changed into a fresh pair of trousers. "Let's go to Morningside Park and sit near your favorite Seligman 'Bear and Faun' fountain."

"I'll tidy, and you peek outside the door."

"All safe," he whispered as he motioned her toward him.

Physical intimacy was only a part of Sophie and Izzy's luscious freedom from the constraints of home. In the fall they spent their free hours walking in Central Park along the bridal path, or feeding the ducks at the Conservatory Pond.

Now in the cold months, they often visited the Metropolitan Museum or drank hot chocolate in a café. Izzy recalled their conversation last week while standing on the balcony overlooking the Great Hall of the museum. They had once again named their four children, two boys and two girls. They planned to buy a house in the Morningside neighborhood of Manhattan, and Izzy would practice labor law.

Then, Sophie had said, "But if we go to war, there will be no children."

"I don't understand," he replied.

"Izzy, I can't raise children in a country that could go to war over Europe's problems. I don't want my children going to another war someday when the president decides to help another country."

*No children?* Izzy hid his concern.

As he recalled the conversation, his agony deepened. Sophie's classmates at Barnard were anti-war. They worked for Wilson's reelection in 1916 because they perceived his intention to keep America out of Europe's war.

Izzy was not so sure that the country could stay out of the conflict. *Those Barnard girls have no idea how close this war is to us. Their petitions won't make a difference.* He was more convinced than ever that America would be drawn into the war. The catastrophic Battle of Verdun with its unholy loss of lives on both sides and Britain's costly defeat of the Germans on the Somme increased his certainty that with America's power, the Allies could put a quick end to the German army.

Izzy continued to dwell on these thoughts as he walked to Brooks Hall to meet Sophie. He had been saving his money to take her to a special restaurant for her nineteenth birthday, and he hoped that his preoccupation with U.S. involvement in Europe's war wouldn't mar their festivity.

The evening, while cold outside, was everything that Sophie might have wished. Izzy had reserved a corner table in a small but upscale French bistro called Le Liaison on the Boulevard near Barnard. When they arrived, Izzy took her coat and handed it to the maître d', who showed them to their candlelit table. They ordered Coquilles Saint Jacques, and felt a rush of sophistication to be eating the wine-sauced scallops in their own shells. It was their first forbidden taste of un-kosher shellfish.

They had a glass of champagne to toast their love and Sophie's birthday. Izzy presented her with a gift that his mother had helped him choose from Hertzl Jewelers in Paterson. He blushed as he handed Sophie the small gold box, who in turn blushed as she opened it. "Oh, Izzy! It's beautiful," she said, extracting a tiny heart-shaped pendant of silver and crystal from its nest in the box. She held it up to her neck. "Would you fasten it?" she asked.

He took the delicate silver chain from her and walked around the table to stand behind her and clasp it. "Next time, an engagement ring," he whispered into her ear. He felt an overwhelming sense of love and desire. "Sophie, you look like a princess tonight in that new dress."

"Do you really like it? Aunt Selma bought it for me at Macy's. She said that the blue complements my eyes."

"It does, Sophie. You look spectacular."

With the gift giving and dinner behind them, Izzy became still and stared downward. The mood shifted with his inward turn of mind. He fingered the red and white checks on the tablecloth and drank his tea in silence.

Sophie watched his demeanor change. She reached out and put her hand over his. He looked up at her with an unaccustomed sadness in his eyes.

"Izzy, what is it?"

Unable to hold back the news that had preoccupied him before dinner, he erupted. "Sophie, the Germans declared unrestricted submarine warfare, and Wilson broke off diplomatic relations. Do you know what that means? They will sink neutral ships that have commerce with the Allies. Open your eyes! We'll be at war as soon as they attack our ships. You can't hide from this anymore."

"Don't holler at me, Izzy," she said as she tried to control herself in public. "I voted with most members of the Barnard Undergraduate Association for a resolution condemning the war."

"I'm only trying to prepare you. The Zimmermann note from the Germans to Mexico says it all. They want to ally with Mexico against us. Our lives will change, Sophie." He reached out to hold her hand, but she pulled it away.

"Please pay the bill, Izzy. I want to go."

He motioned for the bill and while they waited, Isador focused on the cleared table, while Sophie tapped her foot on the floor and squeezed her hands together in her lap. Izzy helped Sophie into her coat and followed her as she twisted her loose hair, stuffed it into her collar, and hastened ahead of him to the door.

Only the cold of that February evening prevented Sophie's total abandonment to tears on their walk back to Brooks Hall. She drew herself into her fur-collared coat and thrust her hands into her pockets. She squeezed her eyes tight, but two tears escaped while the new falling snow covered her eyelashes. Inconsolable, she quickened her pace. Izzy grasped her arm and tried to stop her, but she brushed him off and continued her stride. When they reached Brooks Hall, Sophie opened the door and ran into the building, leaving a stunned Isador outside.

He stood on the sidewalk, distraught and frightened. *How can she hide from reality? I must get her to see.* He waited outside her residence hall, hoping that she would see reason and come back to kiss him good night. *It was supposed to be a perfect night.* She didn't come back.

He waited for as long as he could endure the cold and then turned toward his rooming house. Along the way he contemplated the grisly photographs that he had seen in *The New York Times Pictorial Review* of the hundreds of thousands of war deaths in Europe. He shivered more from fear than the cold, and as he approached his rented room he wondered how this war might alter their dream of marriage and family.

# March 1917

**S**tudy was difficult for Isador and Sophie when the imminence of war was evident. News was full of the tension between America and Germany. By the end of March, seven American merchant ships had been sunk by the Germans.

Sophie busied herself in the suffrage movement to avoid confrontations with Izzy. Feeling very independent, she rode the IRT Broadway line and then walked to the national headquarters of the National American Woman Suffrage Association on East Thirty-second Street and Madison Avenue. Mrs. Catt, the president of NAWSA, organized the suffrage movement across the nation and was close to getting women's right to vote passed in New York State.

Sophie spent many of her free hours at the office where she saw her aunt Selma and helped to write and address campaign literature. This kept her mind occupied and provided an opportunity to forward a cause that was dear to her.

Isador, on the other hand, couldn't help but think about the war and about his love for Sophie. He paced the streets while he pondered his position. *We should marry now, not wait till after graduation. At least we could be together before I go off to war.* He was certain that Wilson would declare war and that he would be conscripted. He wondered about enlisting with the Officers' Reserve Corps at Columbia before the draft tapped him. *How can I convince her to marry now?*

His desperation about marriage so preoccupied Isador that he found himself sitting on the steps of the newly built New York Public Library with his head aching and no memory of having walked there. He meditated on the stately marble lion statues that guard the library's entrance, so like the America that he believed should be the guardian of the seas, guarding against

Germany's plundering. With these leonine images of strength, authority, and leadership on his mind, he ambled back up Broadway wondering what part he would play in the war.

# April 1917

**When** Wilson finally declared war on Germany in April, Izzy faced the inevitable battle with Sophie. They were sitting on the steps of Low Library taking a study break when he said, "Sophie, I've thought so much about this war, and I considered joining the reserves, but I think that I should volunteer to serve now…"

"You should volunteer?" she screamed.

"Hush, people will look."

"I don't care," she said. "How could you think…"

"It's my duty to the country that my parents chose."

Sophie stood up, placed her hands on her hips and nearly shouted, "Izzy, I cannot understand why you would think to risk your life by volunteering to fight in this ugly war. It's not our war. Let France and England fight their own battles."

"Don't you read? Germany has offered an alliance with Mexico against us! That makes it our war. Mexico is here. It is not across the sea in Europe," he shouted in his frustration.

"Don't holler, Izzy." She folded her arms and stood over him, glaring.

Izzy struggled to gain control and stood next to her on the step. He put his arm around her. "My love, our parents came here for freedom. How can I avoid the battle? I want to volunteer."

"Izzy, if you volunteer, I don't think I could bear it. Don't you love me enough to stay with me here?"

"This has nothing to do with our love. I want to marry you now, Sophie, so that we can be together for a while before I have to go."

"But you don't have to go. No one is making you go, and you are barely twenty years old. You're too young to be conscripted, and you know nothing of war. I won't marry you at all if you volunteer to go," she cried, sniffling and dabbing at her eyes.

So many tears these months, thought Izzy as he pulled out his handkerchief to dry her eyes. "You can't mean that, Sophie," he pleaded.

"But I do," she said as her shoulders sagged. She lowered her head and stuffed her hands into her pockets.

Eleanor tired to console her friend, but Sophie was distraught. "Don't cry, dear. I can't think that Izzy would really volunteer to fight in Europe."

"But what can I do to make him see reason? I love him so much, Eleanor."

"Give him time. You have pressured him enough. Would you like to come home with me this weekend?"

"Thank you. I would really like that, Eleanor."

"No, Sophie, thank *you*. You're a good friend to me."

The Reichman house in the Murray Hill neighborhood was familiar to Sophie by now, and she occupied her favorite guest bedroom with its ornate canopied bed. She and her friend spent their time reading in front of the fire or playing cribbage. The weather being somewhat mild, the girls went window-shopping at B. Altman's, Tiffany's, and then farther west to Gimbels and Macy's. Sophie had no thought of ever being able to afford the fine fashions that they lingered over, but she liked to encourage her friend's purchases.

Last February, her aunt Selma had taken her to Macy's for a new birthday dress after their work at the NAWSA office. It was the one she had worn the night of her birthday dinner when she and Izzy had first argued.

The thought of her birthday dinner and the mess that she had made of Izzy's efforts to please her destroyed the pleasure of window-shopping, but she kept up a brave front for her friend.

"Something is wrong, Sophie. I know you well enough by now. Is it Izzy?"

"Yah, Eleanor. I feel so terrible to have threatened him as I did."

"Is it time to let him know?"

"Yes, I think so."

Sophie tossed in her extravagant bed at the Reichman's home, unable to sleep that night. *I was nasty to him, but how can he think about going to war?* She turned onto her stomach and buried her face in the pillow with its delicately embroidered linen cover. *I'll meet him at the library tomorrow and apologize.* The resolve enabled her to roll onto her side, curl up, and drift into sleep.

After breakfast with Ellie and her mother, Sophie took the subway uptown to Columbia. She walked up the wide steps leading to Low Library and hesitated at the monstrous doors. Her head was beginning to ache at the temples, and her resolve of last night wavered. *I came this far. I have to tell him.*

She went into the library, searched for Izzy at his usual desk near the east-facing windows, and found him hunched over with his head on a book, his arms resting on either side of the desktop. She tapped him lightly on his shoulder, and he looked up to see her standing by his side.

She saw that his eyes were bloodshot and that the emerald sparkle, the glow that she treasured, was missing. She put her finger to her lips and motioned him to follow her to the front steps where they could talk.

"I feel terrible. It was awful of me to tell you that I wouldn't marry you. That is all I want in the world. To be with you," she said, looking at him.

He pulled her to the side of the stairway where, hidden by a statue, he embraced her. They clung to each other and cried, suffering the aftermath of their first major argument.

Izzy whispered into her ear, "I tried to believe that you couldn't mean it, but Sophie, I won't enlist. I'll wait until I'm called."

"Maybe the war will end, and you'll never be called," she said.

"Maybe, my love, maybe. Now listen to me. If we want a peaceful life together, we can't be making threats, especially if we don't mean them. It's no way for a husband and wife to live."

"I'm so sorry, Izzy, and I'm frightened."

"I know, love. So am I."

The following day Congress passed The Conscription Act. The minimum age for conscription was twenty-one years, giving Isador relief for the time being.

# July 1917

*July 6, 1917*
*Bedford, New York*

*Dear Izzy,*

*I miss you already, but I am doing the right thing. It was difficult to make this decision, but now that many of our men are fighting in Europe, who else can do the farmwork but women? I hate the war, but I should do something to help feed our country and our soldiers. It is only for the summer, Izzy. You'll have the time to work and study more than when I am with you. Please do not stay upset with me for leaving.*

*Dr. Ogilvie came to the Women's Agricultural Camp with us. She is a Barnard professor, but she is supervising the camp for the summer. It was a muggy day when six of us girls squeezed together in the school's Model T Ford. Although our shirtwaists were damp with perspiration and our hair dripped onto our necks, we were in good spirits, laughing as we jounced around on the bumpy road. Eleanor sat next to me. Her parents let her come, even though they wanted her to stay with them at Sea Bright for the summer.*

*Imagine, Izzy! There are 142 of us up here sleeping in tents at the girls' camp. We get a ride to the farm to work in the fields. It would be too much to ask that the farmers feed us and make room for us to sleep, so the camp is a good idea. I don't think that they really wanted us in the beginning, but they have little choice with all of our men away in Europe.*

*I know that you didn't want me to come here, but I couldn't go home to Paterson for the summer. Mama is still angry with me for going away to live at Barnard. Please don't be angry with me for coming here to work.*

*I send you my love.*
*Sophie*

*July 11, 1917*
*New York, New York*

*Dearest Sophie,*

*I cannot stay angry with you. You know that. I work, and I study, and I try not to think about how I miss you. Maybe I should work on a farm, too. I could be near you and see you sometimes. But that is a silly dream. I have to work here to finish my law degree quickly. I decided to complete three classes this summer instead of the two that we talked about, so I can finish my degree in three years. That way I'll be a lawyer by the time that you graduate from Barnard. Would that make you happy?*

*I think about the night before you left for the farm. You looked so beautiful with your hair down around your shoulders. When you unpin your bun and shake your hair free, when you smile that shy way you do, I feel that I could cry. I held you close, and I smelled the freshness of those curls that cling to the bottom of your neck. I wanted to stay that way forever, not to let you go.*

*Do you remember when we first met at the strike? You were so young, but like today you have a mind of your own. What were you like as a little girl? Did you give your mama trouble? Both of you are strong. I know that you don't want me to say that you are like her, but in that way you are. Strong is good. But to be stiff-necked is not. I wish that your mama would give in. Your papa tries to convince her that you need to be in New York, but she can't seem to forget that you went against her wishes. Meyer told my papa about it. There's nothing that you can do to change her mind, except to give in and go home to Paterson, God forbid.*

*I went home to see my mama and papa. They're lonesome without me, and I wish that I had a little brother or sister to keep them company. They think so much about the war and conscription.*

*Papa and I walked all the way to Eastside Park, and we stopped at Segal's deli for some chopped liver. It was special, because Papa's silk looms are busy day and night with orders for the war, and he has very little time to spend at home.*

*I think it was better when he worked for Doherty's. At least there was an end to the day. Now he works all the time. There's plenty of contract work, and he makes more money, but even together with the few men that he hires, they are all worn out.*

*Here's something good to think about. Maybe I can get a ride to visit you on Sunday. What do you think? When you lie in bed at night, close your eyes and imagine how much I love you. Think about the time when we will be together as husband and wife, my love.*

*Your devoted,*
*Izzy*

*Columbia University*
*July 12, 1917*

*Dear Papa and Mama,*

*I am well and studying my courses for most of each day. You must not worry. I told you that I thought to volunteer, but I have prom-ised Sophie that I will not enlist. Maybe I will miss the war altogether because of my age. Thank God that you are too old, Papa. At thirty-nine you are safe.*

*Did you hear about the selection for national service that happened yesterday in Washington? They picked 10,500 numbers from a glass bowl to see who would have to go first. One by one, they picked little capsules from the bowl. Each little capsule held a group number written in red. It took ten hours, but now they know the order to call all those groups of one thousand men for service. I am too young, and you are too old, Papa, but other men will die for our democracy.*

*Now I miss Sophie and the two of you. She is happy working on a farm with Eleanor and the others from Barnard. It's healthy work, and she does a mitzvah. I have nothing here but to study my law courses. I'll come to see you again next week.*

*Papa, did you talk to Meyer about Sophie's mama? Will she let her come home to visit? How can a mother be so stubborn and cruel? There isn't enough war in the world, so Mrs. Epstein brings it right to her family.*

*Sophie misses her family, especially little Aaron. When she comes back from the farm, I want to bring her home with me. Can you invite her father and brother to visit with her?*

*With love from your son,*
*Isador*

# TWELVE

## May 1918

Isador and Sophie were holding hands on their favorite bench in Morningside Park near a small pond at the foot of the winding steps. In the calm of the park the two had a respite from study and from the clamor of the streets above. Izzy thought it might be a good time to mention what he had done that day.

"Sophie, today when I went to register for the Selective Service, they asked me about insurance."

"What insurance do they mean, Izzy?"

"I can pay sixty-five cents for every thousand dollars of benefit to my beneficiary if I should die."

"How can you even think of such a thing? My God! If you should die!"

"I bought five thousand dollars, but they wouldn't allow me to name you as my beneficiary, since we are not married. Let's marry now, Sophie. Then I can change it."

"What are you saying? That we should marry for money?"

"You aren't thinking straight, my love. This is life. I registered. I will be called, and I will go. I may die, and if I do, you will be without support."

"I can take care of myself, thank God." Sophie jumped from the bench, where a moment ago there had been peace. The skirt of her shirtwaist brushed against the side of Isador's face, as he remained momentarily in shock.

135

He watched her pace back and forth beside the pond. While massaging the nape of his neck, he felt a sob begin to emerge, but he held it in check. Izzy thought that he would do anything if he could get Sophie to marry him now, and he rose from the bench ready to embrace her and plead his case, but at that moment of panic his lawyer's mind engaged, and he sat down again.

Izzy talked himself into calm and resolved to formulate a realistic strategy for them to marry sooner than they had planned. He was accustomed to Sophie's sudden eruptions. Her emotions overwhelmed her for the moment, but he knew that she would reconsider. He consoled himself with thoughts of his love for her independent spirit, without which she would be living in Paterson, and he would be in New York missing her.

It occurred to him that he might be able to complete his law degree if he studied throughout the summer, and then they could marry after his graduation in August. With this possibility in mind, he resolved to look at the courses he would need before making the suggestion to Sophie. *God help me. I hope I don't get called before September.*

Eleanor's sitting room at home opened to Madison Avenue and its bustle of well-heeled women and men going about their Saturday chores. Some men in skullcaps were returning from the synagogue, while others wore the black hats of the Orthodox. Eleanor's home was quiet in observance of the Sabbath except for the gentile staff, who were busy in the kitchen preparing the evening meal.

Sophie and Eleanor had been studying mathematics, but had paused to talk about the guest list for the gala that was planned in honor of Eleanor's birthday. "So far there are only eight men left in town who have not been called to service. If we invite any more of our women friends from Brooks Hall, we'll need more men. Does Izzy have any friends to invite?"

"By the time your celebration comes, he, too, may be gone, but Allen Levy is exempt."

"How did that happen?"

"Ellie, he doesn't have enough molars," she replied, trying to suppress a giggle.

"What are you saying? Enough molars?"

"Izzy read the exemption requirements to me. If a man doesn't have four opposing molars top and bottom, and it can't be fixed by the dentist with a bridge, he can't serve!"

"You should give Izzy a good push and knock his teeth out!"

The two couldn't sustain their moment of lightness. "I wish my mama would forget this party. She thinks of a match for me, but I'm not ready. So many men have gone to war. Max Gold and Harvey Schulman are gone. Harry Gransky, Paul Kriss, Isaac Kristal, and David Kaplan have all passed their physical examinations and may soon be called."

"But our local board reached its quota at the end of March. How many more can be called for Europe's war?"

"Let's hope for an end…Sophie, are you planning to go to the farm again this summer? One car is going soon."

"I feel I should go, but I don't want to leave if Izzy's name comes up. I think it best that I stay in New York, but I'll feel useless here. I have to do some useful work if I stay here, Ellie."

"Years ago before I was born, my great uncle rebuilt some property that he owned on Henry Street and gave it to the Settlement that Lillian Wald started."

"I heard her name at school, and I think I remember that she was on Elizabeth Gurley Flynn's defense committee in 1915 when she was indicted for her agitation during the 1913 strike."

"She does good work on the Lower East Side with immigrant families, with Jews and Italians mostly. She's a nurse, but her work is much more. You haven't been to those tenements or to the factories where they work. Conditions in those factories are worse than in the Paterson textile mills that you told me about. You remember the shirtwaist factory fire? "

"I cried for days about that fire."

"That's what it's like. Worse than slavery."

"Are you suggesting that I might work at the Settlement House this summer?"

"It could be the right thing."

"I would have a chance to make sure it's the right thing for me. Can you get me an introduction to Lillian Wald?"

"We'll ask Papa. He knows her."

# June 1918

**J**une hadn't yet brought the heat and humidity of a New York summer, but regardless, many of the wealthier families had moved to their summer homes on the Hudson River. The Reichmans were leaving for Sea Bright in New Jersey, Eleanor with them. Her father would ferry to the summerhouse for the weekends. Sophie had been invited to spend as much time as she could, having become "a part of the family." She promised Ellie that she would come for some of the weekends.

This weekend, Sophie and Isador decided to go to Paterson. While riding the Paterson trolley, Sophie was silent as she tried to calm the familiar anxious tightening of her stomach. I'm torn in so many directions this summer, she thought as she pressed on her aching stomach with her fists. She pondered her commitments to the Henry Street Settlement, to Izzy and her family in Paterson, and to her anticipation of seeing Eleanor in Sea Bright.

She was glad to have Izzy make the decision to go home to Paterson with him for the weekend. She would see her papa and Aaron at his house, if not her mama, and she would stay with Aunt Selma and Uncle Harry. Selma, too, had tried to talk sense to Emma, who still raged at Sophie's defection almost two years ago.

When the trolley approached the familiar sights of Broadway and the upper Eastside neighborhood, Sophie suggested that she get off earlier than Izzy, who had to ride downtown. She would walk directly to her aunt and uncle's house.

"Maybe this time Aunt Selma can convince Mama to see me, since Papa hasn't had any luck."

"Sophie, I wish this for you, but don't be disappointed," he said when they reached her stop and he handed over the small valise she had brought. "I see you're worried. Your stomach is hurting, no? Relax with your aunt and uncle, and ring me on the telephone later."

Sophie crossed Broadway and strode long-legged to Wall Avenue where she rang the door chimes of the Abramowitz house. Selma herself opened the door and when she saw Sophie, she put her finger to her lips and raised her eyebrows. What now? thought Sophie.

Selma stood mute for a brief moment and then pulled Sophie close to her and whispered, "Your mama is here!"

Sophie pulled away from Selma and made as if to go, but the elder woman caught her arm, opened the door wide, stepped aside, and called into the sitting room, "Emma, you won't be able to guess who is here."

"*Nu?* Who is come?"

As Emma turned to face the hall, Sophie stepped within her view. Emma moved into the entry, and the two faced each other, Emma wide-eyed and mute. Her lower lip trembled slightly. Sophie waited. She saw a tear at the corner of her mother's eye and rushed into her now open arms.

"Mama, Mama," she sobbed as her mother smoothed her hair and whispered, "My daughter, my daughter."

"Let me see you," Emma said, holding her daughter at arm's length. "*Oy,* such a long time I have been without you. Look, you're a beauty! Knock wood! My daughter! Selma, look on my Sophie!"

"Yes, Emma. I told you many times what a good girl she is, how hard she works, how grown up she is become. Sit down, and I'll be right back," said Selma. "I need to go to the kitchen for a minute."

Emma pulled her daughter close again, then held her apart and began to unbutton Sophie's coat. "Take that off, so I get a good look at you."

Sophie complied and put her outer garments on the marble-topped hall tree, standing back for her mother to see.

Emma took a deep breath and released a satisfied, "Aah."

"We go inside, yes?" she said, leading Sophie into the sitting room where the two sat side by side on the settee.

"You came to see your papa at the Shapiro house?"

"Yes, Mama. I see him and Aaron there, but I always hoped you would come someday. I know I left home against your will, but that is long over."

"*Shah*," said Emma as she took her daughter's hand between her own. "What is passed is in the past. We start again."

Sophie leaned over to hug her mother and yielded to Emma's longed-for caress.

After a while Emma released her and called out to Selma. "You don't mind, Selma, we go home now? Papa and Aaron will be happy."

"Come, Sophie. Let's go," she said as she picked up Sophie's valise.

"Let's walk downtown, and we can talk before we get to Fair Street, Mama."

Walking arm and arm, Sophie and her mama spoke for the first time in almost two years. Sophie told her about Izzy and his imminent call to service, and about her studies, but she withheld a description of her Henry Street work. She knew that Emma would find it hard to accept her work in the tenements of the Lower East Side.

Emma told Sophie about her idea of buying a house closer to the east side of Paterson so that Aaron could go to school with "a better class of people." She had been at Harry's house intending to talk to him about the purchase.

Celebration began when they reached the apartment and surprised Meyer and Aaron. Sophie rang Izzy on the telephone, hoping that no party-line members would eavesdrop when she told him the good news. Emma brought out a *nosh*, piling the table with tea things, cinnamon bobka, and Sophie's favorite apple strudel.

When the family adjourned to the front room, Aaron, now four years old, took center stage. "Sophie, Sophie. Mama and Papa want to buy a big house, and Auntie Flora and Uncle Joe would come with us, and I'm going to go to school!"

"Yes, my son. We'll tell Sophie all about it. Now give her a kiss good night and we'll tuck you into bed," said Meyer.

"But Papa, where will Sophie sleep? I'm in her bed."

"Sophie is here to visit, Aaron. She won't need her bed."

"Papa's right, Aaron. It's your bedroom now. I sleep in the residence at school."

"You have a nice room here, Sophie," said Aaron.

"Yah, son. You are a lucky boy," said Meyer as he took his son by the hand for their bedtime ritual.

"What do you think, Sophie, of your mama buying a house?" said Emma.

"Not you and Papa together?"

"Sure, sure. Papa and me together."

"That will be a good thing. Aaron is happy about it."

"And a modern kitchen with a gas stove, and a tiled bathroom yet."

"Oh, Mama, I am glad for you."

"For me only, Sophie?"

"Yah, for you and Papa and Aaron."

"But Sophie, when you come home to live, there will be a big bedroom for you downstairs with Flora and Joe." Emma shut her mouth abruptly.

"Mama, let's not talk about that today."

Emma was obsessed with the idea of moving her family to the "right" side of town. Nothing would do until she could move to the Eastside neighborhood where Paterson's wealthy dwelt.

Mrs. Bingham, the realtor's wife, came into the store on occasion, and Emma used the opportunity to pump her for the sales figures of recent home transactions above East Twenty-fourth Street. Emma had taken take the electric trolley up Broadway from her shop during the quiet periods of the day to see the homes that had recently sold. She was diligent in her research.

Emma had saved five hundred dollars on her own and planned to take a mortgage on a two-family house. It wouldn't fulfill her dream of living on Wall Avenue, but it was a step closer to the right neighborhood. At least Aaron can go to school with the Wall Avenue children, she thought as she scoured the morning paper during breakfast. She would ask Joe and Flora to live downstairs, and her family would be on the top floor. Emma was thrilled to think of the attic rooms that she would also have. "Attic space yet!" she muttered, but not loud enough for Meyer to hear.

Meyer, who was sitting next to her and reading *The Forward* on this half-day Saturday, appeared unconcerned about her frenzy. "Did you say something, Emma?"

"This is it!" Emma shouted in a tone that Meyer couldn't miss.

"Listen, Meyer. 'Lovely two-family house with yard. Each flat with modern kitchen and tiled bathroom. Must see. 749 East Twenty-sixth Street. Four thousand nine hundred ninety dollars.' Meyer, this price is good. I know from this. I can do this with the five hundred dollars I saved from the business. Right away we should call Mr. Bingham, the realtor. His wife buys in the store."

"Emma, you would do this on a Saturday? On *Shabbos*?"

"*Nu? Shabbos* is nothing to him. Bingham goes to church on Sunday, not today."

"You know I am fine in Fair Street, Emma, but if it makes you happy, we look." He turned again to his newspaper, reading the Yiddish in a whisper.

Emma was already at the telephone before he finished his comment, and later that afternoon, Mr. Bingham waited in front of their Fair Street building in his new Packard touring car. She had seen pictures of the luxury car in one of Harry's magazines and was quick to notice it was the Twin-Six Salon model.

She recalled Harry remarking, "It has twelve cylinders to Cadillac's eight!" Emma hastened to sit in the front seat as soon as Mr. Bingham opened the door, thinking that real estate must be a very profitable business. Meyer climbed into the backseat with not a word.

They drove up Park Avenue and turned left onto East Twenty-sixth Street. The white wooden house with brown trim was on the east side of the street near Fifteenth Avenue. Each flat had a screened summer porch adjoining the ample front room and two bedrooms off the kitchen. A formal dining room with French doors opening to a sitting room lay between the front room and the kitchen. The upstairs flat was the sunnier of the two. When Emma saw the new white enameled gas stove, her decision was made. No one on Fair Street had such a prize.

Meyer wanted to see the huge coal furnace in the cellar. He opened the door and looked in. Only ashes from the prior winter. He had seen the radiators in each room of the flat, and he followed the pipes to see the source of the steam heat.

He walked over to the two adjacent room-size bins, open to the basement and full of coal. This would be a bonus for their budget. Meyer admired the gleaming and irregular chunks of coal piled higher near the window in the back of the bin where the deliveryman sent them rushing down a chute from his truck. Two sturdy shovels leaned against the wall, and over on the other side of the furnace were four shiny ash cans.

"Emma," Meyer said as he appeared at the back kitchen door to the flat. "That's some furnace down there. Maybe it's not so bad we should own this house."

"Yah, that's right, Meyer. We move up in the world."

# Thirteen

## September 1918

Auntie Flora allowed Aaron freedom to play outdoors in front of their new house while Emma was away at her store, and Aaron had begun to enjoy his freedom with her, no longer missing his mother during the day. He had learned by now to mask his preference for his aunt, and even at his young age he already knew how to placate his mother.

Aaron didn't need to placate Meyer. He was certain of his father's love, even if he forgot to say, "Thank you," or even if he came inside from play with soiled clothes. The two were as close as Sophie and her papa had been when she lived at home.

In the evenings, Emma allowed Aaron to wait in front of the house for Papa's return from work instead of insisting that he stay in the backyard. The boy waited anxiously. *I hope Papa isn't too tired to take me for a walk.* As soon as he recognized his father's gait and saw the ocher hue of the old meerschaum pipe in his mouth, he would run down East Twenty-sixth Street to greet Meyer.

This night he was lucky. "Papa, can we go…"

"Yah, son. Tonight we walk to the train."

Aaron ran up the four cement steps, crossed the landing with its iron banister, and then mounted the remaining three wooden steps to the outer door. Here in the enclosed entryway was the oak door to Flora and Joe's flat and a winding inside staircase with a mahogany handrail to the landlord's upper flat.

Meyer stood smiling at the foot of the staircase, eyes following his active little boy. When Aaron reached the bend in the staircase, he climbed up after him, went through the open doorway, and stepped into the front room.

Aaron had reached the kitchen where Emma was making dinner.

"Papa and I are going for a walk."

He ran after Meyer across the kitchen and into his parents' adjoining bedroom where he watched every movement of his father's evening routine. Meyer unknotted his tie, removed his collar, and took off his sweat-stained shirt.

"I'll hang your shirt, Papa," said Aaron as he reached for it and then hung the white shirt over the chair back as he had seen Meyer do.

Meyer folded his trousers over the hanger rod, and wearing only his under-clothes, he went to the china washbasin on the bureau that Emma had filled with hot water. He dipped in his hand and flicked the warm water onto his little boy's head.

Aaron giggled and reached for the basin to mimic his Papa. "No play tonight, boy. We must hurry if we want to see the engine pass. It's almost five thirty."

The Erie Railroad crossed Park Avenue at East Twenty-second Street, a little more than four blocks from home. Father and son arrived in time to hear the warning bell—ding, ding, ding, ding—as the man in the tall thin tower lowered the black-and-white striped safety gates. Ding, ding, …ding, ding, ding. After the tracks were secured so that no one could cross them, they heard the rumble of the train in the distance. Aaron felt the rumble in his stomach as the train came barreling toward the Park Avenue intersection.

He jumped up and down, pulling on Meyer's hand. "It's coming, Papa. It's coming." A thick plume of steam pushed upward from the smokestack, and the sound of its exhaust announced its imminent arrival—choo, chooo, choooo.

The engineer waved to Aaron and tugged his whistle. The war had seen an increase in coal coming to Paterson from Pennsylvania. Meyer and Aaron counted the eleven coal-laden cars as they clamored on the iron tracks and whizzed past the intersection. Finally the caboose came into sight, and Aaron jumped and waved with both hands at the rear-facing brakeman in his striped overalls and engineer's cap. He waved to Aaron as the freight train faded from sight.

The gates went up again—ding, ding,… ding, ding, ding—the signal for the two to return home for dinner.

"Aaron, do you know that President Wilson gave those railroad men an eight-hour day? They get overtime, too."

"Will the president give the silk workers an eight-hour day, too, Papa?"

"God willing, boy. God willing."

"Papa, what is the white thing over the engineer's mouth? The caboose man has one, too."

Meyer ran his right hand through his hair and took the pipe from his mouth. "Son, there is a bad sickness come to our country from Spain. They call it the Spanish flu. People cover their mouth and nose with a white mask, so they don't catch the sickness."

"Why, Papa? Why do they cover their mouth and nose?"

Maybe the germs come into the body that way, Aaron."

"I want a mask, too, Papa."

Several days later Aaron was alone in the front of his house, hanging by his knees on the iron banister, arms across his chest. He reached up to the iron bar to disengage his legs, stood erect, and examined his palms, red from gripping the rail. "I'm a strong boy," he said aloud.

"Yeah, you're not so strong, little Aaron," came a boy's voice from behind him on the street. "And you're a sissy with that silly ole mask on your face."

"Am not. I don't want to catch the Spanish flu. And I am too, strong, Dennis. You think you are so big, because you go to school. I'm going to school, too, in January, my mama says."

"Then I'll be in first grade, and you'll still be a kindergarten baby."

Flora's call to him as she thrust her head out of her front-room window put an end to the banter. "Aaron, come inside, boy."

"I'm coming, Auntie," he called as he turned his back on Dennis, walked up the three wooden steps, and struggled to pull open the heavy entrance door.

"Baby," Dennis called after him.

Flora bent down to embrace him when he came inside. "You know that your mama doesn't want you to play with those Cleary boys. Why didn't that boy have a mask?"

"He says I'm a sissy because I wear a mask."

"Don't you mind, my little man. You wear your mask."

Everyone wore masks and stayed indoors as much as possible. Emma refused to close her shop, and Meyer still delivered the bread, but families stayed away from public places and kept to themselves. Jacob Fabian's Regent Theater was closed, and the meeting halls were empty of celebrations. Buses and trains were eerie in their emptiness.

Meyer still attended the Workmen's Circle where he met with his *landsmen* regularly. They wore their masks until they arrived, and then once down in the basement, were relieved to remove the encumbrance. They pulled out their pipes and cigars as if the companionship of *landsmen* was good enough to ward off the flu.

On this evening most of the men knew of a family with a loss. People had begun to hang ribbons on their doors, white for the death of a child, black for middle age, and gray for the old. Fear had gripped the city. *The New York Times* featured pictures of empty streets with a few pedestrians hastening to work, their masks in place. Street sweepers, too, wore their white protection.

"One of those Cleary boys died yesterday," commented Solly. "I saw the white ribbon."

"My Ruthie is wild. She won't let the children out of her sight. She watches over them like a madwoman. Every time someone sneezes, she runs to put her lips to their forehead."

"Meyer, how is Manny doing with his looms?" asked Solly to change the subject. "We don't see much of him here like we used to."

"Busy. Knock wood. The war wants silk, and Manny and his men work

148

day and night. Too hard, but with new men working, at least now Esther can stay home. She isn't built to last in a factory, that woman."

"He has six looms now in that rented mill space, yah, Meyer?" asked Hyman.

"Yah, Hymie. Six looms, a good business and the big guys leave him alone. They get their rent money from him. That's enough."

Isaac stood, preparing to leave. "Well, men. Home to my dinner. I hope there's no new ribbons. It's a bad time when I have to think, 'Who's next?'"

"Such thoughts we never should have. This flu is going to pass soon, I know it," said Meyer as he tamped out the remaining embers from his pipe, put it into his pocket and rose, pulling his coat over his shoulders. He reached into his breast pocket and pulled out the white mask, sighed, and placed it over his nose and mouth.

"Mama, I'm so hot. Mama, Mama, I'm hot," Aaron cried out before dawn.

Emma sat up in bed at the sound of his cry. "What is it, Dolly?" asked Meyer.

"It's Aaron calling."

Emma ran from the bed in her nightgown, not bothering to put on a robe or slippers. "Aaron, my son. What is it?"

"Mama, I'm so hot. My throat hurts."

"Meyer, come quick."

"I'm coming. I'm coming," called Meyer as he roused himself from sleep.

The two distraught parents looked at each other without a word. Both knew what could not be spoken.

Into the morning Emma and Meyer sat tearfully by Aaron's bedside, holding an ice-soaked cloth to his forehead and caressing his hand. When Meyer had to leave the room for a moment, he lingered by the door and heard his wife in quiet prayer.

"Dear God, when have I asked from you anything? Always I work, and do what I must. Now God, help me. Make my Aaron well. No doctor will come when the whole city cries out. It is only you, dear God, who can help."

On that first day Aaron burned with fever and was delirious, mumbling about school, about being a big boy, about being strong. He slept fitfully.

"Yes, my son. You are a strong boy. You will get well," Emma repeated over and over. At times she allowed herself sleep and Meyer wiped the boy's brow. "Be well, *mein zun*. Grow strong, *mein zun*."

Meyer watched his son sleeping and whimpering in his delirium. He thought about what he had yet to teach him, what they had yet to share, and he squeezed his eyes shut. His mind wandered, and he sat on the side of the sickbed dozing. He saw his boy coming home from school to practice his Torah reading. He was about to become a Bar Mitzvah. Rabbi Aronson hovered overhead while Aaron chanted his designated Torah portion. Rabbi Aronson smiled and came to perch on Aaron's shoulder. He wrapped his *tallis* about the young man's shoulders. He hovered behind Aaron, put his thumbs under the boy's chin and his palms on Aaron's cheeks, and he lifted the boy into the air, vanishing…

"No! You can't take him!" screamed Meyer, as he bolted from his sleep.

Emma came running to the bedside, then heard a knock on the back door. When Flora saw Emma's face, she pushed her aside and went into the kitchen. "Where is Aaron? What happened?" Flora went into the bedroom where she saw Meyer's back heaving with silent tears.

"Oh, my darling, my little one," cried Flora.

Flora and Joe, Emma and Meyer sat with Aaron all through the day, but his fever only climbed higher. They put him in a tub of cold water. They mopped his brow. They watched and they prayed.

"Maybe we should call Sophie. There is a phone in Brooks Hall for emergency," said Emma.

"No," Meyer urged. "Let us wait. She can't come here now. It is too dangerous even to travel. Let her be in peace until we know more." They did as Meyer suggested.

For the first time since she bought her shop from Bessie, Emma closed the doors on a workday. Meyer sat with Aaron while she dressed and went to the shop to put a note on the door. "Closed Until Further Notice." Anyone who read the sign would know what that meant.

For six days the four adults sat by the child's bedside and watched the fever rage. He coughed, he moaned, and his body began to turn a bluish shade, but he fought. It was known that the flu took the lives of the young and healthy. Babes and young men and women in their prime were snatched, while the old and the middle-aged were left to mourn their young.

More than two million men were already in Europe with the American Expeditionary Force. More were needed. Though Isador was still in school, he went to the local board of the Selective Service every day. He had recently received notice of his selection for military service, but it didn't mean he had been ordered to report for duty yet.

Izzy was tortured by his need for Sophie and his desperation to marry her. Each time that he went to the Selective Service board he shuddered, not for fear of the draft, but more for the thought of leaving his beloved before they could marry and set up housekeeping.

Today the couple was seated on the edge of Izzy's bed, and he was about to raise the topic again when Sophie gave him an opening.

"Izzy, I am sick from waiting. Every day I wake up, and I think, 'Maybe today will be the day. Maybe today he'll see his red ink serial number there on the list of those to be called.'"

"And for me it is the same. We should marry now before it happens. Please Sophie, be with me. Marry me."

"Oh, Izzy, I want to be with you," she whispered as they reached for each other. The year had seen their lovemaking progress from touching to nude embracing, but the fear of pregnancy had prevented complete coitus. Now as they undressed each other, their fear of separation united them at last, but at the moment that Sophie protested, Izzy withdrew his penis, and the thick milky fluid projected onto the outer lips of her vagina.

"It's fine, *Liebe*. Don't cry. We're safe. You'll see."

"I'm crying because I love you. You make me happy."

"It didn't hurt?"

"Only a little, my dear one. I love you."

They lingered in their embrace and talked of their marriage plans. Given the urgency of the times, they decided to have a simple wedding in the rabbi's office as soon as Isador's training was over and before he left for war. Their families would be disappointed, but they would plan for a big celebration afterward.

The very next day, Isador was called to assemble for transport to Camp Dix.

*September 8, 1918*
*Camp Dix, New Jersey*

*My Darling,*

*I'm glad you didn't come to see me off. It was a sad time. People crying. Officers barking orders. I like to remember you the way we were together in my room the day before I left.*

*Private Parker took charge of our group. He held the "party ticket" with our railroad ticket and our meal tickets. Some party! Why do they call it a party? He counted heads (now I'm a "head"), and then we were off.*

*The train ride was okay for me, because I only thought about you and the smell of your hair, and I looked at your picture. Now I'm here under Corporal Caparelle, a part of the Thirty-fourth Infantry Division.*

*At this training camp we learn about our duties and how to dress and how to shoot. We learn about the weapons. We build our strength. We march. This is not like our walks in Central or Morningside Parks. The parade ground is two miles long! Yet it makes me very strong, and that is a good thing.*

*I am sleeping with nine other men in a "pyramidal" tent. Not so bad. It is made of cloth with a wooden floor. We roll up the sides for air, and we have a little stove to heat and keep the coffee warm. There are no other Yids here, but plenty of good Irish and Italians. You would like them.*

*Sophie, they turned these cornfields into an army camp in only two months! All these buildings! These trucks, tents, headquarters, a hospital!*

*We have our own water, sewage, and electrical system. The roads are paved, and Sophie, there are 1,655 buildings! It's a city here.*

*The camp is close to Hoboken, a train ride away. I hope you can come to see me one Sunday. I miss holding your hand, the coolness of it, your long, delicate fingers.*

*Forever I am your devoted,*
*Izzy*

Sophie lay curled on top of her dormitory bed on this warm September afternoon, the opening week of school. Izzy's letter rested open and tearstained beside her. With the delicate forefinger that he loved, she traced the tiny stitches of the blue and white triangles on the quilt that Emma made for her when she was a little girl. Her stomach ached and groaned. She could feel the tension deep inside. The miserable suspense of waiting for the draft this past year was over. That waiting was nothing compared to the image of Izzy in a uniform with a gun pointed at another human being.

She dozed, but was awakened by her roommate who had recently returned from Sea Bright on the New Jersey shore. When Sophie opened her eyes and saw her dear friend, she reached out her arms, and Ellie fell into them. She was brown from the summer sun. She looked vigorous and rested considering that she, like all New Yorkers, wore protective masks to repel the Spanish flu.

"Oh, Ellie, I am so glad you are here."

"I haven't seen you since July when you came to visit. Tell me about the Settlement on Henry Street. Is it the right thing for you to do?"

Glad of the distraction, Sophie told her friend about the children she taught, the three- and four-year-olds. She sat up and held her palms open, and as if carrying their weight she said, "There are thousands of little children in one city block of tenements. I never knew poverty like this. Ellie, the children have a musty smell, and their scalps are crawling with lice. Lillian Wald says that they are the future of democracy in America. They have such a long way to go. I'll continue to work there at the Settlement house when I can, and I think maybe I'll—"

A knock on the door preceded the appearance of Rose Braverman's wavy blonde head. "I thought I heard you two talking."

"Oh, Rose, Sophie has been telling me about the children at the Henry Street Settlement."

"Tell us about your summer, Rose," said Sophie as she motioned for her to sit across on Ellie's bed.

"I was with my family in Newport for the summer, but it's not as much fun there as it was when I was a kid. My parents are constantly scheming to invite families with eligible sons. I hate it! But Sophie, tell me about Izzy."

For a moment the room was silent, and then Sophie handed over the letter that was lying open on her bed. Both friends reached for it and sat down side by side on Ellie's bed to read. "He's so romantic, but imagine sleeping in a tent with nine men!" said Rose.

They all blushed at the thought, and Ellie laughed, "Of *him* sleeping with nine men."

Sophie got up and opened the window onto the courtyard. She stared outside, and her friends fumbled for words. "Sophie, I would worry, too. But have you been reading the news lately? Maybe the war will end before Izzy finishes his training. Have you thought that he might not have to go to the front?" Ellie queried.

"That's what I pray for. I read that our counteroffensives on the Somme have pushed the German army back into retreat, but they are strong still, I think."

"Don't you believe it, Sophie. The Allies will push them into full retreat. You'll see. Soon they will have to give in," Rose said.

*September 29, 1918*
*Camp Dix, New Jersey*

*My Dear Sophie,*

*The Allies broke through the German fortifications at the Hindenburg line. I know the war will soon be over, and I'll be back in New York to marry Miss Sophie Epstein. While I march up and down I think about you. Will your mama be happy at the news of our wedding? After all, I am a lawyer now. I have only to pass examinations.*

*Have you worked out anything with your mama after all this time? Did your papa tell her that we plan to marry? When you give her a son-in-law, a lawyer yet, she'll forgive you for staying at Barnard instead of the new house.*

*Training isn't so bad. I sleep well after a full day of drill and practice with my Enfield rifle. Training is for two months, so I have another month here, but believe me, the war will be over by then.*

*I knew that you would take to your work in the Settlement. I heard that civilians have died from the flu. Maybe you should not be in public so much, near all of those little children. Will you stop going there until this flu passes by? I'll worry less if you do. Please, for me.*

*You have a mind of your own, dear one, but this time, please listen to me and stop your work at the Settlement house for a while.*

*The guys are getting ready for morning inspection, so I have to go now.*


*I love you with all my heart.*
*Isador*


*P.S. Allen Levy told me that you are wearing my derby. I will think of you that way, but you don't need to wear my vest.*

# October 1918

*October 7, 1918*

*Brooks Hall*
*Barnard College, New York*

*Dearest Love,*

*I stopped going to the Settlement house for now. You are right about that. Conditions are bad, and people are avoiding public transportation. The hospitals are beginning to fill with flu patients. Most of us study here at the library or in Brooks Hall. We are fine here in school. Allen is well, and I see him on occasion. When I read the list of "killed in action" and see the funeral processions here in the city, I don't know which to worry about the most, the war or the flu. May God keep you safe from both.*

*I talked to your folks on the phone last week. They are fine, but there was something in your mama's voice that sounded not right. I called Papa, but he had nothing to say. You shouldn't worry, because our parents are all well. Maybe I feel these things because I worry about you.*

*Remember when I was at the farm last summer? You wrote, "I study and I try not to think about how much I miss you." Now I know how you felt. I dream of the day when you come home, and we marry at last. Would it be right for you to ask Papa for my hand? He expects us to marry, but perhaps they would like the old-fashioned custom. Would you like me to walk around you seven times under the chuppah like our mamas did in the old country?*

*Wait. They are calling me to the phone.*

*It was Papa. Aaron was delirious from the flu for seven days, but he has, thank God, recovered. That was what I heard in your mama's voice. She's not good at keeping secrets.*

*Say hello to your friend Jamie for me. May God bless you and keep you.*

*With love,*
*Your Sophie*

Sophie and her friends were seated in the Brooks Hall dining room. Its large windows opened to a field studded with maple and oak trees. The flaming red maples danced to show off their color, while the sturdier gold and orange oaks resisted the impulse. The air was crisp, and it was a perfect autumn day. Despite the beauty, which might have enraptured them at another time, the girls were listless, picking at their food. They didn't look at the trees. They looked off into space.

Each one knew of someone who had succumbed to the flu. Marci Engel's little brother had died. Ellie knew of several from Temple Emanu-El who had passed on. She had made condolence calls. Rose Braverman told of her cousin, Yolanda, a student in high school. All of the girls knew of Esther Morgan's death. She was a Barnard student who commuted from home. Between the war and the flu, it seemed that no one was exempt from the threat of death.

For Sophie, the anxiety was all the worse. This week she had missed her second menses since the last day that she and Izzy were together. She tried to convince herself that Izzy had done the right thing and that there was no chance of a pregnancy, but the thought nagged at her. Each time she relieved herself, she looked for a bloodstain, but none appeared. She didn't feel pregnant, but what would she be feeling?

Eleanor was her only confidant, and she had suggested that Sophie see her own mother's doctor. Sophie wasn't ready for that, but agreed that she would go next month if she hadn't begun to flow. She was beginning to lose weight, and her skirts were starting to hang at her waist. That didn't seem like being pregnant.

"This will not do, my friend," lectured Eleanor when they were alone on a bench facing the quad. The air held an autumn chill, and Sophie shivered and held her sweater closer. It was the belted golden wool cardigan that Emma had knit for her when she was in high school. She looked downward, and a tear fell into her lap.

"You must eat more, especially if you really are pregnant."

"How can I be pregnant? I'm not married. Izzy said it would be fine. I'll know next month for sure, and if I am going to have a baby, Izzy will be here to marry me. The war will be over. The flu will be over, and it will be all right, won't it, Ellie?"

# FOURTEEN

## November 1918

*November 2, 1918*
*Camp Dix, New Jersey*

*Dearest Sophie,*

*The Turks signed an armistice three days ago! The war is coming to an end and "Johnny will be marching home again." Soon the Germans will sign. To think I will be with you soon.*

*They are not sending soldiers out of Camp Dix now because we are needed to care for the sick. We have so many soldiers in cots, lined up head to toe, that we who are healthy must help how we can. My job is to stuff mattress ticking with straw. We don't have enough beds and mattresses for all the sick men. Don't worry about me, because I am fit from my two months of training. It will be over soon, and our men will come home.*

*This letter is short, because I must work now.*

*I love you,*
*Isador*

"Hey, kike. Wha'ja do on yer day o' leave, m' boy?" asked James Flaherty, Izzy's tent mate and new friend. Jamie, as the guys called him, came from a big Newark family. There were six brothers and three sisters. One Sunday his mother and father and eight brothers and sisters all came to see Jamie at Dix. As an only child, the number of children staggered Izzy. He decided then, when he saw the joking and teasing and hugging and horseplay, that he wanted a large family. Sophie, loving children as she did, would agree, he knew.

"None o' yer business, you mick!" Izzy had toughened in two months. He came to Camp Dix a refined and sober only child. He had learned to be part of a young man's world where epithets were a sign of inclusiveness. He could rassle and name-call with the best.

Jamie leaned over to Izzy's cot from where he lay on his own and tried to grab the tiny box that Izzy was holding. "Whatcha got there? Lemme see, will ya?"

Izzy clutched the little gold satin box to his chest and turned away from Jamie, who jumped on top of Izzy and tried to wrest the box away.

"Okay, okay. I'll show you, but get off me."

Jamie went to his own cot, sat on the edge facing Izzy, and leaned forward with his elbows on his knees and chin resting on his palms. "See, I'm waitin'."

Izzy opened the box carefully and looked at the hidden contents with a faraway smile.

"Com'on will ya?"

"Okay. Look at this."

"Well wha'ja know! A diamond ring! Won't yer girl be proud o' that!"

"She doesn't know about it. I want to surprise her when I get out of here."

"How'ja know she'll have ya, Izzy m' boy?"

"She'll have me. Don't you worry. Look, Jamie. I know this is crazy, but I'm going to write a letter to Sophie and stuff it in this box. If anything should happen to me, will you see she gets it? You could bring it to my folks in Paterson."

"Why ya wanna talk that way, Iz? You'll be home making whoopee before you know it."

"Yeah, but in case something happens, will you promise?"

"Sure, pal."

Four days after writing his last letter to Sophie, Izzy complained of a head-ache. By the end of the day he was in the hospital. His face had turned a dark purplish brown and his feet so black even his mother would not know him. At times blood spurted from his nose. Jamie stood by him, openly crying. Izzy was delirious and moaning for Sophie.

Within twenty-four hours, he was gone. Jamie was by his side. He took Izzy's lifeless hand, closed his eyes, and whispered, "May God hold you in the palm of His hand." Then he reached into Izzy's pocket and pulled out the gold satin box.

Esther and Manny Shapiro sat on the settee in the cramped but spotless front room of their Hamilton Avenue apartment. Esther, speechless and pale, was holding the little gold box that Jamie had delivered, but handed it over to Manny when she noticed that her tears had soaked the gold cardboard. She fumbled in her apron pocket for her handkerchief, the pink monogrammed one that Isador had given her for her last birthday.

Manny pocketed the gold box and stowed the unopened duffel bag of Isador's possessions in his son's bedroom. They had received the telegram, the one that expressed regrets for their loss and assured the bereaved parents that their son was a hero. He had served his country well.

A separate letter was yet to arrive explaining that Izzy had bought life insurance—$28.75 per month for twenty years, payable to his beneficiary, his mother.

"Yah, he served his country by caring for sick boys until he died himself," cried Manny. "He didn't have a chance. A lawyer yet. Our son was a lawyer. Esther, what will become of us without our boy? What will we live for, *Liebe*?"

Esther was silent. The veins on the side of her neck pulsated, and she rubbed her upper arms. Finally she sighed and said, "We'll live for each other, Emanuel, for each other."

"Maybe we should call Sophie now. Give her this little box to remember our boy. This ring. And to think, she would have been our daughter. There might have been grandchildren yet."

While seated on the settee Esther pulled up her cotton hosiery, lifted her yellow flowered skirt, and reached below her knee to roll each stocking an extra time over its garter band. She sniffled, wiped her nose, and strained to raise her bulk from the settee, habitually wiping her hands on the sides of her apron.

*Oy.* Such an effort to move, she thought as she walked to the telephone. The movement across the small parlor to the kitchen telephone tired her. Every step was an effort.

She found her spectacles on the telephone table and put the gold wires over her ears. Esther picked up the blue leather address book, marked Sophie's telephone number with her left hand, and dialed each numeral, impatient for the dial to return to zero between each digit.

"Hello, hello. This is Brooks Hall? Can you get Sophie Epstein to the phone?"

Esther held the phone to her ear, and using her free hand she wiped her eyes with the corner of her apron as she waited for Sophie to come to the phone. "Manny, how can I tell her?" she asked as she tried to stifle a sob.

She nodded to Manny when she heard Sophie's voice. "This is Esther Shapiro, Dolly. I called, I...I called to tell you, mine sweet, that our boy... *Oy* God, Sophie dear. Isador is no more. Izzy is gone. Can you hear me, Sophie? Sophie? Are you there Sophie? Sophie, come to us soon, Dolly. Isador left something for you."

Later that night, Sophie rang the Shapiro doorbell. When Esther opened the door they fell into each other's arms, crying. They held tightly for a long while, and then Sophie went to Manny and hugged him.

"Sit here," Esther said as she patted the settee next to herself. She handed over the box. Sophie held it for several minutes, silent and red-eyed, until she was able to open it. She lifted out a delicate gold filigree band with a small diamond nestled in its bed of gold branches and silently slid it onto her ring finger, stuffing the letter in her pocket for later.

Sophie slept in Izzy's room that night. Before preparing for sleep she opened the letter that had been enclosed with her ring.

*November 5, 1918*
*Camp Dix, New Jersey*

*My Dearest Love,*

*I hope you will never read this letter, but if you do, please know that I longed for you every day of my life since we met so long ago. Do you remember those days of the big silk strike when you sneaked out of school? I knew then that you were for me.*

*I treasure your ideals, your dreams to help the poor, your tender-ness. Now that I am gone, you will follow those dreams without me, but someday I hope you will meet another that you can love as faithfully as you have loved me.*

*I have always loved you, and since that night before I left you for Camp Dix I have considered us as man and wife in God's eyes.*

*Follow your dream, my love. Live long and well.*
*Your Isador*

Sophie folded the tearstained letter and placed it under Izzy's pillow. She lay in his bed, hugged his pillow, and relished the nearness of him. During the night she awoke, thinking that Izzy was beside her, and could not fall back to sleep. She lay thinking about her tender breasts and missed menses. She didn't need Mrs. Reichman's doctor to tell her that she was pregnant, but Izzy had been her confidant, and he wasn't here to help her with this dilemma. She tried to imagine raising a child by herself, Isador's beautiful child, and she thought about the problems she would have to solve. It was too hard, too much. She couldn't think about it yet.

She drifted to sleep and awoke early thinking to fix herself in the mirror, but Esther had turned it to the wall, along with the two other mirrors in the house. It reminded her that the Shapiros respected the traditional *shiva*, the seven days of mourning at home. It was a time for grieving and focusing on their loved one, not to think about themselves or look at their image while in prayer. A deep sense of belonging overcame her, and she resolved to ask the Shapiros if she could stay the week.

When she went into the kitchen, Manny told her that her parents would be coming to pay a call soon. They knew she had arrived. The house would be full of callers for the whole week, and there wouldn't be much time to talk with Esther alone. Sophie asked her to come into Izzy's room and sit beside her on the bed.

"Mrs. Shapiro," she began.

"Call me Esther, Dolly."

"Esther, I feel so at home here. Do you think I could spend this week of *shiva* here with you and sleep in Isador's room?"

"*Vos*? You should ask? Why should you have to ask? We love you like a daughter, *meine sheinela*." The two hugged and cried and wiped their tears away, ready to go back into the kitchen when they heard a riotous hubbub from the street. Esther opened a window and looked down at crowds of people screaming and dancing. "It's over! The war is over!"

Sophie joined Esther at the window. When she realized the irony of her beloved's death, she screamed, "Oh, dear God," and flung herself onto the bed facedown, kicking her bent legs up and down on the mattress whose springs cried out in sympathy.

"Oh no, no, no," she sobbed. Esther sat beside Sophie on the bed, reached over to embrace her, and rested her head on Sophie's back. She too cried, her silent tears spilling onto the shirtwaist of her daughter-in-law that should have been.

Loud knocking came from the hallway and the Shapiros' front door. Esther got up to investigate in time to see Tillie, a friend and neighbor, open the door with a "Yoo-hoo! *Vos* is this sad look? Don't you know the war is over? Here, here is the paper. Read it and give it back to me later. Such a party we will have! Isador will be coming home."

Tillie rushed out to join the throng in the streets, leaving *The New York Times* headline on the kitchen table.

"***War Ends At 6 O'Clock This Morning***" by the Associated Press, Washington, Nov. 11, 2:48 AM. "The armistice between Germany, on the one hand, and the allied Governments and the United States, on the other, has been signed."

"He never saw the war," cried Manny. "He didn't need to go to that Camp Dix. They didn't need him to fight. They took his life for nothing."

Another knock on the door, and a bearded Rabbi Aronson presented himself with the soulful look of a griever. "Manny, Esther. It's right you called me. Let me help you with this lapel. He pulled a small scissors from his pocket and made a tiny snip on Manny's jacket lapel, ripping it further, a symbol of family mourning. He did the same on Esther's collar. When Sophie came forward to have her collar rent, the rabbi said, "Sophie. You don't have to do that. You're not family."

"Yah, Reb Aronson. You should have married her under the *chuppah* with my Isador, but now she is all we have. We say *Kaddish*, not *Mazel tov*."

"Come here, Sophie." He made the tearing, as she held back her sob.

"Emanuel, you will have a *minyen*? You have the required ten men to make prayers?"

"Yah, *Rebbe*. The men from the Workmen's Circle will come every morning."

"And every afternoon and evening?"

"Yah, yah, Reb. Every morning, every afternoon, and every evening ten men will come."

"Good. But Emanuel, what about Isador's body? Will the army send it?"

"We can't reach anyone to talk with us. The nice young man who brought Isador's things said he would try to help, but with the armistice and whatnot… What will we do, Reb Aronson, if they will not return to us Isador's body?"

"It's impossible now to even get a casket. The undertaker is busy. The cabinetmakers are working day and night to make the caskets. I go from house to house with my *Kaddish* prayers. So many ribbons on the doors."

"But his body, Reb. How can we get Isador's body?" Esther entreated. She was now close to hysteria.

"Esther, my dear, I don't know… "

"Even the rabbi fails to help," she mumbled to Sophie, who had moved to be near her.

Esther couldn't remember the day of the week or the meals she had eaten that week of the *shiva*. She and Manny lumbered from guest to guest, room to room, prayer to prayer. Their family and friends came sad-eyed and dour to the door, clutching Esther with tears and moaning. "*Oy*, such a thing," said the downstairs neighbor. "A lawyer yet, and he should die so young," said another.

The apartment was filled with enticing food brought by friends and neighbors, but even Esther with her perpetual *noshing* couldn't take up a bite of the bobka or the ruggeleh. They ate the chicken soup and the pea soup with short ribs, all without pleasure. Corned beef sandwiches piled up. Guests weren't permitted to leave without taking a *bisl* this, a *bisl* that.

Esther overheard her guests in their separate klatches speak with relief and yes, joy about the war's end, and she thought of her own misery. She resented their happiness, especially in this house of mourning, and she berated herself for diminishing her loved ones. "The war may be over, but the flu is not," she had said to Manny. "What cause is there for happiness?" Suddenly her mind cleared. *I am angry. I am very angry. How could God do this to us and to our Sophie?*

The guests kept coming day after day, all putting aside for a moment their intense relief and joy about the end of the war with words of solace. The Barnard girls made the trip to Paterson in twos and threes. One told Sophie about the Barnard snake dance. Almost eight hundred girls from the college had snake-danced through Morningside Heights when news of the armistice broke. They spoke about horn honking, kissing in the streets, shouting and carrying on. A new era of peace had begun even as the Expeditionary Forces in Europe were still in the trenches, making ready for the long, cautious march into Germany.

Esther saw Sophie pace the rooms, handkerchief at the ready, red-eyed and lips aquiver. She noticed how Sophie forced a smile through her tears when she greeted her friends from New York. Esther wondered what Sophie had heard from Emma. While Meyer had been a constant companion in the Shapiro home, Emma had not yet appeared to console her daughter. Maybe today, she thought.

Emma did arrive with Meyer later that day, strudel in hand, coiffed and wearing an elegant black silk dress. "*Oy*, Esther, such a sorrow. May God rest his soul, our poor Isador," she said as she handed over the sweets.

*Since when is he our Isador?* Esther recoiled inwardly. "Let me find Sophie for you. There she is, with Meyer already," said Esther, looking off into the corner of the room where father and daughter stood close together.

Emma approached her daughter with arms outstretched. Esther could see that their recent reconciliation was still holding, because Sophie received Emma with a hug and tears. Yet Esther thought something was amiss. Sophie's stance was somehow stiff, and Emma's embrace a bit overdone. When Meyer came to greet her, she turned her attention away from the reunion that she thought was oddly askew.

At the end of the week when the period of mourning had passed, so too did the hopes of recovering Isador's body. Jamie Flaherty called to report that when he returned to Camp Dix, the bodies had been taken, and he couldn't locate Isador's. In truth, bodies had been piled like logs along the side of the makeshift mortuary, and soon after they were interred in a mass grave.

Esther and Manny told Rabbi Aronson about the loss of Isador's body, and he told them that they could put up a tombstone in the Workmen's Circle cemetery. "Tombstones are for the living to have a place to pray, Esther dear. It will take a while to have a stone made, but you can do this. You can inscribe a stone in his memory."

# December 1918

I t was a clear, frosty day at the end of the month when Sophie and Eleanor sat huddled in their coats and muffs on a bench near the pond in Morningside Park, the one that Sophie and Izzy had favored. A crackle of ice hovered over the edge of the pond, but a pair of mallard ducks dabbled for food on the glistening water.

Sophie slumped into the bench, arms folded within her muff, her eyes dull. She felt what seemed to her the heaviness of pregnancy, but it was rather a heaviness of spirit. Her words were without their musical quality. Flat.

"Look at that duck, Ellie. His shimmering head puts the drab female to shame. Look at him preen. Izzy was like that duck. He sparkled." Sophie held back her tears.

Ellie reached over and hugged Sophie. "It's okay to cry," said Ellie, who continued to hold her friend close until her sobs abated.

"Have you decided what you want to do in January when the new semester begins? I don't think I can go back to Brooks Hall without you there, Sophie. I don't want another roommate.

I wish you would come and stay with us, and I'll commute. You know we always have your bedroom ready, and Mama wants you to be with us. That way we could still be roommates. You could help me with my homework the way you always have. How can I finish school without my smart friend? What do you say?"

"Oh, Ellie. I am so grateful to your family. Your parents are the only ones who know that I am with Izzy's child. Why is it they aren't ashamed of me like my mother? Even though we are talking again and she doesn't know about my pregnancy, I can tell she still believes I'm loose in my ways. What does she think? That I have no morals, because I loved Izzy? She tried to comfort me at the Shapiro's *shiva,* but there was something hollow about her. She didn't feel like my mother, so I'm happier to see Papa at Izzy's house. Izzy's house. It's not Izzy's house anymore."

"It will always be Izzy's house to you. When will you tell Esther and Manny?"

"I'm afraid to tell them, Ellie. Let's talk about something else."

"No. You have to tell them soon. Please promise me. Do you want me to go with you this Saturday?"

"We always talk about my troubles, Ellie. Please tell me about your dinner with Reuben the other night. What did you wear? Where did you go?"

"Okay, if you really want to hear. I wore the dark green silk dress with the drop waist, the one we bought at B. Altman's together. Reuben looked nice.

He had his father's Ford, so after dinner at the Waldorf Astoria we drove up to a Harlem club for a while. Truly, I like him more and more."

"I liked him when we met at your house."

"His father wants him to go into the bank with him, but Reuben doesn't want that. Since he came back from Europe, he continually thinks about his painting. He's talented, Sophie."

"Can he do that? Can he be a painter?"

"He has money from his grandfather, enough to live nicely. His father isn't happy about it, but we'll see. Now, tell me. Will you go to Paterson this weekend? Will you tell them about the baby?"

"This Saturday. I can go by myself. I'll tell them."

"I don't want to push you, but you didn't answer me. Will you come and live with us?"

"I love you, Ellie. Let me think about it after I see the Shapiros."

Manny took his friend's heavy overcoat and fedora at the door. "Meyer, come in. Sophie will soon be here. What does she want to tell us?" asked Manny as the two men embraced.

"We didn't speak yet. Sometimes she rings on the telephone at the bakery, but not this week. *Oy!* Emma, Emma. What makes her like this—to push away her own daughter? Is it so wrong of Sophie to want a life of her own? But Manny, how is it with you and Esther? Is the stone ready yet for Isador's grave marker?"

"*Nein*, it will be a long time. So much death. So much misery."

Esther came into the front room from the kitchen, wiping her hands on her apron. She brushed her palms up and down to signal the end of her cooking and then went to the mirror to check her hair. She stared at her image as if she hadn't seen it for a long time, and in truth, she had changed over the weeks since the mirror had been turned to the wall for the period of mourning.

"*Ach*," she muttered. "The time is up to move on with the living, even though we must pray in our *shul* every day for the first year. But look at this face of mine. A living dead person. With a deep sigh, she examined her face and saw the circles under her eyes. "Look, Isador, can you see your mama? Do you see how she misses you?" she said aloud.

"*Nu*? I should fix my hair." Esther moistened her fingertips with her tongue and quickly ran them back over her bun, patting the hair in place. Before she could study herself any longer, she heard the downstairs hall door squeak. "I hear the door. Manny dear, see if Sophie is coming up the stairs," she said.

Manny opened the door in time to see Sophie plodding up the last flight. She still wore her gauze mask to ward off the flu, but he could see her cheeks, red from the cold, and her breath was still visible. She looked up and smiled at Manny as she removed the mask. Seeing her papa behind him, she rushed up the last few stairs to embrace him.

Esther bustled forward. "Come, come. You're hungry, Dolly? A bagel? A *bisl* cream cheese? White fish I have, too. Come. Sit." Even in her mourning, Esther welcomed guests the way she always had, with warmth and food. She took Sophie's outer clothes and made ready to deposit them on Izzy's bed.

"Please, Esther, let me put them away," said Sophie. Esther had already taken her coat and was on her way, but she stopped.

"You want to be in Isador's room a while? I know. I go there and sit on his bed. I sit. I cry. I remember," said Esther, dabbing at the corner of her eye with her apron. Go. You sit a little time and then you can come and tell us what you want to say."

Sophie's barely perceptible smile didn't cause the muscles to move in her cheeks or around her eyes. She took her coat from Esther and went to lie on the bed in Izzy's room.

Esther went to the front room. "*Nu*? So hard for her. We'll let her rest for a while before we have tea," she said to the men whose quizzical looks demanded an answer. The three sat in familiar silence. Meyer lit his pipe, Manny stared out the window, and Esther fidgeted with her hairpins and her necklace until she rose and said, "She must be rested now. I get her from the bedroom."

Sophie joined them at the kitchen table and they drank hot tea in silence. She gazed at the floral china cup that warmed her hands while Esther observed all of the unspoken communication. Sophie peeked through her lashes to make eye contact with her father and Meyer smiled lovingly back at her. Manny and Esther also fixed their love upon Sophie, waiting for her to break the silence.

The room was quiet except for the pendulum in the mantel clock that counted the minutes. Esther heard the moments tick and wondered what could be causing Sophie to remain speechless. *She seems so far away, thinner maybe, than usual.* She noticed how Sophie fought her tears, seemingly waiting to compose herself.

Sophie looked up and started to speak. "I came...I came to tell you..."

For the moment her quivering lips prevented speech. She tried again and whispered, "I am with child. Izzy's baby."

No one spoke. All eyes were upon her.

Esther leaned forward. "What is that you said?"

"A baby. Izzy's baby."

Esther's eyes widened with awareness. And then, "A child!" she cried. "Did you hear? Izzy's child!" She jumped from her seat and ran to embrace Sophie. "Manny. Meyer. You are sure, Sophie? We are going to have a baby?"

Sophie nodded, and her tears flowed freely as she rose to accept Esther's embrace. Meyer and Manny, both flabbergasted, stood beaming at the women.

A sobbing Esther guided Sophie to the settee in the front room and held her close. "A baby. Isador's child. Our grandchild. Ay, ay ay. Such a thing could happen." Manny and Meyer looked at each other, smiled, gripped each other's shoulders, and followed the women into the front room.

Sophie freed herself from Esther's tight embrace and said, "Before he left, Izzy wanted to get married, but I made him wait. I'm sorry. I'm so sorry. I wanted Mama to come around. I wanted a wedding, I...I forced him to wait."

"In God's eyes you are married. You have his ring. You have his child. We are your parents now, too. Yes, Meyer?"

"Yah. We are *mekhutonim*, a family by marriage. When Sophie? When will our grandchild be born?"

"In May, Papa."

Esther continued to hold Sophie near, her generous arms enfolding this treasure who would bring her Izzy back to her. Do you not remember, Sophie? I told Rabbi Aronson that you are family."

Sophie smiled, a full smile, and groped for a handkerchief in her pocket. She wiped her nose and relaxed into a sigh.

Esther's mind jumped ahead to plans for her grandchild. "*Nu?* Come home to us, Sophie. Stay here and be with us, you and the baby."

"I was afraid to tell you, afraid you would be ashamed…"

"How can you say such a thing? Ashamed. Never. You are our daughter," said Esther to the accompanying nods of the men.

Sophie stuffed her wet handkerchief into her pocket and accepted the dry one her father proffered. She smiled and nestled closer to Esther.

"I can't stay now. I have to finish a week of this school semester, and then I can think about what to do," she told them.

Suddenly she sat up from Esther's embrace. "How can I tell Mama? She is so stubborn. I know she won't be happy."

"We have to tell Emma now," Meyer ventured.

"Yah, you have to tell Emma," the Shapiros agreed.

Meyer rose to go to the telephone, but he said, "I don't think…"

"How can she resist making up now that she is to be a *bubbeh*?" asked Esther.

"Sophie, I don't want you should be hurt. I don't think…"

"Call her, Papa. Tell her to come here."

"Maybe it is best I should go to her," Meyer suggested. "I'll go home now and tell her. You stay, *Liebe*. Let's see if she wants you to come to her."

Meyer left, and within thirty minutes the telephone bell rang in the Shapiro house. When Manny picked it up, Meyer didn't need to say anything. They could all hear Emma in the background. "A shame, I say! It's a scandal. She is no daughter of mine."

# FIFTEEN

## January 1919

**G**eorge and Harry cut off Sophie's tuition and expense money upon hearing about the baby from Emma. Sophie prepared to leave Barnard with one and a half years remaining for her degree, still uncertain about where she would go. She told her dormitory supervisor Miss Weeks that she must leave school, but had avoided details.

Sophie weighed her options, knowing that New Yorkers were still caught in thrall to the flu, although the main impact had subsided by December. Even so, one didn't carelessly spit, cough, or sneeze on the street for fear of being arrested and fined. Public conveyances were fumigated and their windows kept open despite cold weather. Some theaters, taverns, and public buildings remained closed.

Ellie's father, Mr. Reichman, told the family that tens of thousands of New Yorkers had died and that a half million people had been ill since the flu first began in New York last fall. With this dismal reality, Sophie knew that her chances of contracting flu were greater because of her pregnancy, and she was worried for her unborn child.

Esther had pleaded with Sophie to stay with them, but life in the Jewish neighborhood was cramped, doctors were not readily available, and the death toll hadn't subsided.

Ellie and her family convinced Sophie that she would be safer in their New

York home, removed from the daily threat of meeting a contagious neighbor in a close apartment hallway. Meyer and the Shapiros were forced to concede.

Now as Sophie lay in her great canopy bed in the Reichmans' home she thought about her last visit with Esther. "Sophie, *Sheinela*, you can't go to the Reichmans' like a *shnorer* with nothing. You have no money to buy even a toothbrush. Listen, Isador wanted to marry you sooner, because he wanted you to have his insurance."

"He told me, and I refused, Mama Esther. I was so wrong."

"Listen. He called me on the telephone and said that he bought life insurance, but he had to leave it in my name because you were not married. This money is for you and your baby. He wanted it that way. We have enough, Manny and me, with all the looms."

"How can I accept this and take from you what is yours?"

"You need it, and it is yours. It is twenty-eight dollars and seventy-five cents every month for twenty years." Esther went to her bureau and took out an envelope with a check for the amount. She smiled, and with a little nudge she said, "Come, we go to the bank, and we make an account for you. It's settled. Every month I go and put the check in the bank for you, so you have something. My daughter, a *schnorer*, a beggar? Never!"

Sophie smiled as she recalled the conversation, and she rose to ready herself for the day. Ellie would be home from school soon, and today, Friday, Sophie would help with the *Shabbos* preparations. Although the household included a cook and other servants, Sophie felt at home in the massive kitchen, and she loved to prepare the challah for baking. Today she would also make the apple strudel with cinnamon and raisins that she had always enjoyed, a favorite of Mr. Reichman as well.

Even as she was familiar with the Reichman home, she never ceased to wonder how she could be living in an Italianate mansion in Murray Hill. The spacious brownstone had three floors and beautiful bay windows on the first floor. Her room with its own sitting room and bath was on the second floor and overlooked Madison Avenue. It was next to Ellie's suite.

She mused about the house, with its tapestry hangings, paintings, sculpture, and carved furniture, more like a museum than a home. It had a grand ballroom, a music room, a library.

She hadn't visited the house on East Twenty-sixth Street since her family had moved from their downtown apartment, and thus she still had an ache inside, a longing for her cozy childhood home, even though it could easily fit inside the Reichmans' ballroom. She missed her mama and the little brother whom she hardly knew. She missed her Uncle Joe and Aunt Flora, their open-handedness, their joviality.

The ache and the loneliness could bring her to tears at times, but there was another side to her feelings. She felt a sense of pride and expansiveness, a feeling that when she looked into the future it was vast. She envisioned open fields and sky that extended infinitely before her. She saw herself walking fearlessly forward…she and her child.

Yesterday she experienced the first quickening, the stirring inside that made her giddy. At first she thought that her stomach was rumbling, but it came to her that her child had life. It was Izzy's child inside her. Their child. She had laughed out loud. Her clothes still fit even though she had regained her lost weight, but her breasts filled more of the generous shirtwaists that she wore. Soon she would swell and outgrow her clothes.

When Sophie told Mrs. Reichman about the quickening, she reached for Sophie's hands and held them within her own. She developed a faraway look. "It was the most beautiful time of my life," she told Sophie. "I remember everything about those months when I was pregnant with Eleanor. I was never sick, and I know that you haven't felt ill either. I was content, at peace." She laughed. "I'm glad that you are with us, so that you can rest and enjoy this time of waiting. I was shopping today on Fifth Avenue and stopped into a lingerie shop. I thought of you and the things you will need between now and May when your baby comes."

"Oh, I am thinking more of embroidering a layette than what I will wear. I want to go out and buy some embroidery floss."

"Oh, please, Sophie dear, let Maggie buy it for you when she goes to the grocer. You shouldn't be on the streets in your condition. The obituaries are still pages long with flu deaths."

## May 1919

**M**rs. Reichman would not hear of Sophie going to a hospital. When her pains came on a Saturday, she called Dr. Bauman to the house. It was May twenty-fourth, a *Shabbos*. Sophie lay in her canopied bed perspiring and moaning as the increasingly short minutes between contractions passed. Eleanor stood by her side to wipe her brow. Mrs. Reichman held her hand and tried to calm her until the doctor arrived.

Dr. Eli Bauman swept into the room and pushed the ladies away from the canopy bed. Maggie was sent to get water and clean towels. Sophie breathed more freely. For once, something came easy to Sophie. Her pregnancy had been uneventful, and labor was blessedly short. At 6:32 PM the women stood around the bed as Ori Isador Shapiro responded to the slap on his *tuchas* with a grand screech.

"Oooh, my baby, my baby," was the only thing Sophie could say as Ori suckled her breast. Ellie smoothed back her friend's hair while Sophie petted her baby's down-covered head. She uncurled the little fingers and counted them all. She reached for the little toes and counted them as well. When Ori released her nipple and fell into sleep, she and Ellie wrapped him in a new embroidered receiving blanket.

A carved-oak cradle with satin lining stood beside the bed, ready to receive this newborn image of his father. Ellie and her mother tiptoed out of the room as Sophie breathed a deep sigh and fell asleep.

## June 1919

**E**sther was beside herself on this ritual day. "*Oy*, such a party," she cried, waddling from the living room to the kitchen, checking the platters of food and back again. During the course of Sophie's pregnancy, Esther had grown in girth along with her daughter-in-law. Today she had prepared all of the sweets in her repertoire—strudel, mandelbrot, ruggeleh. She had brisket, potatoes, stuffed cabbage, and even carrot tsimmes. The aroma of cooking overflowed the Shapiro apartment and wafted down the halls, welcoming one and all to the circumcision.

This Sunday in June, eight days after Ori's birth, was the first time the family had seen the infant. Ellie and Simone Reichman had driven Sophie to Paterson for the *bris*, and she would be staying with her in-laws for a while until she decided what to do and how she would live.

Sophie sat placidly on the comfortably worn red velvet settee, unable to take her eyes from her son, when Meyer burst into the apartment, "Dolly, Dolly, *mein* Sophie, *mein* daughter."

"Here, Papa. Sit here by me," she said, patting the empty space beside her. "Isn't he beautiful, Papa?"

"Beautiful? Of course beautiful, knock wood. Why not? Look on his mama. Think of his papa. *Mein* grandson. Look, Aaron. Come look on your nephew. Look on Ori, son."

Aaron had followed Meyer into the room and he squeezed in between his sister and Meyer to be close to the baby. "Can I hold him, Sophie?"

"Yes, Aaron," she responded eagerly as she placed the baby on his lap and arranged the boy's hands to support the infant.

"I wish Mama could be here to see him," Aaron said. "Papa, when will she stop being so angry?"

"Soon, *mein* boy. She won't be able to keep away for long."

"Oh, Papa, I hope so. Ori needs two grandmothers, " said Sophie.

The front room filled quickly as all the *landsmen* and their wives arrived to a varied chorus of "*kine-ahora, oy oy oy*, and such-a-*boytshik*!"

All of these people are happy to see me with Izzy's baby, Sophie thought. No one asked, "Did they marry?" It was enough to know that Sophie had always been Izzy's intended and that she wore his ring.

Why couldn't it be enough for my mother to know that we conceived in love and honor? Directions from Rabbi Aronson, who would perform the *bris,* recalled Sophie from her momentary sadness.

She went into the bedroom where Simone and Ellie waited with their gift of a pale blue satin pillow, decorated on the edge with delicate Stars of David. Sophie placed Ori on the pillow and carried her baby like a prince on a throne into the candlelit living room where the rabbi and guests awaited Ori's presentation to his grandfathers.

"Come, Meyer; come, Manny, take your grandson in your arms so we can make the ceremony. Sit here together on the settee and leave the big club chair for Elijah the Prophet to watch the *bris*." Once the drop of wine was placed on Ori's tongue and the blessings made, Rabbi Aronson was quick to make the cut. The baby gave a cry, and shouts of "*Mazel tov*" rang out as Rabbi Aronson gave him his name. Ori Isador Shapiro. Ori, meaning "my light" in Hebrew.

# Sixteen

## July 1919

**S**elma Abramowitz called out, "Yoo-hoo, Emma. Are you in the back?"

"Oh it's you, Selma," said Emma as she came out of the storeroom behind her shop. "Come in. You are well?"

"Yes, and Harry and the boys are fine."

"Sit here on the settee. Do you recall when I was partners with Bessie how we argued over this furniture? It's a good thing we bought it."

"It does look comfortable in here, but I think perhaps it's time to move the wax mannequins out of the window for the summer."

*"Perhaps"…a nice American word.* "Yah, they melt so easy, but I saw in the magazines a new kind of mannequin made of papier-mâché. They are not cheap, but maybe I should invest. That way I change Emma's Fine Foundations to a dress shop with models in the windows. What do you think, Selma?"

"Fashions are changing quickly, Emma. I think you are right to move with the times. By the way, I went to the *bris* for Sophie's baby."

"Yah. Meyer and Aaron told me about this *mamzer*."

"Emma! How could you call this baby illegitimate? Sophie and Isador were as good as married."

"Maybe by you they were married, but not by the rabbi."

"Emma, you are my sister-in-law, and I love you, but this anger is wrong. You are missing a treasure that you will never recapture."

179

*Hmm... "recapture" Born-in-America language* "Selma, this dress you wear is stylish. Where did you buy it?"

"In New York, Emma. Maybe you could go with Meyer one Sunday to see the baby. Ori is beautiful, and Sophie misses you."

"Selma, I can't do it."

"Well, we'll see you and Aaron on Sunday for dinner."

"I'll come. Thank you, Selma," said Emma as Selma rose to leave.

Once the door closed behind her and Emma could see Selma slide into the driver's seat of her Ford parked in front of the store, she let herself slump onto the settee. She took a deep breath and let her shoulders sag. Her head hung, and she removed her spectacles and let them lay in her lap. She rubbed her eyes with the back of her fist. *Oy. Such a sadness.*

Not one to pine for long, she got up, straightened her skirt, and busied herself with sorting inventory. Soon her customers began to straggle in.

Almost every woman who came into the store shunned laced-up corsets with bones in favor of a less restrictive garment. They bought a boneless lace brassiere or a petticoat, but most wanted to try on the new style of hat featured on the window mannequin. While Emma still showed wide-brim hats with feathers and flowers, she showcased a brimless, close-fitting hat to complement the newer bobbed hairstyles, a prescient observation of the coming rage.

Meyer and Aaron spent their Sunday afternoons on outings, leaving Emma to her own devices. On this Sunday, Emma sat at the kitchen table and pored over her catalogues and magazines. The cover of *The American Woman* magazine featured the hat that had caused a stir in her store. The pricier *Red Book* magazine had a luscious photo of a woman with Sophie's beautiful round blue eyes. She pushed the magazine away and reached for her copy of *Vogue*.

As she took in the new designs, her awareness grew and solidified. If she didn't get ahead of the trend, Emma's Fine Foundations would die a pitiful death in its outmoded Broadway shop. Emma rapped the table with the side of her fist. *That's it! I change.*

She began to formulate plans to transform her business from selling only "fine foundations" to selling "fine fashions," and she set aside her magazines to check the real estate section of the *Morning Call*. Emma scoured it for a storefront that could give her more exposure and decided to engage a realtor to find a space on Main Street near Quackenbush's department store.

The great fashion houses of Worth, Lanvin, and Doucet were open to the very wealthy, but Emma knew that good copies could be had from the wholesalers in New York. Paterson department stores and dress shops sold facsimiles that were far removed from the originals. They had less detailing and used cheaper textiles than the only once-removed designs she could offer.

"These Paterson women can't buy Chanel, but some of them can buy from me good copies," she had told Selma. "A cut above those department stores, I think." Then she thought about her own wardrobe and reasoned that if she were to sell fine clothes, she must wear them also, and none too soon. "From these rich ladies I will make the new woman," she muttered to herself. *That's it!* She would have an elegant striped awning above her store, and a sign to read "The New Woman."

The vision of a sophisticated shop on Main Street grew in Emma's mind as she sat at the kitchen table and wondered how she could attract the wealthy Gentiles of Paterson. She was certain she could count on the Abramowitz women and, by extension, the Joelsons, the Barnerts, and other elite Jewish women, but how could she meet the Gentiles like Mrs. Feeny, Mrs. Westerhoff, or the Mayor Radcliffe's wife? What about the doctors' wives and mill owners' wives?

She was so preoccupied that she didn't notice Meyer and Aaron come into the kitchen. "Mama, we went to Eastside Park to feed the deer. Papa took me to the Zucker Delicatessen for a Dr. Brown's Cel-Ray. We had a pastrami sandwich, Mama. Look Mama, I have the bottle. Mama, look. Look at my bottle. I'm going to keep it in my room."

"Yes, Aaron. You do that."

Aaron paused and looked quizzically at his mother. "Mama, why do you speak different? You don't sound the same anymore."

"I am becoming an American, my boy. Like you. You are only five years old and your English is better than mine. I practice to speak like the American women. You don't want a greenhorn for a mother, do you?"

"I don't know, Mama. I think I like the other way better."

"Come, boy, we'll read *The Forward*. Did I tell you what happened at the bakery yesterday?" said Meyer before the conversation could go any further.

"Papa, when can I climb on the bakery truck with you? Can I ride with you, Papa?"

"Sure, Aaron."

"Can I sit in your lap and drive, Papa?"

"Yah, Aaron. You sit in my lap."

"Papa, when can we see baby Ori again? Can Mama come with us?"

Emma turned her ear to the parlor at the mention of her self-exile.

After puzzling over how she would meet the elite women of Paterson, Emma had an idea. On the following Sunday, Emma and Aaron sat at brother George's family dinner table. This time she had a mission, and when she cornered her brother she asked, "George, you're a Mason, no?"

"You know I am a Mason, Emma. Why do you bring it up? Something new is on your mind."

"You go to meetings with all the big shots in Paterson. *Nu?* They have wives."

"Yah. Sure, they have wives."

"George, they have wives. The wives have money to spend. I want to meet the wives."

"What is it I should do? Make personal introductions?  From what do I know about the women? I go to a meeting. I see the men."

"If their men are Masons, the women might be in the Eastern Star. I want to be a member in The Order of the Eastern Star. I'm your sister. You can bring in a sister, no?"

"Emma, Emma, what new scheme do you have this time?"

"George, I'm through with that little shop on Broadway. I need a new shop and a new clientele. I saved, George. I have money for the move. I need an 'in' with the women. Get me into the Eastern Star."

# October 1919

**For** the Grand Opening of The New Woman on Main Street, Emma had invited all of her former customers and her newly acquired friends from The Order of the Eastern Star. She welcomed her guests at the door with a glass of champagne and pointed to the sumptuous buffet tables. Selma had been recruited to circulate and subtly promote the fashions.

Prominent gold lettering on the door below the tasteful striped awning and a sign on the building read "The New Woman." Of the three enticing mannequins in the window, the first featured a periwinkle blue silk crepe-chiffon copy of a Worth dress with a lace collar and drop waist. A black tulle and sequin evening dress glittered on the second mannequin. For the third, Emma featured a daytime suit that proclaimed the beginning of a trend to shorten the skirt length. This skirt exposed the ankles and was designed to hang without impeding the stride of a modern woman.

Inside the shop Emma had hung French lace lingerie on wall hooks. Freestanding display cases held gloves, belts, delicate brassieres, and petticoats. She had placed a rack with day dresses and suits and another with evening wear around the perimeter. Upholstered chairs and a settee in a nook welcomed the weary shopper, and her desk with a client chair sat in a far corner. The fitting room had generous mirrors, as well as an anteroom for admiring husbands.

"What more could you ask for?" Emma overheard one woman say as she circulated. "Look here at this chiffon, Millie," said another. Emma rejoiced at the buzzing of compliments in her new shop.

"Mrs. Radcliffe, I'm glad you could come. If you want something special in the future, ask me, and I will go to New York and get it for you," Emma whispered into her ear as she hooked arms with her guest, exulting in having attracted the mayor's wife.

The afternoon passed with women coming and going, scandalously sipping champagne in the daytime and purchasing ready-made items. Emma collapsed into a chair, exhausted but victorious when the last guest had parted.

"*Nu*, Selma? Thank you for your help. What did you think of the opening?"

"Emma, you will recoup your investment very soon. I predict that The

New Woman with its haute couture right here on Main Street will be the talk of Paterson society."

"From your mouth to God's ears, Selma."

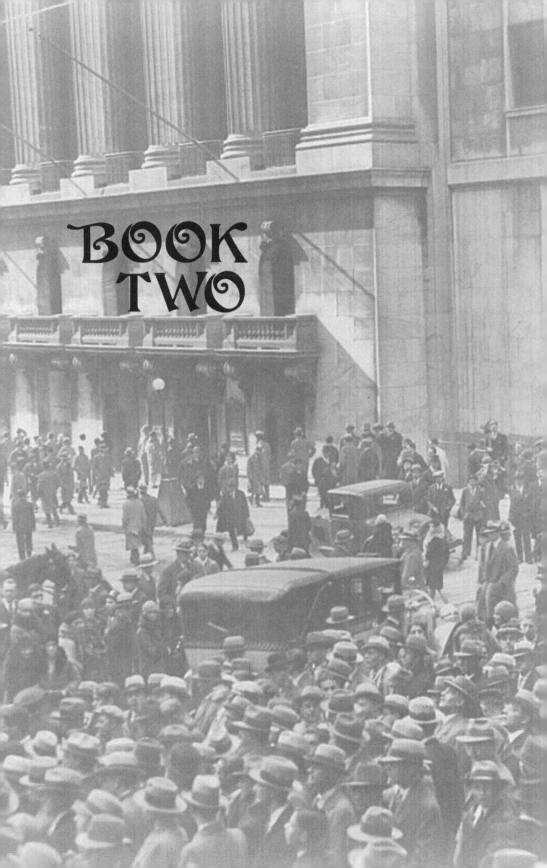

BOOK
TWO

# ONE

## February 1920

**Aaron** Epstein was a beautiful boy, a child who commanded notice. He had Meyer's thick curly black hair and cleft chin, while his thin, tapered fingers were like those of his grandmother, Emma had said. Aaron's eyes were wider set than Meyer's and a sparkling hazel, shimmering and mischievous. He was tall for his age and looked elegant in his short trouser pants and hand-knitted Fair Isle sweaters. His thin frame enhanced the merit of his clothing, as if the garments had been hand-tailored for him.

Emma spared no expense in creating the image of a wellborn young man. Such good looks. People will notice, she thought. Flora took him to the barber every four weeks. When he left for school in the morning, he was spotless. Emma inspected his fingernails and neck on his way out the door. Flora walked with him to school to ensure that he didn't linger, fall in with the wrong sort, or soil his clothing en route.

"Why can't I walk by myself? I know the way," Aaron complained, but he was given no choice.

By the time Aaron entered first grade, Emma had generated enough guilt to ensure his adherence to her standards, and he was finally permitted to walk the few blocks to school by himself.

Following his recovery from the flu, Emma had questioned every sneeze, the regularity of his bowels, and the condition of his skin. Meyer could do nothing to alleviate Aaron's fear of imagined illnesses. The child reported every scratch and every twinge of stomach pain. He was even cautioned not to suck on ice, as he had been told that Emma's twice-removed cousin had died from choking on a piece of ice.

Once after Uncle Joe had taken him to the moving pictures at the new Regent Theater in nearby Passaic, he returned with a stomach ache so severe that he was sent to bed and given a tablespoon of Kepler cod liver oil.

"Aaron, my son, what did you buy in the theater with the two pennies I gave you?"

"I don't remember, Mama," he stammered between his stomach pangs.

"You ate something. What was it?"

"I bought a Reese's Peanut Butter Cup."

He never touched Reese's candy again after the cod-liver oil episode, avoiding it and several other foods that Emma said had "poisoned" his stomach. He became extremely finicky about his food. Having heard of the dangers of undercooked meat, Aaron ate no meat unless it was well done. He separated the food portions on his plate, and never mixed any vegetables with his potatoes. He poked at his food before eating, rolled it over with his fork, and discarded any bite of meat that was not trimmed of fat.

Despite his finicky nature, the boy was sweet tempered, agile, and he had a remarkable sense of humor. At six years, he tried to mimic the voice and mannerisms of people who caught his attention. He remembered jokes and told them with excellent timing. He loved to be in the outdoors and frequently walked to Eastside Park with Meyer to see the deer in their enclosure.

For all of Aaron's charm and obedience, Emma had little satisfaction from her son. "I give the boy everything. I work in that store so he should have everything, and yet he adores only Meyer and follows him everywhere. The child doesn't even work hard in school," she had complained to Harry.

When he came home from school with his first report card in the autumn, he had an "F" in conduct. "I work day and night so you should have a good life, and this is how you repay me? With a 'Fail' in conduct," she had said.

Aaron hung his head, but had no response for his mother.

Seating in Aaron's first-grade classroom was alphabetically arranged. He sat in the first row and the last seat in Miss Levi's class. His teacher, formerly of the Fair Street neighborhood school, had informed him during the first school month that he was no match for his sister, Sophie. "She was an excellent student, and she had an 'Excellent' in conduct as well," goaded Miss Levi.

Although he wanted to please his mother, Aaron couldn't measure up. Whatever was happening outside the window was more interesting to him than what Miss Levi had to say, even if it was only a bird pecking away at discarded scraps of lunch on the sunken cement playground. Today he watched a pigeon flap onto the perimeter wall up to the sidewalk level where a chain-link fence rose six feet into the air, fully enclosing the school property. The bird hopped over the sooty remnants of snow and slipped through the fence to the freedom of the outside world. Aaron followed it with his eye until he heard the shrill voice of his teacher calling his name.

Aaron wished that he could "pay attention" and even earn a "Good" in conduct for his mother. He might have a chance at that, but he worried that learning to read was hopeless. First thing after the morning exercises, Miss Levi called each child in turn to stand beside her desk. The student was to bring his or her black-and-white speckled copybook to her and recite the memorized words that she had written in it the previous day. With that accomplished, Miss Levi would write a new set of words to learn that evening. Meanwhile, the other children were silently intent on practicing their words or reading stories from the primer.

Aaron's head buzzed, and he began to perspire as he waited his turn for Miss Levi to berate him. Knowing that his classmates could hear the interaction, he trembled. *I'm going to get it again.*

"Aaron, didn't you study last night? You haven't learned 'this' from 'that' or even 'these' from 'those.' Read this page to me." After a few agonizing tries, she gave up on his reading for the day and sent Aaron to his seat with a threat to call his parents.

The inevitable note came from Aaron's teacher inviting Mr. and Mrs. Epstein to her classroom early in the morning before school. It had been many years since Emma had faced Sophie's high school principal, and it was the only time she had ever been called to school.

Meyer had never been in a Paterson public school. He anticipated the unimaginable confrontation with Aaron's teacher as any Yiddish-speaking immigrant might, but he had made up his mind not to leave this meeting to Emma alone. He wanted to see for himself why his son didn't measure up in school.

Emma and Meyer entered the unfamiliar, formal first-grade classroom and Miss Levi directed them to sit in the small wooden student chairs beside her massive oak desk. Meyer sat with his legs apart and leaning forward, his elbows pressed to his sides in his heavy outer garments, recalling his own self-conscious *cheder* days in the old country.

Emma perched on the edge of her seat, keeping her long legs together at a deep angle, posing in her high-fashion coat. She kept her hat and gloves on, and with a stern expression, she waited.

The teacher began her soliloquy, offering a litany of Aaron's behavioral transgressions, each punctuated by a wagging finger.

"He doesn't pay attention."

"He bothers other children."

"He looks out the window."

"He fiddles with his pencil."

Finally, as if it were only another infraction, she said, "Aaron hasn't learned to read. He doesn't memorize his word lists."

Emma straightened her back and managed to appear taller than the teacher who was seated on an adult chair at her own desk. "Well, Miss Levi, you haven't taught our son to read."

Meyer reached to place a restraining hand on Emma's shoulder, while Miss Levi was for a moment, speechless.

"This is not about my instruction, Mrs. Epstein. This is about your negligent son. Do you practice words with him every night?"

"Yah," Meyer said. "We do that." *This woman they should lock up.*

"He misbehaves at home, I assume," said Miss Levi.

"No, he does not," said Emma.

"Does he eat a good breakfast?"

"Yah, sure, he eats. Why not eat a breakfast?" said Meyer.

Emma had begun to tap her foot as best she could with her legs folded to the side in the low chair. She gripped her gloved hands together.

Meyer tried to insert a word or two about Aaron's curiosity, his good behavior at home, his excellent recall about what he has heard, but the teacher left no opening in her harangue.

"I can see that you need to spend more time with the boy," said Miss Levi. "Well, you know the truth of 'spare the rod, spoil the boy.'"

Miss Levi rose and guided the pair to the door. As she watched them walk down the hallway, the neighboring teacher came to stand by her side. "If that snooty woman would spend as much time with her boy as she does with her fancy dressing, he wouldn't have these problems."

"A shame," agreed her colleague. "A married woman who owns a dress store! She has no business leaving that child at home while she caters to those fancy uptown ladies."

As the Epsteins made their way out of the building, Meyer burst out, "I will not lay a hand on that boy."

"Then I have to be the one to do it," Emma retorted.

"You will not touch the boy," Meyer said with such force that Emma recoiled.

# June 1920

**B**y the end of the school year, Aaron's conduct had not improved, nor had his reading ability. Worse, he had begun to draw attention as the "class clown." The very attributes that his family so enjoyed, his gift of mimicry, timing, and humor remained a hindrance to his learning and a nuisance to his teacher. As school was about to recess for the summer, the Epsteins were surprised by a note on his report card that Aaron would be "left back" in first grade for another semester.

After reading this appalling news, Emma thrust Aaron into a kitchen chair and held his face upward toward hers. She glared into his eyes. "First your sister goes off and shames the family. And now you!" scolded Emma. "Look at me, Aaron. Now you have another chance in first grade to learn and to begin to make something of yourself. Maybe that other first-grade teacher can knock some sense into your head. After all, you will be seven years old!"

Aaron knew what had caused this catastrophe. Not paying attention was one thing, but bothering other children was something of a different magnitude. He recalled a Saturday in early spring when the streets were still mired in dirty slush. Emma didn't want him to go outside, so he had entertained himself by making faces in his bedroom mirror. He reached inside his cheeks with his index fingers and stretched his lips wide across his face. He tried to see himself looking cross-eyed down at his nose. He raised his eyebrows up and down as fast as he could, then noticed that his ears wiggled when he did that. "Ah! I'll do that again," he giggled. "I bet my friends would laugh at this trick."

That next school day when Miss Levi was writing on the blackboard, Aaron had poked the boy next to him. "Watch this," he whispered. Soon enough the boy began to laugh and point at him. The others were looking and laughing behind their hands as Aaron sat stone-faced and wiggled his ears.

Miss Levi spun around in a fury. "What is this noise?" she demanded.

"Aaron can wiggle his ears, Miss Levi," answered the fawning, beribboned Susie Goodman.

Miss Levi swooped over to Aaron's side, grabbed him by his right ear lobe, and pulled him out of his chair and toward the door. "Go to the principal. NOW. I don't want you in my class," she screamed.

What Aaron had thought might be good entertainment turned into the beginning of one disaster after another. Each time he thought his teacher wasn't aware of his antics, she turned quickly and fixed a frightful stare at him. He could see why Emma was angry, but he enjoyed the attention from his classmates.

Aaron stopped daydreaming and realized that his mother was still very angry and had been lecturing while he had drifted off. With a pleading frown and a pouting lower lip he looked up at his mother, but when he tried to feign a tear he found himself really crying. "I'll be a good boy, Mama. I'll make you proud, not like Sophie."

Even as Emma punished Aaron with her strict silence, Meyer lavished his boy with love. On the Sunday morning following the report card debacle, Meyer put on his vested suit and shirt with a new collar. He placed his fedora at a slight tilt and motioned Aaron toward the door with an almost imperceptible jerk of his head and a roll of his eyes. "Let's get out of here," he seemed to say.

"Good-bye, Mama," Aaron called, but Emma didn't respond.

"Mama, we're going now," he repeated.

"Yah. Go," said Emma without looking up from her bookkeeping ledgers.

Once when Meyer was walking alone with his son he said, "Your Mama is disappointed that you don't work hard in school, son. What you think?"

Aaron hung his head. "It's too hard to learn all the new words, Papa. The kids laugh when I go up to Miss Levi's desk to read them."

Meyer felt all of his boy's pain. He knew that Emma had transferred her aspirations from Sophie to Aaron, her dreams now focusing on this child's success. *Oy. My chest is tight from this aching for my son.*

"Aaron," he said as he stopped walking, knelt down, and gently held the boy's shoulders to face him. "You are my joy, and your mama loves you, too. You know I read good Yiddish and English only a *bisl*. Maybe I help you at night, so we both learn to read good English. What you say, my boy?"

"But Papa, can we still walk to the train when you come home from work?"

"Sure. We'll read together after dinner. Good?"

"Good, Papa. Where are we going today?"

"Someplace new, Aaron. We go to Staten Island on a ferryboat. First, the train to New York."

Meyer reached for Aaron's hand, and they walked to the Erie Railroad station where they boarded the train to Jersey City. Aaron sat by the window with his nose to the glass, making little circles of steam on the window with his lips. Paterson soon disappeared, and they traveled through quiet rural countryside before reaching bustling Jersey City.

"Papa, I don't see a way to cross the river."

"No. This train will take us right under the Hudson River in tubes to Manhattan."

"Sophie lives there! Can we see Sophie?"

"She'll come to Manny and Esther's next week. We'll see her then."

Father and son spoke no more until the train reached the end of the tubes and it was time to get off. They walked to the Staten Island Ferry, Aaron holding Meyer's hand and walking with a hop and a skip to keep up with his father.

"Papa, will they really let automobiles drive on the boat?" Aaron asked, not for the first time, when they arrived at the ferry dock.

"Yah. Come boy. We look."

The two walked into the bowels of the huge Staten Island Ferry where lines of automobiles were parked in rows. Aaron had never seen so many cars in one place. Some drivers abandoned their autos and headed for the open deck and view of the Statue of Liberty above. Meyer and Aaron had begun the ascent when Meyer gripped the iron railing, pulled Aaron's hand, and lowered himself onto the step. He put his hand to his chest, feeling somewhat out of breath.

"Papa, why did you stop? Papa, you're sweating. Let's go up to see the water in the fresh air."

"Wait a bit, son. Let me rest. I feel only a little pain right here. Maybe I'm tired yet from loading the truck on Friday. A big day for delivering challah with no help."

"Your helper didn't come to work again, Papa?"

Meyer shook his head. "Sick."

Soon the moment passed, and they walked up to the deck to see the glorious view of Manhattan, the wondrous Statue of Liberty on Bedloe's Island, and Ellis Island in its shadow.

Meyer thought about his first sight of "Lady Liberty." He remembered the collective cry and the tears of hopeful immigrants as they first laid eyes on this symbol of freedom. He had told Aaron stories of his family's arrival amid the chaos of thousands of immigrants with their baggage, their hopes, and their terror of arriving penniless in this new world.

"Son," he said, squeezing Aaron's hand and looking down at his boy, "America gives us a chance to make good, but not only money. When we help others, we help ourselves to be better. Do you understand, *mein zun?*"

"Yes, Papa." Aaron withdrew his hand and wrapped his arms around his father's hips, squeezing hard.

# October 1920

**The** passage of the nineteenth amendment in August, giving women the right to vote, seemed to Emma to empower them to spend more money. Business was thriving. Women's wear had made dramatic changes since Emma's days of peddling corsets door-to-door, and so too had Emma's fortunes. It had been a year since The New Woman on Main Street near Quackenbush's department store had successfully replaced Emma's Fine Foundations on the less commercially traveled Broadway.

Emma, seated at her dining room table, was reflecting on her coup. Recent copies of *Vogue*, *The Queen*, and *Harper's Bazaar* were open before her. *That Eastern Star bunch is something.* She mused about the "fancy" women who had free time for their charities. At the last meeting they were talking about new books for the Danforth library.

Some of the women remembered Mary Danforth Ryle, who married the son of John Ryle, "The Father of the U.S. Silk Industry." She had donated fifty thousand dollars for the construction of the first library in Paterson, which burned in the great 1902 fire. Then just two years before her death, she donated money to build the new Danforth Library on Broadway.

Emma smiled when she recalled her first meeting of the Eastern Star. She had debated with herself about the suit she would wear, pulled the few gray hairs from her brown waves, and applied Maybelline cake mascara along with her rouge powder. Her care paid off when she appeared at her first meeting wearing a Lanvin suit. Never mind it was a copy, she thought. They paid attention. It didn't take too long before they began to patronize her shop, and Emma learned the size and taste of every woman who came in. She was pleased to have customers who were not above wearing once-removed copies of Paris originals.

While she was occupied with her fashion magazines and her musing, Aaron was sitting nearby in the kitchen, doing his homework. "Mama, help me with my addition practice," he called. "We have to add three numbers in a column, and there are problems, too."

"Go ask your Papa, Aaron. Mama is busy."

The boy went into the front room where Meyer sat in a wing chair reading *The Forward*. "Papa, Mama can't help me. Can you help me with my flash cards?"

"Yah, sure, son. Numbers, I know from. Come to your bedroom where we can work together."

"I want to go out and play with the guys. Let's hurry, Papa. It's still light outside, and all the guys are playing stickball."

"What guys, Aaron?" Meyer queried. "Guys like the O'Neil boy and Jerome and Martin Klein who don't do their schoolwork? You stay here and learn, so you can grow up smart like your sister and go to college."

"But Papa, I want to go out."

A shout came from the dining room. "Aaron, I don't want to hear from that principal again. You make jokes in the schoolroom like a little hooligan. Stay right here and study."

Fuming while turning the pages in *Vogue*, Emma muttered, "A disgrace. That boy is giving me nothing but trouble. No good reports from school. That I should have such a boy! This is what happens with a child of later years."

# Two

## April 1922

**E**mma, impatient to finish her marketing, elbowed her way from shop to shop among the crowded Washington Street markets. As she approached the butcher shop, she happened to look up and catch sight of Esther Shapiro walking toward her, also bound for the butcher's. Esther was looking down at the youngster whose hand she clutched. His deep blue eyes were as mesmerizing as those of her own Sophie, but almond-shaped like Isador's. Yes, this angelic child must be Sophie's, and his dark curly hair was that of Meyer or even Isador Shapiro. And there was Esther, as proud as you please! *My grandson. She's holding on to my grandson.*

Emma changed course and turned the corner toward the greengrocer. *My God, what a beautiful boy.* It had been more than three years since Emma last saw her daughter, and she had never acknowledged her son. To her he was a *mamzer*, an illegitimate offspring of a daughter who left her home to live among the filthy immigrants in New York.

*Meyer tried to tell me about Ori. I couldn't listen to him.*

Emma turned into the greengrocer, but almost tripped on an apple that had fallen from the sidewalk display. "Charlie," she called. "You can't keep your sidewalk clean?"

"Emma, I didn't see you. What can I get you today?"

Emma, still thinking about Ori, looked at the produce inside the shop

197

without making her usual snap decisions. *The family, they call themselves. How could they be family when their son never married my daughter? Family? Nein!*

"Emma, you are well?" prodded Charlie.

"Sure, I'm fine. Business is good."

"God willing, it will stay that way for all of us. Now, what can I get for you? Beans maybe for dinner? We have from New York some good apples."

"I saw the apples, Charlie. On the street. One almost killed me." *How could I forgive Sophie for leaving home and then getting in the family way without even a "how-do-you-do"?*

"Oh, let me take a look," he said as he turned into the doorway facing the street. He got down on his hands and knees, his jacket hiked up above his waistband and showing a roll of smooth white flesh beneath his suspenders. "Ah. Here are two under the stand out here. Looks like I have to give them away. Can't sell bruised apples," he said as he pushed himself to his feet and adjusted his jacket. He held the fruit out to Emma who nodded and put them into her netted shopping bag.

"I'll take the beans for dinner, Charlie, and three more apples for strudel." *Strudel, Sophie's favorite.* Emma imagined Sophie and her grandson at home in Paterson, but the thought of the Eastern Star ladies discovering such a skeleton in her closet unhinged her. *A child born out of wedlock.*

The face of this child haunted Emma. All the way home and into the evening she was visited by the image of this beautiful boy, this grandson. As the days passed, she was still unable to forget the chance meeting. The vision of Ori's face interrupted her work. She sat in the back office of her store, her ledgers open but untouched.

She hadn't taken pen to paper for twenty minutes.

Emma could remember feeling this way only once. It was the year that Meyer first came to her parents' house in Lodz. Almost in the same way, she had a vision of Meyer's face even when he wasn't there. She had ached with her love for him.

*Nu?* she questioned herself. What should I do? Can I go with Meyer and Aaron one Sunday to the Shapiros'?

She was aware that Sophie visited the Shapiros almost every weekend, but Emma had refrained from a visit. Her bitter thoughts and disparaging epithets about the *mamzer* kept her pain at bay. Since the chance sighting, it had occurred to her that she could fabricate a story for her clients or anyone who might chance to see Sophie with the child. She could say that they were married before the war. But every time her thoughts returned to the fib, she stopped herself, knowing that Sophie wouldn't go along. *I know her. Stubborn. So right all the time. Not even a little fib would she say.*

Daydreams of holding her grandson so preoccupied Emma that she often sat mute in her favorite wingback parlor chair. One night when Aaron had gone to bed, Meyer inquired, "Dolly, what is it that is on your mind? You have trouble maybe at the store?"

"No, Meyer. Money, I make plenty."

"You are not right, Emma. What bothers you?"

"*Ach*, Meyer, I am *fermisht*, addled in my mind."

"You, *fermisht*? Never would I think this."

"Meyer, I saw Ori last week. Esther was shopping on Washington Street with the boy. What a beautiful face!"

"Yah. He is a smart little boy. He knows from all his numbers yet."

"He looks like Sophie, no?"

"Yah, and like his father, too."

"Meyer, what does she tell people? Does everyone know that the boy is a *mamzer*?"

"She doesn't lie, and she doesn't say. She calls herself Shapiro for Ori's sake. No one asks. Only the *landsmen* know. Isador bought her a ring before he died. Did you know? She wears the ring."

"I see."

# May 1922

**S**ophie had volunteered at the Henry Street Settlement in the Lower East Side of Manhattan prior to her pregnancy, but after the birth of her son, she was invited to live and work among the few visiting nurses who also lived in the house. Grateful for the opportunity offered to her by Lillian Wald, the Settlement's founder, she and Ori moved into a room on the third floor of the renovated three-story brick home soon after his birth.

While Sophie worked, Ori attended a care program for the predominantly Jewish and Italian children of the immigrant factory workers who lived in nearby tenements.

Today she awakened early and crept over to look at her sleeping child. He had Izzy's lower lip with the little hollow under it. It seems so long ago that we were students together, she thought. Only Ori's resemblance keeps his image alive.

"Wake up, Ori. It's your birthday. Let's get dressed now."

"Mama, I'm three. Three today."

"Yes, sweet one, today is the day you are three, and I have something special for your birthday."

"What is my present, Mama? Can I have it now?"

Sophie opened the armoire, squatted, and pushed aside the shoes that had concealed a small package wrapped in the Sunday funny papers while Ori, still in his Dr. Dentons, leaned on her shoulder and peered into the closet. *Krazy Kat*, Mama. I see *Krazy Kat*, said Ori as he leaned over to point.

"Right, Ori. That's *Krazy Kat*. Here is *Katzenjammer Kids*, and here is *Freckles and His Friends*, but there is something inside, too."

Ori took the package from Sophie and unfolded the paper to extract his gift. "Crayolas! And coloring books!" Ori wrapped his arms around Sophie's neck, and she cuddled him close.

"*Ikh hob dikh lib*, Ori, I love you," she whispered, consciously preserving some of her native Yiddish, although he was also learning it from his grandparents who still spoke it at home.

Ori squirmed to get out of her arms and brought his gifts to the small desk beneath the window. "What should I color, Mama, the ABC or the animal book?"

"You pick one, Ori, while I poke this fire. Maybe I can get it to burn for a little longer. It's still too cold for May."

Sophie set to the task, dressed herself, and began to straighten the cozy little room that overlooked the backyard playground. The room had charm, partly from the brightly colored braided rug on the wooden floor. A cot and nightstand stood on either side of the window, each cot with a multicolored afghan, one long-ago knitted by Emma and the other by Sophie herself. Across the room stood the corner mahogany armoire with its oval beveled mirror. The nearby dresser had a china washbasin on it. Sophie had placed family photos on the wall. The fireplace was centered on the side of the room, facing the doorway.

Loath to hurry her son, but anxious to start the day, Sophie stooped to pull out the dresser drawer and selected Ori's shorts, knee socks, and the cabled sweater knit for him very recently by his grandmother Emma, whom he had never seen.

Sophie caught a sob before it surfaced. Emma had sent the sweater for Ori via Meyer. She's so stubborn she won't even come to the Shapiros' apartment to see Ori. Maybe now is the time for me to visit her, invitation or no, she considered. I suppose this birthday sweater is her peace offering.

"Come, little one, we'll dress and see Auntie Wald in the big dining room."

"Can I have two pancakes?"

"I think Auntie would give you two pancakes on your birthday."

Ori ran to the window to look down at the play yard. "No one is there, Mama."

"It's too early for play. Let's get dressed and wash for breakfast. I think Auntie Wald may have a surprise for you."

"What, Mama. What is it?"

"Wait and see, my little one."

Breakfast this morning was served in the elegant high-ceilinged dining room on the second floor. The immense door with its lovely semicircular window at the top reflected the room's simple Federal-style elegance. The entire staff was assembled around the dining room table when Ori came in with Sophie, ready to celebrate the third birthday of one of their favorite children.

The little boy remained in the doorway of the dining room beside his mother as the singing of "Happy Birthday" welcomed him. He turned to Sophie when the staff sang "dear Ori" and slapped his chest.

"That's me, Mama! I'm Ori."

When the singing ended, he ran to hug each woman in turn, and then "Auntie Wald" made her entrance, wheeling in a shiny red tricycle.

"Happy Birthday, Ori. This new tricycle is in honor of your birthday and is my gift to you and all of the children who visit us here at Henry Street."

He ran to embrace Miss Wald and climbed onto the trike. He held the handlebars, twisted them from side to side, and grinned. "Thank you, Auntie Wald!"

"Mama, Mama, can I ride now?"

"Ask Auntie, Ori."

"Auntie Wald, can I ride now?"

"I'll ask Seth to bring it to the play yard, and you can ride it after breakfast before the others come to play. Then you must share it with all of the boys and girls who will be happy that we honored you with a new tricycle for the play yard."

"No pancakes. Can I ride now, please?"

Sophie enjoyed pancakes with the visiting home nurses and Miss Wald while Seth, the beloved handyman, took Ori to ride his new tricycle in the yard.

Miss Wald had placed Sophie in charge of all of the Settlement's education efforts. After the nurses left for their visits, she and Miss Wald remained at the table to discuss the summer excursions for Settlement house children to visit private estates overlooking the Hudson River, to the Lake Country of northern New Jersey, and to homes on the New Jersey shore, all donated for summer use by the wealthy Manhattan community.

"I have dates for excursions to Riverholm, Camp Henry, Echo Hill Farm, and the Solomon estate in New Jersey," Sophie reported.

"This is good, Sophie. You are doing wonderful work for our children."

Sophie thought of Miss Wald, stocky and now in her fifties, as powerful, yet serene. Her oval face with its wide-set brown eyes, full lips, and cleft chin radiated confidence. She often said that a child who visits the tranquility and beauty of the country carries a dream of something more than the crowded and noisy streets of our Lower East Side. They can build character and a future from these visions, she believed.

Sophie embraced this oft-repeated maxim, and she worked tirelessly to arrange the excursions. Her friendship with Eleanor and other Barnard girls had given her entry to the New York society that Lillian Wald also enjoyed.

"All of the visiting nurses have given me the names of families whose children should get away for at least a week this summer. I'm going to visit them this week to get the parents' permission for their children to go. I should have a schedule very soon."

"Good. How are you enjoying your classes?"

"Oh, Miss Wald, I feel so good to have started back to school at the New York School of Social Work. Now I can finally finish the degree I started at Barnard. Thank you again for putting in a word for me. And for the scholarship."

"What class are you studying now?"

"Two classes—Community Organization and Child Welfare. It worked out well to have completed my fieldwork requirement here at Henry Street."

Miss Wald, rarely demonstrative, embraced Sophie as they rose from the breakfast table.

There was a short knock on the door, and a man walked into the dining room, smiling as he reached to embrace Miss Wald.

Who is this tall man so at ease and handsome in his gray flannel suit? thought Sophie.

She caught herself staring at his warm and open face and his light, smooth, and parted hair, unlike the hair of the men in her family which was dark, curly, and slick-backed. Here was the first man to claim her attention since Izzy's death. Sophie turned toward the window as she felt herself blush, ostensibly to allow Miss Wald and her guest privacy to talk.

"Sophie, come here. Meet Daniel Sheinman who is helping us with our accounting. Another generous volunteer."

"It's a pleasure, Mr. Sheinman."

"Daniel. My name is Daniel. I'm not such a big volunteer. My father is the real help to Henry Street. I just do the bookkeeping."

"Don't underrate yourself, Daniel," Lillian Wald declared in her sonorous voice as she abruptly left the room, leaving the young people alone.

The flustered pair smiled anxiously at each other and then Sophie offered, "It was good to meet you. I have some families to visit, if you'll excuse me."

"I guess I had better get to those books," he replied and headed toward the door.

The meeting left her atremble. I haven't had a thought about any man since

Izzy, she reflected, not even the eligible ones that Ellie forces me to meet. Well, I have no business thinking about romance now, she resolved as she walked across the hall to a landing where she could overlook the play yard.

Ori was riding the bright red tricycle and another little boy was standing on the back of the frame with his hands on Ori's shoulders.

On Saturday Sophie sat with her in-laws and father at the Shapiro kitchen table, the place where she felt most at home. Aaron was with his nephew in Izzy's former bedroom, where Ori once again showed him the framed picture of the man they all said was his father. The boys sat side by side, coloring with Ori's new Crayolas. The familiar smell of chicken soup permeated the air, and the four adult family members sipped tea in the late afternoon.

"Papa, it's time for me to make the gesture to Mama. She sent the sweater for Ori, maybe as a peace offering. Do you think she would receive us well if I took Ori to see her?"

"She misses you still, and she longs to see her grandson, but she won't come here with me. Maybe now is the time you should go to her."

"Your papa is right, Sophie," said Esther. "I think she has many times seen me with Ori on the street and she rushes to turn around. She is so proud, but her grandma's heart must ache. Maybe now she can think less about the shame she felt when Ori was born."

"Before I change my mind, I'll take Ori to see her. He's wearing the sweater she knit, and maybe that would make her happy. She is home, Papa?"

"Yah. She sits at the table with her record books and her fashion magazines, always thinking about making more from her business. Is good. I'll stay here with Manny, Esther, and Aaron."

Sophie went into the bedroom and sat with her legs outstretched on the floor next to Ori. She pulled him onto her lap and held him close. "Ori, *Bubbeh* Shapiro is your daddy's mama," she whispered into his ear.

"I know."

"I have a mama, too. She made this sweater for you. I'd like to take you to her house so you can have two *bubbehs*."

"I love my *Bubbeh* Shapiro."

"Yes, you do, but I think you have enough love for another *bubbeh*, too. Let's go for a walk to see her. This *bubbeh* is *Zaideh* Epstein's wife, like *Bubbeh* Shapiro and *Zaideh* Shapiro are married. You are rich. You have two *bubbehs* and two *zaidehs*."

"Will this *bubbeh* still be here when we come back? Why can't *Bubbeh* Epstein come here?"

"She has her own house, and she would like you to see it. *Bubbeh* Shapiro loves you. She isn't going away."

"Never, Mama?"

"Not for a very long time."

Sophie and Ori took the bus on Broadway and walked the few blocks to the East Twenty-sixth Street house. As they walked hand in hand, Sophie recalled the time four years ago when she and Emma had reconciled for a while, having met unexpectedly at Uncle Harry and Aunt Selma's house. She recalled that it was during her Barnard days and how happy they had been to see each other. The joy had lasted until Emma realized that Sophie wasn't planning to return to Paterson.

Sophie pressed her fist into her stomach as they approached the house that she had never visited.

"This is *Bubbeh* Epstein's house, Ori," Sophie said as the two began to walk the few steps to the door.

"Is this *Zaideh's* house, too?" Ori asked.

"Yes, love, *Zaideh* lives here with *Bubbeh* and your Uncle Aaron."

They went into the front hallway and walked the long flight to the upper flat. Sophie hesitated for a moment at the door, straightened her posture, and rang the doorbell.

They waited, and then heard footsteps approaching. The door swung open and Emma appeared. She stood mouth agape for many seconds, unable to speak. She looked down at Ori who stood wide-eyed and squeezed his mama's hand tighter. Emma looked from one to the other and tears began to flow.

"You came to me. You and my grandson," she voiced through her tears.

"Yes, Mama. Here is Ori. Will you invite us in?"

"My God! Come. Come inside," Emma cried. "Sit. Sit here on the divan. So this is Ori. Your name means 'my light.'"

"Mama says you are my *bubbeh*."

"Yah. That is true."

Sophie sat in silence, unsure of what to say until Emma reached out to her, and the two clutched each other and wept while Ori watched in puzzlement.

"Mama, we must let this unhappiness pass away. Ori needs two *bubbehs*, and I need my mother. I can't change my life, my ideals. Nor will you change yours. Please, we mustn't let this separate our family any longer."

"Thanks to God, my Sophie. Thanks to God."

"You won't always like what I do, but you must understand that my life is different from yours. My work is important to me."

"Yes, but you know some wealthy families. You have 'ins.' You don't have to work with those greenhorns in the worst part of town when you could…"

"Yes. Some of my friends are wealthy, but I live my own life. They aren't 'ins.' They are friends."

"Of course they're friends, but they could help you…"

"Mama, these are things we won't be able to talk about. We are different, you and I. That is all."

"*Shah*. I know. That's all. We won't talk about this anymore."

"Mama, I'm hungry," whispered Ori.

"*Oy*, what kind of a *bubbeh* doesn't give her Ori some cookies? Come into the kitchen and we'll find something good to eat." She looked into the pantry and brought out a red box of Vienna Fingers. "Look, Ori. This cookie is like a sandwich with cream inside. See how long it is, like a finger, no?"

Sophie looked around the kitchen, so different from her childhood home, while Emma separated the sandwich for Ori and he began to lick the filling. Gone were the old gas lamps, the oak icebox, the coal-burning stove—all of them comfortable memories of home. Instead, Emma had realized her dream of a modern kitchen with linoleum on the floor.

"Mama, you have a new icebox and a gas stove!"

"*Nu*, sure. You want I should stay like a foreigner? We live like Americans now. You saw the new furniture?"

"I didn't have a chance…"

"Come, see the salon. All mahogany, right from Friedman's store! Duncan Phyfe, yet. Ori, finish your cookie and come with your mama and me."

"But Mama, what happened to the old settee, the one you saved to buy?"

"Sophie, Sophie. Times change. That old trash we gave away." Emma saw a faraway expression on her daughter's face. "You look around, and Ori will have another cookie in the kitchen."

As Emma took hold of Ori's hand and guided the reluctant child to the kitchen, Sophie said, "Go with *Bubbeh*, sweet one. I'll be right there."

Sophie collapsed onto the "divan." Of course her father mentioned that Emma had bought new furniture, but she wasn't prepared for this barren room. *How could Mama dismiss our old life so easily?* The room with ornate furnishings appeared lifeless to Sophie. As she looked around she noted the loss of all of the things she thought made a home welcoming—a hand-knitted afghan, lace doilies, a book, a magazine. She thought there was nothing to show that someone lived in this house.

Sophie choked up and rose from the divan because she didn't want to cry. She walked through the dining room, noting the formal new furniture there, too, and went back to the kitchen where Emma was pouring milk and foisting another cookie on Ori.

Anxious to change the subject from Emma's new possessions, Sophie asked, "Mama, tell me about the shop."

"Sophie, you would like my new lines. I have designs from all the latest French houses. Of course not originals, but beautiful, well-made copies, not like department store *schlock*." Sophie had seen original designs worn by Mrs. Reichman and her crowd, but she didn't mention these things to Emma.

When Ori had finished his snack, it seemed to Sophie that it was time to go. She was too wise to encourage Ori to kiss Emma good-bye, so there was an awkward moment when Emma, unaccustomed to initiating tenderness to children, bent to kiss him, but held herself in check and patted him on the head. "You'll come to see me again?" she asked.

"Yes, Mama, our whole family will be together again."

# THREE

## October 1922

"**Y**ou can always count on good champagne here at the Reichmans' house, Prohibition or no," remarked Myra to her friend Hilda as they clinked glasses.

"I heard that he has it fixed up with the police. He tells them it's for religious reasons. There are caseloads in the butler's pantry. Did you see them?"

"Mmm. Look there," Myra pointed with her chin. "It's Eleanor's mother in a gorgeous Lanvin evening dress. Silk, with that stunning gold metallic border and a shawl to match!"

"See how it's gathered below the waist and drops so beautifully in folds around her calves," said Hilda. "But your dress is equally lovely, Myra."

"It's Philippe and Gaston. Do you like it? Myra's gown was also silk in shades of pink with luscious beading, metallic lace trim, and even feathers and tortoiseshell.

"Myra, think how those beads will shimmer when you dance the Charleston and Black Bottom with that sheik Daniel Sheinman over there!"

"What a looker! He's the bee's knees, but he's so shy," responded Myra. "Lucky Eleanor. Through with matchmaking parties. I swear, if my mother forces one more eligible young man my way, why I'll just die!"

"You should find your own husband, Myra," said Hilda as she nodded in Daniel's direction.

"Watch me. I'll get his attention." Myra rearranged the hang of her beaded chemise and tottered off in her too-high shoes.

As she neared her prey, Reuben Farber inadvertently thwarted her. He approached his friend who was standing alone in an alcove that looked out on the autumn trees in the corner garden of the Reichman mansion.

"Reuben, congratulations. *Mazel tov*, my friend. It's about time you and Ellie wed."

"Yes. It fell into place when I came home from this last trip to Paris with the new Picasso. I think my father finally realized that my painting isn't an idle hobby. He knew that I wanted to paint, and now that I'm beginning to deal in art, he let go of his hold on me as a business partner. I couldn't ask Ellie to marry me without that settled."

Dan asked about the home that Reuben and Ellie had intended to purchase, but his eye wandered over the crowd as he talked.

"We bought the house on Ninety-second at Fifth Avenue near Ellie's uncle," said Reuben. I have a studio on the third floor with the ceiling open to the sky. I'll invite you to see it as soon as we get back from our wedding trip. We'll be in France for a while. I want Ellie to meet Gertrude Stein. Dan, who are you eyeing over there by the orchestra?"

"Who is that woman wearing the exotic gold and rust print chemise with her hair tied at the neck?"

"That's Sophie Shapiro, Ellie's closest friend."

"But is she the one I saw at the Henry Street house with a child? She has a husband?"

"Ori's father died at the end of the war. Sophie is raising him alone."

"Ah. A child."

"Shall I introduce you, Dan?"

"No," he hesitated. "Not now."

"If you say so. We'll see you when we return from France. Mingle, Dan. Enjoy yourself. Myra Kriss has been eyeing you all evening."

Daniel turned and looked at the place where he had seen Sophie, but she had moved on.

Ellie had spirited Sophie into the music room to say her farewells. The bride had removed her cloche and veil, and with her height and radiance she shone in her deco gown as if encircled by a golden aura. When Eleanor had entered the sanctuary earlier in the day and walked the aisle, gasps of admiration had been audible throughout the room.

Now as Ellie was preparing to leave, the two young women embraced, and Ellie said, "I'll miss you awfully while we're in France..."

"I'll miss you, too, but Ellie...Paris! Gertrude Stein!"

"I know, Sophie. It's going to be an extraordinary honeymoon."

"Thank God, Reuben's father finally understands what he wants to do," said Sophie.

"I'm still in dreamland, Sophie. I can hardly believe my good fortune. And you, Sophie? Won't you let me introduce you to Daniel Sheinman? He's here tonight."

"Ellie, I met him at Henry Street," answered Sophie, feeling her face redden.

"And..."

"And he's very handsome."

"Is that why you're blushing?"

"Miss Wald introduced us. I...I...liked him," admitted Sophie with her characteristic palms-up pose.

"Well, come on. We'll go and talk to him."

"No, Ellie. I can't. Not now."

"Why not?"

"It makes me anxious to think about it. I'm not ready, truly."

"Well then, when we come home."

"Yes. When you and Reuben come home."

# December 1922

**D**aniel stood in a second-floor passageway overlooking the backyard of the Henry Street building, a small dirt yard, but nicely equipped with swings, a slide, tricycles, and a seesaw. His eyes were fixed on a dark-haired little boy who was bouncing with another child on the seesaw. The day was sunny but cold, and the latter boy wore a heavy, tattered hand-knit sweater, woolen kneesocks, and knee-length trousers, exposing his dirty knees. The dark-haired child, whom he knew to be Ori, wore a stylish sweater and clean socks that marked him as different from the other tenement children.

A third child approached the ragged boy, hands on hips and glowering. Daniel could see that an altercation was brewing. Ori got off the seesaw, took the interloper by his arm, and guided him to the seat he'd left vacant, as if to say, *"Don't bother him. You can have my seat."* The would-be bully took the seat, and Ori walked away to watch the others ride trikes.

"He's a lovely boy, no?" inquired Miss Wald as she encircled Dan's waist.

"I didn't hear you come."

"You were quite intent, Daniel. Ori Shapiro is a special child. So is his mother special."

"I saw her at the Reichman wedding."

"She looked lovely that night, didn't she?" asked Miss Wald.

Daniel didn't seem to hear. He remained focused on the playground.

"Daniel, are you listening to me?"

"I'm sorry," he said as he turned toward Miss Wald.

"I said she looked lovely at the wedding."

"Oh, yes, she did. She looked beautiful, but I didn't get a chance to talk to her. She was always surrounded by others." He didn't mention that Reuben had offered to introduce them but he had refused.

"Sophie is here now, and it is almost lunchtime," remarked Miss Wald.

"Uh…I have to be going. The account books are all up to date," he said as he gave her a quick kiss on the cheek and hurried away.

He left the Settlement house and continued onto Henry Street in the direction of the Rivington Street subway. Daniel's pace slowed as he recalled the events in the house, and he ambled onward, rubbing his thumb and forefinger together inside his pockets. *It's not possible. A woman with a child.* He squinted and recalled the scene in the play yard and the diplomacy that Ori had displayed in giving up his place on the seesaw. *Smart little critter.* He walked on a little farther, stumbled over a crack in the sidewalk, and stopped to collect himself. *What am I thinking?*

He was nearly to the end of Henry Street when his thoughts returned to Sophie. *Gentle. Soft.* He wondered why she appeared a little sad-eyed and found himself wishing to make her smile. *A woman with a child. No.*

Then he envisioned Myra and wondered why he had let himself be caught. He felt that he should see it through, just as his parents wished for him. He replayed his father's remark, "A girl from a good family…"

*Sophie's not from our set. I can't break with Myra.*

Suddenly Daniel stopped. He turned an about-face and strode back to Henry Street. *Lunch. It doesn't have to mean anything.* Miss Wald was in the reception room when Dan opened the door.

"Forget something?"

"Well, I'm hungry, and I thought maybe…"

"She's in her office on the second floor."

What am I doing? he thought as he knocked on Sophie's open door.

She turned around in her seat, and seeing Daniel she smiled, a smile that bordered on beaming. Then she looked down, still smiling but slightly reddened.

"I was here working on the accounting, and I noticed that it's lunchtime. Would you like to walk out with me to a restaurant?"

"I…I…Yes! I would like that very much. I'll get my coat."

Daniel watched her as she took her coat from the closet. She wrapped her hand-knit scarf around her neck, and he took her plain navy blue coat and helped her into it, surprised at its simplicity. Myra's coats were fur, or at least fur trimmed. Sophie pulled on her woolen gloves and turned to him with a soft smile. Out went her hands, palms up. "Where would you like to go?"

"There's a deli on Ludlow Street that I go to."

"Near Seward Park?"

"Yes. Let's go," he said, motioning toward the door.

They walked together in awkward silence until they reached the park on East Broadway.

"I wonder if you know that this park is on property that housed the Ludlow Street jail years ago. Isn't it wonderful? This is the first city park to have a permanent children's playground and pavilion in the whole country. You should see the garden in the spring time!"

"I think the jail was before my time, but it's a nice park," said Daniel.

"Oh, it's more than a nice park. It's a model for other cities to build appropriate parks for children. It offers a little bit of green and sunshine for children who usually see nothing but crowded, rundown tenements and cobblestone roads."

"That's important to you."

"Daniel, I work here so that this generation of immigrant children will have opportunities to grow out of these tenements. They need to see beyond this place and play in the open, away from the shadow of smothering rows of buildings. That's why we take them to our patrons' summer homes for a week. Most have never seen a lake or a hillside or a house apart from these flats."

Daniel couldn't force his eyes away from the glowing enthusiasm of Sophie's face. How different from Myra, who took her privilege for granted. When he looked around, he saw that they had reached the deli.

He allowed her to enter first and pointed to a bare table against the wall. "What shall I get you?" he asked.

"A bowl of noodle soup would be good in this cold." Dan put his coat on the back of the chair and went up to the counter where people were three-deep waiting to order.

"Hey, Benny, I want my regular," shouted the man in front of him.

"No Kaiser rolls."

"What do you mean, 'no Kaiser rolls?' What kind of a deli doesn't have Kaiser rolls?"

"*Nu?* The Kaiser rolls are gone. You're too late," countered Benny.

"All right. Rye bread, but don't cheat me on the pastrami like you did last time!"

"Cheat you? Where else can you get a good sandwich like this? You *schle-miel!* You want maybe to go to Zion's? You think there you can get a better sandwich?"

Dan enjoyed the jostling and the jesting and the smells of a Jewish deli. He called out, "Two bowls of soup, Benny! With plenty of rye bread."

Sophie, too, enjoyed the bustle of this eatery patronized by many Orthodox. Men with long sideburns and wayward beards held energetic debates. Always they were shouting about rabbinic questions. Their fur-trimmed black hats and long coats protected an innocent woman's eye from glimpsing the male body, as the *sheitel* covered a woman's head for modesty. Here there were no Orthodox women, however. They stayed at home.

As Daniel approached the table balancing a tray with two bowls of soup and a plate of rye bread, a man suddenly pushed his chair back from the next table and almost upset the tray. Dan raised it and salvaged the soup, which had sloshed only a small amount onto the tray. He managed to squeeze between the closely packed tables to lay his bounty before Sophie.

"I think I saved most of our meal," he said as he removed the bowls and plate from the tray and went to get spoons.

Once settled with their hot noodle soup Daniel said, "Miss Wald pointed Ori out to me while he was playing in the yard. Does he look like his father?"

"Yes. Izzy had dark curly hair and those almond-shaped, sparkling eyes."

"But he has your smile, I think. Does he have your blue eyes?"

"He's the image of his father, but he does have my blue eyes," she said, taking a deep breath.

"How long has he been gone, Sophie?"

"Izzy died a day before the war ended. He never saw Ori or even knew that he was to be a father."

"It must be very hard to raise a boy alone."

"I'm not alone, Daniel."

"But I thought…I thought that you didn't have a husband," Daniel stuttered.

"Oh," laughed Sophie. "I'm not married! I meant that I have Izzy's parents and my own parents and good friends like Ellie Reichman…I mean Ellie Farber, now."

"That was a beautiful wedding party. I saw you there, but you vanished before I had a chance to talk to you."

"I'm sorry that I didn't see you."

Soon the couple left the deli to make their way back to the Henry Street building. Daniel placed Sophie's gloved hand in the crook of his elbow to guide her onto the crowded street. He thought that her beauty deserved finer cloth than the rough wool that he held. He wondered if he could give her a pair of soft kidskin gloves.

Sophie blushed and removed her hand once they were on the sidewalk.

Daniel saw her to the door of the Settlement house and went on his way, pondering Sophie's difference from the women of his social set. Her mind was crowded with her work and her child, unlike Myra's, whose head was filled with thoughts of marriage, family, and status.

# FOUR

## April 1923

**E**llie was dancing from one room to another on the second floor of her new home, pleased to show her dear friend around for her first visit since the Farbers' return from their wedding trip. She and Reuben had been staying with her parents while their home was under renovation.

"Sophie, this will be your room. This room across the hall is for a nursery…"

"Wait, wait. What do you mean, a nursery?"

"Sophie, I think maybe…"

"Oh, Ellie!" Sophie cried as she jumped up and down, pulling Ellie with her. "A baby! When?"

"Wait! We're not sure yet, but I missed my time twice. If this is really going to happen, we think it will be in October, near our anniversary."

"Oh, oh! When will you know?"

"We see Dr. Bauman next week. Uh, do you hear something? Wait. That's the telephone in Reuben's office. Stay here while I run and answer it."

Sophie thought about how the Farbers' child would be raised, likely with a nanny to help Ellie. The baby would have two parents, doting grandparents and trust accounts, private schools…Ori was raised in a tenement childcare center in one room with only one parent.

Sophie had only to think of Ori, nearly four years old, and all thoughts of the Farbers' advantages vanished. Ori's smile, his loving nature, quick mind, and radiant health assured her that money wasn't as important as the love that Ori generated from everyone who knew him. She considered that he might have an advantage in living among children of different backgrounds, poor children with even less than he enjoyed.

Ellie reappeared and jolted Sophie to the present. "Now let me show you Reuben's studio and the paintings that we brought back. Let's walk up, but Reuben's clients will use the elevator."

"How do you feel about having the gallery in your home, Ellie?"

"Oh, it will work out, because guests can use the elevator without coming into the house."

Ellie opened the door and sunlight from the sky above illuminated a studio hung with an array of paintings that made no sense to Sophie. She knew that it had been ten years since the Armory Show had introduced New Yorkers to Cubism and other departures from the romantic landscapes she had come to expect from an art gallery. She even enjoyed the more contemporary painting with broad brushstrokes and lighter palettes, the impressions of a scene rather than the details, and the infusion of light, but these paintings, these strident bold images—she hated to tell Ellie what she thought.

There was no need to break the news to Ellie. "I can see that you wonder about this art, like I did at first."

"You enjoy it now?"

"I understand it a little bit more after meeting the artists."

"Maybe I'll learn, too, but will you tell me more about it next time I see you? I have to get back to Ori."

"Next time, bring him with you. I think that Maggie might come to stay here, and she can take him to the park. My mother hasn't yet agreed to let her favorite housekeeper go, but she was my nanny, and I hope that she'll want to live here."

"That reminds me, Sophie, we are going to have a party for a few friends next Saturday night and Maggie is coming to help. My mother would really like to have Ori visit at her house for the weekend. You know how she loves to take him to the Central Park Menagerie, and I think he has gotten over his upset about Hattie the elephant dying."

"That sounds wonderful. Ori loves to be with your mother, and he has finally stopped talking about Hattie."

When the afternoon came to an end and Sophie had to return to Henry Street, Ellie hugged her tight and whispered, "Dan Sheinman will be at the party."

"I never told you that he took me to lunch in December when he was at Henry Street working on the accounting. You were still in France, and I haven't heard from him again, but I see him now and then in the office."

"He asked Reuben about you at our wedding."

"If he were interested, he would have asked to see me again after we had lunch in December. That was months ago."

"Men! You never can tell!"

Sophie was the first to arrive at the Farber house for the party. She was heading up the wide marble staircase to put her small leather valise in "Sophie's room" when the doorbell rang, and Reuben ushered in Daniel Sheinman, with Myra Kriss on his arm. Sophie turned toward the door at the sound of the bell and froze when she saw Myra. She felt a flash of body heat, and her head began to buzz. She ran up the remaining steps with Ellie on her heels, sat on the edge of her bed, and stared straight ahead, a stony gaze replacing the blush.

"Oh, Sophie," said Ellie. "I didn't know he would bring Myra. I'm so sorry."

"I have no claim on him. We only went out to lunch one time."

"But you like him a great deal, I know."

"Yes, Ellie. He's the first man I have thought about since Izzy. He's a gentle person and so easy to talk to. I didn't know that he was…attached."

"I didn't think he was, but we have to go downstairs and make the best of it. Mark Stemel is coming, and you know how much he likes you."

"I don't want to be unkind, but Mark is stifling. He doesn't stop talking for a minute." She paused to catch her breath. "I don't think I can manage this evening. Could you say that I am feeling unwell and that I'm resting?"

"No. You aren't doing yourself justice. You're not a feeble person! You have strength, you have the ability to face this gracefully, and what's more, you look stunning in that chemise. We're going downstairs now, so perk up!"

"You're right." She looked at the door, considered a retreat, but stood and glanced in the mirror to tuck in a stray hair. Ellie pinched her friend's cheeks to bring back the color, hugged her, and they walked down the stairs and into the small sitting room off of the main foyer.

Maggie was serving hors d'oeuvres when the two women came in. Reuben rose and made the introductions. "Sophie, you know Mark Stemel, and of course Rose Braverman from Barnard. I don't know if you are acquainted with Daniel Sheinman and his friend Myra Kriss."

Daniel responded quickly with a warm smile. "It's nice to see you again, Sophie," he said as he rose from the settee to greet her. "Myra, Sophie works at the Henry Street Settlement where I help with the accounting."

"How lovely," remarked Myra. She flipped her fox boa over her shoulder.

"I've invited Harry Levine, who should be here soon," said Reuben. "You know, Dan, he's the curator of the contemporary art department at the Metropolitan. I thought you would like to meet him, and he wants to see the studio and the work I brought back from this trip."

Mark asked Sophie to join him on an opposite settee from Dan and Myra. Ellie and Rose were busy catching up on their lives in a corner of the room when the doorbell rang, and Reuben went to admit his friend Harry.

Mr. Reichman had sent champagne, and after the first glass, conversation began to flow easily. Mark kept up a steady patter, and for once Sophie was grateful. She didn't dare look across to the opposite side of the cocktail table where Dan and Myra sat close together on the settee. Reuben had pulled a chair to the far end of the table for Harry, and they were engaged in conversation.

Sophie could hear the occasional high-pitched interjection from Myra. "You don't say!" or "Isn't that the truth!" Sophie allowed herself a secret condescension for what she regarded as Myra's inane giggle following each exclamation.

How could he care for her? Sophie wondered. Maybe I was wrong about him. It doesn't seem that the Daniel I met in December would be interested in a frivolous person like Myra. Difficult as it was, Sophie kept her apparent focus on Mark and waited out the evening until the guests followed their host to his studio.

Ellie stayed behind with her wounded friend. "Did you see him looking over at you all night? Couldn't you feel Dan's eyes on you?"

"What are you talking about, Ellie? Daniel sat with *her* all evening while I listened to Mark talk about the fur business, as if I care about fur! He should have been talking to Myra."

"I think Dan is interested in you, Sophie. Mark my words!"

# June 1923

Sophie had not seen Daniel since the Farbers' party in April. Their paths hadn't crossed at Henry Street, and she had tried to put him out of her mind. Now she was preparing for the summer weeks when she would take groups of tenement children as guests to the various country estates that had been offered for the purpose of giving each child a week of fresh air and a first-time view of life outside the tenements.

She was sitting at her desk at the Settlement house looking at the calendar she had created on a sheet of newsprint. She pushed aside a curly strand of hair that had come loose from her bun. Unseen, ink dripped from the nib of her pen onto the edge of the calendar. Her sleeve was a moment away from smearing the blot when Daniel thrust into the room and grabbed her arm.

Shocked, Sophie followed an unknown hand up to the smiling face of Daniel Sheinman. "There's ink on your paper," he said.

"Oh! You startled me. How long were you here?"

"I was passing and I saw your office door open. I stood for a second, ready to knock when I saw your pen drip and you were about to put your sleeve on the spill."

"I should say, 'thank you,' I think!" she said as she rose from her chair to face him.

"I didn't have a chance to talk to you at all when we were at Reuben and Ellie's house. Mark Stemel had you all to himself."

"But I suppose *you* weren't occupied!"

Daniel blushed. "Touché." The two looked at each other for a moment and then laughed simultaneously. "Reuben has sold most of the work that he brought from his last Paris trip, and he may need to go again soon. This work of Picasso and Braque has people mesmerized," he said.

"To be honest, I don't really understand what the artists are doing. The *Three Musicians* painting doesn't look like musicians at all!"

Daniel maneuvered into the hallway and gestured for Sophie to step out of her cramped office. He smiled and said, "You are honest! Most people don't admit that for them, 'the emperor has no clothes.' Reuben explained it to me."

"What did he say?"

"Well, artists see the world in a different way. They see light and form and shadows that are invisible to us as we go through our day without truly seeing. These painters challenge you to look at the subject from different viewpoints at the same time. Objects are broken up, and surfaces intersect at apparently random angles. Everyday sights are transformed so that you see them in a fresh way."

"Yes," responded Sophie. "I wish that we could transform the sights of the poverty in this tenement so that people could see them. They shop here to find a bargain. They walk the streets past the sweatshops. They look, but they don't see."

"You're helping us to see them, Sophie. How many families have offered their homes for the summer? How many more donate money to Henry Street? You are making a difference."

"That's nice of you to say, Daniel."

"But I mean it. I admire your work, your dedication."

A smile grew across Sophie's face, beginning with a little twitch in the right corner of her mouth and growing until it widened, and her deep blue eyes crinkled with the smile. She stood, and Daniel felt the impulse to put his finger on a corner of her lip where the smile had begun. His hand moved in the pocket where he habitually thrust it, but he restrained himself. The moment passed.

"How is your little boy?"

"Ori was four years old in May. He's happy. I'm fortunate that he is the type of child who is naturally at peace. He loves his *bubbeh* and *zaidehs*, and we see them almost every weekend."

"Ah. I remember you told me that your relatives are in Paterson."

"Yes."

Daniel could think of no more to say. He stood with his hands in his pockets. "I guess I should get to work or Lillian Wald will be after me!"

"She's a great woman, isn't she?"

"Speak of—Hello, Miss Wald."

"*Shalom*, Dan. Working on those accounts today, are you?" she asked.

"Sophie, didn't I tell you what a slave driver this woman is?"

"You come with me and let Sophie do her work. We need to get all the summer trips ready to go. I see that your father gave us a week in July. You'll tell him again how much we appreciate the gift to our children."

"I will. Where are we going? Not to my office, I see."

"No, Dan. We're going to the play yard so that you can appreciate how much these summer weeks mean to our children. Right out this door."

Miss Wald led Daniel down the three flights of stairs, around to the back of the building, and outside where the children were riding trikes. "Do you see that little one over there with the green sweater? His mama has pneumonia and can't care for her six children or cut patterns on their kitchen table for pennies anymore. Their father peddles from a cart. Lunch at Henry Street is the best meal the children will get all day.

"That boy, the tall one, is the eldest in his family. At seven years he helps his mother to care for his three younger siblings. Six people in the family live in two rooms."

Daniel stood mesmerized. He thought he knew about the conditions here. He had walked the streets as Sophie had said. But he realized that he didn't know at all. He fisted his hands inside his pockets and his face reddened.

"You're surprised? Most people think they know about the poverty, but it runs very deep, Daniel. This is why we want the children to experience fresh air. It gives them something to dream about, to aspire to. It plants a seed in their minds that they might leave this bleak life someday."

"And there is Ori," Daniel pointed. "He's so different from the others."

"Yes, but he's naïve. He doesn't see that he is different. Not yet."

Daniel left the Henry Street Settlement house without going to the office to work on the accounts. He walked through the streets of the Lower East

Side, trying to *see* for the first time. He looked beyond the quaint Orthodox men dressed in long black coats and black fur hats hurrying along their daily route to pray at the *shul*. They looked neither right nor left. He peered into hallways and dark, befouled narrow staircases with peeling wallpaper. He saw the clothes hanging on lines, worn and tattered, but clean.

*Does Myra have any idea about this other world? I don't think she sees beyond her wardrobe or the next gala.* He thought about his own uninitiated work at Henry Street. His father had asked him to make this contribution of time. While examining his own deficiency of charitable spirit, he continued to walk north on Broadway until it intersected with Fourteenth Street where he stopped, disoriented. The street was wider, devoid of pushcarts. *Ah, yes. Fifth Avenue already.* He turned right onto Fifth Avenue and upward toward his own world with the sweaty smell of poverty behind him.

# FIVE

## June 1923

**T**he table was set with candles. Emma had prepared challah, and the chicken soup was boiling on the stove in preparation for the peace of the Sabbath. "Aaron should be home by now," called Emma as she brought the challah to the table. I don't want him hanging around those good-for-nothing boys. He should go with his own kind, Meyer."

Meyer came into the kitchen after changing from his work clothes. He went to the sideboard to fetch the Concord grape wine that brother Dave brought each week for the *Shabbos*. When Emma began to express disappointment with Aaron, he thought about the wine. *Prohibition or no*, a *bisl wine on Shabbos is a blessing*.

"*Nu*. Who are his own kind?" Meyer asked.

"I don't have to tell you. Other Jewish boys from school, the ones from wealthy families. There is Samuel Goodman, the dentist's son and Leonard Kaplan from the furniture store Kaplans…"

"He has trouble in the school. Those families don't want trouble for their sons."

"How can you say…"

"That is the truth, Emma. He is foolish in the classroom with the other boys. And Emma, he is not a student from books. He wants to do with his hands. He wants to go with me to Sal's garage when I bring the Ford. Emma, he watches everything. He sees how to fix the car. What's wrong he should be a mechanic someday?"

"I'll tell you what's…"

"Soon there will be cars for everyone, and who will fix them?" Meyer continued. "The country will need men who can work with their hands."

Emma busied herself at the stove while Meyer sat at the table and poured the wine in preparation for the prayers.

"Not my Aaron! He's a smart boy. He can go to college and become somebody."

"Emma, he's not smart like that. It's a different smart."

As Emma was ready to retort, the door opened and Aaron burst into the kitchen.

"Look at you! You're *shmutsik*, filthy! Where did you go?"

"Out, Ma. I went out."

"Go! Wash for *Shabbos* and change those clothes," Emma ordered.

"You see, Meyer, what the boy is like?"

"*Nu?* He's a boy. Nine years only. What is wrong with a little *shmutz?*"

"God in Heaven! What will become of such a boy?"

When Aaron came from his room in clean clothes, Emma relaxed, but still she persisted. "Where did you go to get so dirty?"

"Ma, I went to the garage to watch Sal. You should see how he works on those autos. He has two of his own. Papa, you saw his Packard Twin Six touring, didn't you?"

"Yah, boy, that is some automobile!"

"Wish I could drive that auto someday. When can I drive, Papa?"

"Enough with this talk of cars. You went out to play this afternoon. After dinner you must show me your homework for Monday," Emma said.

Again, on Monday after school, Aaron went straight to the mechanic's workshop, which was housed in an alley of rental garages. The alley was narrow with perhaps ten feet of space between two facing rows of wooden sheds, each with its own garage door. The clapboard sheds were attached one to the other with a common flat asphalt roof. Brown paint peeled from most of the sheds, leaving bare wood exposed. For those with no electric pendant lights, a rear window provided the only light when the garage door was closed.

"Can I watch you today, Sal?"

"Your mama, she will be angry. She doesn't like you to come here. What she think, huh?"

"Oh, she wants me to be a lawyer or something like that. It's not for me. I want to fix cars like you, Sal."

"I don't know, boy. I think you come here for my wife's cavalucci cookies," he laughed as he opened his lunch pail and handed the anise-flavored treat to Aaron. "My wife, she come from Siena in the north. She learn from her mama to make these cookies."

"Thanks, Sal. Looks like the gypsies are getting ready for dinner," he commented. Aaron stared at the gypsy family who made their home in one of the garages. The father was sitting on a rickety chair, playing his accordion and watching the women labor over the fire they had built in front of their shed. The fire burned in an ash can lid, and a black cast-iron pot hung over it. The women's red skirts flowed around their ankles as they maneuvered near the fire.

Aaron was mesmerized. His golden eyes glazed over as he stared at the family, envying their imagined freedom to move on whenever they had an impulse. A boy his own age fed the fire with coal. Aaron recalled that same boy hanging around the coal truck to catch the stray chunks that flew from the chute. With summer approaching there would be less coal coming down the chutes into the coal bins. What would they use for their fires? Aaron wondered if they had their own coal bin inside, and he wondered where the gypsies went when the winter wind howled and snowdrifts piled high.

"You come inside here, boy, and don't look at them gypsies. They don't like that."

"Sal, where do the gypsies go in the winter?"

"They move south to a warmer place. Now you come inside."

"Can I sit in your Packard, Sal?"

"Sure."

Aaron climbed onto the running board and over the gleaming black door of the top-down Twin-Six. He settled into the front seat and peered over the windshield. The boy was lost in his own world.

A drawn-out train whistle suddenly punctured the air and interrupted his dreaming.

"Run, boy. You get home before that long freight train comes by," said Sal.

Aaron jumped from the automobile and raced toward the track the moment he heard the warning. Ding... ding... ding. The lowering train gates would close the track to pedestrian traffic in a few moments. The five-thirty freighter signaled the time he needed to be home for dinner. He didn't have time to wait and wave to the conductor, not with his mama on the warpath.

# July 1923

**A**aron's behavior was less of an issue for Emma during the summer months when he spent weeks at a time with his uncles' families at Grossinger's Terrace Hill House, a resort in the Catskills. The women and children stayed there for many of the summer weeks while Harry and George commuted by train on the weekends, leaving town on Friday afternoon to avoid traveling on the Sabbath.

Without the distraction of Aaron's visits to Sal's garage, Emma focused on her business, plotting her next strategy to increase the family's wealth. She was confident that real estate investments would grow in value and bring in rental income.

On this Sunday, Meyer was at the Shapiros', where Sophie was visiting with Ori. Emma hoped that her daughter might come to see her on another day, because today she wanted time to herself. She treasured the solitude at her dining room table, her modern ceiling fan whirring and bringing her relief from the stifling summer heat. She felt contented with her fashion magazines and the newspaper ads until she thought about Meyer.

He still lives in the old world, she thought. His old-fashioned ways gnawed at her, and when she dwelled on his complacency, her jaw tightened, pulling the corners of her mouth downward. These rancorous thoughts about her husband saddened as well as angered her, and she mused for a moment about her youthful love for him now tempered, but still alive.

Meyer's return from his visit jolted her from her reverie.

"Emma, you should see little Ori. Such a loving *boytshikl*. He sits on my lap, and I *kvell*. So proud I am from this boy."

Meyer saw the newspapers spread around her on the table and stopped talking. His wife was deeply engaged in thought.

"Emma, I bother you. Is it money you worry about?"

Emma clenched her fists and turned on her husband. "Meyer, the money is not a problem. I make plenty money, but why shouldn't we cash in on the wealth that is there for the taking? We could buy a six-unit apartment on Park Avenue. I saw one near Thirty-third Street. We could make plenty good rent." She rose from the table and began to pace the room, adjusting the ornaments on the sideboard.

"Emma, sit, Dolly. We have this beautiful house with new furniture. We even have fans on the ceiling, like the rich people. Why do we need to have more?"

"Speak up, Meyer," Emma shouted over the vibrating fans. "Why don't you speak up?"

"Will your hunger never stop?" Meyer rose from the chair he had just taken a moment ago, and he bent over to speak into Emma's ear. "I'm going to the Workmen's Circle where the *landsmen* hear me. Do what you will."

Emma jumped up and put herself between Meyer and the door.

"But Meyer, wait. Everyone is making money. We should make more, too. We need a new car, maybe a trip to the Catskills, like my brothers."

Meyer tried to move around her toward the door, but she held him off. "Aaron is enjoying himself in the mountains with his cousins right now. We should go, too, so we can invite the cousins sometime. We have to put money away for college for Aaron."

"Again with the college! When will you see that our son will not go to college? He isn't made to study. He loves to work with his hands."

"Don't change the talk to some other thing. Aaron will grow bigger and smarter, and he will go to college to make something of himself. He is young yet. In the meantime we must save money for him. That is why we are going to buy an apartment building."

"Emma, Emma. Do what you must do. Your brothers will help you like always. I'm going to the Workmen's Circle. There they have no noisy fans. Now please let me pass."

When Meyer left, Emma began to pace between the empty rooms—into the dining room and through it to the "salon," and then back to the kitchen. She sat at the table once again and snatched up the *Paterson Evening News*. *Where is it? Business, page six.*

She put on her wire-framed spectacles, scanned the stock pages, and gave a shout. "Bingo! RCA at $4.75. That's up from three dollars when I bought it. Hmmm. General Electric. Up! General Motors. Up!" She thought about selling some stock and buying more of another, all on fifty percent margin. *George was right. Such a game to play!*

Ori's sweaty palm rested in Sophie's hand as they walked toward the subway station. The brutal muggy heat of a Manhattan summer didn't appear to slow Ori down, but Sophie took her handkerchief out of her pocket with her free hand and wiped her brow and upper lip. Sweat was beginning to moisten her cotton dress.

"Mama, I don't want to visit *Bubbeh* Epstein. Can I go to *Bubbeh* Esther? You go to *Bubbeh* Epstein."

"Ori, *Bubbeh* Epstein loves you." Sophie struggled to keep her face and voice neutral, the less to show her irritation with Ori's feelings than with her own. *I can't cope with all of this now. Such heat.* Sophie was annoyed with her mother who claimed she wanted to see Ori, but when they arrived would lose interest. Business dominated her life.

"But I don't love her!"

"What makes you say that, Ori?"

"She pats my head all the time. She gives me too much candy. You said candy isn't good for me. I don't like Milky Way bars."

"My sweet one. She is only trying to make you happy. She thinks all little boys like Milky Way bars."

"She should ask what I want, like *Bubbeh* Esther."

As Ori skipped over the subway grate on the sidewalk, a huge burst of steam from below whooshed at the edges of Sophie's short hemline. "Let's hurry, Mama!' I hope we get a seat on the subway. I don't like to get squashed between legs!"

"Ori, do you think a big dragon is under the street blowing all that steam up to us?"

"Silly! That's the train, Mama," giggled Ori.

The Rivington Street subway station was ahead of them, raised above the pushcart frenzy and reached by climbing one of two flights of stairs located on either side of the street.

"I smell knishes. Maybe we should buy some for *Bubbeh* first," Sophie said.

"Mama, look at this pushcart. Please, Mama. It's better than knishes. Look at the halvah and the pretzels and ooh, Mama. Can we buy chewing gum?"

"Ori, the last time you had gum, I found it on your bed sheets."

"I'll be careful this time. I promise, Mama."

"Ori, my Ori. Okay. Here is a penny for Juicy Fruit."

The two made their way squeezing through the crowds of shoppers, past the pungent Italian carts with olives and garlic and the Jewish carts steaming with chickpeas and knishes. Sophie made a quick purchase for Emma, and they rushed up the staircase hoping to catch the next train.

With luck they pushed the turnstile barely in time to board the waiting northbound train. When it jolted forward, Sophie nearly fell onto a tan woven seat whose springs creaked as she landed. She pulled Ori onto her lap, encircling his waist, and the two looked out into the blackness of the underground.

An hour later after the subway and a subsequent bus ride through Paterson, they were on Broadway and walked the few blocks to the Epstein house.

"*Shah*," Emma signaled with a finger to her lips as she opened the door. "Meyer is sleeping."

"*Zeideh* is here?" asked Ori.

"Yah. He was tired, so he went to lie down."

"I'll go see if he is awake," said Ori as he started off in the direction of the bedroom.

"Wait a minute, son. You don't want to wake him."

"I'll be quiet. I won't wake him if he is sleeping," said Ori. And off he went before anyone could stop him.

"Mama," Sophie asked. "Why is Papa in bed on a Saturday afternoon? Didn't he go to the Workmen's Circle after synagogue?"

"It's nothing. He gets a bit tired, and he goes to bed."

"Since when, Mama, does he go to lie down in the middle of a day?"

"I don't remember. Come. I'll show you my new designs for the fall line. I have pictures from the showrooms. Yesterday I went to look at the new fashions. My customers are asking already about what they see in the magazines."

"I'll look in on Papa first."

Meyer was sitting up in his bed with Ori snuggled beside him when Sophie popped her head around the door. "Papa, why are you in bed?" asked Sophie.

Meyer reached out with both arms. "Oh, my daughter. Come. Give Papa a kiss. Such a boy you have! You look like your Papa, Ori, with your nice straight nose and curly hair."

"But Papa, is something wrong?"

"*Nein, nein.* A *bisl* tired. Not more. I'm getting like an old man now. Fifty years!"

"You should see the doctor."

"What do I need with a doctor? I work. I play cards. No trouble."

"Yoo-hoo, Sophie. Come in the kitchen. I want to show you something."

Sophie reluctantly left Meyer to be alone with Ori while she visited with Emma. When she came to the kitchen table, Emma didn't have her fashions spread out on the table, but instead sheets of paper with numbers. "Look here." Emma stood over the table and pointed to the pages. "These are my investments. I make good in the stock market."

Sophie sat down and pulled the sheets toward her. "It says here, 'margin.' What does that mean?"

"Oh, I learned a thing or two. You can buy stocks with such little money and pay the rest when you sell the stocks. The price goes up, I sell, and I make money. With this I buy property."

"I see. It's like borrowing. Aren't you happy with this fine house and all of your new furniture? What more do you want to buy?"

"Exactly like your Papa and Joe! Aaron should go to college, and this time I pay!" she exclaimed, pointing to her own chest. "I can be smart like my brothers, too."

"Yes, Mama. You are very smart," Sophie whispered under her breath. "We should have some tea and then go, I think, so Papa can rest."

# Six

## July 1923

Ellie was visiting Sophie in her Henry Street office. She often had occasion to be there in her role as administrator of her father's charitable donations. The friends were looking over the calendar for the children's summer trips to country homes. "The Henry Street children will be at Sea Bright twice this summer," said Ellie, "but we have the house all to ourselves next weekend. Will you bring Ori and come for the weekend? It's time he learned to swim, you know. The pool is ready for the season."

"I can't teach him, Ellie. I never learned to swim as a child, and to be honest, I'm a little bit afraid, but we love to be on the beach."

Ellie desired that her friend broaden her outlook. Ori was four years old and Sophie had done little else than care for him, work at Henry Street, and visit family since his birth. Ellie had offered introductions to available men, party invitations, and even short vacations without Ori, but Sophie held back, and she wasn't at all adventuresome. Today she was determined to get Sophie away from the city.

"He won't drown in our swimming pool! I'll teach him."

"I guess. No one in my family ever learned to swim except Aaron. I think he goes in the water when he visits the family in the mountains."

"Would you like Ori to swim?"

"Well, if I don't have to go in the water!"

"Reuben and I will come for you in the car after you finish here on Friday and we'll take the ferry to Sandy Hook. Say yes."

"I'll bring a bathing costume."

"Reuben has a new Jantzen swim costume that stretches."

"Oh, one of those ribbed wool ones. And I suppose you have a red Diving Girl, like the billboards?"

"You'll see."

"Okay. I'll see you Friday…with Ori and swim costumes, not red," said Sophie.

"I'll see you then."

The Reichmans' caretaker met Reuben, Ellie, Sophie, and Ori at Sandy Hook pier and drove them to the summerhouse. As they walked up the long birch-lined path to the front door, Ellie said, "Sophie, I don't think I ever told you that Grandfather's architect for this house also designed Low Library at Columbia. Maybe that's why you love that building. Oooh, watch out, Ori!"

"It's all right, Ellie. That low, stone wall is precisely Ori's cup of tea. He's a good climber."

Ori backed down off of the wall, his belly on the edge until his feet touched the ground, and then he ran to Reuben who grasped his hand. The two trotted ahead, leaving the girlfriends to talk.

"Mama, there's a man here," Ori cried as he raced back toward the women, Reuben in his wake. "He's a friend of Uncle Reuben, and we saw him at Henry Street."

Sophie paled. With eyebrows raised and a flash of her deep blue eyes, she assaulted Ellie. "How could you do this to me? You arranged this without my knowledge?"

"Ori, is it Daniel?" asked Ellie.

"Yes that's his name. I remember now," he answered.

"Ellie, you didn't tell me! Why would you do this without telling me?"

"Sophie, I didn't know," she whispered as she looked toward her husband who was approaching her with a smile. "Reuben must have invited him."

"Well, I guess I forgot to tell you that I invited Dan. I'm sorry."

"Mama, is he the man that I saw at Henry Street?"

"Yes, Ori. Come and meet Mr. Sheinman."

By this time Daniel had reached them and stood beside Sophie with his hands stuffed into the pockets of his tan summer trousers. "Reuben said you would be here."

Sophie turned to glower at Reuben, but he had walked away with Ellie, leaving her alone with Ori and Dan. She felt a warm flash, clenched her fists, and blinked her eyes in rapid succession at this unexpected closeness to Daniel. *Why do I get nervous around him?* As Sophie took note of her body sensations she fought to control them. She let her eyes rest for a moment, took a breath, and with Ori's hand tightly within hers, she looked up at Dan.

He towered over them, and smiling, he squatted next to Ori. "Ori, I've seen you playing at Henry Street. You're a swell tricycle rider. Do you like to swim, too?"

"I don't know how to swim. My mother doesn't know how to swim either. Not even my *zaidehs* know how to swim, but Uncle Aaron does."

Okay, Ori, that's enough, thought Sophie.

"I can teach you in the morning if you want to learn," said Daniel.

"Mama, can I? Please? I want to swim like Uncle Aaron," said Ori, jumping up and down.

"If you promise to do exactly as Mr. Sheinman says."

"I promise, Mama. I can, Mr. Sheinman. Did you hear her?" he said with his blue eyes sparkling. "I'm going to tell Uncle Reuben." He ran toward the yellow wooden house with its white trim and fieldstone base and scrambled onto the wraparound porch. The simple Doric columns and the hanging porch swing belied the size and luxury of the thirty-room Stanford White country mansion. Ori went inside, leaving Sophie and Dan alone.

"Let's walk around to the back of the house," suggested Daniel. A rose-lined path along the south side of the house led to the main part of the grounds. Sophie lingered over the old English shrub roses, inhaling their fruity, old-world scent. Daniel watched her as she bent over the low bush, her light summer skirt revealing the backs of her long legs. She turned around to see him gazing at her, and she looked up at him with her broad smile.

For a moment all was still. They could hear the sound of the ocean waves beyond the gardens. Some bees hummed on the roses. The waters of a nearby garden fountain bubbled sedately, in contrast to the tumult of the ocean below.

"Sophie, I wanted to talk to you…"

Before Daniel could finish his sentence, Ori reappeared. "Mama, Uncle Reuben said we could make a campfire after dinner! We could pop popcorn and…"

"Ori, your manners, sweetheart."

"I'm sorry. Excuse me. I have something to say," recited Ori.

"Well, a campfire sounds swell, Ori," laughed Daniel.

The moment of solitude was lost as the three made their way back to the house where Ori and Sophie went to freshen up for dinner.

At dinner, Ori chattered about how *Dan* would teach him to swim the next day. He emphasized Dan's name, feeling proud of his newly acquired familiarity with Mr. Sheinman. After the sorbet, Sophie excused herself from Daniel's side saying, "Ori, it's time for bed."

Speaking to the Farbers and to Dan she said, "I'll be back in a while." Ori kissed each adult as he and his mother left the dining room. Daniel turned to follow her with his eyes as she ascended the carpeted spiral staircase that led to the guest suites.

Soon afterward, Ellie excused herself from the table to say good night to Ori. Sophie had hardly tucked him in when Ellie came into the room. "Good night, my love," she said to Ori as she bent to kiss him on the forehead.

"Thank you for inviting us, Auntie Ellie. I love you."

"Me, too," she said.

As they left Ori's small room and entered the adjoining bedroom, Sophie exclaimed, "Ellie, that was some trick of Reuben's to invite Daniel here."

"Reuben said that Daniel asked about you, so he invited him. I don't think he initiated the matchmaking. It was Dan. Don't pretend that you aren't happy to see him."

"I am, Ellie, but what about Myra?"

Dan waited for Sophie to come back downstairs after tucking Ori into bed. He stood alone at the foot of the stairs. Ellie and Reuben had disappeared. "Will you try that stroll through the rose garden again?"

It was dusk, but the warmth of the day lingered as they walked side by side out to the porch and around to the garden. They retraced their former steps through the roses and talked about Ori and the beauty of Sea Bright. Sophie wondered about the casualness of Dan's attention. *Why is he here without Myra?* This thought disturbed the comfort of their companionship and her stomach tightened.

Daniel stopped walking, turned toward Sophie, and reached for her hand. Despite her discomfort, she quivered at his touch.

"I'm sorry, Sophie. I am too forward."

"Daniel, I'm confused. I'm enjoying the time here and Ori is eager about your teaching him to swim, but why are you here without Myra and..."

"I should have said something, Sophie. It's not easy for me to speak to you."

"You seem to be doing fine. We've talked about so many things."

"No, Sophie. I am not doing fine. I'm having a very difficult time trying to tell you that I broke it off with Myra, much to my parents' chagrin."

"But..."

"Sophie, after the last time I saw you at Henry Street, I walked home in a daze. I'm impressed with you, uh, I mean I admire your commitment to your work."

"Thank you, but that doesn't explain..."

"I'm not expressing myself. Your gentle loveliness left me wondering what I was thinking in marrying Myra."

"But she is beautiful, Dan."

"Your beauty is much deeper. You radiate warmth and goodness..."

"But..."

"Let me speak, Sophie, while my nerve holds up. I can't be led into a marriage based on family status and convenience. My folks have been so fretful about my single life that I finally gave in to Myra's pursuit. She chased me, and I let myself be caught, but once I saw your depth, I knew that I couldn't go through with it."

"Why didn't you tell me sooner? You never gave any hint."

"I watched Ori in the play yard, you know, and…"

"You didn't like him?"

"Shh," he said, gently covering her lips with his hand. "I was worried that I couldn't be a father to someone else's child, and I didn't want to start anything with that fear. I had to be sure that I could be a good father to him."

"And…"

"And he is charming, and you are charming, and you are charming together!"

Sophie smiled, her face averted. *Could it be true?*

"I've been in love with you without admitting it. Lillian Wald knows it. Reuben seems to know it. And now you know it."

Sophie looked up at Daniel's face, shadowed in the emerging darkness, and her smile grew from the corners of her mouth outward. This time Daniel reached out and followed his impulse to touch those very corners, the genesis of her beaming face. She held his gaze while her smile broadened and her deep blue eyes crinkled. Daniel bent down to kiss her mouth, and she reached up to embrace his neck for her first kiss since Izzy left for war.

Stone steps led from the elegant formal gardens and fountains on the east side of the mansion across a terrace, and then to the swimming pool and cabana below. Sloping beyond the pool, massive bayberry clumps bordered a great lawn, separating the wild ocean beach from the decorum of the landscape.

Sophie sat by the side of the swimming pool late the next morning in one of the newly popular Westport Adirondack chairs. While talking with Ellie, she felt Daniel's presence nearby and focused on Ellie's face to avoid staring at him. Ori stood on the edge of the pool swinging his arms and yelling, "I'm going to jump now, Dan!" while Daniel stood in the pool close to the edge with his arms held out.

Sophie tensed and squeezed her fingernails into her palms so as not to turn and shout, "Careful, Ori." She knew that if Ori saw her panic, it might be the end of swimming for him.

"He's doing well, Sophie. It's okay. Daniel will watch out for Ori," said Ellie.

"I'll be most happy when they stop for the day. Maybe I should go inside. I can hardly keep myself from crying out."

Suddenly Ori screeched and Sophie jumped up. "Calm down, Sophie. He's having a good time. You haven't told me anything about last night."

"Ellie, he kissed me." Sophie reached for her friend's hand. "He wants to see more of me."

"And what did you say?" They both laughed.

# SEVEN

## September 1923

"**S**ophie, Sophie, come down here quick! There's a phone call for you."
The shout came from the front hall of the Henry Street house.

"I'm coming. Who is it?" Sophie asked as she pulled her robe over her nightgown and looked for her slippers. "I was just going to sleep."

"He sounds anxious, Sophie. I don't know who it is."

Sophie rushed down the stairs and put the receiver to her ear. "Hello?"

She could hardly distinguish Manny's voice on the other end. It seemed to her that he was crying. "Sophie. I'm at the synagogue. Sophie…"

"What, Papa Shapiro? Tell me."

"Meyer is no more. Your own papa is dead."

"What…what?"

"Meyer, my beloved friend, was working late at the bakery. It was his heart. They brought him here and I came."

"But my mother? Where is she?"

"Emma came here, and then went home. Don't worry, Sophie. I'll stay with him until the burial."

"I'll dress and be there as soon as I can." Sophie knew that she could waste no time in making the long trip by ferry and bus to New Jersey, and it was already eight in the evening. The family observed the Jewish tradition of burial within a twenty-four-hour period, and her father's

241

body had to be accompanied between the time of his death and the burial.

She held on to the banister for support as she made her way slowly up the creaking stairs. Ori was still sound asleep. She looked at him through clouded eyes and whispered, "Your *zaideh*. What will you do without your *zaideh*, my Ori?"

She stood in front of the open armoire unable to select something to wear. She searched for a black dress, but couldn't recall having one. She knew that her mother would see to that. She dressed with little awareness, her mind on Ori. I can't leave him here to wake up with me gone, and I can't bring him to Paterson in the cold of night.

She went down to the telephone to call Ellie. Maybe she could take Ori for the night. "Ellie, Ellie, my papa is gone. He's dead, Ellie. My papa." She could no longer hold in her tears.

"Sophie, stay there and we'll come for you and Ori. No, I'll ring Daniel. He's closer to you and he can take you on the ferry. We'll come for Ori. Stay there."

"I can manage to get to Paterson if you come for Ori."

"You can always manage, Sophie. That is who you are, but that's not the point. You need to be with people who love you. Pack up some things, and we'll ring Daniel and come for Ori." Sophie found herself holding the dead receiver in her hand for several moments until she realized she should replace it on the hook.

Upstairs again, she put some of her clothing in her valise and packed a separate case for Ori. She went to Miss Wald's room to ask that she watch Ori until the Farbers came. Miss Wald, still dressed and with a book in her hand, opened her door to see Sophie in tears, hugging herself and trembling. "Sophie, what happened?"

"My papa. My papa."

"Come here and sit." She guided Sophie to her settee and sat beside her. She reached out and pulled Sophie close to her as the young woman struggled to gain composure.

"Papa died. It was his heart. I need to go to him. Daniel is coming for me."

"Of course, you should go now. We can watch Ori for you."

"Ellie and Reuben are coming for him. Can you sit with Ori until they come?"

"Certainly, Sophie. What else can I do for you?"

"I don't know. I don't know. My papa is dead."

"You didn't expect it. He was well?"

"I thought so, but maybe I should have known."

They walked toward the door and into the hallway. Miss Wald embraced Sophie and walked her back to her bedroom.

Soon after, Daniel found her sitting on the edge of her bed with Ori, still asleep, cradled in her arms. "Come, sweetheart. Put Ori back in his bed until Ellie and Reuben get here. We'll take the Barclay Street Ferry to Hoboken."

"Daniel, Papa's dead. He had a heart attack. My papa."

Daniel drove his Packard onto the gangway of the ferry and they stayed in the car for the crossing. Sophie dabbed at her tears, and when Daniel reached to take her hand, she grasped it and took several deep breaths.

"Why is Mama at home?" Sophie said. "Why isn't she with Papa's body? The *hevra kadisha* must have washed and purified his body already."

"Excuse me, Sophie. The *hevra kadisha?*" asked Dan.

"I forget that you weren't brought up with the same old-world customs that I was. These are the 'holy society,' women who come to the home or the funeral parlor to ready the deceased for burial, to wash the dead person, wrap him in a white cloth, and pray. I'm grateful for Manny. Who would be with my papa if not him?"

"Izzy's father. He's your Papa's closest friend from the old country?"

"Yes. They were young men together in Lodz."

Sophie and Daniel drove up the Paterson Plank Road along the west side of the Hudson River and then west to Broadway and into Paterson. They went directly to the *shul* on Godwin Avenue and to the rooms behind the sanctuary where they found Manny, wearing his long white silk prayer shawl draped over his head and shoulders. He was fingering the blue tassels on its ends and praying over his linen-shrouded friend. As he rocked back and forth, Sophie heard him recite the Hebrew words associated with death.

"Sophie, my daughter," Manny cried as they embraced. Daniel slipped away into the next room while the mourners grieved.

Sophie broke from Manny's embrace. "I have to talk to Mama. Why isn't she here? She should be here with her husband. I can't understand."

"Ring her telephone," suggested Manny.

Sophie went into the room where Daniel was waiting and gave her mother's number to the operator.

"Mama, why aren't you here?"

"Rabbi Aronson was there, and he made arrangements for the afternoon at two o'clock."

"Yes, but why aren't you here?"

"Me? I told you. Rabbi Aronson made arrangements, and Manny is there. Why me? I have to prepare the house for people who will come after the burial service. What will people think if the house isn't clean? Who will make the plans for the food? Do you have what to wear? I'll bring you a dress."

Sophie hung up the receiver and sank into a cushioned wing chair. She hadn't the strength to confront her mother.

"What did she say, Sophie?" asked Daniel.

"Her house is more important than her husband. She is home cleaning the house! Cleaning the house!"

"Don't be quick to judge, sweetheart. Maybe it is too much for her to face now."

"I'll call Aunt Flora," she replied as she dialed her number.

As she suspected, Flora and Joe had Aaron with them, and they had made several phone calls, as did Mama Esther. Most of the family knew about the death and the time of the funeral service. The family would take care of everything.

"Daniel, you should go back to New York and rest for work tomorrow," Sophie said.

"I'll stay with you until the morning and doze on this davenport while you are with your father. Go, sweetheart. Be with Meyer." He paused and took her hand. "I wish I had known him."

Throughout the night Manny and Sophie alternated tending their beloved Meyer's body. When dawn broke, Daniel went to buy some *bialies* and cream cheese for their breakfast before leaving for New York.

The morning passed in quiet prayer, and then the entire family came for the service. The *shul* was packed, and people were standing on the street. Sophie was gratified, but not surprised at the huge number of mourners. All of the men from the Workmen's Circle were there, as were the former silk mill strikers from IWW Local 152. The Purity Bakery staff and all their customers were well represented.

A man whom Aaron didn't recognize approached Sophie and Aaron and said, "It seems that all of Paterson loved your papa."

Sophie stood with her arm around her little brother, who answered, "Papa was the King of Paterson."

After the service Sophie went to Emma's house with the other family members and mourners to pay the traditional visit. She was aghast at the care taken to arrange the rooms with splendor. There were extra chairs placed near the parlor furniture and in the dining room, and silver trays of food decorated the linen-clad dining table. Even though Sophie recognized the need for a "spread," she couldn't forgive her mother for avoiding her duty to her husband before his burial. *Flora and Esther could have done the preparations.*

Sophie turned to watch Emma greet her guests, wearing a fine navy blue silk dress, appropriate but evidently expensive. She flourished her lace handkerchief and dabbed at the corners of her eyes. She hugged her brothers and embraced the few women who were present. "Try the pickled herring from the S & Z Deli. Theirs is the best," she offered.

Cousin Bessie, whose small business selling corsets had launched Emma's now elegant clothing shop, tearfully stuffed lox canapés into her mouth. A few of the Workmen's Circle wives had come out of respect for Meyer, and they crowded together in the parlor with plates of cold cuts on their laps, whispering about the fashionable furnishings and the expensive ornaments.

Flora bustled in the kitchen with Esther and the hired girl from the delicatessen. The Abramowitz brothers adjourned to the back porch to avoid Meyer's workingmen friends. Meanwhile, Aaron and Uncle Joe huddled together on the back stoop wearing their wool sweaters against the early autumn air.

"Uncle Joe, can I sleep downstairs with you and Aunt Flora tonight?"

"Yah, Aaron. Your mama won't mind."

Sophie came outside to sit with them, still wearing her outer clothing. "It's cold," she said as she sat down. "Aaron, will you go and get me some tea?"

After he left Sophie cried, "How could she behave this way? She didn't pray over her husband before he was buried, and now she behaves like the bereaved wife. Did she even love my father?" Joe leaned over to embrace her, but was silent.

When Aaron came home from school the week after the funeral he found Emma cleaning the wardrobe. "What are you doing with Papa's clothes?" he asked.

"They are no use to me. Somebody who is needy will like them," she replied.

"But Mama, he died only a week ago. I went back to school only today, because you said we must stay home so that people will know we are mourning. You're getting rid of his things already?"

"No, Aaron. We stayed home because that is the Jewish tradition," she reiterated as she pushed another pair of trousers into a sack.

"I'd like to keep some of Papa's things. Can I pick some of his clothes?"

"What do you want with his old clothes? They wouldn't fit you. When you finish college, you'll be wearing new suits with a tie."

"I want to keep his gray derby, and I want his suspenders and a tie. I want some of his things from the box on top of the bureau, too."

"Take what you want, Aaron, but mind you, make sure you put it away somewhere."

Emma got up from the footstool to make room for her son to inspect the armoire. She brushed her palms together in her "I'm finished" manner, yet she squeezed a tear from her eye and hurried out of the room.

Aaron chose the hat, tie, suspenders, and a white shirt, things that Meyer wore on Sundays when the two of them went out together. Then he took the small inlaid wooden box from the dresser and brought the treasures to his room to inspect. He slouched down on the rug and leaned against his bed. *Papa, Papa. Why did you leave me?*

He took two small lapel pins from the box. One was gold. It said *Industrial Workers of the World* around the edges, and *IWW* above an image of the globe. There were gold stars on both sides of the *I*, and a third star between each *W* on the next line. Another pin said *IWW Local 152*. There was a pair of black cuff links with the same *IWW* on each one. He held the jewelry and turned the pieces over in his hand.

Papa never wore these. I wonder what they are, he thought. The boy replaced the jewelry and put the box in his drawer beneath a pile of sweaters. *I wonder if Sophie knows about these things?*

Aaron put Meyer's derby on his head. He brought the shirt to his nose, inhaled the familiar smell of his papa, and sobbed.

The next day Emma rang her daughter. "Sophie, I'm getting rid of Meyer's things. Aaron took his box with the IWW pins. I don't suppose you want anything?"

"Mama, so soon? I didn't think…"

"*Nu?* I should keep his old rags, his *shmatahs*, when I could use the space?"

"Mama, please wait until I come to see if there's anything I'd like to have. I'll be there on Sunday."

Sophie left Ori with the Shapiros when she went to visit her mother. "Where is my grandson?" Emma asked when she saw Sophie standing alone at the door.

"I thought he might be in the way while we look at things, so I left him with Esther and Manny."

"Always Esther and Manny." *That boy clings to Esther like a monkey around her legs.*

"You know why he spends more time with them."

"We won't talk about that now. Would you like to have something to eat? Sit down and we can talk."

"I'm sorry. I don't have time. Let me see the carton of things Papa saved. I'd like his certificates from the IWW and some of the papers that he saved about the strike."

"There is something from under the bed that I didn't look at." She handed Sophie a Zimmerman's Department Store suit box.

"Mama, I'm going to take this downstairs to Uncle Joe and Aunt Flora to look at."

"You can look here, no? You're angry?"

"Mama, I am so angry that I can't talk to you. How could you treat my father's life and death with so little respect? Your own husband of twenty-six years! You didn't sit *shiva*. You don't go to pray."

"I gave a nice party. Everyone came. Esther said that a young man brought you to the *shul*. You have a gentleman friend? A nice Jewish boy?"

"My friend Daniel is Jewish. I'm going now." Sophie picked up the box and left the flat to join her brother downstairs.

Emma stood by the door for a moment after Sophie walked out. I *never understood that girl from the time she was thirteen.* Then she walked slowly back to her kitchen, alone. She sat on one of the bentwood chairs and leaned her elbows on the enamel tabletop, resting her head in her palms. She recalled her litany of complaints, thinking that it is always something with her daughter. First she has a child out of wedlock, and then she goes off to live in a ghetto. *Now she picks on me.* Emma sighed and got up to resume discarding Meyer's possessions.

Sophie brought Meyer's box of mementos downstairs to her aunt and uncle's flat. After a kiss for each of them, she went into the spare bedroom and sat on the walnut slipper rocker with its embroidered seat. She felt at home in this cozy Victorian room with the rose-flowered wallpaper and lace curtains. Here, feeling the abundance of Aunt Flora's warmth, she began to explore Meyer's past.

She balanced the brown suit box on her lap, its cover bent at the corners and brittle with age. Taking care not to tear it, she lifted the cover slowly, revealing an array of yellowed papers. For a moment she sat still, inhaling the mustiness of memories. *Why did you abandon us?* She ached with missing her papa and grieved for the emptiness of life without him while she wondered how she would explain his death to Ori. She thought about Aaron left to find his way without his father and resolved to be a more motherly sister. Oh, *Papa. Papa.*

She finally turned her attention back to the box on her lap. Piece by piece she uncovered the remains of Meyer's life, his passport from Russia and the Declaration of Intention to become a citizen of the United States of America and "to renounce forever all allegiance and fidelity to any foreign prince…" She handled his Certificate of Naturalization. There were photos of his mother and father in the old country. They were seated on either side of a small table, his mother with abundant black hair parted in the middle and pulled back over her ears in waves. She was smiling gently into the camera, while his bearded father gazed with penetrating eyes into an unknown distance. *Is there a trace of Ori that I see in his great-grandfather's face? His mouth?*

Sophie picked up a packet of letters and saw that they were addressed from Emma in Poland. The tissue-paper page was written to Meyer in Yiddish. Translating the native tongue of her parents she read,

*My Love,*

*It is good you got out of Poland quickly. The conscription is getting worse, and soon Joe and Dave will have to leave Lodz or they will be forced into the Russian army.*

*Last time I wrote I was worried that maybe I would have to come to you in America sooner than we planned. Now I must leave here as soon as you can send the passage money. It will take time to get to Gdansk on foot, but Joe and Dave can be with me on this trip to the port. The three of us can manage the trip together. Mama suspects something when she looks at me. She will have terrible shame on her head if I don't leave soon.*

*Yours,*
*Emma*

Puzzled, Sophie inspected the date on the letter and on the envelope. She read the date with difficulty. September 22, 1897. *I was born on February 10, 1898.* Sophie held the letter in her shaking hand. She shut her eyes tight and tried to think through the timing.

She opened her eyes and shook her head. Mechanically, she lifted the box of memorabilia from her lap and leaned over to place it on the floor near the rocker. She went into the kitchen with the letter. "Uncle Joe? Did you know this?" she said as she appeared in the kitchen, showing him the letter and envelope.

Joe saw that her face was pale and that she was trembling. "What, Sophie?"

"Look at this letter," she said, holding the fragile sheet of tissue paper out to him. "Did you know this all the time?"

It didn't take Joe a second to realize what Sophie had found.

"How can this be? She had the same love for Papa as I had for Isador, yet she couldn't accept me or my child. And they lied to me all these years. I wasn't born in Lodz. I was born right here in Paterson. When did they marry?"

"Sit here, *Liebe.* Flora, you should hear this too. We all sit. There was no time to marry. Meyer's name was on the conscription list, and he had to run. No one knew about her condition. Emma herself didn't know when he left that she was in the family way."

"But Uncle, why didn't they tell me? Why did Mama punish me for the same thing she did?"

"I only know that Emma wanted it that way. I had to promise not to tell anyone, not even Flora. Meyer, too, wanted to tell you, but Emma…well, Emma was ashamed."

# EIGHT

## October 1923

Sophie normally enjoyed the thrill of the Third Avenue El racing high above the city streets. She boarded on The Bowery and rode all the way up Third Avenue to within a few blocks of Ellie's house on Ninety-second Street. The rumbling elevated train passed so close to tenement buildings that she could look into the windows. The vibrations of metal on metal and the screeching brakes thrust her forward in her seat. She felt the pulse of the city in her gut.

This day Sophie was brooding all the way to Eleanor's house on the train, oblivious to its rumbling. Three months had passed since Dan had declared his love. Ori had grown to rely on him, and Sophie dreamed of marriage. Now she was uncertain of his intention.

She left the train and walked a measured pace to the Farbers' home, reluctant to mar Ellie's joy in the forthcoming birth of her child. She loved Eleanor and was grateful to partake of her privileged life. She had never envied her friend's wealth or attractiveness, but now Ellie had the one thing that Sophie wanted—marriage.

Sophie knocked and entered the Farbers' unlocked door, calling out to her friend, "Ellie, I'm here."

Ellie had been sitting in a chromed-steel and red-leather chair in the nearby salon. Sophie wondered about the modern furniture that she and Reuben had selected in Paris for their home. She resonated with its spare lines as little as she did their Picassos.

Sophie shook off her gloom, gave Ellie an impish grin, and cradled an imaginary baby. "Baby's here. Isn't she adorable?"

"You think I'm carrying a girl?"

"Who knows? Let's go upstairs to the baby's room. You fixed it up so beautifully. Careful now, Ellie. Let me help you up."

As they walked up the wide carpeted stairway together, Sophie reached to support her friend's arm. "I'm not all that fragile," said Ellie.

"No, I wasn't either when I was carrying Ori, but I feel very fragile now."

"What is it, Sophie?" asked Eleanor as she propped up her bulging abdomen with her arms and sat down on the step. "Sit here."

Sophie hesitated and her lower lip began to tremble.

Ellie leaned over her large belly and tried to hug her friend. "Tell me what's hurting you."

"It's Daniel. I think he's getting cold feet. I haven't even met his family yet, so I wonder if he will ask me to marry him. For a while I was so certain, but...I don't know. Do you think his family objects?"

Ellie leaned back on the riser and eyed her friend with squinty eyes. "To you? To my remarkable, dearest friend? I doubt it. They don't even know you."

"But I'm not from their social set, and I have a child."

"It hasn't made a difference to Dan, has it?"

"Not yet, but last week he came to the Shapiros' with me. Manny met him before the funeral last month, you know, and he wanted us to bring Daniel to meet Esther. Aaron was there, too. It must have been very hard for them to see me with another man, not their son."

"They are loving people, and I think they realize that Ori needs a father."

"Esther did take me aside to tell me how much she likes Daniel. Ori showed him Izzy's room. He still calls it Papa's room. It must have been a shock for Daniel to see that side of my life. He was quiet on the way home. He hasn't mentioned it since then."

"Sophie, he needs time..."

"But Ellie, what if he doesn't want someone else's child? What if he can't bring himself to marry me? Maybe I should break it off. I don't want

Ori to be hurt. It's been four months. He should know by now. Don't you think so?"

"But he only recently met Esther and Manny. Give him a little more time, Sophie."

"Did I hear voices?" interrupted Reuben as he jogged down the last flight of stairs to where the friends were sitting. "Sophie, what should we name this little darling?" he said as he sat down next to his wife and patted her stomach.

Sophie smiled at Reuben while noting his adoration for Ellie. She remembered how Ellie and her mother, not her beloved Isador, had seen her through her own pregnancy.

"Reuben, Sophie is talking about breaking it off with Dan," said Ellie.

"Wait a minute! Why would you think about that, Sophie?" asked Reuben.

"I took Daniel to meet Esther and Manny. He saw Izzy's house, and he saw Ori in his father's bedroom. I think it was too much for him. I don't think he wants someone else's family."

"Is that how you feel about yourself and Ori? That you are someone else's family? Do you and Ori belong to a man who passed away years ago?"

Sophie sat up straight and looked at Reuben. She tilted her head and held out her hands, palms up as if to weigh the idea. "Well I didn't mean…I hadn't thought…No, Daniel is real to Ori, and Ori loves him."

"And what about you, Sophie? Are you still someone else's family?" asked Reuben.

The questioned caused Sophie to reflect. "A family is more than a child and a husband. A family is a way of life."

"A way of life?" asked Ellie.

"Besides my relatives, Henry Street Settlement is my way of life. In a way, the people who work for the neighborhood are my sisters, and they're a part of Ori's family, too. I've been afraid to question Daniel's way of life for me. It's not only about him accepting me."

Sophie began to cry. Reuben pulled out his handkerchief and moved to sit on her other side, encircling her shoulders. "What if we aren't right for each other?" she sobbed.

"Do you think that he wouldn't support your work?" asked Ellie.

"I don't know, but we haven't talked about it. I can't give up my work."

"Sophie, that changes things. I thought that you would stay home once you were married. Oh, I go to Henry Street to work on the charitable foundation, but that's not the same. And now that we are planning a family…"

"But Ori has never been in the way of my work."

"Won't you want Ori to go to school with our children? He can't stay at the Henry Street child program forever," said Ellie.

"I hadn't thought that far."

"Sophie, I guess you have more to think about," said Reuben. "Maybe you had better do it before either of you is hurt more than you would be if you ended it now."

"Sophie blew her nose and blurted, "End it now? But I love him!"

# December 1923

Sophie was dressed in an elegant teal silk chemise that Simone Reichman had given her as a gift while she and Ori waited in the Henry Street dining room for Dan's arrival. They were going to meet Dan's parents.

Sophie was too nervous to drink the tea she had poured, and Ori, who was coloring a picture, got up again to ask, "Mama, when is he coming? I remember what you told me."

"What is that, Ori?"

"I must be extra polite to Mr. and Mrs. Sheinman. I'll use my best manners to make Dan proud."

"I know you will. You are my beautiful boy."

"I hear him, Mama. I'll go downstairs to see."

Sophie got up and smoothed her dress. She had recently cut her thick wavy hair into the popular French bob with a side part that came just below her ears, but she was still reaching without thought to tuck loose wisps into her bun. *What if they don't like me?*

She looked up to see Dan grinning at her. He gave her the eye and said, "You look smashing, my girl!"

Ori followed behind him and giggled, "Yes, Mama, smashing."

"I'm nervous, Dan. What if they don't like me?"

"They like you already after hearing all I have to say about you…and Ori," he answered, reaching for Ori's hand. "They are very anxious to meet you, and, you know, I think they are a little nervous, too."

"Why would they be at all nervous?"

"They know how much I love you, and they want you to like them. After all, Sophie, they're parents like any other. Is it the house? The money?"

"No, Dan. I don't think so. I'm accustomed to that with the Reichmans."

"Can we go up to your room?" Sophie gave him a questioning look but led the way, with Ori on her heels. Once inside, Daniel said, "Sophie, sit here next to me on the bed for a minute. I have a Hanukkah gift for you. I have one for you, too, Ori, at my house." Ori climbed onto his own bed opposite Sophie's.

"Oh, Dan, adults don't give gifts on Hanukkah! I don't have anything for you."

"This one time, I want to give you a gift," he said as he reached into his jacket pocket and withdrew a small box. He opened it slowly to reveal an exquisite Cartier diamond ring. Looking into her eyes he reached for her left hand and asked, "May I?"

Tentatively, she put forth her hand and he slipped the diamond onto her finger. She looked up at his questioning face and said, "Yes, Daniel, yes."

Ori jumped off of his bed. "I want to see, Mama."

"This ring means that Daniel wants the three of us to be a family and live together."

"Can we, Mama? Can we?"

"Yes siree!" said Daniel.

# January 1924

Flora's usual calm was ruffled as was Joe's, but they appeared composed as they sat at their kitchen table, nodding while Emma paced back and forth.

"Finally she brings him to me! I knew she was seeing someone when Meyer died last fall. I asked about him, and what kind of answer did I get? 'My friend is Jewish,'" she said. "Now she calls to bring him here! And she's coming with him next week."

"But Emma, did you expect more?" said Joe, thinking about Sophie's anger over the funeral and most of all how Emma had concealed the story of her birth. Joe didn't mention that the Shapiros had invited the two of them to meet Daniel and celebrate one of the nights of Hanukkah together.

Flora lowered her voice to a whisper and said, "Sit. Sit here and have some schnapps." She proffered a bottle and a shot glass.

"Schnapps? From where you got schnapps? You got maybe some rye bread to eat with the schnapps?" asked Emma as she sat at the table. "I don't take my schnapps without a dunk of bread."

"Yes, I have bread, and you know where I get my schnapps, too," said Flora as she smoothed the red Christmas tablecloth and laid out a napkin."

"I don't want to know from where you get it."

"You know our brother Dave gets it from his friend at the Cotton Club," said Joe. "You'll make a nice dinner for Sophie and her friend?"

"Yah. You and Flora can come? With Aaron that will be six. A good number, no?"

Joe nodded. *I better remind Aaron not to let on that he knows Dan.*

Emma was quiet as she tore off bits of rye bread and dipped them into the schnapps. The flush of anger left her cheeks, and she began to breathe more slowly. She looked down at the table, taking note for the first time of the tablecloth. "Christmas, still, Flora? You didn't put Christmas away yet?"

"It's only the first week of January, Emma. My mother always left our Christmas decorations up in January. A little festivity goes a long way," Flora replied.

"Yah. I suppose so. What should I make for them? Pot roast?"

"Pot roast is good, Emma," said Flora.

"You'll be there and Aaron and the two of them," said Emma, knowing that Flora and Joe would make a good buffer should the conversation go awry. "I'll need to get help in the store on a Saturday."

The Packard's wipers removed the lightly falling snow from the windshield as Sophie and Daniel drove off the car ferry and headed north to Paterson. Sophie was wrapped in a heavy green plaid woolen blanket over her winter coat, but her left hand was peeking out. She had removed her glove to look at her engagement ring and remind herself once again that she was to marry Daniel.

Sophie was uncomfortable with the size of the ring. She had imagined something simple, and much smaller, but Daniel wanted her to have a Cartier design, something like his mother's ring.

"I do appreciate this ring, Daniel, but I can't get used to the size of the diamond."

"I know, sweetheart. We'll have to work out any other differences that we have about what you see as ostentation, but for now, enjoy your ring. It's special, because that's how I feel about you. I've never known a woman who demands so little."

"Don't underestimate what I demand, Daniel Sheinman. Fidelity, companionship, and compromise are far more valuable than diamonds. Remember all of your promises about Henry Street. I'm holding you to it, you know. I do plan to work there after we're married, at least a few days a week…And I want to bring Ori to see his friends."

"I love you very much, Sophie. You might change your mind about Henry Street after we're married."

"I don't think so, Dan."

"We'll work it out. I promise. We'll also get over this hump with your mother. We solved some other issues, didn't we?"

Sophie nodded and let the tension go from her stomach. "You'll charm her, and my aunt and uncle will keep things jolly. Remember that she doesn't know you've met Aaron."

"I know how you hate deception. This isn't easy for you, Sophie."

When the couple parked in front of number 749 East Twenty-sixth Street, they reached for each other and embraced. "I'll be patient with her. I promise," said Sophie.

Aaron heard the car door slam and greeted his sister and her husband-to-be before they climbed the outer steps to the door. When they entered the flat, Sophie inhaled the memorable smell of simmering pot roast with its bay leaves and sweet carrots. The aroma with all of the early childhood memories it evoked helped her to feel more charitable toward her mother.

Emma rushed to greet them at the door, but stood apart for a moment to look at her beautiful daughter and her tall, urbane, future son-in-law.

Sophie rushed to fill the gap. "Mama, this is Daniel Sheinman."

Daniel bent over to Emma and took her hands in his. "Mrs. Epstein, I've been looking forward to meeting you." He sniffed the air. "Is that pot roast I smell?"

"Yah, pot roast. Sophie knows my pot roast. Please come in and sit down. Flora and Joe will be here soon. Where is Ori tonight?"

"He's with Esther and Manny."

Emma squeezed her lips together.

"Hey, Aaron. Sophie tells me you dig cars. Seen any spiffy new ones lately?" Daniel was quick to smooth things over in the jargon of the day.

"I notice you have a nifty Packard. I'd like to ride in it sometime."

"Aaron, mind your manners," said Emma.

"And you shall! Maybe even drive it. It's fine, Mrs. Epstein."

"Daniel, can I really?"

"Why not?"

Flora and Joe arrived soon after and were happy to see the couple again, but they were careful not to mention the Hanukkah celebration.

"Sophie, may I see your ring?" asked Flora, who had seen Emma staring at the ring without comment.

Sophie took Flora aside and whispered, "It's a little too big, no?"

"Don't be foolish. Dan gave you a beautiful ring, and you should enjoy it!"

Sophie wore a soulful smile, and her eyes misted.

"Are you about to cry, my niece?" asked Flora. "What is it, dear?"

Now one teardrop did escape from the corner of her eye, and she brushed it aside. "Oh, I'm so fortunate to have a man like Daniel who knows and loves me in spite of my foolishness, my pigheadedness and…"

"Don't talk about yourself like that! He loves you because you are lovable. You have a beautiful soul, a blessed *neshima*. I know that, even if I am not Jewish!"

Sophie smiled then. She turned her softly glowing face to Flora and kissed her.

"You are like a daughter to me, Sophie. The daughter we couldn't have."

"What are you two doing in there," called Joe. "Time to sit down to eat."

The group sat down to dinner. Emma had laid out her fine Limoges china and new sterling silver utensils. Irish linen draped the table. While Sophie held her fork midair, glimmers of the old tarnished silver plate from Poland and the worn rose pattern on Emma's crackled china came briefly to mind. Sophie squeezed her eyes to shut out memories of the warmth that once enveloped her family...*sitting at that old oak table on Fair Street...long before their fighting and anger. When Papa was alive.*

She returned to the present and noticed Daniel eyeing her quizzically.

The conversation had turned to the wedding plans, as Sophie thought they would. She and Dan had talked about it with his parents, resolving their differing expectations about a society wedding.

"*Nu*, when is the wedding? You have a date maybe?" asked Emma.

"Mama, we are thinking about a June wedding before people leave town for the summer. June twenty-second."

*Only the wealthy leave town for the summer, not the Epstein family.* "You think maybe of the Sheinmans?"

"Yes, they often go to Grandview where they have a house, but—"

"I see," interrupted Emma.

Sophie reddened and felt a wave of prickly warmth spread throughout her body when she sensed the turn of the conversation.

"Mrs. Epstein," Dan quickly added. "We had in mind two wedding parties. There are ample friends and relatives on both sides of the Hudson to manage two celebrations."

"Mama, I have many friends in Manhattan from the eight years I've been living there, and we—"

"You don't have friends here in Paterson?" said Emma.

"Mama, please let me speak."

"Tell us about your plans, kids," said Joe.

"Of course, Mama, you may not want to do this. I know we haven't been close these years, but we want to get married in New York and then..." Sophie hesitated as she noticed her mother's lips tighten. "We want our close families at the wedding service—you and the Shapiros and the uncles and their families. Dan is an only child, but he has aunts, uncles, and cousins. After the service we can have a lunch at the temple."

"My mother would like to have an evening reception at our house for a wider number of friends," Dan hastened to say. "We expect the Paterson clan to come, too."

"But Mama, I thought maybe, well, maybe you could host a reception here, so our friends wouldn't have to travel to Manhattan. I understand that maybe you don't want any part…"

"You are my daughter, Sophie. I will give a big party for your wedding. That's settled," she said as she brushed her palms together.

Much later, after an evening of small talk, Sophie and Dan left for New York. Joe turned to Emma. "I know what you are thinking. You want to give a party in that house. The one near Eastside Park on Wall Avenue that you went to look at."

"Ma, you didn't tell me that you are buying a new house!" shouted Aaron.

"I was only looking, but things have changed. I can't have a party for Sophie in our little flat."

Ma, you could have it at Temple Emanuel. It's not too far from here," said Aaron.

"You don't know from what you are saying, son."

Early Sunday morning, Joe and Flora went upstairs to talk to Emma. They had a plan to present to her, and they decided that the time had come to talk about it. Their idea would be good for everyone, except maybe Aaron. But that, too, could be arranged to suit him.

Emma answered the door wearing a housecoat. "Joe, Flora, I didn't expect you to come up this morning," she said as she pulled her housecoat around her and sat down at the kitchen table.

"You'll offer us some tea, Emma?"

"Yah, tea I have on the stove," she said as she got up to pour them a cup. "You have something to say so early in the morning?"

"Emma, Flora and I have a proposition."

"A proposition?" Emma asked as she poured tea.

"Yah. Sit Emma. We have been putting aside a little money. We had some good luck."

Flora nodded.

"You play the market, Joe?"

"A little, but we got out. We don't like to take chances. But Emma, listen. We want to buy this house from you. We saved enough to put down on the house, and we can get a mortgage for the rest. The rent from the other flat would help."

Emma pushed her tea aside and leaned forward toward Joe. Her eyes widened as she began her internal calculations.

"You see, Emma. You own this building outright. If we buy it, you might have plenty money to buy the house near the park."

"You don't have to explain that to me!" she replied.

Emma remained at the kitchen table after Flora and Joe went downstairs. When the thought of owning the coveted house on Wall Avenue became a reality, she began to look inward. *Ay, meine kofp. So much regret. My shame and Sophie's.* She prayed that the upcoming marriage would ease her burden. Emma was still tortured with her memory of that night in Lodz, her forwardness, and her unforgivable behavior.

She envisioned the exact scenario over and over again. *Meyer went out of the shtetl to the edge of the forest on that summer night where he plotted in secret with the other socialist workers against the mill owners. I waited by the path to see his lantern after the others left, and then pulled out my hairpins and shook out my long brown curls to play in the summer breeze. How could a proper Jewish girl do this?*

Emma flinched as she recalled how forward she had been, how much she had wanted him to love her, and to take her away from that crowded *shtetl* to America.

Unable to stop herself, she continued to replay the scene. *He saw me in the light of the lantern. He rushed to my side, put his arm around my tiny waist, and guided me a few steps into the woods, where he placed the lantern on the ground and embraced me with both arms. I put my head on his shoulder, and he buried his face in all of that freshly washed hair.*

"Ah," she said aloud.

*We stood that way for a while and then I let him lead me farther into the woods. I didn't resist. I made it easy for him. After that he asked if he could approach Papa about marriage. Too late, I think. Too late.*

Emma put her head down into her folded arms. For the first time in so many years, she cried. Her body heaved with the release of years of guilt and shame.

# June 1924

**E**mma recalled the April day two months ago that she had taken possession of her Wall Avenue home. She had gazed up from the sidewalk, key in hand, ready to survey her property. The three-story brick façade with a columned portico above the front door delighted her. This is a house for a *Somebody*, a person of importance, she had thought.

She strode up the marble steps inspecting the terraced lawns on either side of the walkway. Red azaleas bloomed beneath the windows, and a plaque on the white lantern post proclaimed the house number "199." Emma held her breath as she approached the front door to her new home for the first time, then exhaled audibly as the knob turned beneath her hand.

Once inside the entry hall, her steps echoed across the bare hardwood floors of the spacious front room, through the dining room with its built-in sideboards, to the kitchen where she turned on each appliance with a satisfied smile. Modern, clean, new, she thought.

She retraced her steps to visit the sitting room on one side of the main front room and across it to the library on the other side. She walked out to the screened summer porch along the right side of the house.

Still entranced, Emma gazed at the second-floor landing, reached by a winding mahogany staircase that could be accessed at the front entry hall or by the simple servants' flight in the back of the house. She stroked the newel post and then floated from room to room, feeling the textures of the wallpapers, admiring the wood below the chair rails, and noting the ornate crown moldings. *Mine. My own.*

Sophie's wedding party will be everything that she should have from a mother who is an important businesswoman in Paterson, she thought as she began to plan where her furniture would be placed when delivered. *Sure, I had to borrow to furnish the house, but with my earnings and investments, I'll soon pay it off.* She was satisfied with her good decision making.

The only thing that spoiled her complete delight was the unfinished rear yard, a simple lawn with nondescript hedges. She dreamed of flowers and a patio, exquisite outdoor furniture, maybe a gazebo. That would have to wait, but she resolved to replace the existing lawn with lush landscaping, fit for a house of this stature.

Since that April day, Emma had mustered all of her resources to pull off the extravaganza she hoped would impress her guests, the Sheinman family among them.

On the afternoon of June twenty-ninth, one week after Sophie and Dan's formal wedding and reception in the Sheinmans' New York mansion, she stood couture-ready in anticipation of her guests. *Ach! I must relax.* She waved her hands quickly before her as if to ward off any possible unpleasantness and to reset her escalating emotions.

*My manor is not so grand as the Sheinman mansion,* she thought, *but even with all her money, Iris looks like a lump in her clothes. A drop-waist silk Worth evening dress straight from Paris yet. I got more attention in a Lanvin copy.*

Aaron called to her from his upstairs bedroom window, where he could see the Abramowitz cousins walking toward the house.

"They're coming, Mama," he shouted. Emma shivered. She checked the hall mirror to adjust her dress, pulled back her shoulders, and opened the door to face her family. *Thank God for my good legs with these new short styles.*

Sophie, Dan, and Ori arrived just as the Abramowitz families approached on foot from their nearby homes. Joe and Flora drove up in their Ford with Esther and Manny in the backseat.

"Mama, there's *Bubbeh* Esther," said Ori as he ran to meet them.

Charlotte embraced Sophie. A Bryn Mawr graduate, she had married well and lived in Manhattan not too far from the Sheinmans. Her husband, Mort Offenberg, trailed with their toddler, Rebecca, in tow.

The big house began to fill up and Emma was everywhere at once, smiling, preening, offering refreshments and a tour of the house.

Eleanor, Charlotte, and Sophie found a quiet place in the library where they relived the wedding ceremony and reception of last Sunday, but Emma soon found them.

"Sophie, come. Meet my guests," she said, dragging Sophie by the arm toward the dining room buffet where several of Paterson's Jewish elite were congregated.

Sophie looked back at her cousin and close friend, rolled her eyes, and followed Emma.

"This is my Sophie," Emma said to each person, squeezing Sophie's arm to encourage her forward. When five-year-old Ori appeared at his mother's side, Emma paused and said, "...and this is her son, Ori, from her first marriage. You remember poor Isador who died a hero in the war."

Sophie smiled and presented herself with the charm that Emma desired.

"Emma, we didn't know you had such a beauty!" they oozed while she, in apparent ignorance of Sophie's irritation, beamed and turned her daughter toward other guests.

Sophie bent down and whispered into Ori's ear, "I see *Bubbeh* Esther over in that corner with no one to talk to her."

"And she's eating cake," Ori said, heading in her direction.

When all of the introductions had been endured, Sophie went back to revisit Charlotte and Eleanor. They saw her face, red and stiffened, with eyes wide and glaring.

"Oh dear," said Charlotte. "I know that look."

"What happened?" asked Eleanor. "You look furious."

"What happened? What do you think happened? She introduced Ori as my son from my first marriage, not even as her own grandson. Marriage. She can't accept that I wasn't married to Izzy."

"I thought that she and Ori had become closer," said Charlotte.

"No. She doesn't seem to have the *bubbeh* instinct, so he is content with Esther."

The friends commiserated for a while longer, and then Sophie exchanged her scowl for a smile and left them to greet her other family and friends.

Charlotte leaned over to whisper in Ellie's ear. "She never mentioned the letter to Aunt Emma, the one she wrote to Uncle Meyer when she was with child in Balut."

Ellie nodded. "I don't understand how Emma can be self-righteous when she did the same as her daughter. No wonder Sophie is so frustrated with her."

The doorbell rang, and Emma passed the young women on her way to answer it.

"Iris, Max. Welcome to my home. Let me get you something to drink after your drive from New York."

"We're glad to be here, Emma," said Mr. Sheinman. "It was a splendid wedding ceremony, and now your generous reception."

"Max, the party in your home was everything Sophie and Daniel could have wished for. Please, I see Dan talking to some of my friends. Let me introduce you."

Emma took Iris's elbow and guided her into the great front room, handing a glass of champagne from the buffet to each of them.

Ori noticed his new grandparents with Emma and ran to greet them. Iris handed the champagne glass to her husband as she bent to embrace the boy.

# NINE

## May 1925

Emma chose a hopeful spring day to visit the Garment District's showrooms where copies of the latest Parisian couture were available at wholesale for hungry fashion buyers. She was among the throng of store owners who came to select their new fall lines.

Emma had walked from Penn Station to Seventh Avenue where she found herself in the now familiar midst of a great building boom. New high-rise buildings for garment manufacturing and showrooms were in various stages of completion, causing thunderous construction noise and windblown dust. Emma put a protective handkerchief over her nose and looked up to see the construction high overhead. A worker in his bib overalls and peaked cap sat precariously on a girder with a sandwich in his hand. He gazed straight ahead into space and took a bite.

Almost one hundred new buildings had been erected and rented since 1920, making New York one of the world's leading garment manufacturing cities. Emma smiled inwardly, anticipating the familiar argot of other newly successful Jewish immigrants who had become a majority among the members of the rag or *shmatah* trade.

She smiled as she absorbed the hubbub and the bustle of the side streets where Ford trucks delivered material and loaded finished garments, frequently blocking traffic. Horns honked, and deliverymen pushed and shoved their way between parked vehicles. Push boys, elbows to the crowd, shoved racked garments through the streets, making life difficult for pedestrians, but Emma didn't care.

"Hey, boy," she shouted, when one of them bumped into her. She reveled in the banter and in carving a place for herself among the buyers. She flushed in her eagerness to handle the newly designed garments, and she hastened to the showroom floor. A silk tulle evening dress, a velvet coat, a beaded lace tea dress, and most elegant of all, a black silk crepe evening dress with bands of Oriental patterned gold lamé caught her eye. She fingered the gold lamé and closed her eyes. *I wish I could see my own Sophie in this dress.* Emma chased away the fantasy and let the fabric drop. She picked up her pencil, thought about which of her clients might buy which garment, and began to fill in her order.

After she struggled to make her selections from among the replicas of the glorious new Parisian styles, she decided she would need to return another day to select daytime dresses and lingerie. Now it was time for her treat, a stop at Horn and Hardart's Automat.

For her, a trip to Manhattan was only complete when she savored a cup of their famous New Orleans-style drip coffee and a slice of cherry pie. Emma still thrilled at the bank of windows, each displaying an individual portion of pie, cake, or a sandwich, most of which could be had by depositing a mere nickel in the slot and lifting the glass door to remove the serving. She took her meal to a long table and sat down amid a crowd of office workers, men and women alike, rich and poor as well.

I'll sit here for a minute and rest with my coffee, and then see what B. Altman and Bergdorf are showing, she thought. Her clientele didn't often visit New York to shop, but she always told them, "I bring you the best couture from New York, so you should look as glamorous and up to date as the Warburg, Loeb, and Schiff women. I know exactly what they sell in their fancy Fifth Avenue department stores, and I have it right here just for you."

After lunch Emma was quick to hail a cab for Wall Street, where she intended to go to the visitors' gallery of the New York Stock Exchange. *Why not see how my money is traded?* She sat back in the plush interior of the taxi as it wended its way down Sixth Avenue to Church Street, and then walked with a determined stride toward 11 Wall Street where the new Exchange building had been erected in 1922.

Emma slowed to a tentative pace and then resumed her stride after reassuring herself. *People should see I belong here. I know where I'm going.* After a few more steps she arrived at the imposing façade. She peered up at the six Corinthian columns, took a deep breath, straightened her posture, and walked in.

The Garage, as the trading floor was known, closed at three o'clock PM, and she had planned to be there for closing. Her hands began to tingle and she felt light headed as she walked up the steps and into the grand arena of capitalism. The New York Stock Exchange! In the packed visitors' gallery she stood elbow to elbow with people who were all scouring the screens that displayed quotations from the ticker tape. Miles of ticker tape crinkled underfoot as the traders scurried from post to post around the perimeter of the vast floor, delivering buy and sell orders. *My order could be among them.*

A hush came over the visiting crowd as Mr. William R. Crawford, superintendent of the mechanical department of the New York Stock Exchange, walked into the gallery a moment before the market's close for the day to greet the visitors and explain the trading below.

"Shh," Emma said to those around her as she strained to hear him enumerate the Exchange's statistics.

"Five hundred miles of ticker tape for every million shares bought or sold! All those unraveled rolls of narrow white paper register every trade. There are eleven hundred forty-five telephonists, five hundred page boys, two hundred eighty tube attendants, and two hundred clerks. These, all in the service of nine hundred brokers, each with a seat on the Exchange."

It was hard for her to take in all of the activity on this first visit. Then one man whooped and jumped into the air. "RCA up again!" Thanks to God I didn't sell, she thought.

Mr. Crawford left the gallery and advanced across the padded floor of the Exchange, nodding to the famous, until he reached and ascended the rostrum that was suspended in midair from the south wall. He picked up his hand-tooled gavel, paused, and then banged it against the fluted gong, a resounding order to close trading for the day. While the hubbub didn't stop immediately, it tapered off until the floor finally cleared.

Pummeled along by the departing crowd, Emma found herself on the street, her cloche pushed back on her head. She needed to find a place to recover her poise before leaving for home, and she recalled a conversation about Trinity Church with one of her clients. Its tall Gothic spire at Broadway and Wall Street was an unmistakable beacon. Emma slowed her pace as she approached the church, unsure whether a Jew would be welcome, but the bronze door was open and she peered inside. It was empty. Uncomfortable about entering any church, her fatigue won, and she sat in the last row on the farthest corner where she could take a breather and straighten her hat and suit, oblivious to the architectural beauty surrounding her.

She mused about the Stock Exchange and recalled the men scurrying across the floor from broker to broker, perhaps carrying her order. *I'll make more money than I ever dreamed!* Her eyes closed briefly, and her countenance softened as a quiet smile appeared.

In this mood of contentment, she thought of her two children, her little grandson, Ori, and Sophie's new baby on the way. She rarely saw Sophie's family, and Aaron at eleven years was more often with Flora and Joe than at home. *They'll come around when I have more to offer them.* She imagined that the stock market investments would elevate her position so that Aaron would go to college and be proud to bring his wealthy friends home for a visit. Sophie would bring her family and even her in-laws to visit Emma's own grand manor.

# August 1925

**D**aniel and Sophie's first child was born on August 19, 1925. Both sides of the family were invited to her naming ceremony, which was to take place at their home on the last Sunday of the month so that Emma could attend without having to close her shop.

Sophie had been adamant about owning a more conservative home than Ellie and Reuben. She told Daniel, "It hurts me to think that we have so much when others are needy. It's difficult to come from the poverty of Henry Street to our home."

Daniel agreed, but both had wanted to be near the Farbers on East Ninety-second Street. They had decided on a three-story brownstone row house, less grand than that of their friends' detached mansion. Emma greatly admired this home built in 1898 on Carnegie Hill, but Sophie was ambivalent.

It was the architecture and the location near Central Park that most impressed Emma, but she was unsure of the décor. Whereas she had selected copies of European period pieces for her Wall Avenue home, Sophie's décor, counter to her own cluttered mid-nineteenth century taste, was American. Corresponding to her love of nature, Sophie had chosen flowing curved lines with asymmetrical arrangements of forms and patterns—grasses, lilies, vines, and the like. Her home made a statement that was unique in her mother's experience, creating a puzzling and daunting impression on her.

Emma detected a hint of the old Sears catalog oaken furniture, but the cabinetry was handcrafted with inlay, much finer than her old catalog pieces. There was a copper fire screen and a tiled fireplace. There were stained-glass lamps and even a stained-glass window. Sophie had chosen very plain-looking pottery to ornament her shelves, not the silver Emma desired. Nothing about her daughter's possessions spoke of luxury to Emma. It bewildered her.

She couldn't explain her feelings, but she knew that when she entered her daughter's home a terrible longing overcame her. It was part of her desperate craving for style and wealth that had haunted her since her childhood in Lodz. Now she wondered if she had been wrong about her conception of elegance. Perhaps other wealthy New Yorkers decorated in this understated style.

These thoughts plagued her as usual when she and Flora and Joe arrived first at the party. Sophie greeted them at the door and she ushered them into the parlor on the right of the entry where Dan and Ori were seated at an oak game table. Ori was studying a picture book. He looked up and said, "Hello, *Bubbeh*" when he saw Emma.

Flora went to Ori and kissed him on the top of his head. He looked up at her and reached for a hug. Joe sat on a sofa and Daniel joined him. Sophie brought baby Molly to Emma, who gingerly took the infant in her arms and went to sit on a sofa opposite the men.

The doorbell rang, and there was a "rap, rap," a pause, and a "rap, rap, rap" on the door. Ori knew his *zaideh's* familiar knocking pattern, and he ran to open the door for Esther and Manny. He reached up to hug his *Bubbeh* Esther, who bent to enfold him in her arms, warm from the August sun. Manny, strong and wiry, laughed and crouched to pick up the boy.

"*Zaideh*, your mustache is longer! Look at it twist," he cried as he reached to embrace his grandpa.

"I let it grow only for you to twist, my child."

Soon the Sheinman grandparents arrived from Murray Hill, and Emma readily gave up her granddaughter to Iris. Dan's father, Max, joined the men for a cigar in the library across the hall. Manny hoisted Ori onto his shoulders, at six years almost too big for a piggyback, and they joined the other men. The women remained in the parlor.

Emma withdrew into self-reflection, thinking that she had never seen Sophie happy like this. There had been the ever-present conflict about Meyer's socialist beliefs during her teenage years, and then Sophie left for school. She hardly knew her grown daughter. *And the boy hugs Esther like his own mother.*

Sophie observed her mother's mournful look with tenderness.

# TEN

## June 1926

**B**y the seventh grade, Aaron had outgrown his boyhood mischief and was an avid reader, but to Emma's chagrin, most of his reading matter consisted of auto magazines, not the loftier books she had hoped for. He had a well-worn copy of the *Automobile Trade Journal* borrowed from Sal. He collected automobile ads from Emma's magazines, and he spent most of his free time after school at Sal's garage.

Daniel had given him a copy of *The Great Gatsby*, the one book he seemed to enjoy, returning every night to the same dog-eared page that described Jay Gatsby's Rolls-Royce. "It was a rich cream color, bright with nickel…" He imagined the length and shine of the fabulous automobile in which he would chauffeur his own Daisy. This fantasy released him for a time from the tedium of school life and the empty hours in his mother's desolate mansion.

He mourned the loss of the house on East Twenty-sixth Street since he and Emma had moved to Wall Avenue two years ago after a frantic rush to prepare for Sophie's wedding party. Without much attention coming from his mother, the loss of daily nurturing from his Aunt Flora and guidance from Uncle Joe left him feeling adrift.

"She loves the house more than she cares about me," he had said to Flora one day. After the excitement of the move and his sister's party, life had come to a standstill for Aaron in this oversized house with hardwood floors that

273

resounded with each step, curtains that never fluttered, and shuttered doors to rooms that no one used. It felt to him like a deserted tomb. Dry. Still. Hollow.

When they moved to the Eastside not far from his uncles on Wall Avenue, Aaron had begged to be allowed to remain at Public School Number 13. "Ma," he had said, "it would be hard to make new friends, and don't you want me to be near family when I get out of school?"

"Yah," she conceded. "Flora watches over you like a…"

"Mother," Aaron inserted without thought.

Emma drew herself up into her familiar erect stance, her jaws tight and her eyes cold. Like a shut door without a keyhole, Aaron thought.

With endless hours to fill, Aaron spent many evenings in his bedroom reading about automobiles and listening to the radio. He pined for a motor vehicle of his own, and Daniel had convinced Emma that he should be given a 1925 Harley-Davidson JD motorcycle for his fourteenth birthday next year. It was the one concession that gave Aaron hope for freedom. For now, he could practice driving his mother's Ford with Joe riding shotgun, or Daniel might let him drive the Packard while on a visit to his vacation home.

One evening when school was nearly out for the summer, Aaron thought of something that might save him from those lonely times when he was not in the Catskills with his uncles. He asked Flora, "Can I come here and live with you?"

"Aaron, that would hurt your mama very much. Already you are here for dinner most of the time."

"I don't think she would notice, Aunt Flora. She comes home late from the shop and then she fusses over her papers."

"Joe, what do you say? We can't hurt Emma like that."

"Tell you what, I'll talk to Emma and see how she thinks. She won't like it, I'll bet."

"I know how she thinks, Uncle Joe. She doesn't care. If she sees my good grades at school, that is all she cares about. Papa was the one who cared."

"You miss him, son. We miss him, too. Every day I go to the stores to deliver the bread and at each place I think, "Meyer was here. This was his job.""

"When I go to the *shul* to study with the rabbi, I do it for Papa. I know he would be disappointed if I don't make my Bar Mitzvah." Aaron's voice rose louder. "He wouldn't mind that I want to be a mechanic, either. You two don't think it is wrong for me. Only Mama."

He was almost shouting when suddenly he stopped talking. His shoulders drooped, he put his chin on his chest and began to sob. Flora got up and stood by him, silently stroking his head.

# July 1926

Considering so little time that Emma had spent with her grandchildren, Daniel and Sophie invited Emma and Aaron to visit them in the Sheinman family's summer home. They would be the only guests that week. "It will give your mother a chance to know us better without the other relatives," Dan had reasoned.

Emma accepted the invitation, and for the first time in Sophie's memory, except for the dark period when Aaron had the Spanish flu, her mother closed the shop.

Although Aaron had become increasingly able with Joe's teaching to drive the Ford, Emma was reluctant to cede control of it to her young son. Perhaps if Aaron had been less avid about choosing auto mechanics as a career, she might have been willing to allow him an opportunity to drive, but today he was slouched in the passenger seat, silent during the two-hour trip to Grandview.

"Such a house!" Emma exclaimed as they entered the driveway on the right and drove around toward the back to a restored barn with a view of the Hudson River beyond. The three-story masonry and brown wood-shingled summer retreat stood on a rise overlooking the river, and it overshadowed the ancient wooden barn on its right. Emma stopped the Ford and marveled, "The front of the house is in the back!"

Aaron jumped out of the car and ran round to help his mother. Before he could reach her, Sophie and Dan came out, followed by Ori who was holding Molly's hand. Ori let go of his sister and ran to his uncle. "Aaron, Aaron, come and see my playroom," he cried as he grabbed Aaron's arm and tugged him in the direction of the house.

"Whoa, there, Ori. Let Aaron catch his breath. He just got here," said

Dan, who fetched their oversized valises and stepped onto the wide porch toward the front door where Molly teetered barefoot in her striped yellow-and-white piqué sunsuit. Sophie ran to snatch her up, and she brought the eleven-month-old to Emma. "Say hello to *Bubbeh* Emma, Molly."

"*Bubbeh*," she said as she reached out to Emma with both arms.

Before Emma could decide otherwise, she accepted Molly from Sophie's arms and walked toward the house with the child on her hip. "Where did you get that curly blonde hair, little girl?" Emma asked as Molly reached for the amethyst pendant around her *bubbeh's* neck. *Thanks to God. Molly likes her bubbeh. She came to me.*

The group went inside and Dan took Aaron upstairs to his bedroom, put Emma's valise in an adjoining room, and asked, "Aaron, how would you like to go out on the river? Only the two of us. We have a new rowboat down at the dock." In response to Aaron's smile he said, "Why don't you change into a swimming costume and meet me out in front of the house?"

Meanwhile, Emma had released Molly to Sophie, and she stood in the great front room taking in every detail. A second-story balcony overlooked the immense living space on all sides. On the wall across from the entrance was a massive stone fireplace. Despite the enormous height and size of the room, it was intimate. Large Oriental rugs and groupings of comfortably aged leather sofas and chairs softened the effect of a two-story beamed ceiling, wood-paneled walls, and oak floors.

"Mama, you look as stunned as I was when I first saw this room," said Sophie.

"It's a big room, but I like it," said Emma.

"I'm happy that you like it, Mama. I hope that we'll see more of you here. Would you like to see the rest of the house? Ori, take Molly and come with me and *Bubbeh*." They walked around to the dining hall beyond the great room, and Sophie led her mother through the kitchen and through several smaller rooms on the first floor as well as a screened summer porch. As they walked the stairs to the bedrooms, Ori raced ahead to show his bedroom and playroom. Molly reached up to her mother to be lifted.

"Mama, would you like to sit on the sofa by the fireplace with the children? You must be tired from your trip." Sophie went into the kitchen to fix a cool drink and returned to see Molly sitting next to Emma with her array of dolls. Ori was sitting on the floor constructing a bridge with his wooden Tinkertoys.

"Sophie, such a house as this I have never seen! So different from the city."

"Mama, it took me a long time to feel comfortable here. I'm not at home with wealth, even though I've known Eleanor and her family for so many years. It was someone else's house. Now such a house belongs to my husband's family, and it takes getting used to."

Emma thought carefully about what she was about to say. Her lips tightened and her jaws clenched. Words of compassion or inner motivations had never been easy for her. "Sophie," she finally began, "I always wanted you to have the best. That is why I was demanding with you. You know this?"

Sophie did not reply at first, but then nodded her head almost imperceptibly.

Molly crawled up on Sophie's lap and handed her Baby Peggy doll to Emma. "*Bubbeh*," she said.

"Molly, come here to *Bubbeh*," Emma said as she reached out to the child. The toddler responded with such warmth that Emma was startled for the second time. She held her granddaughter close and her lower lip began to quiver. She bit it. "You didn't think I remembered how to hold a little girl, Sophie?"

Sophie smiled and sat back in her seat.

Not to be left out of the snuggling, Ori climbed onto his mother's lap. The four were quiet for a few moments until the children became restless.

"Mama, are you rested enough to go out for a walk? You haven't seen our forest," said Sophie.

"Yah, why not."

Ori jumped from Sophie's lap. "*Bubbeh*, I know the names of all the trees. I'll show you!" He took Molly's hand and the little girl reached to Emma with the other. She was learning to walk and enjoyed being carried along by the two of them.

They walked a path to the far side of the wide lawn beyond the grounds-keeper's cottage where Donald O'Brien and his wife, Madeline, lived. They had worked for the family and lived in the cottage since Daniel was a small boy. Madeline came outside when she saw them, and Sophie introduced her to Emma. "I'm pleased to meet you, Ma'am. Miss Sophie, I'm making your dinner in my house, and I'll bring it to your kitchen later. I know you want to serve it yourself."

"Thank you, Madeline. I appreciate it," said Sophie. After a bit of conversation about her history with the house, Madeline went back inside and the family continued to the wooded area.

Ori had been patient, but now he began to narrate the history of the land. Sophie beamed as Ori told the story that Daniel had explained to him. "A long time ago, people from uh…oh, Dutch people came here and made farms. They cut down the oak trees and built their houses."

"How smart you are, Ori!" said Emma.

"I know more, *Bubbeh*. After a while they went away from here and Daniel's grandpa built this house. The lawn and the trees on this path are on the Dutch people's farm. I mean it used to be their farm."

Molly had enough of the talk. "Up, up," she cried.

"*Bubbeh*, let's swing Molly. She likes that. When I say three, we lift her up and swing. One, two…three!"

"Up," giggled Molly.

"Ori," Sophie called. "It's time for Molly's nap. Would you like to get her ready?"

"Okay, Mama. C'mon, Molly. I'll take you upstairs for a nap, and I can read to you, too." Ori clutched Molly, and with both arms around her waist he hoisted her a few inches off the ground and half carried, half dragged her into the house with cheerful compliance on her part. Ori had grown tall for his seven years, but lifting this robust little girl was still a feat.

"Mama, while the children are inside, let's sit down on this bench for a while."

"It's a dream, this mansion on the river. Who would have thought that a foreign-born daughter of mine could live like this?" said Emma.

At the phrase "foreign-born," Sophie sat up. Her nostrils flared, and she reddened. She held out her hands, palms up as if to say something, and dropped them into her lap. No words came out.

"What is it, Sophie?"

The daughter sat quietly for a moment, her face hidden and contorted.

She pulled at a button on her sweater, and almost twisted it off, then folded her hands in her lap.

"*Nu*, Sophie?"

"Mama, how can you still say 'foreign-born' when I know that I was born in Paterson, New Jersey? You came to America to marry Papa when you were already expecting me. Why did you lie to me all of these years?" she blurted.

"You knew?" asked Emma.

"You remember when Papa died I took his suit box from under your bed?"

"Yah. That was almost three years ago."

"Papa saved your letters from Poland. I read them."

Emma looked toward the porch to see if Ori was coming back.

"Don't worry, Mama. Ori will be with Molly for a while."

Emma looked down at her hands, tightly clasped in her lap. "I thought that when you married Daniel the shame would go away. Your good marriage might cross out our disgrace, and you wouldn't have to know."

"What are you saying, Mama?"

"I hoped I would never have to tell you this. My shame was so great."

"Your shame? Why did you force me away?"

"Wait, my daughter, mine own. When I was a girl in Poland we lived so poor. I loved your father, but we were never alone in that cottage or by the looms where he worked. Always someone was nearby. Neighbors, brothers, parents. The only time we could talk was in front of others, and I wanted to hear his voice away from the crowding and the dung smell and the tumult of the looms.

"I could tell that he loved me, but he had not said so. I believed that we would marry and go to America to be with my brothers, but we hadn't talked. I knew that he often went at night to the forest to meet with the workers from the big mills. They plotted a strike like in Paterson. One night I got the nerve to sneak out of the house in the dark and wait for him after the other men went away. He lingered with his lantern to say good-bye to each friend. When they were gone, I left from the house and went to meet him. I didn't mean for it to happen, but that is how it was."

"But Mama. Why did you reject me for the same thing? I loved Izzy, and we planned to marry, too."

"Oh, my love. I was dishonored. Meyer had to leave for America all of a sudden. His name came up for the Russian army, and he ran away to my uncle in Bialystok and then to America. We didn't have time to marry. Before he left, he promised to send for me, but we didn't know that I was in the family way. When I was sure, I wrote to him. By then I was beginning to show. Only your grandmother could tell, I think. She didn't say a thing, but she was shamed. If the neighbors saw, even if my Papa knew, the dishonor to the family would be great."

"Did you tell her?"

"No. I couldn't bring myself to hurt her, but it was time for Joe and Dave to leave, too. Soon they would be old enough for conscription. We had to get to Gdansk where the ship would leave. By then, the Russians tracked young Jewish men who could be called. They couldn't leave so easy. At night we left for the long walk across the country to the port. Meyer sent money. So did the other brothers. We had enough to bribe the farmers with carts to carry us little by little to the north. Sometimes we walked in the night. Sometimes we rode in carts. We got there."

"And you came to Paterson?"

"Yah. Still the humiliation was so great that we couldn't ask the rabbi to marry us. We went to the city hall and got married there, so the neighbors shouldn't know that we weren't married in Lodz. I wanted to spare you. I didn't want you to be disgraced by your birth that came so soon after our marriage."

"You loved Papa when you were a girl like I loved Izzy. Why did you push me away? Why, Mama, did we all have to suffer?"

"Why, why? I don't know why. I was so mixed up in my mind. The dishonor would come to our family in Paterson like it almost came to my parents in Lodz. I saw it happen over again."

"And now everything is fine because I married a rich man?"

"I only hoped that my own guilt would go away. I thought I could stop thinking about my mistake in those old days in Lodz."

Emma was quiet and looked up from her lap to face her daughter. The look in her eye was pleading. Sophie reached for her mother and pulled her close. Emma whispered into her daughter's ear, "Forgive me, my daughter. Forgive me."

# November, 1926

**A**aron Epstein was called to the *bimah* of Temple Emanuel to recite his Torah portion as a Bar Mitzvah on this Sabbath day, the thirteenth of November. Now at thirteen years, he was said to be a man, and was honored with an *aliyah*, his first "going up" to read from the sacred scroll. In his new tailored suit he stood up, straightened Meyer's prayer shawl around his shoulders, and felt the crown of his head to make sure that his yarmulke was in place.

Then, quivering with a mixture of anxiety and pride, he strode from the family pew up to the *bimah* where the Torah rested on its lectern. *Please God, don't let my voice crack, and please while you are at it, don't let me trip on the steps to the bimah with my big feet.* He shook hands with Rabbi Bronfman and turned to the lectern where he faced all of his family and Paterson's Jewish elite who were seated on pews in the octagonal sanctuary. He looked out with awe at the stained-glass panels and the shimmering chandeliers. As he faced the expectant audience he took a breath to prepare for the ordeal of the recitation.

"Papa, I'll make you proud," he whispered.

Aaron inwardly mourned the comfortable *shul* of Rabbi Aronson in the old neighborhood where his father had lain before his burial, and he silently apologized to his papa in heaven for this ornate chapel. *Temple Emanuel means so much to Mama. You know she is proud to be a founding member.*

In fact, this newly opened deco-style Temple Emanuel on Broadway near the elegant Eastside Park neighborhood marked Emma's arrival into the wealthy Jewish community of Paterson. She had contributed to the addition of the bronze filigree entrance doors, and her name was etched on a wall plaque among the other supporters.

Aaron chanted from the Torah without missing a word. He opened his subsequent speech with the ritual theme, "Now that I am a man," and continued with his personal interpretation, "I have the gift and also the responsibility of self-choice…" Looking at his mother to the very end, his voice held strong. Emma smiled and looked around at the audience, making eye contact with family and guests and receiving their smiling recognition.

The boy, on the other hand, thought only of his papa, for whom he had endured endless lessons with Rabbi Bronfman in order to perform these required rituals as his father had wished.

Later that unseasonably warm November afternoon, family and friends adjourned to the Epstein home on Wall Avenue. Emma had petitioned the rabbi for an early Bar Mitzvah, her ostensible reason being that Aaron would have more time to study his Torah portion in the summer. But Rabbi Bronfman had been unyielding. "A twelve-year-old is not yet a man."

As her guests began to arrive, Emma inwardly lamented that most of the party would be indoors rather than in the garden or on "the grounds." The prior year she had employed brother George's gardener and spared no expense to enhance the space that she imagined would be the backdrop for Aaron's Bar Mitzvah. Tall privet hedges now provided Emma's coveted privacy on each side of the yard.

In summer, flowerbeds had blossomed in front of the hedges lush with peonies, dahlias, and hydrangeas for perennial color. A plethora of spring and summer bulbs had sprouted in turn, according to precision planning. Lilacs flourished in profusion along the back fence, their heady aroma evoking a sensuous boudoir.

In fall, however, she had to have the gardener rake the last of the decayed leaves from the lawn, the stone pathway, and the octagonal marble patio. Fall flowers were withering, but Emma had kept the glass-top table and twelve dainty French garden chairs from winter storage. Maybe, she thought, the weather would still allow some time in the garden.

In honor of her son's coming-of-age celebration, she was dressed in a navy drop-waist silk dress with a myriad of covered buttons down the front, revealing her still lovely figure as she approached age fifty. Her newly prescribed gold-wired spectacles remained on her dressing table. Bejeweled and coiffed anew with a Marcel-waved shingle cut, she glowed as she welcomed family and friends to her home and showed them out to garden where it was warm enough to sit wearing fall wraps if they so chose. *Those Abramowitz women always wear their furs anyway.*

Sophie and Daniel, with Molly and Ori on their laps, were seated around the table with Flora and Joe, along with Sophie's cousin Charlotte Offenberg and the other Abramowitz boy cousins. When Aaron appeared in his new suit, the family applauded.

"Well, Aaron, you pulled it off!" laughed Daniel. "What are your plans for the winter vacation?"

Aaron took the empty seat on one side of his sister and reached over to kiss her and then Molly. "Sal promised that I could help him in the garage for a few weeks. He has the contract for all the city cars, and that's a lot of work. Imagine! Every automobile that Paterson owns will go through Sal's garage. And he still has his regular customers."

"What does Mama say about this? Will she let you spend so much time there?"

"You know how she is! She wants me to work with Uncle George at the mill. Says I should begin to learn the silk business, but I won't. Uncle Joe will stand up for me."

"Would you like to join us at Grandview for a weekend to celebrate Hanukkah if there's no snow on the roads?" asked Sophie. "I was hoping that Mama would come, too."

"Did you ask her yet?" queried Aaron.

"Well, she's been very busy planning for your Bar Mitzvah," answered Dan. "But we'll invite her soon."

Sophie turned to Aaron and whispered, "She's only been to Grandview once, and that was last summer."

"I know. She's always so busy."

Aaron shrugged his shoulders, got up, and took Ori's arm. "Ori, want to come and see my bedroom? Come on, everyone. Let's all go upstairs," Aaron said to his cousins.

Ori jumped from Daniel's lap and followed the troop of his older cousins who ran through the garden, onto the porch, and into the mudroom, clambering up the two flights to Aaron's room. The adults were left to coo over little Molly. Sophie held her closely on her lap, relaxed among her loved ones.

Esther and Manny would soon arrive to make her family complete. Sophie looked adoringly at Daniel and reached over to whisper in his ear, "Thank you for being a part of my family, for fitting in. I love you."

She hugged Molly closer. The little girl was the double of her father, with creamy skin and round, light blue eyes, opposite of her brother Ori's deep blue almond-shaped eyes and olive complexion. Ori's chiseled features gave him an exotic look. Molly, with her blonde curls and ready smile, was round and delicious.

# Eleven

## September 1927

Emma had driven home from her store and changed into a chenille robe, feeling an unaccustomed contentment after making herself comfortable with the *Paterson Evening News* and a cup of tea. She walked across the kitchen to the radiator and held her hands over the warmth generated from the natural gas furnace. *No more shoveling coal.* Then she pushed aside the kitchen curtain and gazed out the window where icicles, aglow from the streetlamp, hung from the eaves. Crystal drops decorated the bare branches of the maple tree.

Her thoughts ran to the huge profit she had made from the sale of her General Motors stock. Now she would be able to update this splendid house. At the exact moment she was imagining a newly remodeled kitchen with a coveted Roper four-burner gas stove and electric refrigerator, the back door burst open and slammed against the wall. Aaron stormed into the room and threw his books on the table. "Mama, I'm going to quit school."

"What did you say?"

"I'll be fourteen in November. I can quit then. Plenty of boys quit school to work at fourteen."

"Nonsense. You are not 'plenty of boys.' You're Aaron Epstein, and you are going to college as we planned."

Aaron closed his eyes for a moment and then ran his fingers through his black combed-back curly hair.

285

*Just like his father he looks, but taller.*

"You planned for college. It's your dream, not mine. I'm not going to college. That's not for me. I want to work with Sal at the garage."

"You dare to talk to me that way? I worked only for you all these years. I bought this house so you would be proud to invite your friends. I made a good life for you, and you dare to tell me this? A dropout! A good-for-nothing."

"You really do think that I am good for nothing, don't you?"

"You will not quit school. No more talk."

"That's right, Ma. No more talk. I'm going to our old house," he cried, slamming the door as he raced out.

After nearly running the entire mile to get there, Aaron arrived at the East Twenty-sixth Street address and sat collecting himself in Uncle Joe and Aunt Flora's kitchen. He sipped the hot cocoa that he had come to expect from Flora whenever he was upset, and he inhaled the comforting aroma of her stew. While he sipped his drink, Flora looked over at Joe and discreetly put a finger over her lips and turned to the stove to tend to her pots.

Joe sat at the table next to his nephew and opened the newspaper. "Look here, Aaron. It says that Robert Benoist was first on the podium at the Italian Grand Prix. That's a 500 kilometer race."

"Yeah. Over 300 miles. He drives that French Delage I read about. What was his speed?"

"Says here that he made it in 3:37:3."

"I'd love to see that car!"

The words hung in the air as Aaron assumed a faraway look. He sighed and pushed his cocoa away. The only sound was that of Flora's spoon scraping the sides of her stewpot.

"Ma wouldn't let me move in with the two of you when Papa died. I'd like to come now if you'll have me. I'll do my share of the work and…"

"Do you want to talk about what's bothering you now?" asked Flora as she turned from the stove and prepared to set the dinner table for the three of them.

Aaron placed his long thin hands flat on the table, the tips of his fingers gripping the surface, his arms and shoulders tense. He squeezed his eyes shut. Flora and Joe knew to keep silent when Aaron struggled this way. They knew that he would talk when he could release the tension he felt.

Aaron expelled his bottled-up energy with a huge burst of air. "I'm going to quit school and work for Sal. I don't care what she says."

"You don't think you have much left to learn in school?" asked Joe.

"Sure I could learn more, but not anything I would need to be a good automobile mechanic."

"And you want to live here because your mother is against this?" asked Flora.

"Well, you know she doesn't understand…"

"Let's think, boy. How can you have what you want and make your mother happy in the bargain?" Joe asked.

"There's no way to satisfy her unless I go to college and become a doctor or something like that." Aaron balled his fists and shook them. "She doesn't care what I really want. Since Papa died she spends even more time in her shop."

Joe got up from the table and began to pace. He started to say something and then stopped himself. He rubbed his rapidly balding head in thought and then looked at Flora, who nodded with complicity.

"Aaron, you heard maybe of Paterson Vocational School? I know a guy at Purity Bakery. His son goes there."

"It's near Eastside High, but I don't know much about it."

"Good school to learn the trades. They take boys at fourteen years and keep them for two years or however long they need to learn a trade."

"You mean they would teach me how to be a good mechanic?" Aaron's eyes widened with hope. He jumped up from the table and moved closer to Joe. The boy had reached almost six feet in the past year and he towered over his shorter, rotund uncle. "Do you think I…"

"It's something to find out about, no?"

"Let's sit and eat dinner and then we can talk more," interrupted Flora as she brought dinner to the table and made her prayer. "Thank you, God, for this great country and for the food that we are about to eat."

Aaron asked Joe to ring his mother and let her know he wouldn't be home that night. He was jittery for the rest of the evening, and he went to Sal's garage the next morning, a Coke bottle in hand.

"Thank you, Aaron. It's good, this Coke. Sit," he said as he pointed to an upended wooden crate among the greasy rags. "Have a cavalucci cookie from my lunchbox. When you bring a Coke, I think you have something to say." Aaron smiled. *Sal knows me pretty good.*

Aaron blushed and searched his mind for a neutral topic to engage Sal. "My mother is buying a new Stutz. She said it's a Safety Stutz. What's safe about it? She didn't know."

Sal knew. "She's a long, low baby, no slipping and sliding on the road. That Stutz has wire-glass windows. They don't break so easy. She's a beaut, Aaron."

"I hope she lets me drive it, but I bet I'll have to borrow Uncle Joe's Model T when I start to drive."

Sal took a long swig of his Coke and nodded.

"You know, Sal, I'm getting older now, and uh, and well, I have to start thinking about my life."

Aaron got up from the crate and stuffed the last of the cookie into his mouth. After a pause, he wiped a trace of crumbs from his lips with a fresh handkerchief from his back pocket.

"Sal, I've been helping you and learning from you for a long time, ever since I was a little boy," he said, reddening. "So I thought, uh…when I quit Eastside High, can I work for you? You know, a real job."

"Hold on to your horses. You wanna quit school? Why?" he said, wiping his hands.

"I hate sitting there when I could be learning something important like fixing autos. I'm not going to college, no matter what my mother says."

"Maybe you finish high school and then you work for me."

"Sal, my uncle Joe told me about a school right here in Paterson where they teach auto mechanics." Aaron began to stumble over his spate of words. "See, I wouldn't, I wouldn't be quitting school, only changing schools."

Sal furrowed his brow and took another swig of his Coke. He scratched his ribs. Aaron waited for him to speak. He knew Sal's habits as Sal knew his.

"I know about this school. Many new cars built, eight million last year. We need more mechanics," said Sal.

"If I wait too long, you'll find someone else to help you with your new Paterson contract. I want to start Paterson Vocational now."

"You talk to your Mama and then we talk," countered Sal.

"Uncle Joe will talk to her, too. He'll help me."

"I like your uncle. He's a happy man. No work too hard like your mama."

This year when Daniel and Sophie invited her to Grandview for the Labor Day weekend, Emma was too distraught to go. She had seen the family on holidays, and they had even come to visit her on Wall Avenue, but she hadn't been alone with her grandchildren for more than a year, even though she had often been invited.

Sitting at her desk on the porch, Emma pushed aside the ledgers she had been attempting to balance and thought about the emergencies that continued to crop up and prevent her from enjoying her family. *Something always interferes with seeing the children.* There was a call from a tenant with a broken toilet, and then she lost her apartment building "super." She had to waste time trying to find a good manager, and they were hard to come by. She worried that she would have to pay more for a new one. Last week when she wanted to invite the family, her salesgirl didn't come to the store, and Emma had to work on the sales floor.

*I would like to go to Grandview, but how can I go with Aaron this way? Oy! Such a mess!*

Emma paced from room to room muttering to herself and wringing her hands. *It can't be. It can't be.* She rubbed her temples and pulled at the roots of her hair. *How could he quit school when I have plenty money to send him to college?*

Yesterday's argument with Aaron had been the final disastrous blow to her plans for him. He announced that he would move in with Flora and Joe to be close to Sal's garage and enroll in the winter semester at Paterson Vocational School, after he'd turned fourteen.

She had shrieked, "You will waste your life and everything that I worked to give you. You will amount to nothing. You want to wear overalls and come home greasy at night, smelling from oil and gasoline when you could be wearing fine suits?"

This had been her coup de grâce, intended to end the argument. Instead it fueled Aaron's anger. "That's what you thought of my father," he yelled. "You don't want me to be a workingman like him."

Emma drew in her breath and opened her mouth in shock, covering it with her hand. She raised her eyebrows and gave a stare that said, "You must be crazy." She rushed from the room and vowed to herself that silence would bring him around. She would stop talking to him.

Even when Joe came today to plead Aaron's case, she hadn't assimilated the truth of Aaron's move. "He's in the Classical Course, not even the Commercial," she had said. "He's with the smart ones in school, no dummies getting ready for the trades. He wouldn't throw away his future."

"Is that what you still think, Emma, that doing something he likes will ruin his life? I love you, sister, but this time you are wrong."

The next day, Aaron packed a valise and went to stay with his uncle and aunt. Sal had agreed to hire him as a part-time helper for now, and Flora and Joe's flat on East Twenty-sixth Street was convenient to the garage. He worked for token wages, but he would begin to learn auto mechanics even before the start of vocational school.

"Your mama is not so happy," Sal said when Aaron first came to work. "She came here early in the morning and told me not to give you work."

Aaron pounded the workbench with his fist. "She can't do that. What did you tell her, Sal?"

"I gave you a job. Could I go back on my word?"

"I'm sorry, Sal. She might take her Stutz somewhere else."

"Maybe," said Sal. He turned to look under the hood of a black Ford

Model A and Aaron hopped up on the running board to look over his shoulder.

Later in the day when Sal and Aaron ate their lunch on two chairs in the alley in front of the shop, Aaron returned to the topic most on his mind. "I moved in with Uncle Joe and Aunt Flora. Ma isn't talking to me," he said. After a pause he added, "She'll get used to it, I guess, and then she won't be so angry."

Sal grunted and handed him a cavalucci cookie.

# TWELVE

## May 1928

**E**mma emerged from Penn Station wearing a light wool wrap coat and decided to walk to Fifth Avenue on this warm spring day. It wasn't far to the doomed Waldorf Astoria Hotel, which was soon to be razed to make room for the tallest building in the world.

Her first stop in the hotel was the cavernous ladies' room with its marble sinks and an attendant to hand her a towel. She removed her kid gloves, arranged her windblown hair, and applied a bit more face powder. She leaned forward and examined her lips, pulling them over her teeth. She sighed. Her lips, she knew, were too thin for the style of the day, so she set about repairing a rose-colored Cupid's bow on the upper lip and widening the lower. She felt better when she looked in the full-length mirror to admire her low-waisted couture dress. Its below-the-knee, softly pleated skirt showed her shapely legs and ankles. *Not bad for fifty*. Feeling generous, she reached into her handbag for a twenty-five-cent piece to tip the attendant.

Emma walked down the hall and entered a lush, drapes-drawn suite where the elite women of Manhattan congregated in this private club permanently rented by a firm on the Stock Exchange. Some women, young among the older, partially reclined on overstuffed davenports. Others sat in deep armchairs. Regardless of where they sat in the room, all eyes traveled between indecipherable symbols gliding across a narrow wall screen and a blackboard upon which two female attendants chalked similar ever-changing figures. All hands were busy making notes.

Emma stood at the entrance and surveyed the room. She put her gloves in her handbag. *Nu*, she thought as she looked around for a seat, *I fit in here.* She handed her reference note to the receptionist, and with a commanding entrance that belied her mild discomfort, Emma found a vacant emerald green Florentine armchair amid a cluster of similar seats. She lowered herself with all the poise she could muster, crossed her legs, adjusted her skirt, and turned to smile at the women nearby.

Then she busied herself with her handbag, withdrew her cigarette holder, and placed a long Turkish cigarette in it. Instantly a waitress appeared to light it for her. Emma thanked her and ordered a coffee. Now she could comfortably study the room.

The ticker-tape machines made a familiar "tick" sound while the reeled paper of the telegraph-printing instrument displayed data on stocks, bonds, and commodities from the exchanges. Good that I learned to read the tape from that broker Levine in Paterson, she thought.

Acting as if the women who messengered the tape from the machine to the clients were familiar, she took a pencil, a list of her assets, and notepaper from her handbag. She was ready to participate for the first time in this ritual that her busy schedule seldom allowed. She wouldn't have to look at her list of holdings, however, because she had committed them to memory. Emma drew in her breath and exhaled a deep sigh. *Luxury.* She patted her hennaed hair waves with the outer edge of her right hand, wondering if it wasn't a bit too modern for an older lady. *Now I'll look for a new stock to buy, or maybe something I should sell.*

"I'm glad I listened to my husband," confided a nearby woman to her friend. "After that frightening drop in the market last week, he was more adamant than ever. He made me promise never to buy on margin and never to sell short. 'I tell you how much money to invest, and that's what you have,'" he says. "No brokerage loans, and no fancy trading. Buy what we can afford."

"Imagine, Doris, if we owed money to the broker and the market hadn't corrected. We'd bankrupt our families."

"Well, that won't happen. The market is going nowhere but up. Look how fast it turned around."

I got money in the bank and apartment buildings to back my loans, thought Emma. Mentally she enumerated her outstanding mortgages and cash on hand, thinking it would be safe to bet on a sure thing.

"Eeeee, look at this tape!" Everyone turned to look at the source of the scream. A very young woman jumped up and waved her arms as if shouting for a Babe Ruth home run.

"RCA hit 420!" A cacophony of women cheered the wild ride. "I'm holding it!" "I doubled my money!" "From 85 at the beginning!" "Horace will be proud of me!"

Emma sat back in her armchair, overwhelmed by the headiness of the atmosphere. She crushed her cigarette and allowed herself an unguarded moment. Thoughts of her childhood in Lodz swept into the momentary lapse. She wasn't so different during her childhood in the Balut ghetto of Lodz when she had to draw water from a well and owned only two dresses. She was strong from the start. *And now I have everything.* Self-assured, she spent another two hours watching the screen and the chalkboard before she left to find the Horn and Hardart's Automat.

# August 1929

"**R**euben, it's time to get out of the market. I know that your father manages your trust for you, but if you have any other cash invested, sell now," Daniel urged his friend.

Reuben nodded to the waiter to remove his empty plate. "Is that the reason you invited me to lunch today? I appreciate it, but for an artist, I'm not so dumb, my friend. Paul Warburg has been talking to my father and to Eleanor's, too, about the market. Ever since the collapse of last May, both Warburg and his friend Giannini from Transamerica have been claiming that stocks have risen beyond their worth. He's been saying all year that the market has signs of intrinsic weakness."

"Righto! It's been up and down all month," said Dan.

"Even so, there are hordes on Wall Street clamoring to get in on a deal.

Have you seen the crowds? It's almost like a circus on Wall Street. Those same people will be banging down the doors to sell before long. Let me tell you, this is no time for the small investor to be playing the game."

Reuben looked around for a speakeasy waiter and ordered another highball.

Dan became quiet while Reuben sipped his second drink. He looked around the backroom restaurant, one of hundreds of speakeasies in Manhattan, and felt a sense of foreboding. Well-groomed, well-fed bankers, brokers, and corporate managers drank and laughed with abandon. *Have they no sense of impending doom?*

He thought of his conversation about Emma that morning with Sophie. They had been concerned for the last two years about her leveraged position but had not been able to convince her to be more conservative in her investments.

Now Sophie was frantic. "Mama is caught in a fantasy," she had said. "It's as if she's a child on a merry-go-round screaming to be pushed faster and faster. She closes her eyes and loses herself in the reckless speed."

With these thoughts in mind, Dan looked at his friend and confidant. He and Reuben had been prep school and college buddies, were raised in the same social and religious milieu, and were devoted to the same family charities. Their comfort level was so strong that they could talk about most anything. Reuben and Ellie both knew of Sophie's ongoing conflict between continuing her work, albeit volunteer, at the Henry Street Settlement, and her position as the wife of a wealthy banker. Now he wanted to talk about Emma.

"Reuben, Sophie's mother is up to her neck in debt. When the broker calls her loans, I don't think she'll be able to back them. Sophie and I have tried to persuade her to cash out, but she is determined. She thinks her real estate is the cushion, but the housing units have mortgages. I'm worried about her. Any ideas, Reuben?"

"Has Sophie tried to talk to her uncles? What are they doing?"

"She talked to her Aunt Selma. Harry and George are the smart ones. They're getting out of the market, but Sophie thinks that Harry left some money that he can afford to lose in the big companies, RCA and such."

"What about the others, Dan?"

"The twins aren't in the business with the other two. Joe is happy without investing. He's an unpretentious sort, someone to trust. And Dave...well Dave is a bootlegger. He makes money enough without playing the market. Bathtub gin keeps him going, along with his Harlem connections at the Cotton Club where he works."

Reuben squinted, his forehead wrinkled. "Can't Sophie get the uncles to talk to Emma?" he said as he looked at his watch.

"Emma listens to them, but not this time."

"Don't know what else you can do short of covering her when the time comes," said Reuben.

"We won't do that. Sophie and I talked about it. So we'll wait."

Reuben stood and made ready to leave. "Client is coming at two to look at a Miró. I received a new one—*Spanish Dancer*. Art is where the money is, my friend. We'll see you at Sea Bright next weekend? Ori is getting to be a good swimmer!"

"We'll be there, Reuben. Maybe I'll be able to get Sophie in the water yet this year."

# September 1929

"Look, Levine, I take your advice and sell the RCA to pay the margin calls on Montgomery Ward and General Electric, but the rest I leave to make more money before I sell."

"Emma, I'm your friend. Sarah buys dresses from you. Listen to me. More margin calls are coming. Today the "big boys" sold, and they're holding only cash. If you don't sell now and they call your margin loans at eight percent, you'll be broke. The rate has been as high as twelve percent, for God's sake!"

Emma tightened her grip on the telephone as she listened to her friend and broker speak of doom. "*Nu*, who are these 'big boys'?"

"Bernard Baruch and Michael Bouvier, for example. I tell you, Emma, sell, sell, sell."

"Not yet, Levine," said Emma. "George and Harry sold. I thought they had more *chutzpa*," she said as she paced the floor of her office behind the shop, untwisting the telephone cord with one hand and holding the receiver in the other. "Levine, I'll hold what I have. I know a lot is on margin, but every time the market has a little break, they all panic. Not me."

"Emma, you make me very sad. But I'm only your broker. I do what you say. Good-bye Emma, but please think it over."

"No selling, Levine. I'll call you soon for a trade. So long," she said and placed the receiver in its cradle.

Emma knew that the stock market would not fail her. She thought about all that she had—her home debt free, income property, some money in the bank, clothes, jewels, sterling silver service, an expensive automobile… all that and a profitable business. Suddenly she became aware that her dress was moist under her arms. *I'm perspiring like I'm nervous. Why should I be nervous?*

She heard someone come into the shop and she walked to the showroom. "Good afternoon, Mrs. Silverberg. It was nice to see you at the Eastern Star meeting last week."

"Yes, we accomplished a great deal for our charity." Her eye wandered to the display of suits to her left. She ambled toward it as if she were not overly anxious and began to examine the suits, holding one up to herself while looking in a mirror. I see you haven't sold this little Chanel suit that I was looking at a few days ago."

"I think it is waiting special for you. You didn't try it on, I remember. I'll put it in the changing room, and I have some tea ready if you want a cup before you go inside."

"How nice, Emma. Such a pleasure to come here."

# October 1929

**D**espite her staunch attitude about remaining in the market, Emma had not been immune to the talk of the past month. She knew that her brothers had taken the market instability seriously. They had either sold their shares or they planned to sell short. By selling short they hoped to "make out like bandits," speculating that the prices would drop. Sophie had reminded her that Reuben and Daniel had urged her to sell. Yet Emma held fast.

Early this Tuesday morning she lay awake in bed, unable to sleep. It was too early to get up and look for today's newspaper, but she went to the window and drew back the luxurious damask hangings that she had purchased last month. The streetlight in front of her house still glowed in the near darkness. *Never have I had such trouble with sleep. It's too early yet for the birds to wake up. I'll try to sleep more.* But she could not sleep. She turned on her side and smiled as she felt the smoothness of her satin sheets, but the smile faded as she recalled the newspaper headlines of the past week.

*The New York Times* and the *Herald Tribune* had featured daily headlines that changed from doom to euphoria. On October twentieth, the *Times* headline read "*Scare Orders From All Oover Country Halt Ticker an Hour in Feverish Day.*" Then on Thursday, October twenty-fourth, all hell broke loose and the bottom seemed to have fallen out of the market. Emma was certain that she would get a margin call to pay off the loans from the brokerage house, but no call came.

On Friday morning she had awakened with the thought, *Today I sell everything*, but then she read the day's newspaper account. "*Brokerage Houses are Optimistic on the Recovery of Stocks—Brokers in Meeting Predict Recovery.*"

The article continued, "…much of the selling of the last few days, the brokers felt, was induced by hysteria. The views of all of the brokers present were heard, and none knew of anything disturbing to the general market situation…"

*Yah. This is all that talk of "market correction." Now everything is correct.* Once again the lure of wealth overwhelmed her sense of propriety, and she discarded the thought of selling.

On Sunday she read in the *Herald Tribune*, "*Brokers Believe Worst is Oover and Recommend Buying of Real Bargains.*"

On Tuesday, October twenty-ninth, when sleep continued to evade her, Emma thought of the conflicting headlines that alternated between doom and assurance. The terror of losing all of her wealth overwhelmed her. She pushed the bedding aside, reached for her robe, and rushed to her desk barefoot, pulling on her robe as she went. She was shaking when she pulled out her list of accounts, and she could feel her face and scalp tingling with anxious perspiration.

A few of her holdings were without loans on them, good blue-chip stocks that she had purchased long ago, but the more recent holdings were all lever-aged. She began to pace and pull at the roots of her hair. *What should I do? Maybe I call Levine now.*

She went into her home office and sat at the desk staring at the receiver of her telephone. *Yah. I call Levine and sell. Lambert 3-7600.* She lifted the receiver and turned the instrument toward her face. She looked at it and waited for a mild nausea to pass. She put the receiver to her ear and used her index finger to rotate the dial. It seemed to take an eternity for the dial to rotate between digits.

Then she realized that it was too early for Levine to be in his office. She put the telephone back on the cradle and decided to make breakfast. She sat in front of her toast and tea, unable to eat. She got up and paced. She looked at the clock. *Too early still.* She paced some more and sat at the table willing herself to eat the cold toast. *No good.*

The dawn passed and eight o'clock finally arrived. Emma dialed Levine and waited. *Ach. Busy.* She slammed down the receiver and went to the kitchen to make fresh tea. Impatient, she went back to the desk and dialed again. Busy. After several more tries, she decided to go downtown and see Levine in person.

Her awareness turned to the blaring radio in the front room where she had turned it on expecting soothing music for her breakfast hour. "I bet my money on a bobtail nag, somebody bet on the bay. Doo-dah, doo-dah. Oh, doo-dah day!" *Damn that Al Jolson.* She switched off the radio and strode into her bedroom.

Emma dressed in her most impressive suit and drove her Stutz down to the broker's office. The traffic around the Main Street building was much busier than usual, and it took her a longer time to park her car.

As she walked closer to the office she noticed a clutch of suited business-men and a few women milling around the entry, and upon reaching the stairs she heard their murmurs. "The office is closed up." "Levine's not answering the door."

"What's going on here?" she asked one of the bystanders.

"I tried to sell this morning, but he couldn't find buyers for my shares. Now he can't even get through to New York."

"Nobody can get through. We can't sell anything and what we have is worthless anyway."

Emma was dazed and couldn't process what she was hearing. She turned from the crowd and crossed Main Street toward the city hall plaza, unaware of the honking horns. By the time she reached a bench, her pulsating temples overcame her. She leaned forward and allowed her head to hang over her knees but quickly rose, fearing a faint. She sat upright and looked ahead, seeing nothing. She passed ten minutes this way, and no one in the crowd took notice of her.

A tightening headache replaced the throbbing at her temples, and she felt as if she had been seized by a *dybbuk*. *What evil spirit is pressing my soul?* This supernatural sensation harkened to the Jewish superstitions of her ghetto days in Poland. She staggered to her automobile and drove unsteadily home.

That evening when she looked at the newspaper she read, "***Stock Prices Slump $14,000,000,000 in Nation-wide Stampede to Unload.***"

# THIRTEEN

## October 31, 1929

Joe and Aaron stayed home from work, and Sophie came to Joe's house to talk about Emma's situation. The newspapers hadn't been too much help, but Sophie knew that Rockefeller and others were buying up stocks, supposedly to stabilize the market.

Sophie read the front page of *The New York Times* aloud.

> ### Stocks Mount in Strong All-day Rally
> ### Rockafeller Buying Heartens Market
> ### 2-Day Closing Ordered to Erase Strain

"Even if the market recovers it won't help Mama. She must be agonizing over a flurry of margin calls," said Sophie. "I ache for her."

"How can you say that after the way she treated you?" asked Aaron.

"She's Mama. She suffers."

Joe moved his teacup out of the way and leaned his elbows on the table. "We all feel sad for her, my darling, but what can we do to help her?"

"Here's Ma in that big house all by herself with no money," said Aaron. "That's what she deserves. All these years telling me how much money she has. She only talked about business and money. My whole life she never cared about who I was unless I fit into her life the way she wanted it. Well, I am who I am. I saved up from my pay at Sal's these past two years. I didn't throw it away like her."

Flora had been listening from the front room. "Aaron, she's your mother!" Flora called to him as she came to sit at the kitchen table with the others.

"That's right, Aaron," echoed Joe. "Longest speech I ever heard from you," he said under his breath.

Aaron flushed. He passed his fingers through his curly black hair from forehead to crown. Sophie recalled how Meyer had always raked his hair back when he was upset. Then he would pull out his pipe.

"I know," he said aloud. "I didn't really mean it. I have to help her. It's what Papa would say. Do the right thing. But how? She would never take money from me. She'd die first. I know that." He stood and put his hands into his front pockets, fingered the loose change, and sat down facing his sister. "Are you and Dan going to give her money, Sophie?"

"No, we don't think it's the right way to help her." She picked up her teacup and cradled it in her hands. "I'm angry with her, too Aaron. For the past. I'm angry that my children hardly know her. But that doesn't really matter now, does it?"

Aaron hung his head. "No. It doesn't matter anymore."

"She's expecting the two of you this afternoon. What do you think you'll say?" asked Flora.

"I guess we'll have to talk it out, see what she thinks. Right, Sophie?"

"Right, Aaron."

"I bought a new sidecar for my Harley. You can open a door and climb in. It even has an upholstered seat. Are you game to try it over to Ma's house?"

"Aaron, why did you buy a sidecar? Tell Sophie."

"Oh, Aunt Flora," he said, reddening and averting his face.

"Enough," said Sophie. "Let's see that sidecar and get to Mama's house. You can tell me about it another time."

It was a short drive up Fifteenth Avenue and left onto Wall Avenue, with Sophie holding down her hat. Aaron ran around to help his sister out of the sidecar. "How'd ya like it?"

"Nifty, Dan would say."

Their mood changed as they walked to the front door, and when Aaron stepped under the portico he couldn't help but sneer. Sophie knew the look. It was his sneer of disgust, distaste. He squeezed his lips and turned them downward like his mother.

Aaron knocked on the door. They waited, but there was no response. "Is she expecting us, Sophie?"

"Yes. Ring the bell." Again there was no response. He pressed the buzzer. They waited. All was still but the breeze. The smell of fall leaves, usually evocative of joyous childhood romps, this day smelled of decay. The last of the red and orange maple leaves fluttered to the ground and blew onto the entryway. Three bare trees waited for winter.

Sophie took a deep whiff of air and said, "Burning leaves."

"The neighbor down the street is burning leaves in the gutter. See him there with his rake? I wonder if the gardener will come to rake and burn Ma's. Who's going to take care of this place if she has no money?"

Sophie pulled her coat closer. "Where is she?" She began to mutter to herself. "Be calm. No arguing."

"What did you say, Sophie?"

"Oh, I was reminding myself to be calm. Don't argue with her. I was thinking about getting a lawyer to work on her finances, maybe bankruptcy."

They waited a moment more and listened at the door. Finally Sophie turned the immense brass doorknob, which she found unlocked, and they walked into the darkened front parlor. Emma was slumped in her favorite upholstered fan-back chair. Her forearms rested on the sides of the chair, and her wrists hung loosely over the front of the armrests. Her head lolled forward, and for the first time Sophie saw her mother's gray hair growing out beneath the henna. Several newspapers were scattered on the floor near the chair. Carpet slippers lay askew.

Aaron and Sophie looked at each other, fear on both their faces. Sophie walked over to her mother and shook her shoulder. "Mama, Mama, are you asleep?"

"Asleep? Sure, I'm asleep."

"Mama, you didn't get dressed today? You're still wearing your bed robe," said Sophie.

"What's to get dressed for? I closed the shop. I have nothing. I am nothing."

"Ma, what are you talking about?" said Aaron. "You lost money, not your life."

"Not yet. Plenty people are jumping from buildings," she responded as she sat up in the chair.

Emma's children moved chairs from the dining room to sit close to their mother. Sophie leaned very close to Emma's face and stared into her eyes. "Yes, Mama. People are doing horrible things to their families. They choose death, not responsibility. They leave their families without a father or a husband to care for them, but you couldn't do that to your family. You wouldn't leave your children without a mother or your grandchildren without a *bubbeh*. And what about your brothers and their families? You are not that woman who would choose the easy way out."

"My children? You, Aaron, leave your mother and become a car mechanic. And you, Sophie, with your hoity-toity family in New York. What time do you have for an old mother?"

"Ma, that's all I want to hear. You are ashamed of a son who is making his way in life with a good salary and the promise of more? We came here to help you, to give you our love and support, and you can't even see that."

Sophie glanced sideways at Aaron with a look that said, "Enough." Aaron sat back in his chair and continued to rake his fingers through his hair.

The pendulum was silent behind the mantel clock's glass door. Aaron's hair raking was the only movement in the stagnant room. Emma and Aaron slouched, but Sophie sat on the edge of the hard dining room chair poised to say something, anything to ease the burden of the moment.

She held out her upturned palms. "Mama, let us help you to get through this period."

"I should take money from my own children? Never!"

"We didn't have money in mind," said Sophie.

"What then? What will become of me? I had it all, and now I have nothing. No stocks, no money in the bank. I don't know if I can keep my house or my buildings or even my business. I had nothing when I came to Paterson, and I have nothing now. For what was my lifetime of work?"

Sophie said no more. She knew that Emma had to answer her own questions. She got up and went toward the kitchen to make tea. "Mama, get dressed and we'll sit down and have a *nosh* together."

"Yah, a *nosh*. You want ruggeleh maybe? Not my ruggeleh, from the bakery."

"Yes, we do. Right, Aaron?" Aaron nodded his head. "Mama, why don't you go up and get dressed while I fix us a *nosh*?"

As soon as Emma left the room Aaron said, "Sophie, what do you think? Was she putting on a show for us? She can get wound up, and she says things she doesn't mean."

"I'm not sure, but it seems to me that maybe the drama is over for a while. After all, people who are ready to die don't think about pastry."

Sophie went to the stove to get the teakettle. She brought it to the sink and registered shock at what she saw. "Dirty dishes. This I have never seen. Mama doesn't leave anything undone."

Aaron had found the ruggeleh and brought it to the dining room table.

"Come here. Look at this, Aaron."

"I never saw a mess in Mama's kitchen before," said Aaron.

Sophie was thoughtful. She started to run water into the sink for the dishes, but stopped and turned to Aaron. "You said before we came here that you would be willing to move in with her for a while until we can resolve her finances. How do you feel about that now?"

Aaron hesitated. "You know I don't want to, but if I did move in, she would have to agree that I'm my own man."

"My 'little' brother is a man, a real *mensch*," said Sophie as she looked up at his fine-boned face, his olive complexion, and mass of curly black hair brushed back from his forehead. Today she noted stubble on his chin for the first time. "I wish Papa could see how you've grown up. Except for your height, you look like him."

"I think I am like him, but…"

Sophie nudged Aaron and pointed with her chin toward Emma, who was striding down the stairs fully dressed and coiffed. "You look much better, Mama."

"It's what I tell my customers. Clothes make the mood. Good clothes."

The family, cautiously revived, sat down at one end of the ornate mahogany dining table to have tea. Sophie got up and kissed her mother on the cheek, wound the mantel clock, and then opened the drapes to let the afternoon light stream in.

Aaron's deep breath and exhalation broke the silence. "Ma, I was thinking maybe I could move back to my old room until things are settled. I pay Flora for my keep. I could pay it here instead."

"No money from my children."

"Okay, if that's the way you want it. What do you think about my coming back for a while?"

"Not now. I can't think now, Aaron. We talk again?"

"Yeah, Ma. We'll talk again."

"Mama, what are you going to do now? Will you go to the shop?" asked Sophie.

"I don't know, Sophie. I'll wait to hear from the broker or his lawyer about my debt." Emma spit out the word "debt" as she might if an insect had flown into her mouth.

"Mama, would you like us to hold some of your silver and valuables at our house?" asked Sophie.

Emma flinched and turned to face her daughter. "It could come to that? I didn't think…"

Sophie responded with a look of despair and held up her palms.

"Not now, Sophie. Don't take them now."

"Mama, it's time for us to leave. Daniel and I would like you to visit with us for a few days next week. The children miss seeing you. Ori remembers the last time he saw you, and he asked about you."

Emma was silent.

"I don't think people will be flocking to buy dresses for a few days more. You can keep the shop closed for a while longer," continued Sophie. "Think about it."

A week later, Emma had recovered somewhat from the initial shock of her loss. Nothing had been decided, but she began to ruminate about her options, and gradually her mind again could focus.

This morning as she came downstairs she gazed from the dining room into the parlor where she saw that she had neglected to put things away. *Ach! Such a mess.* She straightened the newspapers and plumped the cushions, taking care to order her surroundings. Then she smiled tenderly at her creation, her lovely room.

She had selected each piece of furniture and ornament with personal care. The Oriental rugs, the crystal vases, the porcelain figurines. Could all of this be taken from her even before she had sufficient opportunities to show them off?

She wandered into the dining room, fingered the silver tea service, and opened the lower sideboard drawers to examine her supply of table linen edged with Irish lace. She closed the drawers and sighed, wiping a tear from the corner of her eye. Her scalloped, gold-rimmed Limoges china was arranged behind glass doors. *Will they take these beautiful things away from me? This house too? Gornischt! Nothing left.*

Emma started to go into the kitchen for breakfast, but on second thought returned to the sideboard. She opened one of the glass doors and withdrew a plate, a cup, and a saucer. *Why not enjoy Limoges while I have it?* She carried the few pieces of china into the kitchen with such care that the place setting might have been a precious newborn. She set them on the kitchen table and, as an afterthought, went back into the dining room for a silver teaspoon and butter knife. She prepared a piece of toast with butter and a cup of tea, sat down, and began to relish her elegant meal.

She passed the time lingering over what she thought would be the last use of these treasured possessions. She raised the now empty cup to enjoy the translucence and turned it to catch the light. On the bottom the tiny gold lettering read *Limoges, Made in France.* Emma sighed. She brought her shoulders up and let them drop. *That's all.* She would not cry again.

At last she gathered her breakfast dishes and brought them to the kitchen sink.

With both hands submerged in the sudsy water, she looked outside the window above the sink, noting the bare maple branches that faced the coming winter.

The years of desperate struggle passed before her—the corset *schlepping,* the partnership with Bessie, the hard-won success with The New Woman, and the heady years of investing in real estate and stocks. *And for what?* She nearly lost her entire family. Yet they came back to me, she thought. *My Aaron and Sophie. They came to me when I have nothing.*

As she wiped the fragile saucer, she thought of Ori and little Molly. *I could take them for a walk in Central Park…maybe the zoo.* Her shoulders straightened. *And nu? They have never been to see The New Woman.* She dried her hands, and with lifted chin, ascended her grand staircase.

# Acknowledgments

**Thanks** to my husband, Bill, for his enthusiastic support throughout the research and writing of this book. He accompanied me to Paterson, New Jersey, and to various New York City archives, museums, and the Lower East Side neighborhood, holding the umbrella, checking out the subways, and even turning archival pages with gloved hands. He read my drafts, comforted me when I doubted myself, and cheered for my successes.

I am indebted to Professor Steve Golin for his research on the Paterson Silk Strike of 1913 and for his careful reading of my manuscript for historical accuracy. Thanks to Evelyn M. Hershey, Education Director of the American Labor Museum, Botto House National Landmark in Haledon, New Jersey, for making the resources of the museum available to me and for her critical reading of my manuscript.

Grateful thanks go to author and teacher Camille Minichino, and to my critique group members Sheryl Ruzek, Ann Damaschino, Sunny Solomon, Joanne Furio, Sally Tubach, and Marlene Miller, who supported me as my writing evolved. Joanna H. Kraus deserves special thanks for her ongoing support and critical reading of the final manuscript.

Many other dedicated readers provided insight through various iterations of the manuscript. I am grateful to Barbara Grossman, Marilyn Friedman, Jody Sahlin, Ellen Taner, and Alaine Joseph for early and frequent input. Others who provided critical suggestions to improve the final draft are Paula Schiff,

Jo Mele, Ellen Israel, Sue Monje, Paula Tint, Phyliss Loonin, Helene Casella, Cindy Silver, Susie Reisfelt, and Dorian Fine.

Thanks to the archivists in the Barnard College Library and the Paterson Public Library for their generous help.

# Discussion Questions

1. Many readers see Emma as a controversial figure. How did you feel about her at the beginning of the story, and did you feel the same at the end? If not, why not, and what influenced your change of opinion?

   What motivated her response to Sophie's life choices? Why was Emma having a hard time giving Sophie the freedom that she had taken for herself?

2. What part did her admiration for her successful brothers play in shaping Emma's life?

3. Consider that the 1920s era was a first step in freeing women from societal constraints. How was Emma's entrepreneurial behavior affected by the constraints of the early twentieth century?

4. Activism in the 1960s expanded women's rights. What has happened since the 1960s, and what might yet come for women? How might Emma have approached her entrepreneurial efforts differently had she been a contemporary of ours?

5. How was Sophie affected by her parents' conflict, and what choices did she make based on them?

6. How did Emma view Meyer's politics, and how did it influence her decisions and their marriage?

7. How did you view Meyer's character with respect to his personal values and also with respect to his marriage?

8. What attracted Sophie to Izzy? Why did this relationship grow, and do you think it would have flourished had Isador lived? Why or why not?

9. Meyer's advocacy for the workingman was fed by the earlier industrial revolution. What comparisons can you draw between the labor movement in the early twentieth century and the contemporary labor issues? What form would Meyer's zeal for workers' equity take in today's labor environment?

10. For Aaron, Meyer was a counterforce against his mother's demands. How did Meyer's death affect him? How were Sophie and Emma each affected by Meyer's death?

11. What predictions would you make for Aaron's adulthood?

12. What drew Sophie to Daniel? What would you predict for their marriage? Why?

13. How can you imagine the relationship between Emma and her children changing in future years, if at all?

Please consider inviting me to speak with your book group via Skype or in person if I am in your area. I'd enjoy your responses to the book, and would be happy to answer questions about my writing process, research, or publishing experience. Contact me through my website at http://www.leslierupley.com or by phone at 925-383-2330.

# About the Author

**L**eslie Rupley, oral historian and memoirist, turned to fiction with her debut novel *Beyond the Silk Mills*. She draws on her childhood experiences in Paterson, New Jersey, the one-time capital of the silk textile industry, where the former mills and Great Falls of the Passaic River that powered them inspired her writing. Leslie lives in Walnut Creek, California, adjacent to an extensive trail system where she likes to spend her early mornings hiking. Her husband Bill, family, and friends are central to her life, but she also reads, knits, travels, volunteers, and has begun work on her sequel novel.

Made in the USA
San Bernardino, CA
13 December 2014